No
RESERVATIONS

"Sheryl Lister's beautiful women's fiction debut is filled with emotional hills and valleys. This heartfelt and uplifting story of friendship and perseverance is told with depth and humor, and the characters will sit with you long after the book is complete."
—Lacey Baker, *USA TODAY* bestselling author of
Snow Place Like Home

"Wonderfully engaging and un-put-downable. A celebration of sisterhood, friendship, and love. *No Reservations* captured me from the first sentence. A beautiful examination and tribute to women and the limitless power of friendship."
—Anna J. Stewart, *USA TODAY* bestselling author

"Warm and wise—a feel good story. Sheryl Lister's *No Reservations* is a heartfelt tribute to sisterhood and found-family. The feelings linger long after the last page."
—Vanessa Riley, award-winning author of *Island Queen*
and *Queen of Exiles*

"At times both deeply emotional and heartwarmingly funny, *No Reservations* encapsulates the beauty of the unbreakable bond of enduring friendships and true sisterhood."
—Farrah Rochon, *New York Times* bestselling author of
The Hookup Plan

"*No Reservations* is a tale of triumph, which showcases the treasure of female friendships. Sheryl Lister hits us with an emotional page turner."
—Kwana Jackson, *USA TODAY* bestselling
author of *Real Men Knit*

"In *No Reservations*, Sheryl Lister has captured the true spirit of sisterhood with characters who celebrate one another's highs and are there to help make lemonade with life's lemons. Joy, Diane, and Rochelle's enduring bond even after losing their other sister-friend, Yvette, pulled at my heartstrings and stuck with me long after the story was done."

—Tiffany L. Warren, bestselling author of
The Replacement Wife

No RESERVATIONS

SHERYL LISTER

HARPER MUSE

No Reservations

Copyright © 2023 Sheryl Lister

Published by Harper Muse, an imprint of HarperCollins Focus LLC.

This book is a work of fiction. The characters, incidents, and dialogue are drawn from the author's imagination and are not to be construed as real. Any resemblance to actual events or persons, living or dead, is entirely coincidental.

Any internet addresses (websites, blogs, etc.) in this book are offered as a resource. They are not intended in any way to be or imply an endorsement by HarperCollins Focus LLC, nor does HarperCollins Focus LLC vouch for the content of these sites for the life of this book.

ISBN 978-1-4002-4579-6 (trade paper)
ISBN 978-1-4002-4580-2 (epub)
ISBN 978-1-4002-4582-6 (audio download)

Library of Congress Cataloging-in-Publication Data
Names: Lister, Sheryl, author.
Title: No reservations / Sheryl Lister.
Description: Nashville, Tennessee: Harper Muse, 2024. | Summary: "Four friends, three struggling relationships, and one final wish: find your happiness. Both heartwarming and heart-wrenching, Sheryl Lister invites readers to take a trip of a lifetime with her new women's fiction novel that reminds us all to live without regrets"—Provided by publisher.
Identifiers: LCCN 2023031716 (print) | LCCN 2023031717 (ebook) | ISBN 9781400245796 (paperback) | ISBN 9781400245802 (epub) | ISBN 9781400245826
Subjects: LCSH: Female friendship—Fiction. | LCGFT: Novels.
Classification: LCC PS3612.I863 N6 2024 (print) | LCC PS3612.I863 (ebook) | DDC 813/.6—dc23/eng/20230714
LC record available at https://lccn.loc.gov/2023031716
LC ebook record available at https://lccn.loc.gov/2023031717

Printed in the United States of America

23 24 25 26 27 LBC 5 4 3 2 1

This book is dedicated to my sister-besties. They know who they are.

Prologue

YVETTE STEPHENS WISHED SHE COULD BE HAVING THIS conversation from the comfort of her home, but life had other plans. A wave of pain hit as she tried to adjust herself. Her husband rushed over to help, and she gave him a grateful smile. Joseph had been her rock since high school, and she loved him with every beat of her heart.

"I'm good, babe," she said with a small smile.

How she wished they had more time. Yvette stared at the three women surrounding her hospital bed with tears in their eyes. Best friends since age eight, they had laughed, cried and seen each other through every challenge life threw their way.

"No crying allowed—or at least save it until I've had my say." They smiled at her. "I just wanted to tell you how much your friendship has meant to me all these years. You've been the best sisters of the heart a girl could have." She reached for Joy's hand. "Joy, your mama named you right because you've been that and more to me. You've sacrificed your dreams long enough, sis. It's time for you to start that business because every woman needs a place of respite."

Joy laughed through her tears and gave Yvette's hand a gentle squeeze. "I know, and I promise."

Yvette shifted her gaze to her second friend. "Diane, you've been the best godmother to Ebony and Ian—all three of you have—and I know you'll be an even better mother. Jeff will come around, just keep working on him."

Diane's pained gaze met Yvette's. "I'm working on him. One way or another," she added with a wry smile.

"Rochelle," Yvette started.

Before she could continue, Rochelle lifted a hand. "I already know what you're going to say."

Joy laughed. "Probably the same thing we've all been saying."

Yvette chuckled, then moaned in pain. "Don't make me laugh. Chelle, girl, I know your sorry ex is enough to make a woman stay single for the rest of this life and the next, but you're a beautiful woman, and you can't do that. Warren is a good man, and he really likes you."

Rochelle raised an eyebrow. "How do you know?"

"I asked. What did you think? Let him in, sis. He can love you like you deserve to be loved." She grasped Rochelle's hand.

"I'll see."

Yvette gave her a look.

"Hey, it's the best I can do."

"Joy and Di, make sure she doesn't mess it up."

"We will," they chorused.

"Watch out for Joe and my babies, okay? And if he finds somebody else, be nice to her." She smiled at Joe. "Well, unless she's a gold-digging heifer. Oh, one more thing. We never got around to taking that trip back to Jamaica. Don't put it off any longer. Make those reservations, and take that trip."

Joe returned her smile, bent to kiss her softly and stroked her brow. "That's enough, baby. You've given a bellyful of advice tonight."

Staring up into his eyes, she felt his pain as surely as the pain coursing through her own body. "I know. I just want my girls to enjoy their lives and live to the fullest like we talked about while growing up. And we promised we'd go back. I need y'all to take that trip, sisters," she said once more.

"They'll be fine. We all will."

Yvette didn't believe him for a moment. Her eyes drifted shut. Lord, she was so tired.

"To the sisters of my heart . . ."

Chapter 1

Joy

JOY WEST CHECKED HER WATCH FOR THE TENTH TIME and wished the man talking would hurry up. She should have been gone fifteen minutes ago for her Saturday brunch meetup with her girls Diane Evans and Rochelle Winters. She sent her husband a look, which he pointedly ignored while continuing to show photos of home renovations they'd completed. When they'd started West Home Renovations ten years ago, shortly after their marriage, she had been all fired up. Now, she just wanted out. Of both. She mouthed, *I'm leaving in five minutes.* He must have gotten the message because he did a quick wrap-up.

She stood and extended her hand. "Thank you for coming, Mr. Kelly. We look forward to working with you."

"The pleasure is all mine, Mrs. West." Mr. Kelly shook her hand, then Robert's. "Robert, I'll call you on Monday to get on your schedule."

Robert grinned. "Good enough. I'll walk you out."

As soon as they walked out, Joy gathered up all the folders and the contract and made her way to her office. She locked everything in a drawer and grabbed her purse.

"Could you have made it a little less obvious that you wanted to leave?"

Joy glanced over at the door where Robert stood glaring with his arms folded. "You knew I had somewhere to be at eleven, yet you still scheduled the appointment, and on a Saturday when the office is closed." She hesitated before handing him a small envelope.

"What's this?"

"Just open it." She bit her lip anxiously as she waited.

He tore open the envelope and pulled the card out. "An invitation? To dinner?"

She had made a card inviting him to a romantic dinner that evening. "Yes. After I get back later, I was hoping we could go out to dinner tonight and talk. We haven't done anything together outside of work in months." Their marriage had been steadily unraveling over the past year. Despite her best efforts to get it back on track—from planning romantic dinners and overnight getaways to trying to surprise him with lunchtime picnics—nothing had gotten his attention. She seemed to be the only one trying to make it work, and she was tired.

"I can't," Robert said, tossing the card aside. "I want to get things going for this new project. You know the summer months are our busiest, and June is only two months away."

Her spirit sank. She couldn't even interest him in a simple dinner. "It's *Saturday*, Robert. Even when we were just starting out and had to work long hours, we still managed to find time to do some fun stuff." The man standing before her was so different from the one she had fallen in love with years ago. No doubt he was still ambitious, intelligent, and handsome. At over six feet tall with a slim, muscular build, his clean-shaven, mahogany good looks still turned heads. However, the funny and engaging man— the one whose smile made her weak—had somehow disappeared over the past few years. "Speaking of making some time, did you place the ad for another business manager?"

He sighed heavily. "No. The customers love you. Why are you so quick to mess up a good thing? Anyway, I thought you didn't want to be late," he said.

She opened her mouth, then closed it. Clearly, he didn't want to spend time with her. Memories of them cuddling together in bed watching movies while stuffing their faces with popcorn, taking long walks on the beach while holding hands, and having candlelit dinners at their favorite restaurants surfaced. She missed those times with him. She missed them. Not for the first time, she wondered if he might be having an affair. Each rejection cut a little deeper, and the love she used to have for him had waned considerably. For the past year, they had been nothing more than polite strangers in their home.

"I'm more concerned about our marriage than this company, but it feels like I'm the only one who's been trying to make it work these past several months. I've asked you to talk to me, I've tried to get us to spend more time together, but I don't know what else to do," she said. "If you want out, just say so," she added softly, hoping he'd say he didn't want their marriage to end.

"That's the third or fourth time you've mentioned that or threatened to leave, so maybe you're the one who wants out," Robert snapped. "And didn't you say you had somewhere to be?"

"If I wanted out, I wouldn't be trying so hard to save this marriage." Joy rolled her eyes and strode past him out the door. "I'll see you later."

In the car, she took a deep breath and willed back her tears. She was so tired of being the only one making an effort to repair their relationship and wondered after his response—or lack thereof—if she was fighting a losing battle and should just call it quits. Clearly Robert didn't seem to care one way or another.

7

After sending a quick text to her friends, she started the car and drove off.

Thirty minutes later, she parked, rushed inside the Mimosa House and scanned the area. Diane threw up a wave, and Joy started in that direction. She hugged Diane and Rochelle.

"I'm so sorry I'm late." She dropped down into a chair and picked up a menu. "Have you guys ordered yet? I need a mimosa or maybe something stronger."

Rochelle eyed her. "That bad?"

"Worse." Her entire life was falling apart, and she'd lost one of her best friends. She glanced over to the empty fourth chair at their table. That it would be vacant from here on out only made her sadder. It had been two weeks since they'd buried Yvette, and Joy still couldn't get used to the fact that she was gone. She had been only thirty-eight, and cancer had stolen her life.

"I hear you. And it's hard knowing Yvette isn't coming." They fell silent. Rochelle blew out a long breath. "Man, I miss her."

"She was always the one who gave us good advice. Now who's going to keep us in line?" They had often teased Yvette about having an old soul because she had been wise beyond her years.

They ordered their drinks and food, and as soon as the mimosas hit the table, Joy took a big gulp.

"You want to let us in on what happened, Joy?" Diane asked after taking a sip of her own drink.

"Robert. He deliberately scheduled an appointment for a new client this morning after I told him I was meeting you guys. We haven't worked on a Saturday in over three years, and now, all of a sudden, he's acting like we need to be available every day of the week." Joy took another healthy swig.

Rochelle reached over and snatched the flute. "Give me that. If you don't slow down, you're going to be passed out under the table."

Joy rubbed her temples. "I know, I know. It's just that since I told him I was ready to start working on opening the spa, he's changed. We *agreed* that after West Home Renovations was on solid footing, that it would be my turn. We've been in the black for three years running."

"You've been talking about expanding for over a year."

Joy reached for her glass and saluted Rochelle. "Exactly." The conversation paused as the server returned with their food. They thanked the young woman and dug in. "I asked him about placing an ad for a business manager to take my place so I can devote my time to getting my business off the ground, and do you know what he said? He told me all the customers like me, and he didn't know why I wanted to mess up a good thing." Just the thought of his audacity made her angry all over again.

They ate in silence for a few minutes, then Diane said, "I hate to say it, but Yvette might've been right." She cut into her omelet and forked up a portion.

Joy finished chewing a piece of toast. "I've been thinking a lot about what she said, and I don't think Robert's going to get on board." The conversation she'd had with Yvette a few months ago played in her mind.

"I've been listening to Robert lately, and it seems as if he's really happy about the company's growth. He doesn't strike me as wanting things to change."

Joy stared at Yvette. "I know. Every time I bring up the spa, he shifts the conversation."

"There's going to come a time when you're forced to decide if opening your place is what you really want or if you'll be content with the way things are now. I just hope it doesn't come down to you having to choose between it and your marriage."

"If I have to choose, then the decision is obvious."

A touch on her arm brought Joy out of her thoughts.

"Well then, he needs to get his ass out of the way." Rochelle lifted her glass in a mock toast. "You know we've got your back, sis."

Diane followed suit. "Chelle's right. Whatever you need, we'll help you."

"Thanks." She could always count on them. "What about you two? Have you thought more about what Yvette said?"

Diane set her fork on the plate. "Honestly, I've done nothing but think about it. The wait for adopting a baby is so long and, lately, I've been wondering, at my age, whether an older child might be a better option."

Joy smiled. "That's wonderful. There are so many of them who need a good home. Is Jeffrey okay with that?"

"I thought he was, but every time I try to start the conversation, he claims he's too busy or it's not the right time."

What is it with these men? "Whatever you decide, I'll be ready to don my godmother hat." Joy had never wanted children and was perfectly content with her current role as godmother to Yvette's two children and Rochelle's daughter, and aunt to her brother's two sons. It had taken years for her family, particularly her mother, to come to grips with Joy's belief that not all women had to be mothers. "What about you, Chelle? Have you talked to Warren lately?"

"Not since the funeral, and we didn't really have a long conversation."

"Maybe not, but I saw him bringing you water and holding your hand."

"And that little kiss on the forehead," Diane added with a wide grin. "You do know what they say about a forehead kiss, right?"

Rochelle divided a wary glance between Joy's and Diane's smiling faces. "No. What?"

"It means that he cares a lot about you, and it's not all about the sex. He wants you to know that you're special and he respects you and wants to protect you."

"I think you're reading way more into it." Rochelle shook her head.

At five eight, Rochelle was the tallest of the group. With her full figure, clear mocha complexion, dark brown eyes and long hair, she was absolutely gorgeous, but she didn't see herself that way. Joy's friend's self-esteem had taken a beating from her ex in ways Joy suspected Rochelle hadn't even shared with them. If anyone deserved some happiness in her life, Chelle did.

They continued to converse while finishing the meal and for another hour afterward.

"Have you thought about the other thing Yvette said?" Joy asked the group.

"What other thing?" Diane asked.

"Going back to Jamaica."

The four of them had made the first trip there right after graduating from college. While they'd been childhood friends, it had been there on the beach where they'd pledged to be sisters for life. They'd promised to go back every five years to recommit. Somehow, life always got in the way, and those reservations had never been made. Sure, they'd gone on day trips and weekenders, but with everyone starting jobs, getting married and having children, and navigating through life's ups and downs, the trip hadn't happened.

Rochelle clasped her hands together on the table. "Not really. With everything going on at work and Haley finishing up her first year of high school . . . But you're right, we need to make this happen."

Diane nodded. "I agree. It's been pretty stressful at work and home, but we should think about doing it this summer. I know we haven't wavered in our commitment as sisters, but there was something special and magical about the little ceremony we had in Jamaica."

"Yeah," Joy said.

Silence stretched between them, and she wondered if they all had the same regrets. They shouldn't have kept putting off the trip, and now it would never be the four of them. Once again, Joy's eyes strayed to the empty chair. The women chatted for a while longer, and when it was time to leave, they shared strong hugs, made a promise to meet again in a couple of weeks to start planning the trip and went their separate ways.

The house was quiet when Joy arrived, and a part of her was glad Robert hadn't made it home. After changing out of her black slacks and silk printed blouse and into a pair of comfortable sweats and a T-shirt and putting her shoulder-length hair up into a ponytail, she powered up her laptop. She'd been working on her business plan for over three years and felt it was solid enough to take to the bank. She only hoped she'd be able to secure the loan on her own now that she knew for sure she wouldn't be able to count on the promised assets from their company. The next step was to find the perfect spot for her dream spa. She had initially thought about buying the old community center that had been vacated after the city built a new one ten miles away. It already had ample parking and an industrial-sized kitchen. The grounds connected to a park, which would be ideal for a small walking trail or a couple of gazebos, but the noise from children playing would defeat the whole purpose of it being a retreat, so she'd nixed the idea.

For the next hour, she searched for properties that would be a good fit for what she wanted—something relatively small and intimate but could accommodate at least six treatment rooms. Her fingers froze on the track pad when she saw a ten-thousand-square-foot space that had originally been a small women's gym in El Dorado Hills. Joy quickly clicked on each picture, and her excitement rose with each one. There were seven large rooms that she could use for the various treatments and another space that she could have reconfigured into an industrial kitchen, as she planned to offer a limited menu. It also had a locker room, showers and plenty of bathroom stalls.

Joy read further and saw that there were an additional ten acres of land on the property that could be developed. Her smile widened, and her mind went into overdrive. She opened her wish list document, and her fingers flew across the keyboard. She was so engrossed in the task that she didn't hear Robert come in until he appeared beside her desk. She jumped and clutched her chest.

"You scared me."

Robert mumbled something that sounded like, "Sorry." He peered over her shoulder. "Are you researching ideas for Mr. Kelly's project?"

"No. This is for the spa. Do you want to see?"

"No." His deep voice was curt as he pivoted on his heel and stalked out of her office.

Get his ass out of the way, indeed. She'd sacrificed her dreams long enough.

Chapter 2

Diane

DIANE EVANS SAT ON THE SIDE OF HER BED FRIDAY evening reading the latest test results from Dr. Fields. Her fertility specialist had called to share the information earlier, but seeing it in black and white made it all too real. *Premature menopause.* The phrase played in her mind over and over. How could she be entering menopause at thirty-eight? She swiped at the tears flowing down her face. Even though she knew there was a slim chance of her being able to conceive and carry a child, this blow hit her hard. She hadn't mentioned it to Chelle and Joy last weekend during their brunch get-together because they were dealing with their own problems.

That never stopped you before, her inner voice chimed.

Truthfully, she hoped that by not saying the words, they wouldn't be true. Adoption was still on the table, but in a perfect world, she would have been able to do both.

"Why are you still sitting here? You're not even dressed yet."

She glanced over her shoulder at her husband, Jeffrey, as he rushed into the room and over to the walk-in closet.

Jeffrey looked down at his watch. "The guests will be here in less than an hour, and we need to make sure everything is ready."

"And the reason you can't do it would be what? They're *your* guests." Surely he could see that she'd been crying, but he didn't even ask why.

He took down a tie and walked over to the mirror to put it on. "Can we not do this tonight, Di, please? We can talk about whatever you want tomorrow, but my boss is coming, and you know I'm up for asset manager this quarter."

"All the more reason for you to host this dinner yourself." Diane rose from the bed and went into the bathroom. For the past three months, Jeffrey had been working longer hours and hosting one business dinner after another. But Diane always ended up doing all the work while he stood by and accepted the praise. Tonight, she didn't feel like it. Tonight, she wanted to take a long bath, put on her pajamas and crawl into bed with a book and a bowl of her favorite chocolate chip ice cream. Instead, she settled for a quick shower. She applied light makeup to her tawny-brown face and recombed her short, layered hair, then slipped into her dress and smoothed a hand down the front. At five six, she'd maintained her size ten frame.

Her hand stopped on her belly, and Diane felt her emotions rising once more with the knowledge that it would never be filled with the baby she desperately wanted. Sighing, she pushed the thoughts away and headed downstairs. And by the time the six guests arrived, she had her smile firmly in place.

Diane made sure the service staff she'd hired for the night replenished the hors d'oeuvres, kept the glasses full and served each one of the dinner courses on time.

"Everything tastes so good, Diane." Jeffrey's boss's wife, Adele, said halfway through the last course.

"Thank you, Adele."

Jeffrey shot Diane a look, which she ignored. The woman had called Diane by her first name, and Diane didn't see any reason not to do the same, particularly since Adele wasn't much older. The conversation flowed around the table, and they all laughed loudly at the many bad jokes Jeffrey's boss told. She figured more than one person must have been up for a promotion since his boss wouldn't have been able to tell a good joke even if Bernie Mac walked up and handed the man a script. She had never been so glad to end a dinner in her life . . . unless she counted the last four times they'd hosted Jeffrey's work colleagues.

Jeffrey stood. "We can all adjourn to the living room for after-dinner drinks."

How about they all adjourn somewhere else? An old saying popped into Diane's head: *You ain't gotta go home, but you got to get the hell out of here.* She allowed Jeffrey to help her up and led the guests into the next room. Once again, Adele tried to engage her in conversation.

"What is it that you do again, Diane?"

"I'm the director of a preschool and day care center."

"Oh, that must be challenging."

"Some days it is, but I love the kids."

"Are you and Jeff planning to have any children of your own?" Adele asked with a sly grin.

Before Diane could answer, Jeffrey slid an arm around her waist and said laughingly, "We're working on it."

It took everything inside Diane not to knock that fake smile right off his face. They weren't working on anything. She couldn't get him to *talk* about fostering or adopting a child for five minutes, let alone *work* on it. She discreetly pushed his arm away and pasted a smile on her face.

"I need to go check on dessert. I'll be right back."

Instead of going to the kitchen, she made her way down the short hallway to the half bathroom. After closing the door, she leaned against the counter and drew in several calming breaths. How dare he stand there and lie? She'd had to beg and plead for him to accompany her to one doctor after another for five years, in the hopes that she would be able to fill that missing piece in her life by having a child. She'd had her life all mapped out—career, marriage, then children. Never in her wildest dreams did she think she wouldn't be able to have it all. But as her mother often said, we plan and God laughs. Only she couldn't find one thing funny.

Diane stood there a moment longer before going back to the front. She stopped in the kitchen and asked that the dessert be served now instead of later, as had been planned. The quicker they finished, the quicker she could curl up in her bed and begin her pity party. She donned her polite mask once again—the one that said everything was okay—and announced dessert.

Forty-five minutes later, the last of the stragglers were leaving, including Jeffrey's boss and his wife.

"Thank you for coming, Mr. Paulson," Jeffrey said, shaking the man's hand. "It's always a pleasure to have you and your lovely wife in our home."

Diane barely suppressed an eye roll.

Mr. Paulson turned to Diane. "Everything was just wonderful, Diane."

"Thank you. I'm glad you both enjoyed yourselves. You two have a good evening."

Jeffrey paid the staff, and they departed. As soon as the door closed, she breathed a sigh of relief, but it was short-lived.

"How could you embarrass me like that in front of my boss by calling his wife by her first name?"

This time she did roll her eyes. "She called me by mine. And as far as being an embarrassment, that honor goes solely to you."

Jeffrey's eyes narrowed. "What the hell are you talking about?"

"That whole *we're working on it* crap when Adele asked about us having children." Diane stepped around him and went upstairs to their bedroom. She removed her jewelry and dress.

"What was I supposed to say?"

17

She spun around and glared at him. "How about the truth! You know what hurts the most? When you came in earlier, you *knew* I'd been crying, but you didn't bother to ask why. The doctor called me today and said I've started menopause prematurely. Do you know what that means?" she asked, her voice and emotions rising. "It means that I will *never* be able to have the babies I wanted."

"Diane—"

"Are you ready to discuss being foster parents or adopting, or did we take all those classes for nothing? Every time I bring it up, you conveniently find something else to do."

"I'm forty years old and at the peak of my career. Besides, you said the waiting list for newborns is long. It could be three or four years, and I don't know if I want to deal with a baby at that point."

"I know that, and I've been thinking we could adopt an older child instead."

Jeffrey waved a hand. "*No.* I'm not bringing that kind of drama into my house. There's no telling what kinds of problems those kids have."

"Are you kidding me right now?" She was done with this conversation. Snatching her nightshirt from the drawer, Diane strode toward the bathroom.

"Look, I didn't know."

She stopped, faced him and chuckled bitterly. "Of course you didn't. The only thing you were concerned about was that dinner. I guess I know what's really important to you these days." She waited for him to say something, *anything*, but he just stood there. Her heart breaking, she continued to the bathroom and took a long, leisurely candlelit bubble bath. Afterward, Diane trudged back downstairs, got that bowl of ice cream and went back up to her bed.

Jeffrey watched her every move, but he still didn't utter a word.

Finally, after what seemed like forever, he said, "Regardless of what's going on between us, Diane, I really am sorry about the news from your doctor."

"I appreciate you saying that," she said, moving the ice cream around in her bowl. Tonight she would eat her dessert and indulge in her pity party. Tomorrow, she planned to find a way to fulfill her dream. One way or another.

Chapter 3

Rochelle

ROCHELLE WINTERS DROPPED DOWN ON HER BED AND groaned. Some days she felt as if she had nothing left to give, and today was one of them. Her day had started at seven thirty, and with the second registered dental hygienist calling out sick, she'd had to take up the slack and stay half an hour past her normal four o'clock time. She had never been so glad to see Friday, which seemed to be how she'd felt for the past several weeks. Taking a moment to kick off her shoes, she laid back against the pillow and closed her eyes. Fifteen minutes. That's all she needed.

"Mom, can you sign my trip slip? Oh, and am I still getting my hair braided next weekend? Don't forget we're supposed to go shopping on Sunday."

Rochelle cracked open one eye and stared at her fourteen-year-old daughter. "Haley, leave the trip slip on the nightstand and I'll sign it. Yes, you're getting your hair braided, and I didn't forget."

"But why can't you just sign it now?"

"You're not getting on the bus in the next five minutes, so there's no rush. Can you just give me a few minutes to catch my breath? It's been a long day. We'll do dinner in a little while and talk."

Haley placed the paper on the nightstand. "Okay. You're not sick, are you?"

Good grief. How many questions does this child have today? "No, baby. Just tired." More like two weeks past exhaustion if she were being honest. Rochelle closed her eyes again as soon as Haley walked out. She didn't realize she had dozed off until she felt a gentle shake.

"Mom, are you awake?"

"I am now," she murmured. She glanced over at the clock. Only ten minutes had passed. "I can't even get fifteen minutes. What is it?"

"Can I spend the night at Ebony's house?"

Rochelle's eyes snapped open and she sat up. "Honey, I don't know if that's a good idea with everything going on." The god-sisters usually spent one weekend night together during the school year, alternating houses, and this month was supposed to be at the Stephenses' home. It had been three weeks since Yvette died, and both Ebony and Ian were struggling with the loss. They all were.

Just yesterday, Rochelle had picked up her phone to send Yvette a text, and it wasn't until she'd typed half the message that she'd remembered that her friend was no longer here. It had taken a good thirty minutes for the tears to stop and for Rochelle to get herself together. She wondered how long it would take for the un-expected bouts of grief to become manageable.

"*Please?* Uncle Joe said it was okay."

She sighed. "I'll call him in about thirty minutes, *after* I relax, and see what he says."

"Yes!" Haley did a little dance out the door.

She wanted to tell her not to get her hopes up because Joe had his hands full, but she didn't have the heart. Maybe she'd offer to let Ebony stay here instead, to give him a break. Resuming her position, she adjusted the pillow beneath her head, set the alarm on her watch and drifted off.

When she woke up, Rochelle felt marginally better. She made

her way to the kitchen and saw Haley curled up on the sofa in the family room rewatching one of the *High School Musical* movies. As she pulled out the ingredients to make spaghetti and preheated the oven to make cookies, she remembered she was supposed to make a call. She sliced enough of the homemade cookie dough she had in the freezer to make a dozen, placed them on a pan and stuck it the oven when it got to the correct baking temperature, then went back to the bedroom to call Joe.

"Hey, Joe. It's Chelle," she said when he answered.

"Hey, Chelle. You calling about Haley staying over?"

"Yep. Are you sure you're okay with it? They can stay over here instead."

"I appreciate that, but I'm trying to keep as many things normal for the kids as possible, and it's no trouble. I was just going to order pizza and let them watch a movie—*Captain Marvel*, I think."

"Okay, if you're sure. But if it gets to be too much, call me, and I'll come get them."

Joe chuckled. "Hey, you know I will. Ian and I will probably watch another Marvel movie. He told me he didn't want to watch with them because they giggle too much."

She laughed. Ian was two years younger than Haley and Ebony and still in the "girls are yucky" phase. "What time do you want me to bring her over?"

"If it was left up to them, an hour ago, but whenever you want. We'll be here."

"We'll see you in a little while." Rochelle disconnected.

She could hear the sadness in Joe's voice. He and Yvette were a perfect match, and they brought out the best in each other. Too bad Rochelle couldn't say the same about her ex.

Picking up her phone again, she sent a text to Joy and Diane: **Talked to Joe, and I'm a little worried about him. I'm dropping**

Haley off in a little while and was thinking you can meet me there for a few minutes.

A couple of minutes later, Joy replied: I'm leaving the office now and will meet you there. Do you need me to stop and pick up food?

Rochelle: No. They're ordering pizza and watching a movie.

Diane: Hey. I can stop by for a couple of minutes. Will pick up some drinks and popcorn on the way.

Rochelle pocketed her phone and smiled as she walked down the hall to the kitchen. She knew she could count on them. "Haley, get your stuff together, and as soon as these cookies are done, I'll take you over."

She sometimes had to repeat herself for her daughter to get moving. This time, the words were barely off her tongue before the child was up and sprinting down the hallway. Shaking her head, she placed the ground turkey back in the refrigerator. That was one less thing she had to do today. She'd figure out something to eat for herself after she got back. The oven timer sounded a minute later, and Rochelle removed the cookies. She had just placed them on a plate when Haley returned.

"I'm ready." Haley held up her bag.

"That was fast."

"I had it already packed, just in case."

Smiling, she handed her daughter the foil-covered plate and said, "Let's go, girl."

She put on her shoes, passed a mirror and realized her hair was sticking up all over her head. Rochelle redid her ponytail and debated on whether to change out of her scrubs. She'd only be gone long enough to drop Haley off, so she kept them on.

The normal twenty-minute drive took almost double the time with all the traffic. Rochelle noticed Joy's and Diane's cars there as she parked in front of the house. Haley nearly jumped out of the car with excitement. Apparently, Ebony felt the same way, as she came barreling out the door. The two girls embraced as if they hadn't seen each other in months. In reality, it had been less than two weeks.

"Hi, Aunt Chelle." Ebony wrapped her thin arms around Rochelle.

Rochelle hugged her tight. "How are you doing?"

"Okay, I guess." She held the door open. "Daddy is in the kitchen with Aunt Joy and Aunt Diane. Come on, Haley."

Rochelle watched the two girls disappear around the corner and made her way to the family room, where she found Ian. "Hey, Ian."

"Hi, Aunt Chelle." Ian stood, gave her a quick hug and flopped back down on the sofa.

Joe rounded the corner and gave her a hug. "Hey, Chelle. I see you called in reinforcements."

She gave Joe a strong hug and chuckled. "Hey, that's what we do. We're family."

"Di and Joy are in the kitchen."

She followed him there, hugged her two friends and took a seat at the table.

Joe took the vacant one.

"How are you holding up?" she asked, studying the weary lines etched around his light brown eyes. He looked as if he hadn't slept in days.

He shrugged and ran a hand over his close-cropped hair. "Some days I think I'm doing okay and others, not so much. I thought I was ready, but . . . I miss her so much. I keep expecting to hear her laughter. I still talk to her in my mind and wish she was here, but my heart and soul know she's at peace."

Rochelle felt his pain as if it were her own. At two years older, he had been like a big brother to her, Joy and Diane, and she wished she could do something to help. "I know you do. We all do. Is there anything you need me to do?"

Joy reached out and took Joe's hand. "You know we're here for whatever you all need."

Diane nodded.

He shook his head. "Not right now. You all have been lifesavers bringing food and checking on us." Joe paused, then said, "I have something I'd planned to give you later, but since you're all here, now is as good a time as any." He stood, left the room and came back a moment later. "Yvette left this for you all."

Rochelle, sitting closest, accepted the large envelope he handed her. She took a deep breath, opened it and pulled out a sheet of paper and three smaller envelopes with her, Diane's and Joy's names on them. Scanning the sheet of paper, she felt her emotions rising. "This note is from Yvette. 'Sisters,'" she read, "'I figured you three would still be talking about making those reservations ten years from now and never get the trip done, so I made them for you. Remember how we used to love hanging out at the beach, laughing, gorging ourselves on too much chocolate and sipping on wine coolers? It's time to enjoy it again. Before any one of you starts, I booked the trip for the second week in July. Chelle, I made sure it was during the summer so you don't have to worry about school for Haley. And since she spends a couple of weeks with your parents, you'll be free.'" Rochelle chuckled and continued reading. "'Diane, there are far less students at the day care, and I know you have your summer program laid out right down to the smallest detail. You have an assistant director, so let her earn her money for a week.'"

"That girl," Diane said, shaking her head and smiling. "She knew me well."

"She knows us all." Rochelle smiled and lifted the paper again. "'Joy, I know you'll be ready with your bags packed. You were always the one to help me get the other two in line. I'm counting on you to do it one more time.'"

Joy released a deep breath and swiped at the moisture in her eyes. "I've got my girl on this."

"'Since you all love me, I know I can count on you three not to waste my money. Y'all better have your butts on that plane to Jamaica. Make sure to buy some cute clothes and have a drink on me. If you don't, I'll be waiting for you when you get to heaven, and it's not going to be pretty. Until we meet again, Yvette.'"

Rochelle set the letter down. No one spoke for a lengthy moment.

Joe broke the silence. "She loved you all." He reached over and gave them each their plane tickets and Visa gift cards worth two hundred dollars each.

Diane held up the gift card. "What's this for?"

"To get your shopping started."

Joy ran her hand over the ticket. "She was one of a kind. So I guess that means we're going to Jamaica in about three months."

Rochelle smiled. "I guess so."

"And we're going to look good while we're there," Diane added as she stood. "I need to get going. Joe, if you need anything, let me know."

Joe nodded and rose to his feet. "Thanks for the popcorn and drinks. I think we should have enough for about ten movie nights," he said with a chuckle.

"I need to get going too," Joy said.

Rochelle gave both her friends a strong hug. "Thanks. We'll have to schedule a time to go shopping."

Joy laughed. "You ain't said nothing but a word."

Diane smiled. "Probably not, Miss Shopaholic."

While Joe led them out, Rochelle went to check on Haley and Ebony. "Haley, where are those cookies?"

"Oh, sorry, Mom." Haley grabbed the plate off the bed and handed it to Rochelle.

Shaking her head, she took the plate into the kitchen, placed it on the table and reclaimed her seat. Joe returned as she sat. "I made a few chocolate chip cookies to go along with the other snacks."

"My favorite." Joe immediately lifted the foil and snagged one. He bit into it and let out a moan. "These are so good. Whenever you made them for Yvette, I rarely got one."

She smiled, recalling how much her friend had loved the cookies. "No one got any if she saw them first." From the first time Rochelle had made them when they were juniors in high school, Yvette had always told her how good they tasted and tried to come up with a million reasons Rochelle *had* to bake more. It became standard for Rochelle to bake her some for every celebration, from birthdays and holidays to work promotions and just because. She drew in a deep breath and wondered if she'd made a mistake in bringing them.

The doorbell rang, interrupting their conversation. "Excuse me. Probably one of my neighbors. They've been stopping by regularly."

While he was gone, she bowed her head and prayed for help. She needed to keep it together and be strong for Yvette's family, although she didn't know how she'd do it with her own grief still so fresh and raw.

"Hello, Rochelle."

Her head came up sharply. "Oh. Um . . . hey, Warren."

Warren McIntyre smiled and sat in the chair next to her.

Rochelle eyed Joe, who still stood behind Warren.

He held up his hands in mock surrender and mouthed, *I didn't know he was coming over.*

She threw him a look that said she didn't believe him. Now she wished she had taken time to change, especially with Warren staring at her the way he always did. He had on a pair of nice jeans and a polo shirt, and at forty-two, the man was drop-dead fine and could pass for someone a decade younger. His mahogany-colored face remained unlined, and his body was toned and tight. She, on the other hand, needed to lose a good twenty-five pounds.

Rochelle's gaze dropped. *Great. Is that a toothpaste stain on my shirt?*

She clasped her hands in front of her and leaned her forearms on the table, hoping to hide it.

"I'm going to check on the girls. I'll be right back." Joe made a hasty exit.

Warren covered her hands with one of his. "How've you been?"

"Alright. Just working a lot." She resisted the urge to pull her hands back and shift in her chair. Every time she was around him, she felt like a sixteen-year-old girl on her first date. After her short-lived marriage, Rochelle had shoved men and dating to the farthest corner of a closet and shut the door firmly. The few times she did venture out to date had turned out disastrous, sending her right back to her simple, single and safe life.

"When are you going to let me take you out to dinner?"

Rochelle stared at him. He'd been asking her out for the past three months, and she'd turned him down each time. Any other man would have walked away long ago, but not Warren. Whenever they had some get-together, he would always do nice stuff for her.

"Let him in, sis. He can love you like you deserve to be loved."

Yvette's words came back to her. Rochelle didn't know about the whole love thing, but she figured one dinner couldn't hurt. "How about tonight?"

His eyes widened in surprise. "You wouldn't tease a brother, would you?"

She couldn't stop the smile that curved her lips. "No."

He studied her a moment, seemingly searching for some hint of guile. Finally, he said, "It's a date."

"What's a date?" Joe asked, coming into the kitchen.

Warren grinned. "Rochelle finally agreed to let me take her out to dinner tonight."

"I see. Well, she's free the whole evening since Haley is spending the night here."

Rochelle's gaze flew to Joe's. Was he trying to take up the matchmaking mantle his wife had initiated?

Warren stood and extended his hand. "Then we should get started. I don't want to waste one moment."

She hesitated briefly before placing her hand in his and letting him help her up. "I'm going to tell Haley I'm leaving. I'll be right back."

Around the corner, she let the wall take her weight. She'd been out of the game far too long and started to have second thoughts. "I can do this," she whispered under her breath repeatedly. *It's only dinner.* In control again, she said her goodbyes to the girls and Ian and went back to the kitchen. "I'm ready. Where do you want me to meet you?"

"Meet me?" He shook his head. "Rochelle, a real man picks his date up and drops her off at her door. Always."

Oo-kay. "*Um* . . . that's fine." She gave him her address. "I need to go home and change." His gaze made a slow tour from her face to her feet and back up again, making her breath catch in her throat and her heart race. And she wanted to hide. Did he see what she saw every time she looked in a mirror—a tired, overweight woman?

"You look fine to me, but if you'd like to change, that's fine too. I'll follow you home and wait for you. Will that work?"

"Sure." Rochelle hugged Joe and whispered, "I am so going to get you."

Joe merely smiled. "Take good care of her, Warren. She's like a sister to me."

"Oh, I will." Warren spoke the words to Joe, but his eyes never left Rochelle's.

As soon as she got into the car, she engaged the Bluetooth and called Diane. "Hey, Di. Call Joy. I need help."

"Hang on." Diane came back on the line. "Joy, are you there?"

"I'm here. Hey, Chelle. What's going on?"

"Warren showed up after you two left."

"Alrighty now."

"I knew you were going to say that, Joy. Anyway, he asked me out to dinner and—"

Diane cut in. "Girl, please don't tell me you turned the man down *again*."

"Can you guys stop interrupting and let me finish, please? Now, for the record, I didn't turn him down. And we're going tonight."

Joy's and Diane's screams came through the line, followed by "It's about time" and "Finally."

"I can't remember the last time I went out, and I just don't know if it's a good idea."

"It's a great idea, Chelle. What are you going to wear?"

"I don't know, Di." Since she had gained weight, none of her clothes fit well. She had never been small, but lately she hovered between a size eighteen and twenty, depending on the style. It was the one thing that made her self-conscious, and she wondered what Warren saw in her.

"I know it better not be those scrubs you still have on," Joy said. "Where are you going?"

"He didn't say."

"Well, a nice pair of slacks and a cute top will work. I would say bring a blazer just in case, but these mid-April temps here in Sacramento are already acting like it's summer."

Joy was right about the weather. It had been in the mideighties all week. Rochelle mentally tried to recall what she had in her closet and sighed. "I'll see what works. I'm pulling into the driveway, so I have to go."

"Whatever you decide will be fine. Go and have a good time. We'll be expecting the details tomorrow," Diane added with a little laugh.

"Thanks, and I'm sure you will." She ended the call and reached for the door handle, but Warren was already there and opening it. "I need to change clothes. Where are we going?"

"Somewhere casual, so don't worry about getting dressed up. We'll save that for next time."

He reached up toward her face, and she instinctively drew back and gasped. Clutching her chest, she closed her eyes as a fear she hadn't experienced in years rose up and nearly overwhelmed her. When she opened them again, he was staring at her with a mixture of shock and concern.

"Are you okay?" Warren slowly dropped his hand and moved a few steps away. "There was a piece of lint in your hair, and I—"

"Y-yes. Fine." Or at least she would be as soon as her heart rate returned to a normal pace and her hands stopped shaking.

"Are you sure?"

Rochelle nodded but knew he had questions. They stood there a moment longer.

He opened his mouth and closed it again, then scrubbed a hand down his face.

"Go ahead and ask your question."

"Joe mentioned you were divorced, and I'm not trying to get into your business, but . . ." He paused before continuing. "Did he hit you? I just want to know what I'm up against."

Her brow lifted. "What does that mean?"

"It means I really want to get to know you, but I also want to be careful not to frighten you or make you uncomfortable in any way."

Rochelle hesitated. "Once, and I walked," she said softly.

In one of her ex's rages, he'd backhanded her, and although it caught her off guard, she'd managed to dodge most of the force, and his hand merely glanced off her cheek. The impact had been far less than the blows she'd taken from his words.

His concerned gaze met hers. "I can wait outside for you if it'll make you more at ease."

"No, that won't be necessary."

He had been nothing but kind to her. Inside, she directed him to a seat in the living room.

"I won't be long." She continued to her bedroom and cursed under her breath. She hadn't reacted like that in years and had no idea why it had happened today. *Probably some leftover memory from all the times my crazy ex threatened to hit me . . . or the one time he did.*

Shaking her head, she quickly searched and settled on a pair of black jeans and a short-sleeved button-down top that fit reasonably well. After freshening up, she dressed, brushed her hair out, applied eyeliner and lip color, then went out front. "I'm ready."

He stood. "You look beautiful."

She wished she felt that way. "Did you decide where we're going?"

"Have you been to that soul food place in Oak Park called Fixins?"

"No, but I've heard of it. The food is supposed to be pretty good."

"We could go there, if that's okay."

"Sure." On the way out the door, she caught her reflection in the mirror and tugged on her shirt. She wished she had something else to wear.

By the time they arrived at the restaurant, Rochelle was still a little nervous because it had been so long since she'd been on a date. But when he placed his hand in the small of her back to guide her, something about the soft pressure seemed to calm and excite her at the same time. A hostess led them to a booth near the back. The paintings on the wall and the music playing in the background made her feel as if she'd stepped into somebody's big mama's house. It had a true southern vibe. They pored over the menu for a few minutes, and she chose the shrimp and grits, while Warren opted for the fried chicken with collard greens and red beans and rice. Both chose sweet tea.

Over dinner, he told her about his job as a high school psychologist and some of the challenges he faced.

"I don't think I could deal with that many teenagers. The one I have at home is enough."

Warren laughed. "I feel the same way sometimes, but I like to think I'm making a difference in a few lives. The best part is when one of my students graduates from college, then comes back to tell me how much my support and advice helped them." He shook his head. "I can't tell you how proud it makes me."

The emotion in his voice gave Rochelle another glimpse into his personality and provided one more piece of evidence of him being a good man. Until now, she hadn't let herself think of him as anything but a friend, even though she could admit that she'd been secretly attracted to him. However, tonight she could feel the chemistry between them rising with each passing moment. Every sweet gesture, the soft touch of his hand on hers and his magnetic smile pulled her in.

The server returned with their food a moment later, and she waited until the young man left before continuing the conversation.

"You're obviously really great at being a counselor. Do many of them keep in touch?"

He nodded. "More than I would've ever imagined. I've been invited to and attended college graduations, weddings, and even a few christenings." Warren took a bite of his chicken.

"That's pretty amazing. Any advice for a mother of a teen?" she asked with a smile.

"You're already doing great. From what I've seen, you're a wonderful mother. Haley has grown into a lovely young woman."

Rochelle pretended to concentrate on her food, not wanting him to see how uncomfortable she had become. Ever since her disastrous marriage, she'd had a hard time accepting compliments, always expecting the other shoe to drop in the form of a negative comment.

He's not Kenny, she reminded herself. Just the opposite, and like her older sister, Valerie, always said, Rochelle had to stop judging every man's intent by her sorry ex's. She lifted her head and stared into Warren's eyes. "Thank you."

Warren smiled. "No thanks necessary. You've done all the work." They both laughed, then he leaned forward and asked, "How are you all doing with losing Yvette? I know it has to be hard on you."

Rochelle drew in a deep breath. "Harder than I ever anticipated. The grief pops up out of nowhere, and then there are times when I forget and pick up the phone to call or text her." She shook her head as she felt her emotions rising.

"I understand. It's been tough. Rochelle, if you ever need someone to talk to or just a shoulder to cry on, I'm here. No matter what time it is, you can call me."

She met his sincere gaze and nodded. "Thanks. That means a lot."

He took a sip of his tea. "So, what do you do for fun when you're not being Mom?"

"I don't have much time for fun, but I hang out with Diane and Joy."

"You have to make time. It's important for your mental health."

"I know. When it's basketball season, I try to get to at least one Warriors game. Does that count for fun?"

His eyes lit up. "You like basketball?"

"I do."

"So do I, along with football. We'll have to go to a game when the season starts. So, are you Team LeBron or Team Jordan as to who's the best of all time?"

"Neither. I mean, they're in the conversation for best of all time, but until I see somebody hit a hundred points in a game or average fifty points for an *entire* season like Wilt Chamberlain, then I can't consider them to be the best. But LeBron being the all-time scoring leader is definitely up there."

"I wholeheartedly agree."

Over dinner, they continued to converse about their favorite players, then everything and nothing. Then the conversation turned to music. She was surprised to find they liked a lot of the same artists. And every time he stared at her with one of those heated looks, her pulse skipped, and she had to resist the urge to fan herself.

Eyes shining, he picked up her hand and placed a soft kiss on the back. "Basketball, music. You, Rochelle Winters, are a woman after my own heart. I'm going to enjoy finding out what else you like."

The heat from his soft lips on her hand sent all kinds of sensations flowing up her arm. *Breathe. Don't swoon under the table, girl.*

She wasn't used to such frank male scrutiny, and by the time he took her home, she was still a mass of nerves. Was he planning to kiss her? Would it be another one of those sweet forehead kisses or something more intense?

Taking her hand, he walked her to the door. "I really enjoyed dinner tonight and hope we can do it again soon."

Part of her wanted to tell him no because trusting another man was hard, and she didn't want to be hurt again. However, the other part—the one that had enjoyed his company—wanted nothing more than to see him again. The latter won. "I'd like that."

"Would it be okay if I kissed you goodnight?"

She appreciated him asking. Most men would expect it. "Yes."

A small smile tilted the corner of his mouth. He lowered his head and brushed his lips across hers once, twice, and the sweetness poured over her like warm honey. He touched his mouth to hers once more, gifting her with butterfly kisses all over her lips before slipping his tongue inside and swirling it around hers. Sensations she hadn't felt in a long time, if ever, flowed through her, and her arms came up and wound around his neck. Her knees went weak, and she probably would have melted to the floor if Warren's arms hadn't been securely around her. A soft moan escaped as desire flooded her entire being. After another second, she eased back. *What was that?* "Um . . . so that's what you call a goodnight kiss, huh?"

Warren's deep chuckle floated through the air. "That was just a *taste*, baby." He pressed a soft kiss to her forehead. "We'll save the rest for another time." He tossed her a bold wink.

A taste? If that was only a taste, she wondered what a full good-night one would feel like.

Warren kissed her once more. "Sleep well, beautiful."

She nodded, her heart racing a mile a minute. "You too." Rochelle closed the door behind him and leaned her forehead against it. *The man could kiss!*

Chapter 4

Diane

"CHELLE, I CAN'T BELIEVE YOU'RE JUST NOW CALLING to tell us about your date with Warren." Diane got up to close her office door. "It's been three days."

"For real," Joy said. "How did it go?"

"It went well. Actually, it was the best date I've ever had, hands down," Rochelle said with a laugh. "He took me to Fixins, and the food is pretty good. I'm really glad I decided to go out with him. Not only is he fine, Warren is a true gentleman, makes me laugh, opens doors. Oh, and the brother can kiss!"

Diane adjusted the phone on her ear, paused in filing the new children's emergency contact forms and grinned. "That's what I'm talking about, girl."

Joy's excited squeal came through the line. "I am so happy for you, Chelle. Now about that kiss, was it one of those that made you warm all over?"

"Girl, more like a five-alarm blaze and melted me on the spot."

This time, Diane let out a little shout, then clapped her hand over her mouth. Thankfully, her door was closed. "Girl, that's what I like to hear."

"Exactly," Joy said. "It sounds like he's just the man you need to get you back into the dating world."

Chuckling, Rochelle said, "Joy, you sound like Yvette, but you're right."

"I'll take that as a compliment. Is Kenny still popping up?" Diane frowned. "I hope not." Rochelle's ex had a habit of showing up out of the blue supposedly to see Haley. However, his true intent was to remind Rochelle why she would never be any man's fantasy, knowing it would send her self-esteem spiraling down.

Rochelle sighed. "Yeah, but he hasn't been by in a couple of months, so I'm sure he'll be making an appearance soon. Thankfully I've succeeded in keeping him away from Haley. Anyway, how are things with you and Robert?"

"Ugh. Don't ask."

"Sounds like my situation," Diane said. "Tonight, we have a social worker coming for the home inspection. Jeffrey isn't too keen on someone walking all through the house, but I'm just glad he said he'd be there."

"Hopefully, everything will be fine and you two can move forward with finding a little one," Rochelle said.

"I sure hope so. But with all the tension between us, that Jamaica trip can't come fast enough."

"Amen," Joy said. "I've already done a little online shopping, and I found some cute sandals."

Rochelle laughed. "Of course you did."

Diane shook her head. Before she could respond, the receptionist knocked on the door. She covered the receiver. "Come in."

"Mrs. Bell is here."

"Thanks." To her friends, she said, "I have to go, but I'm glad things are going well with you and Warren, Chelle." They spoke a moment longer, then said their goodbyes. Diane stood and went out to meet the woman. "Mrs. Bell, I'm Diane Evans."

"It's nice to meet you."

She smiled down at the toddler nearly hiding behind his mother, his large blue eyes assessing the room.

"This is Connor." Mrs. Bell moved him to stand in front of her. "Connor, say hello to Mrs. Evans."

"Hi, Mrs. Evans," he mumbled.

"Hi, Connor. Would you like to look around the school?"

Connor glanced up at his mother, as if seeking permission, and she nodded. "Yes."

Diane showed them the three-year-old classroom where he would be and pointed out the different learning stations through the open door.

"This isn't like those programs where the kids can choose whichever one they want and are left to figure out how to do the task on their own, is it?" Mrs. Bell asked.

"No. Each class has a teacher and an assistant, and we focus on a little more structured learning. With the ever-changing school system policies, we want the children to be adequately prepared for any next steps."

"Great."

They stopped by the lunchroom where the afternoon snacks were being prepared, and she got permission from Connor's mother to give him a small cup filled with pretzels and Goldfish crackers. The shy smile he gave her warmed her heart. She continued the tour, showing her the playground and lastly, the computer lab. Diane realized she couldn't control what happened once the children left the school, but the center limited screen time in an effort to minimize some of its negative effects—eye strain, headaches, disrupted sleep patterns, ineffective hand strength and dexterity.

"We also have a school-age program that serves students first through fifth grades. The staff walks the students to and from the elementary school across the street. After school, we help with homework, provide snacks and relaxation time. They can also attend full-time in the summer."

"I really like your program, and I'm hoping Connor will do well here."

"I hope so too." Diane glanced down at the little boy still clinging to his mother. "Connor, would you like to meet some new friends?" She extended her hand and was more than pleased when he took it. They walked back to the classroom, and she led him over to a table where three other children were doing a tissue paper art project. Each student had a shape and used their fingers to crumple the paper and glue it on. She lowered herself into one of the small chairs and showed Connor how to do it. She clapped when he finished the first one.

"Look, Mama. I did it!"

The excitement in his voice moved Mrs. Bell to tears. "You must be a child whisperer or something, Mrs. Evans. I have never seen him take to someone so fast. Your children are blessed to have you."

Diane felt a pang of sadness. She stood. "I don't have any children, just my babies here. Maybe it's because I've been doing this for over fifteen years."

"Well, if you ever decide to have some, you're going to be a fantastic mother."

Successfully concealing her pain, she smiled. "Does this mean Connor will be joining us here at Journey Preschool?"

Mrs. Bell smiled. "Yes."

"If you like, we can leave Connor here while we take care of the paperwork. He'll be fine, and Ms. Katie will bring him to the office if he gets a little uncomfortable," she added at Mrs. Bell's look of uncertainty.

"Okay."

Once the paperwork was completed, they went back to collect

Connor. Diane had to laugh when the little boy didn't want to leave. After assuring him that he would be back, he reluctantly gathered up his finished project, and they departed. Diane spent the remainder of her day observing the teachers in preparation for the yearly performance reviews.

By the time she made it home, she still felt a little melancholy. Ever since she found out that she couldn't have children, not a day went by without someone mentioning children or babies. Each time broke off another piece of her heart. The only lift she had these days was the upcoming trip to Jamaica. Diane still couldn't believe what Yvette had done, but she knew they would honor their friend's last wish.

After putting her tote away, she went to make sure everything was ready for the visit. Jeffrey came through the garage and entered the kitchen just as she did.

"Hi."

"Hey."

They had been walking on eggshells around each other since the night of the business dinner a week ago. "I'll do dinner after the social worker leaves."

"You don't have to. I already ate."

Her stomach dropped. "Oh." The first question that came to mind was who he'd eaten with. But, as far as she knew, he had never cheated in the eight years they had been married—although, there had been that one thing a few weeks before their wedding. She shoved the thought aside. He'd made a promise.

Jeffrey stood there staring, as if he wanted to say more. Finally, he asked, "What time is the social worker coming?"

"She should be here shortly." As soon as the words were off her tongue, the doorbell rang. She started toward the front, but Jeffrey held up a hand.

"I'll get it. I still don't understand why all this is necessary," he added as he walked out.

She sighed. In the beginning, Jeffrey had been just as excited and fired up about having children, and Diane had no idea why or when he'd changed his mind. She wanted to understand, but he bit her head off every time the subject came up. However, she was glad that he showed up and hoped it meant something positive. Smoothing a hand down her dress, she headed for the living room just as Jeffrey and the social worker entered. She smiled at the woman.

Jeffrey made the introductions, then gestured for them to sit.

Diane masked her surprise when he came and sat close to her on the sofa. The social worker, Ms. Hughes, sat across from them in one of the armchairs.

"This is a lovely home," Ms. Hughes said as she withdrew a clipboard and pen from her tote.

"Thank you," Diane said, trying to calm the butterflies dancing in her belly. They'd finished all the required hours of training, completed their certifications in CPR and first aid and had their fingerprints, background and financial checks done, something Jeffrey hadn't been too happy about.

"As you are aware, this home inspection is to assess whether you're prepared and suitable to provide a safe and welcoming home for a child." She flipped through some papers in a folder and rattled off all the information that they'd completed. "We seem to be missing your references, but everything else is in order."

Diane slanted a quick glance at Jeffrey, whose expression barely masked his irritation. "I can get those for you before you leave."

Ms. Hughes smiled. "Great. Now let's get started." She stood.

Diane and Jeffrey led her throughout the house, pointing out all the things on the woman's list—smoke and carbon monoxide detectors, fire extinguishers, locks and screens on all the windows, first aid kits, fireplace safeguards. By the time they made it to the two potential bedrooms, even she had started to become weary with the process. The only thing the woman hadn't asked was the color of their underwear.

Ms. Hughes crossed the space, opened and closed the closet, then peered at the walls near the floor. "Do you have outlet covers?"

"Yes, we do. They just haven't been covered since no one uses the room. I'll be right back."

"I'll get them," Jeffrey said and quickly exited. He came back a minute later with the package of outlet covers and drawer locks. "Here they are."

"Oh good." She noted something on the paper she'd been carrying around.

It took another fifteen minutes before the woman packed up. Diane and Jeffrey thanked her and saw her to the door.

"I should have this written up and submitted within the next two weeks. You all have a nice evening."

"You too," Diane said as she closed the door. She turned to Jeffrey. "That was interesting."

"To say the least. I don't know if it's worth it to go through all this trouble." Jeffrey dragged a hand down his face. "They've been through our bank accounts, done background investigations and fingerprinting like I'm some kind of criminal." He frowned. "Now they're searching the house."

She understood where he was coming from, and yes, they had been put under a microscope, but finding a child who could bask in the love she knew he could give—*they* could give—made the process worth it in her mind.

"I know it feels that way, but it's only to be sure someone doesn't adopt a child who could potentially be dangerous. We're just about finished with everything now."

"I'm just not sure if it's worth all this now." Jeffrey threw up his hands, shook his head and left the room.

A churning started in her belly. Was he really going to change his mind? She didn't know what she'd do if he did. All she could see was her dream of becoming a mother going down the drain.

Chapter 5

Joy

AFTER A WEEK OF BEING IGNORED BY ROBERT, JOY WAS in no mood to pretend to be happy. Sitting next to him at the business luncheon Friday afternoon, listening to him go on and on about them being a team and how successful their company had become because of it while holding her hand, made her even angrier. It took everything inside her not to snatch her hand back and knock him out of the chair. But she had more class than that, and more than likely, she would need at least one or two of the people in the room when it came time to open her spa.

Joy scanned the area and made a mental note of the companies represented that did commercial renovations. She'd seen the work of at least three of them and would make sure to get their business cards before leaving. The woman seated to her right asked Joy a question, pulling her out of her thoughts.

"I'm sorry. What did you ask?"

"How long have you and your husband been in business?"

"Almost ten years."

"Wow. Sounds like West Home Renovations has had a lot of growth since then. Are you guys thinking about expanding into other areas, like interior design?"

"We—"

"Absolutely," Robert said. "Joy and I have been discussing branching out so we can keep everything in-house."

Joy slowly faced Robert. *Ain't this about a—?* Once again, the urge to curse him out rose up hard and fast. She turned back to the woman. "We've definitely been discussing *branching out* and will be talking more about it as soon as we get back to the office." She skewered her husband with a look. "I can't wait for you to hear what I've come up with, *honey*."

Robert's smile wavered for a brief moment before he recovered. He kissed the back of her hand. "I know that whatever it is will be brilliant, baby."

"It will be, especially since we've decided to go in a different direction and open a day spa," Joy said sweetly. "It's going to be wonderful, and I can't wait for it to open."

The woman seated next to her said, "That's fabulous. I know I'd love to spend a day at a spa."

"Same here. I'd happily spend a day being pampered." Joy smiled over at her husband.

Robert looked as if he wanted to spit nails. "I guess you have been thinking," he said tightly.

A man sitting across from them lifted his glass in a mock toast and said, "Happy spouse, happy house."

Robert leaned over and whispered, "I don't know why the hell you told them that lie."

Lie? "The only liar at this table is you."

Joy really hoped the smile plastered on her face looked real because she was so irritated, she could scream. She had to get out now before she did something to embarrass herself. Pushing away from the table, she stood. "Excuse me for a moment." She hightailed it out of the ballroom and made her way to the nearest exit, the angry staccato of her heels clicking on the highly polished floors. Once outside, she paced and drew in several deep, calming breaths. There was no way she could go back in there, not without doing something that would put her on the evening news and every social media network known to man. Thankfully, because Robert had been out of the office that morning, they had driven separate cars.

Calmer now, she returned to the luncheon. "I'm sorry. Something came up at the office, and I need to get back." Robert made a move to stand. "Oh, you don't have to leave, Rob. Stay and enjoy. I'll take care of it and see you back at the office."

Robert scrutinized her for a long moment. "Are you sure?"

"Positive." Joy smiled at her dining companions. "It was a pleasure to meet you all. Enjoy the rest of your lunch." She slung her purse on her shoulder and strolled out, feeling the tension leave her body with each step. On her way to the exit, she stopped by the tables of the three people who could potentially help her with her business, got their cards and promised to be in touch.

Instead of going straight to the office, she decided to pay her mother a visit in the hopes that she might have some good advice about what to do. Her parents had divorced when she was four, and she rarely heard from her father back then. According to her mother, he had walked out one day and never came back. Joy and her father had reconnected once Joy reached adulthood, and they spoke on the phone or got together for an occasional lunch, but she didn't have the same close relationship with him as she did with her mother.

Joy thought about calling first but changed her mind. Her mother would be right where she always was from eleven to two every day—sitting in her floral-print recliner watching her soap operas. When Joy arrived, she let herself in, walked back to the family room and found her mother exactly where she thought. Marsha Chandler had retired from the post office three years ago, and at age sixty-eight didn't look a day over fifty.

"Hey, Mom."

"Joy. Hey." Her mother frowned. "It's the middle of the day. What are you doing here, and why are you all dressed up?"

She kissed her mother's cheek, then sat down on the sofa. "I just left a business luncheon. I wanted to talk to you for a few minutes about something."

"Girl, now you know I'm trying to watch my stories. And this is the good part. I need to see if Peter is going to kill Willow."

"Mom, just pause it. When I leave, you can hit Play and fast-forward past the commercials. As anxious as you always are, I don't know why you don't just record them. It would be faster."

"Maybe, but then I'd have to wait at least half an hour later." Marsha reached for the remote and hit the Pause button. "What's on your mind?"

"I'm having . . . Rob and I are . . ." Joy blew out a long breath, struggling to get the words out. "We're having problems—have been for a long while now—and I don't think my marriage is going to last," she said softly as her voice cracked. Saying the words out loud made her heart clench.

Marsha's eyes widened. "What are you talking about? You guys have that business that's doing well, a nice house and everything."

"Not everything." She would take going back to the way they were at the beginning—struggling to make ends meet and living in a small two-bedroom house—any day. Back then, even with things being hard, they had each other, and they had love.

"Is he cheating on you?"

"No—or at least I don't think so." She didn't want to believe on top of everything else, Robert would betray her in that way. "But we're barely talking, unless it's about the company. I'm ready to start my business like we talked about, and he's trying to talk me out of it because he'd rather I stay."

"If business is good, why rock the boat? A bird in the hand is worth two in the bush. Isn't that how the saying goes?"

Joy stared at her mother, momentarily at a loss for words. While they butted heads often when Joy was a teen and had gone through a few rough patches during her college years and because she hadn't agreed with Joy and Robert moving in together before they married, Marsha had been mostly supportive. "Are you saying you agree with him? You remember the agreement he and I had about me opening the spa retreat once the renovation company was solid. You even said it was a great idea and that it would be a nice place for women to escape and relax."

Her mom waved a hand and leaned back in the recliner. "I know what I said then, and it's still a great idea. You still have time to open your spa. I'm just saying a lot of women would love to be in your shoes. Robert is a good man who provides whatever you need and takes good care of you. I would think you'd rather hold on to that than mess it all up." Something like regret flickered across her face. "Women need to stop being all fired up about having everything their way right at that moment. Sometimes it's better to compromise, be happy with what you have and take up the fight another day. I'm sure you two will be able to come to an agreement."

Anger bubbled up inside Joy. She could hardly believe her ears. *Compromise? Having everything their way?* As far as Robert taking care of her needs, he'd done a poor job of that emotionally and physically over the past year. She tried to wrap her mind around her mother's words. "Mom, I have compromised. Actually, I'm the only one who has. I can't believe you're taking his side. And as far as him taking good care of me, that hasn't happened in a while."

"I'm not taking anyone's side, honey. You can still try to work it out. Don't be so quick to end things." She slanted Joy a quick glance, turned away, then added, "It's better than wondering what if. Trust me."

"Are you suggesting I stay in a relationship headed nowhere, and what does 'wondering what if' mean?"

"I am not telling you to stay in a dead-end relationship, if that's what this is. I'm simply saying you should really think this through and be sure the marriage can't be salvaged before deciding. Don't make the s—" She cut herself off and turned toward the television.

Was she saying this because of what happened with Joy's father? The first several months after he'd left, Joy remembered constantly asking about her father—why he had left and when would he be coming back—and wanting him around. Every time she'd ask, her mother would shut the conversation down, and she had never understood why. Only after Joy had gotten older had she chalked up her mother's reluctance to discuss her father to the hurt and devastation of him abandoning his family. It took more than two years to stop asking and wondering, and Joy herself had begun to despise him for leaving as well. However, her mother's words now seemed to contradict everything she'd told Joy in the past. But that wouldn't make sense, unless . . .

"Be sure the marriage can't be salvaged before deciding. Don't make the s—"

Then it dawned on her. Her heart clenched. *No, no, no.* "Mom, Dad didn't leave, did he?" She hesitated before saying the next words because she didn't want them to be true. "You did."

Her mother didn't reply immediately. "Yes," she whispered finally. "And it was the biggest mistake of my life. I don't want to see you do the same thing."

She didn't know what to say. All her life she had grown up being angry at her father for leaving them, and it had been a lie. Memories of the years she had ignored his calls as a teen and the indifference she'd shown him whenever he tried to reach out came back with such force, it snatched her breath away. And not once had he ever said a harsh word about her mother or tried to tell his side of the story.

"All this time . . . Mom, *why*?"

She stared at a spot on the wall briefly, then faced Joy. "It was a long time ago, and this isn't about me right now. I just don't want you to have the same regrets later."

"I can't even process this right now," Joy said, laying her head against the sofa and closing her eyes. "And our situation is totally different. I'm not asking him to bow to my wishes, just live up to the promises he made and be the man who said he loved me. He's not doing either of those things right now, and I'm tired of always being the only one trying to make it work. How long am I supposed to stay in a relationship that's going nowhere?"

"I can't tell you that. Your vows say until death do you part, but only you and Robert can make the decision to end it."

Well, she should have no problems getting out because she was dying inside. She stood. "I have to leave. You can go back to your stories." Although, the conversation they'd just had would rival any one of those television dramas.

"Honey, I hope you and Robert can work things out."

"I don't think so, Mom. I'll see you later." Her mother didn't try to stop her, but Joy heard her sigh and saw her lift the remote and push Play while shaking her head.

A moment later, Joy sat in her car and leaned against the headrest. The visit hadn't gone anywhere near how she expected. In fact, it only served to add more anxiety. Tears blurred her vision, and she swiped at them. No way could she go back to the office. She took a moment to get her emotions under control before calling her assistant.

"Hey, Stacey. It's Joy."

"Hi, Joy. How was the luncheon?"

Enlightening. Irritating. "Oh, it was okay. I'm going to work from home for the rest of the afternoon."

"Okay. You don't have anything on the schedule or any urgent messages. Is Rob going to do the same?"

"He's stopping to check on a couple of project sites." Or at least that's what he'd told her this morning when he'd left.

"Okay. See you on Monday."

"Have a good weekend."

Joy disconnected, started the car and drove home. She walked straight to the kitchen and poured herself a glass of wine. It was after three, so she called it happy hour and went to sit on the swing she'd had Robert build on the backyard deck. For a long while, she sipped her drink and enjoyed the peaceful surroundings. It made her think of the upcoming trip to Jamaica and how she couldn't wait to go. Lounging on the beach, inhaling the scent of lush island flowers . . . It would be heaven. The sound of the water flowing over the waterfall at the far end of the backyard further relaxed her.

The conversation with her mother played over and over in her head. She had been four at the time, so she only had memories of her father being there one day and then gone the next. She'd loved him and had cried for days afterward. She wondered if her brother knew the truth. Five years her senior, Brent Chandler had stepped in as the man of the house by the time he turned sixteen. In some ways, he still held the role. She planned to call him and ask, but not today. Today, she'd had enough.

Joy started a slow sway and thought more about the potential properties she had located for her dream. She still liked the El Dorado Hills space as her first choice, but she had also found a couple of existing day spas for sale. Going with the latter would eliminate the need to purchase all the equipment and hire employees, but it would also make it harder to bring her vision to life in a fully established space.

After her first visit to a day spa with her friends while in college, she had been hooked by the ambience, serenity and services. She'd vowed to open one someday. She'd even gone through the nine-month program to become a massage therapist and practiced her skills on Yvette, Diane and Rochelle every chance she got. Joy loved the thought of being able to provide a place of respite for women just like she'd received and, although she envisioned herself as the owner, she wanted to have the knowledge to be able to pitch in if necessary. She'd decided to simply call it Amani, which meant peace in Swahili. Lord knew she needed that and more.

"So what was the big emergency? I called Stacey, and she said you told her you'd be working from home for the rest of the afternoon."

She sighed upon hearing Robert's voice. She had hoped to enjoy her quiet time longer. Without opening her eyes, she said, "The big emergency was leaving so I didn't lose my mind behind all those lies you were telling about us being a team."

"I didn't lie. We are a team."

She snorted. "A team that works for only one person. When was the last time we sat down to eat together or went out to dinner, just the two of us? Every time I ask, you always have an excuse. And let's not even talk about the last time we had sex." She downed the rest of her wine and got up to get more.

He followed her into the kitchen. "That has nothing to do with this conversation."

"Sure it does. We're talking about being a team, right?" Joy gave him the side-eye. "Unless you've found a new team member." She filled the glass up to the brim.

"We're talking about the business right now, and no, I am not cheating," he gritted out.

The fact that he wouldn't even discuss their marital problems let her know that she was fighting a losing battle. "Then by all means, let's continue talking business. For the record—to clear up the other lie you told earlier—we haven't talked once about expanding *anything*."

He glared, and his jaw tightened, but he plowed on as if their marriage meant nothing. "We should think about it. A full-service renovation company is a good move. People would love not having to contract three or four different companies to do plumbing or interior design."

Joy placed the wine bottle on the counter with a *thud*. "What about *my* company? I gave up my job in finance to support your dream, but you can't do the same for me? I'm not even asking you to give up your job, just to support me in mine. I guess we have very different definitions of what being a team means. You're all fired up about expanding but not about keeping your word. I've been trying to talk to you about this for over a year, and you keep putting me off!"

Robert threw up his hands. "Well, if you wanted to start a business that complements what we already have, like interior design, instead of this . . . this crazy spa idea, maybe we could talk."

"Wow. Just, *wow*. Now that's what I want to hear from the man who's supposed to be my life partner." She pointed a finger his way. "No. What's *crazy* is me thinking that the man I married would have my back just like I had his when he wanted to pursue *his* passion!" She took a step closer. "What's *crazy*," she said, her voice rising, "is me thinking that you loved me as much as I loved you."

She stood there waiting for him to say something. To tell her she was wrong and that he did have her back or at least say that he loved her, but he didn't. He just stood there with his arms folded. Joy hurled her glass across the room and didn't even flinch

55

when it shattered against the stainless-steel refrigerator, the trail of red wine cascading down much like the tears in her heart. She couldn't say the same for Robert. He'd jumped nearly five feet in the air. The shock on his face was priceless, and had this been any other time, she might have found it hilarious.

"You know what? I can't do this anymore. I'm done."

Chest heaving and biting back tears, she gave him one last glare and stormed out. She wouldn't give him the satisfaction of seeing her cry. In her bedroom, she pulled out a suitcase with one hand and dialed Rochelle with the other.

"Hey, girl," Rochelle said when she answered.

Joy could barely talk around the tears that came in waves. "Chelle, I need a place to stay for the night."

"You don't even have to ask. Do you need me to come get you? I don't know if I want you driving like this."

"No. I'll be fine. Thanks, sis. I'm going to drive around for a bit first, though."

"Okay, but if you take too long, I'm sending out a posse."

"See you in a while."

She tossed in enough clothes for a week, added her toiletries, then zipped the suitcase. Taking a last look around the bedroom she had designed, with its custom bookshelves and reading nook, she turned and walked out. She didn't see Robert when she got downstairs, and that was just as well because he had just effectively killed their marriage.

Chapter 6

Rochelle

ROCHELLE FINISHED CHANGING THE SHEETS ON THE bed in her guest bedroom just as the doorbell rang. She rushed out front and snatched the door open. "Oh, thank goodness!" She grabbed Joy in a tight hug. "You should've been here a long time ago. It's after nine. I was seriously about to send out that posse."

"I'm so sorry. I know I should've called, but I started driving west on Interstate 80, and the next thing I knew I was in Vacaville. I stopped at the Nut Tree shopping plaza and walked around for a while."

Pulling Joy inside, she said, "I'm just glad you're here. Come on in. Have you eaten?"

Joy shook her head. "I couldn't muster up an appetite."

Rochelle led her to the kitchen. "Sit. I'll fix you a plate." She had finally gotten around to making the spaghetti that she'd planned to do the night of her impromptu date with Warren.

"Where's Haley?"

"I called Val and asked if she could spend the night." Her older sister, Valerie, hadn't hesitated when Rochelle called to tell her that Joy and Robert were having problems and Joy needed a place for the night. "I figured you needed some time."

"I do. Thanks."

Her heart went out to her friend. Just as Joy, Diane and Yvette had been there when Rochelle was going through her drama with Ken, she planned to do the same for Joy. Things were strained with Diane and Jeffrey as well, and she hoped they'd be able to work out their differences. It was times like these that made her miss Yvette even more. The woman always knew the right thing to say.

She placed a slice of garlic bread in the toaster oven, and when it was almost done, she filled a plate with spaghetti and stuck it in the microwave. Minutes later, she set the plate in front of Joy.

"Thanks, sis. It smells good."

"What do you want to drink?"

"A shot of something strong," Joy said with a wry smile.

Rochelle chuckled and went to the cabinet. She came back to the table with a shot glass and a bottle of tequila. "One shot. Can't have you dancing on top of my table."

This time she laughed for real. "I forgot all about that."

"Yeah, well, I haven't. It took all three of us to get you off that table."

The four of them had decided to celebrate graduating from college by going to a club. After one shot too many, Joy had stood on top of their table and started singing at the top of her lungs while dancing. Rochelle, Diane and Yvette had begged and pleaded with her to come down, but ended up carrying her out. That had been right before their Jamaica trip.

Joy wiped away tears of mirth. "I needed that laugh." She picked up the glass, tossed back the liquor, then set it down. "Now I can eat."

Rochelle smiled and shook her head. She took the chair next to her friend and waited until she had finished eating before speaking. "You want to talk about it?" When Joy hesitated, she added, "It's fine if you want to wait."

"I think my marriage is over. Things haven't been good for a long time, and when I was driving around today, I realized the change began the first time I mentioned working on the spa. Everything came to a head today. We were at a luncheon, and Robert was going on and on about us being a team and acting all loving, all while lying about us discussing expanding the business." She leaned back in the chair. "I said that I couldn't wait to share my ideas, and he had the nerve to kiss my hand and say, 'I know that whatever it is will be brilliant, honey.' Then I mentioned opening the spa, and he had the nerve to ask me why I'd told that lie. I wanted to sock him."

"I'm confused. You called me late this afternoon, not at lunch."

"The argument didn't happen until after he got home. I left the luncheon early because I couldn't take it one more moment."

Joy clasped her hands on the table and recounted how Robert had told her expanding into a full-service renovation company would be a good idea and his response when she asked about starting her business.

"What about the agreement you guys had?"

"Chelle, he actually said my idea was crazy. But what hurt me more was when I told him maybe I was crazy for believing he'd have my back and thinking he loved me as much as I loved him, he didn't say a word. *Nothing.*"

Rochelle gave Joy's hand a gentle squeeze. "I'm so sorry. Do you think you'll be able to fix the relationship?"

"I don't think so. I just feel like he never intended to help me once he saw how well our business grew. And like I said, it's been bad for about a year, but this was the final straw. I finally realized he's never going to support me. And the fact that he didn't even reassure me that he loved me says it all." She swiped at the tears rolling down her cheeks. When Joy's cell buzzed, she picked it up, read for a moment, then tossed the phone back on the table. "That was Robert asking me if I was done pouting."

Rochelle shook her head, not believing the guy she had come to love as a brother would be so callous and not even ask if his wife was okay. "Wow. I'm sorry, sis. You've had a long day, and I have the room all fixed up for you."

Joy stared at her with tear-stained eyes. "I can't tell you how much I appreciate this." She stood.

Rochelle followed suit. "You know I'm always here for you. You've done the same for me countless times. Get some rest, and we can talk more tomorrow. I'll call Diane, and maybe we can do breakfast before Haley gets home. Do you need anything?"

"No. I remember where everything is. I'll see you in the morning." She picked up her suitcase from where she had left it near the door and slowly made her way down the hall.

Rochelle felt her own emotions rising. She knew the feeling. Her own marriage had barely lasted three years, and half of that time, she wondered how she could have gotten involved with a man she clearly never really knew. She tried to recall if there had been signs beforehand, but couldn't say. Kenneth McClendon had played the game well and been a perfect gentleman for the year and a half they dated and the first year of their marriage. It wasn't until their daughter was born that his cruel words began. From her cooking and cleaning to her postpregnancy weight gain and style of her hair, he'd found fault with it all. She had tried to stick it out, hoping and praying that things would change because she knew all couples had their challenges, but the day he raised his hand to hit her, she walked out and never looked back. When it was all said and done, Rochelle severed every tie and reclaimed her maiden name. Though she still had some work to do on her lingering self-esteem issues, she'd finally gotten most of her life back in order and enjoyed not having to always be on pins and needles waiting for the next explosion.

Rochelle was up by eight the next morning and in the kitchen preparing breakfast. She'd already talked to Diane, and before she could finish her sentence, Diane had said she'd be over in an hour.

"Morning."

She turned at the sound of Joy's voice. "Morning. How did you sleep?" She noted the tired lines etched in her friend's face and already had the answer.

Joy shrugged. "Not that great. Kept waking up hoping that this was just a bad dream and not my reality." She came over to the stove where Rochelle was taking bacon out of a pan. "What do you need me to do?"

"You can put the biscuits in the oven. Di should be here in about twenty minutes."

"Okay."

As they busied themselves with the breakfast preparations, Joy didn't offer any conversation, and Rochelle didn't push. Diane arrived just as the biscuits were ready, and Rochelle went to answer the door. "Hey, girl. Come on in." They shared an embrace.

"Hey. How's our girl?"

"Not too good. I think she and Robert may be done."

Diane's eyes widened. "Oh no."

Going to the kitchen, Rochelle said, "Breakfast is almost ready."

She held up a bag. "I brought champagne and juice for mimosas. After the ones at Mimosa House, I've been craving them again, so thanks for the excuse."

They laughed.

Diane hugged Joy. "I'm so sorry, sis."

"Hey, girl. So am I, but I'm glad you're here." Tears shimmered in her eyes.

Rochelle placed a comforting hand on Joy's arm. "Why don't you sit? I'll have the eggs done in a moment, and we can eat."

"I'm going to clean my face, and I'll be right back. I'm tired of crying over that man."

While she was gone, Rochelle cooked the eggs, and Diane helped bring everything to the kitchen table. Diane poured the mimosas, and by the time Joy returned, they were ready to eat. After reciting a blessing, the three women dug in. For the first few minutes, no one spoke.

Diane said, "Chelle told me what happened and that you don't think you two can work it out."

"Not this time." Joy divided a glance between Rochelle and Diane. "And after yesterday, I'm not sure I want to."

Rochelle took a sip of her mimosa. "Joy, are you thinking divorce?"

"I am. Enough about me. I spent all night thinking of me. How are things going with you and Jeffrey? Any closer to finding a little one?"

Diane blew out a long breath. "It's still the same. And I just found out that I've gone into early menopause, so any hopes of having a child of my own are gone. We did have the home evaluation, and hopefully everything goes as planned and we're approved, because adoption will be the only way we'll have children."

Joy reached over and grasped her hand. "I am so sorry. I know how much you wanted to have your own."

"Is there anything you need us to do?" Rochelle asked. It broke her heart hearing the pain in her friend's voice. From miscarriages to fertility specialists, Diane had done it all. Now this.

"No. The only thing I need right now is that trip to Jamaica. Funny, Jeffrey had nothing supportive to say about the early menopause, but he thought the trip was a good idea."

Rochelle shook her head. Seemed like life kept throwing curveballs one right after another. Her cell rang, and she got up and retrieved it from the counter where she had left it, thinking it might be Valerie or Haley. Her finger stilled over the Accept button when she saw Warren's name on the display, and she debated whether to answer it. Joy and Diane stared at her curiously, and she went ahead and connected.

"Good morning, Rochelle," Warren said in response to her greeting. "What are you doing this beautiful morning? If you're not busy, I was hoping to take you to breakfast."

"Hey, Warren. I'm already having breakfast with Diane and Joy. Sorry." She met both her friends' smiling faces and turned her back.

"Guess I need to get up early in the morning in order to get on your schedule," he said with a low chuckle.

The sound of his voice, deep and smooth, floated over her like a gentle caress. "That's not true." She didn't have a schedule outside of work, Haley and the time she spent with her friends.

"Then can I interest you in dinner sometime next weekend?"

She really wanted to say no because he made her feel things that scared her, but once again, the parts of her that enjoyed his company overruled the other parts of her that were afraid. "Sure. Which night?"

"Whatever works best for you, and you can decide where we go."

"How about Friday?" She'd ask Val about coming to stay with Haley. Although she allowed her daughter to be home alone for a couple of hours after school, she wasn't comfortable leaving her at night. "I don't have a preference for a restaurant, so whatever you choose will be fine."

"If you're sure. I'm thinking of a nice steak house."

She sighed inwardly. That meant finding something to wear other than her oversize scrubs. Again. Maybe she needed to bite the bullet and go shopping. "That works."

"I appreciate you agreeing to go out with me. I'll let you get back to your friends. Tell them I said hello, and I'll call you later in the week to confirm the time."

"Okay." She disconnected, went back to the table and picked up her fork. "I don't want to hear one word."

Both chuckled, and Joy said, "One of us needs to be able to get their happy on, and it might as well be you. Does this mean we need to add shopping for date clothes to our list? I mean, we did kind of promise Yvette we'd make sure you gave Warren a chance."

Diane nodded and wiggled her eyebrows. "*Mm-hmm.* We sure did, and that means finding you an outfit that will make his eyeballs pop out."

Rochelle just shook her head and reclaimed her chair, but she couldn't hide her smile. "Y'all are lucky I love you. And yeah, add it to the shopping list. I still can't believe Yvette bought us those tickets."

Joy nodded. "I can't either, Chelle. We have to do this for her. And for us. We can start each day with our favorite cup of coffee while gazing out at the water from the suite." She sighed dreamily.

"Sounds good to me," Rochelle said. The last trip they'd taken had been shortly after her divorce. Between Rochelle adjusting to life as a single mother, Joy working to get the home renovation company on solid ground, Diane moving up the ladder and into the director's position at the day care center, and Yvette balancing a full-time job with a husband and two children, time had gotten away from them. They were way overdue. "So, when are we going shopping?"

Joy gestured to Rochelle's nearly empty plate. "As soon as you eat those last two bites."

Her mouth fell open.

Diane reached over and gently pushed Rochelle's chin up. Chuckling, she said, "Hurry up. Didn't you say Haley would be home around noon?" She glanced at her watch. "That means we have less than two hours to power shop."

"I wasn't talking about going *now*. I mean . . . never mind. Okay, let's do it." The women quickly finished eating and grabbed their purses.

"I'll take care of the kitchen when we get back," Joy said, getting her keys out. "I'll drive."

The three of them piled into Joy's SUV and headed to the mall. Rochelle couldn't recall the last time she'd done something spontaneous. She'd forgotten how much fun it was to just "do" without thinking, planning, weighing, and made a mental note to add more spontaneity to her somewhat staid life.

Once at the mall, they went on a mission.

"Okay, since we're pressed for time, let's find Chelle an outfit for her date first, then get a head start on a few things for Jamaica," Diane said.

"You ain't said nothing but a word, and I have on my power-shopping shoes." Joy lifted her foot clad in purple-and-black sneakers.

Rochelle laughed and rubbed her hands together. "Let's get this party started." In the first store, she didn't know what she was looking for, but nothing caught her eye. Rummaging through the racks of dresses, she picked up and discarded at least ten.

Joy approached with a few garments draped across her arm. "Find anything?"

"Sure, if I was shopping for my grandmother."

She burst out laughing. "They can't be that bad." Joy held up a dress and made a face. "I stand corrected. Who still wears dresses with all this lace around the collar and on the sleeves?"

"Please tell me you weren't thinking about that dress," Diane said, poking her head around the aisle.

"Absolutely not." Rochelle snatched the dress and shoved it back on the rack. The women broke out in a fit of laughter. "I think I'm going to pass on a dress for now because this right here," she waved her hand in front of the rack, "ain't happening."

"Agreed," Joy said, still chuckling. "Let me try these on real quick, then we can hit the next store."

Rochelle and Diane followed her over to the fitting rooms.

While waiting, Diane asked, "Did I say how glad I am that you finally agreed to date Warren?"

Playfully bumping her shoulder, Rochelle said, "Only about a hundred times. He's so . . . so different from every guy I've dated, in a really good way. His calm presence is exactly what I need. Yvette was right."

"Girl, you're gonna make me cry."

"Alright, ladies. I'm ready for Jamaica." Joy danced out of the fitting room wearing a blue tie-dye maxi halter dress with a thigh-high slit, singing "Mr. Boombastic" by Shaggy.

Rochelle threw her hands in the air and joined in. "Oh my goodness. I love it! Where did you find it?"

"There were a bunch of them near the shoes."

"You change. Chelle and I will meet you over there," Diane said.

Rochelle didn't hesitate. "I was definitely in the wrong section," she said once they found the dresses in varying lengths. "These won't work for a date, but they're perfect for the beach." She held up a sleeveless maxi dress tie-dyed in orange and yellow with black accents. "I'm going to try this one on." She smiled over at Diane, who held up a purple printed one that stopped a few inches below her knees, and they both rushed back over to the dressing room giggling like teenagers. By the time she and Diane came out, Joy was waiting.

"Well?"

Rochelle stood in front of the mirror, turned one way, then another. The dress skimmed her curves and had a knee-high slit. And she looked good in it.

"You look amazing, Chelle. Maybe you ought to wear it for your date with Warren. I guarantee his eyes will pop out," Joy said with a sly grin.

Taking one more glance in the mirror, she smiled. "You're right."

"Yvette would say work it like you own it." Diane snapped her fingers and did a little shimmy in the calf-length sundress.

For the next few moments, in the spirit of their friend, they strutted around, moving their hips to a popular Bob Marley song they all knew and worked it like they owned it, drawing stares from passersby.

Afterward, Rochelle fanned herself. "I can't believe y'all have me in this store cutting up."

Grinning, Joy raised a hand. "Guilty. And I'll do it again."

The three women shared a smile, and Rochelle hooked her arm in Joy's. "Come on, before you get us in trouble. And I think I need to go get a couple more of these dresses."

They changed back into their clothes, searched and found more sundresses, then went to pay.

"Since Warren mentioned this being a dress-up kind of date, I'll have to save these for another time." Rochelle wiggled her eyebrows, drawing more laughter from her friends.

"Yeah, can't have you wearing just anything," Diane said.

No, she couldn't. Not when Warren was becoming special to her. It was time for her to let go of her insecurities and enjoy being with a man who treated her like a queen and made her heart beat a little faster with just a smile.

Chapter 7

Diane

SUNDAY AFTERNOON, DIANE SAT RECLINING IN HER family room talking on the phone with Joy. After their breakfast yesterday, she had spent much of the day thinking about her friend's predicament.

"I've decided to file for divorce."

"Are you serious? I know yesterday you mentioned not thinking you guys could work it out. Have you talked to Robert since then?"

"No. And that's why. He hasn't called, texted or emailed asking where I am. You'd think after I left the house and didn't come back all night, he'd at least send a damn text to see if I was alright. I could've been in an accident or something. Obviously, he doesn't care. And I've decided it's time for me to stop caring too. I need to move on with my life."

"What about the company? You'll have to see him there." Diane didn't know if she would be able to work with him on a daily basis with all the tension.

"I've already put an ad out for someone to take my position. As soon as this person is hired, I'm giving my notice. I have an attorney friend, and I'm going to call her tomorrow and see what options I have, then I'm going to look for my own place, maybe an apartment. You know Chelle said I could stay as long as I need, but I don't want to put her out, especially now that things with her and Warren are starting to heat up."

"An apartment? What about the house? With the way he's been acting, he should be the one moving, not you."

"There are too many memories tied to that house, and I'd rather start fresh with a place that belongs to me. We were supposed to find another house, but that's another thing that never happened. Another promise broken."

Diane listened and couldn't help thinking about her own situation. Would she and Jeffrey end up the same way? She closed her eyes. She didn't even want to go there. Yet, the only thing causing tension in his mind was her desire to have children, and she couldn't say whether she would be able to give up that yearning. She wanted to talk about it with her husband, to maybe figure out what to do, but he couldn't be bothered. Then that nagging suspicion that he might be cheating kept popping up in her mind as well.

"Let me know when you're going to start looking, and I'll come with you."

"I'm thinking it won't be until next Saturday. We have a couple of new project bids that need to get done. I'll see if Chelle is available, too, then we can do lunch afterward—my treat. We might as well do some shopping for our trip while we're at it."

She mentally went over her schedule for next weekend and didn't think she had anything planned. She and Jeffrey certainly didn't. "I'm good for Saturday. Have you talked to your mom about what's going on?"

"Girl, that's a whole other story. She basically told me I should think about it before doing anything."

"I can't believe she wants you to stay in a relationship that's hurting you like this." Glancing up, she noticed her husband standing there. She wondered how much of the conversation he had heard. He stared at her as if he wanted to say something.

"She also said she's not going to tell me what to do, so . . ." She let the sentence hang. "But I found out some other stuff about my dad that we can talk about on Saturday."

"Okay. Is Chelle there?"

"No. She took Haley to get some things for a school project and to get her hair braided. I need to go back over to the house and pick up some things I left. I'm hoping I can get in and out without another confrontation."

"I hope so too. Let me know if you need me to do anything else." They spoke a moment longer about Saturday's meeting time, then ended the call. Diane met Jeffrey's eyes. "Hey."

"Hey." Jeffrey sat on the sofa next to her recliner. "What's going on with Joy and Chelle?"

She wasn't sure she wanted to tell him, especially with what they were going through, but she had never withheld information before. "Chelle is fine. Joy and Robert are . . . Joy is thinking divorce."

"I see," he said slowly, as if digesting the information.

Diane really wished she could see inside his head and know his thoughts. Was he contemplating the same for them? The last couple of weeks had been strained, to say the least. They'd walked around the house talking only when necessary, outside of the standard "Hello, how was your day?" greeting.

"How is she doing?"

Her brow lifted. "She's having a hard time."

"I heard you say she's going to look for an apartment."

How long has he been standing there? "Yes. She's staying with Chelle right now, but wants to go apartment-hunting next Saturday. We don't have anything planned, do we?"

"No. Do you want to go out to dinner?"

"I . . . *um* . . . today? Now?" She was so stunned, she could barely get the words out.

71

"Yes. But if you'd rather not—"

"No, no. I mean yes, I want to go." Diane lowered the footrest. "I just need to change. Are we going somewhere dressy or casual?"

"Casual, if that's okay."

"It's fine." Still trying to process what he might be up to, she went upstairs. Her mind went into overdrive trying to figure out why, all of a sudden, he wanted them to go on a date. Any other time, she would have jumped at the chance and been excited. Today, however, she felt only an overwhelming sense of anxiety. Once again, she had a hard time keeping her mind from going down a dark path that led to her thinking he might be planning the same thing as Joy, or worse—that he was seeing someone else.

The old memories rose up again, and she tried to push them down, but they came anyway.

Diane followed Yvette to the front of the restaurant, still laughing at her friend. Her laughter died when she spotted her fiancé on the far side of the room sitting with a group of men and a beautiful woman. As Diane took a step in that direction, the woman leaned over and engaged Jeffrey in a lip-lock that was definitely not professional. Her heart nearly stopped, and tears filled her eyes.

"He was supposed to be at a business dinner with colleagues, and that doesn't look like anything resembling business," she said, choking back a sob. "I'm going over there and telling him it's over. He can have her."

Yvette placed a staying hand on her arm. "No, you're not, Di. Don't do that here. I admit I want to follow you over, take off my earrings and slather on the Vaseline, but we both have far more class than that."

She rolled her eyes. "Class, my ass. The only thing I want to hear is why he lied about the damn dinner."

"Again. Later. We're leaving now." Yvette ushered her out the door and to the car.

Diane fumed all the way home. Once there, she cried. "I thought I had found a man who loved me."

"I believe Jeffrey does love you. I'm not going to tell you whether you should call the wedding off or not, but I am going to tell you to talk to him about it. Talk, not yell." She shrugged. *"Who knows, he might want to open up."*

"Whatever."

Always the wise one, Yvette had been right. Had Diane stooped to his level, she would have never forgiven herself. Jeffrey had shown up at her house fifteen minutes later, and when she asked how the dinner went, he lied. She told him she'd seen him and the woman, and he finally confessed that the woman had propositioned him for one last night of sex as a free man. He said he turned her down because he loved her and the kiss was the only thing that had happened. Diane had been close to calling off the wedding, but he'd begged, pleaded and even suggested they go to counseling together to work things through. She'd relented and ended up following through with their plans.

A part of her couldn't help but wonder, with everything else going on, whether there was some other woman making him a proposition. Then again, despite all their problems, he'd never really given her a reason to think he'd been cheating. No, the only thing she noticed was his sudden reluctance to discuss having children.

"He asked me to dinner, so that's a step in the right direction," she mumbled under her breath while pulling on her jeans and a three-quarter sleeved buttoned-down blouse. She recombed her short layers and noted that she needed to make an appointment to get her hair done. At the last minute, she decided to add lipstick, then went back down to where her husband waited. "I'm ready."

Jeffrey glanced around, then felt his pockets. "I think I left my phone upstairs." He went to get it and came back a moment later.

Diane followed him out to the car and got in on her side. He got behind the wheel and got them underway. She searched her mind for conversation but was afraid that anything she brought up might cause an argument and mess up the evening before it got started. Work was a safe topic, so she started there. "Any word on the promotion?"

"Not yet. Hopefully, I'll hear something within the next couple of weeks. I do think I have a good shot."

"I hope you get it. I know you'll be great." The man knew his job. She'd give him that.

They rode the rest of the way in silence and ended up at Black Angus. She hadn't been to the restaurant in a while. Her next shock came when he walked up to the hostess station and announced they had reservations. She wanted to ask when he'd made them but decided to go with the flow for now.

It took only a few minutes for them to be seated, and the server came shortly after to take their drink order. Diane chose iced tea, while Jeffrey opted for a beer.

"A beer? I can't remember the last time you had one of those."

Lately, he seemed to always order something more sophisticated.

Jeffrey smiled a little. "Every now and again it's good to go back to the basics."

What is this man up to? She studied her menu.

"How're Joe and the kids doing since . . . ?"

Diane glanced up. "I talked to him on Tuesday, and they're doing as well as can be expected, I guess. Ebony has fits of crying, and Ian hasn't been talking much." She still had a hard time accepting her friend was gone, and she knew her grief didn't compare to theirs. The server came back with the drinks and took their food order.

"I can imagine," he murmured, picking up the conversation. "I'll have to give him a call this week."

"I'm sure he'd like that." All the guys had become friends over the years.

He sipped his beer but didn't comment further.

She scanned the room and noticed several other couples laughing and talking. They all seemed so relaxed, and she wished she and Jeffrey could experience the same. While all couples had their ups and downs, the last two years of their marriage seemed to be plagued with one problem after another, from the miscarriages and her most recent health problems to his lack of communication and unwillingness to have a simple conversation.

They'd met through mutual friends, and there had been an instant attraction. With his six-foot, three-inch height, nut-brown skin and hazel eyes, she thought him the most handsome man she'd ever met. She still did. But now Diane had no idea how to bridge the gap that was widening daily. After a few minutes passed, she thought it might be a good time to bring up the adoption. Hopefully, being in a public place would make the conversation go smoother.

As soon as she opened her mouth, the food arrived. After the server departed, she asked, "So how do you think the results of the home evaluation will turn out?" They'd been going through the process for almost four months and the inspection had been the last hurdle.

Jeffrey shrugged. "I don't know why there would be any problems." A moment later, Jeffrey's cell rang. He dug it out of his pocket, checked the display and resumed eating.

"You're not going to answer that?"

"No. It's just work, and it can wait until tomorrow." Jeffrey gestured toward her plate with his fork. "Just enjoy your dinner."

Diane eyed him for a lengthy moment, then resumed eating. "Do you have a preference of a boy or girl?" she asked, picking up on the previous conversation.

He eyed her over his glass. "Do we really need to talk about this right now?"

"I was hoping we could—or at least talk about what has changed with you."

Ever since they underwent the medical testing and started the classes to become foster-adopt parents, he'd pretty much gone silent on the subject. His phone rang again. This time he answered.

"This is Jeff . . . No, Mr. Paulson, this isn't a bad time."

Diane paused with her fork in the air and lifted a brow. *It's a Sunday*, she mouthed. *I thought work could wait.*

Jeffrey frowned, shifted slightly away from her and talked for a few minutes about one of the accounts he oversaw. "I'll be in early tomorrow to take care of it, and no apologies are needed. You didn't interrupt my evening. Good night."

"Since when did your boss start calling on a Sunday evening? And I thought whatever it was could wait." She was so irritated, she'd taken only about three bites of her food the entire time he'd talked, each one turning her stomach a little more.

Cutting into his prime rib, he said, "Since he wanted to give me a heads-up about something I need to deal with tomorrow."

"Key word *tomorrow*."

"He's my boss. Am I not supposed to answer? It's not like he calls all the time, so it's no big deal. Let's just try to enjoy dinner."

Diane bowed her head and drew in a couple of calming breaths. She really wanted them to try to reclaim the closeness they'd once shared, so she let it go for the moment and took another bite of her baked potato. After a few moments she said, "You never answered my question."

Jeffrey frowned. "What question?"

"About whether you want a boy or girl."

"I don't know, and I don't want to talk about it right now. When are you guys supposed to be going to Jamaica?"

She sighed inwardly, disappointed that he still wouldn't make an effort to discuss children. Deciding to let it go for now so as not to completely ruin the evening, she said, "July, and it's for five days."

"It was pretty cool of Yvette to leave the tickets."

"Yes, it was." As they continued to eat, no matter how many times she tried to engage him in a conversation about adopting, he deflected and brought up something else. She had no idea what she'd do if he didn't come around.

Jeff will come around, just keep working on him. Yvette's words came back to her.

I plan to, she vowed.

Chapter 8

Joy

"IS THERE ANY CHANCE YOU TWO MIGHT RECONCILE?"

Joy stared at her attorney and friend, Sondra Harris, and wished she could say yes. In her mind, she replayed the last week of her married life—the argument, the feeling that she wasn't important and the devastating knowledge that her husband didn't love her, or at least not enough to make their marriage work. Once again, the thought crossed her mind that he might be seeing someone else. He'd said he wasn't cheating, but with the way things stood now, she didn't know what to believe.

They used to be so good together, and it broke her heart to know things would never be the same. Robert's caustic words came back to her in a rush. *Well, if you wanted to start a business that complements what we already have like interior design, instead of this . . . this crazy spa idea, maybe we could talk.*

Squaring her shoulders, she said, "No, Sondra. There's no chance."

Sondra gave her a bittersweet smile. "I'm sorry."

"No sorrier than I am. I wish this could be simple, but with the business, I'm not so sure."

"Depends on what you want to do. If you plan to maintain your position in the company, it may not be as difficult."

"I'd rather him buy me out." Joy had thought about staying,

but she wouldn't be able to take seeing Robert every day and having to pretend she wanted to be there. She could also use her share toward building her own business.

"Okay." Sondra continued to take notes on her tablet. "We'll need to determine what the business is worth and—"

She handed Sondra a folder. "Already done."

"You're prepared." She opened the folder and scanned the papers inside. "I assume you're looking for half."

"Yes. I was there from the ground up. If you look at the last sheet, I've detailed everything about the start-up."

Joy had always been organized and tended to keep every receipt and scrap of paper, but she never imagined she'd be using them for something like this.

She nodded while glancing at the indicated page. "I'll read through this thoroughly and let you know what we're up against. I assume he'll secure his own attorney after being served, so we'll wait to see if there is a counteroffer." She stood, rounded the desk and sat next to Joy. "This is always hard, but even harder when it's a friend. I'll do everything I can to make this as easy on you as possible."

"Thank you." Joy sighed. "Hopefully, it can be my Christmas present," she added wryly.

Sondra laughed. "At least you still have your humor."

"At the rate I'm going, that'll be gone next." She grasped Sondra's hand, gave it a gentle squeeze, and then stood. "Thanks."

Sondra followed suit and went back to her desk. "You're welcome. I'll see about having Robert served. It may end up being at the office, so I want you to be prepared."

"I know."

She also knew he would blow a gasket and hoped by having it done at the office, it would keep the drama to a minimum. A queasy feeling started in her stomach.

"Give me a call if you need anything before we meet again next week."

"I will."

Joy hurried out to her car and sat a few minutes to get herself together. She felt as bad as she did the day Yvette died. After taking a couple of deep breaths and letting them out slowly, she felt more in control. Joy started the car and drove off to meet her brother for lunch at their favorite bar and grill.

Brent was already there when she arrived and waved her over. He rose from the booth, kissed her cheek and hugged her. "Hey, sis."

She held on to him, needing to feel her big brother's protective arms around her. At length, she stepped back and slid into the seat.

He reclaimed his seat and scrutinized her for a long moment.

"Have you ordered already?" Joy picked up her menu.

"No. I just got here a couple of minutes ago."

"I already know what I want."

Brent chuckled. "You always order the same thing."

"So do you."

The server came to take their drink order.

Joy really wanted something straight and strong, but it wasn't even noon, and she had to go to the office, so she opted for iced tea. Brent ordered a Coke. "I'm ready to order."

"What would you like?" the young man asked, looking at Joy.

"A bacon cheeseburger with french fries."

"Okay. And you, sir?"

"The same. And can you add mushrooms on mine?"

"Sure. I'll put this in and be right back with your drinks." The young man smiled, collected the menus and departed.

"How are Tammy and the boys? I haven't been over there in almost a month. I need to see them."

A grin spread across Brent's face. "My wife is good. She's happy school will be out in a couple of weeks." Tammy worked as a nurse at a high school. "I need to figure out a way to bottle and sell my kids' six-year old energy. Otis and Jace are driving us crazy with all these sports. First it was basketball. Now it's baseball, and they're supposed to be starting karate lessons in the summer."

Joy laughed. "Wow. They are busy. I have to come see them play."

"Pick a weekend. There's always something going on. I've been meaning to ask how Joe and the kids are doing."

The server returned with their drinks, and Joy waited until he left to answer. "They're hanging in there. Yvette left us tickets and reservations for a girls' trip to Jamaica this summer because we kept putting it off. I still can't believe she won't be there."

"I hear you, but I'm glad you, Rochelle and Diane are going to go. It'll be good for you all." Brent gave her hand a reassuring squeeze. "How's the business?" he asked a moment later.

She added sweetener to her tea and stirred. "Business is fine. Summer is always busy."

"I hear a *but.*"

She didn't even know where to begin.

When she didn't say anything, he said, "Okay, sis. What gives? You rarely call me to have lunch during the week. Is anything wrong?"

"Everything is wrong. I just left an attorney's office, and I'm filing for divorce."

Brent leaned back. "Oh, wow. I didn't know you and Robert were having problems." He reached over and grasped her hand. "I'm sorry. What happened?"

Joy told him about how the relationship had been strained for over a year and that she and Robert had been nothing more than roommates for the past five months.

He lifted a brow. "You mean y'all aren't . . . ?"

She gave a quick shake of her head. "Things came to a head last week when he called my idea to open the day spa crazy. He said if I wanted to do something that was more in line with the renovation company, then maybe we could talk." She felt her anger rising once again.

"Wait. I thought you guys agreed that you'd get your business going once the renovation company was solid."

"We did, but every time I mention it, he brushes me off or changes the subject. He always has an excuse when I ask about us going out or doing something together." She shrugged. "It takes two to make a relationship work, and clearly he doesn't want to put in the effort. I'm done." She took a sip of her tea.

The more she thought about it, the more she realized Yvette had been right about the fact that Joy would have to make a hard choice. Joy didn't want to waste her entire life waiting for something that would never happen.

Brent ran a hand down his face. "I don't even know what to say right now. If you need a place, you're more than welcome to stay with us until you find something."

Before she could comment, the server returned with their meals. She thanked him and waited for him to leave before continuing. "Thanks, but I'm staying with Chelle. I've been looking online, and she, Diane and I are going to check out a few places available to rent next weekend." She added ketchup to her burger and put some on her plate to dip her fries. A moan escaped her with the first bite. "This is so good," she said around a mouthful.

"It would've been even better if you added mushrooms."

Joy made a face. "Ugh." She liked mushrooms on her pizza and in stir-fry, but not on her hamburger.

Brent laughed.

They ate in silence for a few minutes, and she felt some of her tension drain. Being with her brother always seemed to calm her.

Growing up, whenever she cried he'd wrap his arms around her and tell her everything would be okay, then get her a Snickers bar, her favorite candy.

"Does Mom know?"

His question drew her out of her thoughts. "I stopped by last week to tell her I was thinking about it, and she told me I shouldn't rock the boat and that my vows said until death do us part." She dipped a fry in ketchup, then paused to ask the question that had been on her mind ever since the shocking revelation from her mother. "Brent, did you know that Mom left Dad and not the other way around?"

He let out a deep sigh and set his burger on the plate. "Yeah."

She froze with the fry halfway to her mouth. "What? And you didn't say anything to me?"

Brent leaned back against the seat. "I found out years later only because I overheard one of Mom's friends asking her about it. Believe me, Joy, I wanted to tell you, but I didn't know how." He shook his head. "Especially after I heard Mom telling you more than once that Dad had left and we all had to go on. I asked her about it once, and she nearly took my head off and told me never to bring it up again. So I didn't."

"I thought I was the only one she'd forbidden to ask about it." Obviously, their mother had shut him down the same way she'd done with Joy. "I don't even know how to deal with this. And the way I treated Dad . . ." Joy closed her eyes briefly to get control of her emotions.

Her brother reached across the table and grasped her hand. "You were *four years old*, sis. It's not your fault, and I know that Dad never held it against you. Even though I was nine at the time, I had a hard time dealing too."

She gave his hand a gentle squeeze. Since he had always taken care of her and pretty much became the man of the house, she had never considered how much he had been affected. "I'm sorry."

"It wasn't until I turned fifteen that I brought up the subject with Dad. I asked him why he never set the record straight, and he told me he would never put us in a position that forced us to choose one parent over the other. And apparently, he had no idea where Mom had moved for the first year or so."

Joy felt even worse. All the years she believed her father had cast them aside and didn't love them had been one big lie. He had paid the highest cost to prove his love. After all the times he'd told her he loved her, she'd reciprocated only a few times. "I need to call him and apologize."

"He'd like that, and I know he wants to have a closer relationship with you. Now, we need to stop this conversation and eat. I hate cold hamburgers."

She laughed. He always knew how to lift her spirits. "I love you, Brent, and I'm glad you're my big brother."

"Love you, too, baby girl."

They finished the meal, and Brent snatched the bill as soon as it hit the table. "I'll take care of this. You're going to need every penny to get this new venture off the ground, and you know Tammy and I will be happy to invest in your business."

"I can afford to treat you to lunch."

"Maybe, but since I am the big brother, I'm pulling rank." Brent slid out of the booth and extended his hand. "I'm sure you need to get back to work."

"*Ugh.* Don't remind me. We have a meeting with a new client, and I don't want to be in the same room as Robert right now." They made their way to the front where Brent paid the bill, then walked her out to her car. She hugged him "Thanks for lunch."

"You're welcome. I do have a question, though."

"What's that?"

"Robert hasn't put his hands on you, has he? Not getting along is one thing, but that's a totally different story, and I will kick his punk ass if he has."

"No, he hasn't." Joy appreciated his concern, but even if Robert had raised his hand to her, she'd be hesitant to tell Brent. He'd end up in jail for sure. She unlocked the car door by remote and got in.

He studied her for a lengthy moment, as if searching for the truth. Apparently satisfied, he nodded. "If you need me, call. Let me know what happens after he's served."

"I will." She wasn't looking forward to Robert's reaction. "See you later," she said, closing the door. Brent waited until she had driven off before walking the short distance to his car. She threw up a wave as she passed.

Joy didn't see Robert's truck when she arrived at the home of Charles Kelly, their new client, so while waiting, she took a moment to scan her emails. Not seeing anything urgent, she closed the page and tossed the phone on the seat. Then she picked it up again and sent a text to Diane and Chelle to let them know she'd met with her attorney and filed for divorce.

A moment later, Chelle's message popped up: **Hey, girl. You know I've got you. We can talk when you get here.**

Diane: **Are you okay? Do we need to meet tonight? I can bring the wine and tissues.**

Joy smiled and hit the reply button: **Not tonight, but I have another bombshell that will definitely require wine on Saturday.**

Diane: **Wait! What?**

Chelle: **Oh, hell, no! I'm not waiting until Saturday.**

Both texts popped up almost immediately, and Joy smiled. She knew they'd respond quickly. They always did. Subconsciously, part of her had been waiting for Yvette's reply as well. The three of them had toyed with starting a new group text with just the three of them, but couldn't bring themselves to do it. Even though Yvette was no longer here, she would always be part of their sisterhood. Joy released a deep sigh.

She didn't have time to go into details at the moment, so she typed back: **Meeting a client. Will talk to you guys later.**

She tapped the phone against her chin. With everything going on, she needed her own retreat. Jamaica would serve two purposes—relaxing and finding inspiration for her project. Most resorts had well-run day spas, and she planned to ask lots of questions. She'd make some notes once she got home.

Her thoughts shifted to her conversation with Brent, and she found herself more than a little upset with her mother. How could she have threatened her own son that way and lied to her daughter? Her mother could have simply told them things didn't work out between her and their father and left it at that. The guilt that had plagued Joy since finding out the truth surfaced again. She eyed her phone. Seeing that Robert still hadn't arrived, she hesitated briefly and picked it up before she lost her nerve. Taking a deep breath, she scrolled to her father's number and hit the call button. Normally, she'd just send a text, but with their estrangement, she felt a phone call would be more appropriate.

"Joy? Hey," her father said when he picked up.

"Hi, Dad." She had no idea where to begin, and the emotion clogging her throat made it difficult to talk without breaking down completely.

"How are you?"

Willing back the tears, she said, "Okay. *Um* . . . I wanted to come by and talk to you if you're going to be home later."

"Sure. I'll be around." He paused. "Honey, is everything alright?"

"Yeah, Dad. We'll talk when I get there. I should be there by six or six thirty."

"I'll fix us some dinner. Is Robert coming with you?"

"Not this time."

"Well, I'll be glad to see you. You working today?"

"Yes. I'm at a client's home waiting for Robert to arrive, so I should probably get off this phone. I'll see you this evening."

"I'm looking forward to it, baby girl."

They said their goodbyes, and she disconnected. Joy closed her eyes and held the phone to her chest. She had no idea how to fix things with him, but she was going to try. She jumped and her eyes snapped open when she heard the sharp tap against her window. Robert stood next to her car with a frown. She'd been so lost in her thoughts, she hadn't heard him drive up. Sighing, she turned off the engine, grabbed her leather tote and got out.

"Did you get my text?"

"Hello to you too. And no, I didn't. What did you want?" Just the sight of him irritated her, she realized. She needed time and space to process everything going on, and working together every day didn't allow for it to happen.

"I sent you a message to tell you I'd be a few minutes late and to go ahead and start going over the cost estimate with Charles."

"Well, you're here now." She started up the walk, leaving him to follow. When Charles answered the door, Joy pushed aside the riot of emotions swirling in her belly and, giving him a smile she didn't feel, said, "Good afternoon, Charles. Hope you're ready to get started."

Charles Kelly reached out to shake her hand and then Robert's. "More than ready. Come on in."

They followed him to the kitchen where he gestured for them to sit at the eat-in table.

"I'd like to start taking the measurements for the flooring and windows while Joy is going over the paperwork, if that's okay," Robert said. "That way we won't take up too much of your time."

"Sure."

Relieved that she wouldn't have to spend more time than necessary with her soon-to-be ex-husband, Joy sat and removed a folder
from her bag. Charles had questions for Robert and followed him
to the back. By the time Charles came back, she had everything
laid out. She waited for him to sit, then began. "This first sheet
outlines everything that we're going to be doing and the costs of
each." She went line-by-line, and when he gave his approval, had
him sign.

"The work will begin next Monday, a week from today, on the
bathroom flooring, backyard deck and sunroom. Since the windows are made to order, we'll schedule the installation once we
get a date from the company."

Robert came back as she ended. She placed copies of the contract in the two-pocket folder bearing their company's logo.

"Sounds good. My wife is going to be ecstatic about enlarg-
ing the master bath. She's been complaining for a good fifteen
years."

Joy smiled. "I hope she'll be happy with the final results. This is
your copy. If you have any questions, our cards are inside."

"Oh, I have no doubts. I've seen some of your work, and my
neighbor's wife can't stop raving about her bathroom."

"We do our best," Robert said. "I'll see you next week."

"Have a good rest of your day," Joy added.

As soon as they got to her car, Robert started in. "How long are
you going to continue with this whole leaving thing? And another
thing, you've been out of the office all day. Are you planning to be
there this afternoon?"

She took that as him trying to ask where she had been, but she
wasn't biting. "I can do my job from anywhere, and you never had
a problem with me working from home before. Why start now?
As far as me continuing with this *leaving thing*, as you put it, I'm

done trying to fix this relationship when you clearly don't care one way or another."

The few texts he'd sent all had the same tone as his last statement. No apology, no "let's try to work things out," nothing. Without waiting for his answer, she slid behind the wheel, started the car and drove off. Her intention had been to go to the office, but after that little stunt, she toyed with just going back to Rochelle's instead. However, her father lived closer to the office, so she went there and worked the rest of the afternoon ordering the windows and lining up the team who would be working at the Kelly home.

By the time she drove up to her father's house that evening, Joy was a mass of nerves. But she was ready to put on her big-girl panties and do the right thing. She rang the bell, and the door swung open a few seconds later.

"Hi, baby girl. Come on in."

The feel of Gregory Chandler's strong arms wrapped around Joy filled her with myriad emotions—grief, comfort and, most of all, guilt. "Hi, Dad."

He peered down into her face, and his concerned gaze met hers. "Let's sit and talk, sweetheart. I know there's something on your mind."

She followed him to his spacious family room and perched on the edge of the sofa. He took a seat in his favorite recliner and leaned back, seemingly waiting for her to start the conversation. She wrung her hands while the knots in her stomach tightened. Finally, she said, "I'm so sorry, Dad."

He frowned. "Sorry for what?"

"For all the years I blamed you for leaving me when it wasn't the truth," she said as the dam broke and tears streamed down her face. All of the things she'd said, done and felt over the years poured out of her. She buried her head in her hands and apologized over and over. Then those same arms that had consoled her when she'd fallen on her skates and skinned her knees at age four were around her.

"Baby, none of that was your fault. I don't blame you." He held her, whispering that there was nothing to forgive, telling her he loved her and letting her know they were going to be okay as father and daughter.

At length, Joy's tears slowed, then stopped. They sat in silence for a while. "Dad, why didn't you tell me?"

He eased back. "There was no need to put you and your brother in the middle of grown folks' mess."

"But, Dad—"

"No buts. Just like I told Brent, I would never make you choose between me and your mom. You loved her and had to live with her. I'm just glad she didn't deny me the opportunity to see you."

"All the times I thought you didn't love me . . ." She'd told herself that if he didn't love her, she wouldn't waste her love on him either.

He took out his handkerchief and wiped her tears. "I never stopped loving you, even while we were going through our rough patches."

Another wave of shame washed over her. "I'm so sorry for everything I said to you." She threw her arms around him and said the words that she hadn't uttered in over thirty years. "I love you, Daddy." She felt him stiffen.

He leaned back and stared, emotion filling his eyes. "I never thought I'd hear you say those words again," he whispered.

"I didn't think I'd ever say them, but I do love you." Over the past week, Joy realized the love she held as a little girl still existed. However, it had been buried deep beneath all the anger and hurt.

"I love you, too, babycakes. So much."

Hearing him call her the nickname he'd given her as a child put a fresh sheen of tears in Joy's eyes. She laughed softly. "I haven't heard that name in a long time."

After a few minutes, he said, "I'm glad you came. Let's eat."

Joy followed him to the kitchen, and her mouth fell open when she saw the fried pork chops, broccoli with cheese sauce and sautéed potatoes. "How did you know this was my favorite meal?"

A smile creased his face. "I called Brent after I talked to you."

She shook her head. "Well, if you talked to him, then he probably told you that I would try to hurt myself eating."

His booming laughter filled the room. "He might have mentioned that I should fix my plate first."

Joy joined in his laughter. At least one thing in her life was headed in the right direction.

Chapter 9

Rochelle

ROCHELLE'S DAY HADN'T GONE ANYWHERE NEAR smooth, and she would've given anything to be settled on a Jamaican beach. However, their trip was still more than two months away. She had two back-to-back irate patients—one who'd been angry about having four cavities, but probably hadn't flossed since the last visit, and another one who had been twenty minutes late for her appointment and was angry that she'd had to wait. After that, she'd watched a mother break down when told her toddler had to have eight teeth capped because they had rotted due to her letting him sleep with a bottle filled with milk or juice.

Thankfully, Rochelle hadn't been the hygienist on the case.

"It is only Wednesday," she mumbled under her breath, going to the next room. *Two more patients to go.* She grabbed the chart out of the wall file and went still. *What is Warren doing here?*

They hadn't talked since their short conversation on Saturday morning, and every time she thought about their upcoming date, butterflies started dancing in her belly. No denying she had enjoyed his company when they had gone out. Even now, she could recall his gentle voice, soft touch and the sweet forehead kiss when he brought her home. Voices behind her snapped Rochelle out of her reverie, and she realized she was still standing outside the treatment room. Shaking herself, she drew in a calming breath and stepped inside.

"*Rochelle?*" Warren's eyes lit with surprise. "What are you doing here?" He chuckled. "I mean, judging from your outfit, I guess I know what you're doing here. I just had no idea you worked here."

She smiled. "I know what you meant. I've been here for twelve years. I see you're a new patient."

"Yes. My dentist just retired, and I wasn't too fond of his replacement. Joe mentioned this place, and since it's only fifteen minutes from my house, I thought I'd try it."

Figures. Obviously, Joe had ignored Rochelle's quit-trying-to-matchmake speech. "I see."

"I have to say, I'm pretty much sold on coming here now."

Ignoring the sparkle in his eyes, she tried to muster up every ounce of her professionalism. She scanned the history he had provided. "Since you're a new patient and it looks like you haven't had X-rays done in a year, I'll have one of the dental assistants take care of it, and then we'll go from there."

"Sounds good," he said, still smiling.

She flagged down one of the assistants and asked her to take care of the films. While waiting, Rochelle sent a text to Joe: **Warren just showed up. I thought we discussed you stopping this matchmaking campaign.**

Joe: **Hey, I promised my girl, and you know I keep my word.**

Yeah, she knew. She typed her reply: **You're lucky I love you like a brother. Otherwise . . .**

Joe: **LOL! Yeah, I love you, too, sis. For what it's worth, Warren is one of the good guys, and you deserve some happiness.**

That remained to be seen. Though, so far, Warren had proven to be every bit of a "good guy." She shook her head, shoved the phone back into the pocket of her lab coat and made her way back to the room just as he slid back into the chair. She brought the X-rays up on the screen and fastened the paper bib around his neck. While doing so, Warren never took his eyes off her, and it made Rochelle somewhat nervous, but not in an uncomfortable way. She couldn't remember the last time a man had stared at her with such intensity, as if she meant everything to him. Once again, she wondered what he saw.

"The dentist will come in and do her examination, then I'll clean your teeth."

"I'll be waiting."

The sexy grin and low tone in his voice made her heart skip a beat. "I'll be back." She quickly exited. Rochelle needed to talk to her girls about how to deal with this man. Clearly, she had been out of the dating game for far too long. Once the dentist finished, Rochelle returned to the room to do her part. Even though Warren wore the protective glasses, she could see him watching her with that same passion. Being this close to his mouth reminded her of the kiss they'd shared, the multitude of sensations that had accompanied it and the slow slide of his hands on her sides. And he smelled so good.

Warren jerked and brought his hand up to his face. "Whoa."

"Oh my goodness! I'm so sorry." Rochelle had been so into her musings that when she went to rinse his mouth, she missed and splashed water across his face. She quickly wiped up the mess.

He removed the glasses, and she dried them off. "Thanks for the cool spritz. I was a little warm." When she handed the glasses back, he smiled and settled back into the chair.

She tried not to laugh but couldn't help it. It took great concentration, but she managed to get the cleaning done. "Okay, rinse one last time, and you're all set."

This time, she made sure not to miss his mouth.

Warren complied. "This has been the best dental visit I've ever had. I'm looking forward to our date on Friday. I'd planned to call you tonight to confirm, but seeing you in person is much better. We're still on, right?"

"Yes."

He nodded. "I made reservations for seven so you wouldn't have to rush after work."

"Thanks, and that works." Silence crept between them. "So . . . you're all done. You can schedule your next appointment with the receptionist on your way out." She reached down to remove the bib at the same time as he sat up, and their lips were a mere inch apart. Rochelle jumped back and mumbled, "Sorry."

He stood, towering over her five eight height by more than six inches. He gave her hand a gentle squeeze. "I'll see you on Friday, Rochelle."

She followed him out front to drop off the chart. The man had a damn sexy walk. "See you later." She found herself attracted to everything about him, from his tall, fit body and megawatt smile to his calm demeanor and respectful ways. At four years her senior, Warren was most likely far more experienced when it came to relationships. Rochelle's ex had been only her second boyfriend, and since her divorce, she could count on one hand the number of men she'd dated. Her friends teased her and said she'd been out of the game too long, but Rochelle had never really been in the game. Shaking her head at the remembrance of her splashing water all over him, she grabbed the chart of her last patient and headed back down the hallway.

By the time Rochelle made it home hours later, her back and neck were stiff from working with a patient who refused to be reclined. However, she couldn't complain too much. Her job paid well, and the flexible schedule allowed her to drop Haley off at school and be home no more than an hour after Haley arrived in the afternoons. She stuck her head in her daughter's room and found Haley sitting at her desk scribbling furiously.

"Hey, Haley. How was school?"

"Hey, Mom. Fine, but these teachers act like none of the other teachers give homework."

She crossed the floor and placed a kiss on Haley's temple. "What are you working on?"

"An essay for English. I hate writing," she grumbled.

Rochelle laughed. "I know, but it's probably one of the things you'll use most in life. Give me a few minutes, and we can talk about it."

"Okay."

"Look on the bright side: you only have five more weeks of school before summer vacation."

Haley rolled her eyes and groaned. "That's not a bright side, Mom. I still have finals and papers and everything." Haley was completing her first year of high school, and the workload difference from middle school had been a big adjustment, forcing her to learn time management. It hadn't been easy, but Haley had done well.

Still chuckling, Rochelle headed for the door. "You'll survive." As soon as she made it to her bedroom and kicked off her shoes, her phone rang. Rochelle groaned at the name flashing on her screen and connected. "Hey, Mom."

"Hey, Chelle. Long day?"

"You could say that. I just got home."

"I won't keep you long," her mother said. "I just wanted to see if you are coming over next Friday to help me get everything ready for the family reunion."

That was one event she wished she could skip. "I'll be over. Is Val coming?"

"Yes. Your sister will be here. Your grandmother is flying in from Louisiana and staying with your cousins. They'll bring her over."

She rolled her eyes. She couldn't wait to see the family matriarch but wouldn't say the same for her three cousins. As far back as she could remember, they had spent every gathering snickering and laughing about Rochelle's weight and calling her names. Now that she had picked up another twenty-five pounds, she figured it would be even worse. Growing up, she always ended up crying and hiding out in the house. She just hoped to get through the weekend without wanting to knock them into the middle of next week. "I'm looking forward to seeing Grandma. I should make it there by six or so."

"I'll fix something, so don't worry about cooking. How's my grandbaby?"

"Fussing about all the homework she has to do, but other than that, she's good."

"Give her a kiss for me."

"I will." She activated the speaker, stripped out of her work clothes and put on a pair of comfortable stretch pants and a tee.

"Have you talked to Joe?"

"A couple of weeks ago. They're doing the best they can. I'll probably see if Ebony wants to spend the night this weekend. She's really missing her mom. Ian isn't saying a whole lot, but I know he's hurting too." The way Ian had held on to Rochelle when he hugged her tugged at Rochelle's heart. She felt her own pain rising again.

"That'll be good. And boys tend to be closemouthed about their feelings. You should invite them to the reunion."

"I'll see," she said, knowing she probably wouldn't ask. They were already grieving and didn't need to be around all the negative vibes some of her family members gave off. Rochelle sat on the bed and rubbed her neck to try to relieve some of the kinks from being hunched over all day. "I need to go and help Haley with her homework. If you think of anything you need me to bring, let me know."

"Okay, baby. See you later."

After disconnecting, she placed the phone on her nightstand and plugged it into the charger. She sat there a few minutes longer, then went back to help her daughter. Afterward, she fixed a simple dinner. Tonight it was just the two of them. Joy had been invited to share dinner with her brother and his family. Throughout dinner, she studied Haley. "Something on your mind?"

Haley looked up from pushing her broccoli around the plate. "You're just going to say no."

She cocked her head to the side. "How do you know if you don't ask?"

"Do I still have to wait until I'm sixteen to wear makeup?"

Rochelle paused with her fork halfway to her mouth.

"I mean I'm not asking about foundation, fake eyelashes and stuff," she rushed to add before Rochelle could comment. "Just lipstick and eyeliner."

"Sixteen, Haley." They'd had this conversation more than once, seemingly more often in the past few months.

Haley slumped back against the chair and pouted. "All my friends' moms let them wear it. I'm the only one in high school who can't. Just like being able to go on social media."

She didn't believe that for a minute. "I'm not everybody's mama, and I don't care what they let them do. You have an Instagram page, and that's enough for now. In this house, I set the rules, and the rules are no makeup until you're sixteen." Taking in the mutinous glare on her daughter's face, Rochelle tried to explain. "Sweetheart, you are only fourteen, and I don't want anyone thinking you're anything other than that."

"Are you talking about boys? I don't like any of the boys in my class."

"Maybe not now, but remember what happened to your friend Pam?"

She dropped her head and slumped farther in her seat. "I'm not going to do that. It's not like I'm on there all the time anyway."

Wearing a full face of makeup, Pam had opened a second, secret Instagram account and pretended to be eighteen years old. A sexual predator doing the same had befriended her and convinced the teen to meet him at a local coffee shop. Pam had bragged to her friends, Haley included, about the hot senior she planned to hook up with after school. She might have been lost forever had it not been for a family friend who happened upon the man trying to force Pam into an unmarked van.

"You don't have to go on those apps all the time. All it takes is one time, and these days, they'll just approach you on the street, engage you in conversation and tell you how pretty you are. If they think you're older, they may push a little harder, and I don't want anything to happen to you." Rochelle reached over and covered her daughter's hand. "You have your whole life to be grown up, so just enjoy where you are for now." A wry smile curved her lips. "In about ten years, you're going to come whining to me about wanting to go back to being a kid. Being an adult isn't all it's cracked up to be. *Trust me.*"

Haley sighed, and a small smile peeked out. "Okay. I get it. I don't want anybody trying to snatch me off the streets either. Pam was scared for months, and she deleted all her social media pages."

"It was a very scary thing, but I'm glad she's safe."

"Me too." She picked up her fork and continued eating.

After they finished, both cleaned the kitchen, then tackled the essay.

Two hours later, Haley read over the paper and grinned. "Thanks, Mom. I'm glad you like writing; otherwise, I would've been sitting here all night."

Rochelle laughed. "I don't think so. You did most of it yourself. I'm proud of you." She gave Haley's shoulders a squeeze. "Are your friends still coming over Friday to work on your biology project?"

She leaned away and frowned. "They aren't my friends. I don't like them like that, and they get on my nerves. I hate having them in my group. Can't I just say we have something to do after school or tell them you have to work late?"

Her daughter had inherited Rochelle's sister's blunt speech, and Rochelle worked hard to temper her daughter's responses. "No, you can't, but I will be going out later that evening. How long do you think it'll take to finish?"

"No more than an hour, if they quit playing around. When we were over at Erin's house last week, we barely got anything done because she and Tiffany kept checking their Snapchat and Instagram pages, scrolling on TikTok, taking selfies and giggling. I don't have time for that mess."

Patience had never been one of Haley's strongpoints, particularly when she felt as if someone was wasting her time.

"How about letting them know to come from about four thirty to six? That's an hour and a half, and you won't be lying about me having plans," Rochelle said with a smile.

"Okay."

"I'll even make a few snacks for you to have."

"Don't make too much. I want them to finish this project and go home."

Rochelle shook her head. "I don't know what I'm going to do with you. In life, you're going to have to deal with all kinds of people, so you need to learn some patience."

"I do have patience. I just don't like wasting my time." Haley made a face. "Oh, Ebony is having her birthday party on Saturday at five. *Um* . . . are we still going to do our mani-pedi? I think it might make her feel better, and I know she wants to go."

Ebony's birthday had totally slipped her mind. However, she did agree that continuing to do some of those special things might be helpful. "I'll talk to her dad about it."

"Thanks, Mom."

Joy stuck her head in the kitchen. "Hey, guys."

"Hi, Aunt Joy." Haley got up to hug her, then gathered up all her work. "Mom, after I text Erin and Tiffany about tomorrow, can I finish my movie?"

"Yes." They watched her go.

Joy claimed the chair Haley had vacated. "Why is Haley looking so down?"

"She has to do a project with two of her classmates, and apparently they get on her nerves."

She laughed. "I remember having a few of those back in the day."

"Same. She reminded me that Ebony's birthday is tomorrow and wants us to still do the mani-pedis. Joe's having a party later in the afternoon on Saturday."

"That would be nice. We need to do something fun for her because I know she's missing her mom. Since I have only three appointments to look at houses that day, we can go early and be done looking at rental properties around noon, which leaves plenty of time before the party." Joy already had her phone out calling the nail salon and spa where they always went.

While Joy made her call, Rochelle sent a text to Joe and received a reply a minute later.

"Viv said one thirty on Saturday for the five of us. I'll send Diane a text to let her know." Her fingers flew over the keys.

"Okay. How was dinner?"

"Good. I can't believe how fast my nephews are growing. I promised to attend one of Otis's baseball games."

"And at work?"

Joy shook her head. "Nothing's changed." Her phone buzzed. She picked it up and read. "Diane is good." She paused for a moment, then picked up on the previous conversation. "Robert and I don't say anything outside of what's necessary for the job. I'm sitting on eggshells waiting for him to be served because I know it'll end up in another blowup. I expect it to happen tomorrow or Friday." She waved a hand. "I don't want to talk about it anymore. Did you have any crazy patients today?"

"No, but I got the shock of my life when I walked into a treatment room and saw Warren sitting in the chair."

Her mouth fell open. "Are you *kidding* me?" She burst out laughing. "How did he end up at your office?"

"He said his dentist retired, and Joe *conveniently* told him about our office. I could barely get through the cleaning." Even now, Rochelle could recall his intense gaze and how being so close to him made her heart race. And the fact that she'd tried to give him a shower.

Joy shook her head. "Yvette is still running things, even though she's not here."

They fell silent for a moment. "Damn, I miss her."

"Me too. But you know if she were here, she'd be telling us both to get it together."

They smiled and Rochelle said, "Yes, she would."

"You and Warren are still going out on Friday, right?"

"I told him yes, but I feel like a fish out of water, and I don't know what to do. On one hand, he's a really nice guy, and I like being with him. On the other, I'm not sure I can let another man get close to me."

"Sis, don't punish him for Kenneth's mistakes. Warren is a good man. He has to be, otherwise Joe would've shut him down cold before he could even say hello." Joy stood. "You deserve to have a man who will show you what it's like to be desired." A shadow crossed her face, as if remembering better days. "I'll see you in the morning."

"Good night." Rochelle sat there awhile longer trying to convince herself that she did, indeed, deserve a good man.

Chapter 10

Joy

JOY HAD SPENT THE ENTIRE WEEK AVOIDING ROBERT. Thankfully he'd been out of the office for the most part, which left her time to type up instructions for whomever would be taking her place. It hadn't taken long for the applications to start rolling in after posting the job announcement, and she had whittled down the list to three candidates. She sent them each an email with a date and time to be interviewed, then made a list of questions. She would stay around for a couple of weeks to make sure the transition went smoothly, which was more than Robert deserved, but after that, he'd be on his own.

"Why are you doing this to us?"

Joy glanced up to see Robert in the doorway. He came in and closed the door. "Doing what?"

Robert waved a hand. "This . . . this sulking. You're acting like a child who can't have her way."

She rotated her chair to face him. She'd never considered herself to be a violent person, but lately she found herself wanting to punch Robert in his face every time she saw him. "I'm not sulking. This is me thinking about the direction our relationship is going to take. If you're not man enough to honor your word on this, I have to wonder what else you'll fail to honor."

"You're willing to throw away our marriage for something as

trivial as a disagreement about starting another business? You're messing up the best thing we've got going. Business is picking up, and now's not the time to start something new."

"Trivial? And is that all you're concerned about . . . the *business*?"

Just like last time, she waited to see if he would say anything about saving their marriage, but he didn't. Again. Obviously, their marriage wasn't included in his "best thing going" statement. And did he really stand there and accuse her of "messing up" the business when it was the only thing between them going well?

Joy shook her head. "You just don't get it, and it's not like we've had a *real* marriage for a long time. This isn't about the business; it's about you being a selfish jerk."

Robert sighed and ran a hand over his head. "Look, Joy . . ."

She jumped up from her chair. "No! *You* look." She braced her palms on the desk and pinned him with a glare. "I'm tired of being the only one trying to make this marriage work. The only thing you seem to be concerned about is this company. Tell me I'm wrong."

Before she could comment further, Stacey knocked and stuck her head in the partially closed door. Joy was sure the woman had gotten an earful. Usually Joy tried to keep her private life just that. Today, she could care less.

"I'm sorry to interrupt, but, Robert, there's a young man here to see you."

"Did he say what he wanted?"

Stacey shook her head and divided her gaze between Joy and Robert. "I tried to get him to talk to one of the other project managers, but he refused and said that he needed to see you specifically."

The process server? Joy's heart started pounding. She had planned to be out of the office when Robert was served and would have been had her earlier appointment not canceled.

"Have him wait in my office," Robert said. "I'll be right there." As soon as Stacey left, he closed the door and turned back to Joy. "We need to finish this conversation."

She shrugged. "It's finished. I have nothing else to say." She dropped back down in her chair and rotated it toward her computer. "Isn't there someone waiting for you?"

Robert stood there a moment longer, then snatched the door open and strode out, slamming it behind him.

Joy leaned her head back and released a long breath. If the man waiting was indeed the process server, she hoped Robert would have sense enough to wait until later to bring it up to her. Then again, if he had any sense, she wouldn't have had to file for divorce in the first place. Sitting up, she refocused on the document in front of her. She had a meeting with the human resource director later to discuss the salary and pertinent information needed for whichever candidate would replace Joy. Joy dearly wanted to just hire the person and leave a folder with some notes, then throw up the deuces and say she was out. However, the professional in her wouldn't allow it.

She was halfway through her list when the door burst open and Robert stalked over to her desk and slapped some papers down.

"What the hell is this?"

She glanced over and saw the court address. "Divorce papers," she answered mildly.

"I can't believe you're doing this."

"I don't know why not. You haven't given me one reason *not* to do it." Joy stood, rounded her desk and went to close the door. She leaned against it and folded her arms. "Are you here to give me one now? Tell me you don't want out of this marriage?" For a split second his features softened, and she saw a glimpse of the man she had fallen in love with all those years ago, but it disappeared so quickly she couldn't be sure whether it was just wishful thinking.

Robert scrubbed a hand down his face and paced. He came back and stood in front of her. "Was this some impulsive decision because of the disagreement we're having about you wanting to start your spa?"

"Impulsive?" Once again, he seemed to lay the blame at her feet. "There was nothing impulsive about my decision. I've thought about it for the past six months. *Six* months, Robert! You keep canceling our date nights, and we haven't eaten dinner together at home in I don't know how long. You haven't touched, kissed or made love to me in months. I guess it's a good thing I have my battery-operated boyfriend, otherwise I'd be shit out of luck," Joy said with irritation. "I asked you if you loved me, and you didn't answer. What am I supposed to think? I moved out, for heaven's sake, and you've never even *asked* about it or apologized for the things you said to me." She released a deep sigh. "I'm tired, Robert. Tired of being the only one fighting for this relationship. Tired of being the only one fighting for *us*." Her shoulders slumped, and the sting of tears burned her eyes. "I can't do it anymore." Joy pushed off the door and started back to her desk.

Robert placed a staying hand on her arm. "Joy." Her glare made him drop his hand. "Let's talk about this."

"We are talking about it. And it's done."

"You don't mean that, baby."

The endearment caught her off guard.

"Can we go somewhere and talk for a few minutes? The coffee shop is right down the street."

The softness of his voice and the plea in his eyes also caught her off guard. It was the first time in a long while that she felt the tiny tug on her heart. She wanted to hope, but with everything that had gone on before . . . Again, she wondered if it was just wishful thinking that somehow their marriage could be salvaged. When she met Robert fifteen years ago, she had been halfway through her MBA program, and he'd been finishing his construction engineering degree. They'd bonded over the woes of school and were soon inseparable. They'd shared their dreams and grew closer and, two years later, were headed for the altar.

He moved closer to her. "Just for a few minutes."

The heat of his body surrounded her, reminding her just how long it had been since they'd had actual contact. Her traitorous body reacted, and she heard herself agreeing. "Okay. I need to be back for a meeting with HR in an hour."

Robert nodded. "I'll let Stacey know we're leaving and meet you out front."

Joy nodded. When he left, she saved the document on her computer, got her purse and went to wait.

They stepped outside and she tightened her jacket around her to ward off the cool temperatures. It had dropped by a good fifteen degrees over the past two weeks and she sincerely hoped that when the calendar turned to May next week that it would warm up some. The walk to the nearby spot was accomplished in complete silence, and once seated with their drinks of choice, neither seemed anxious to begin the conversation. Finally she said, "You said you wanted to talk. I'm listening."

"Not sure where to begin." Robert held her gaze for a moment before dropping it and staring into his cup.

Joy had always been the one to start the conversations in their relationship. Lately she'd stuck her neck out there too many times, only to have it chopped off. But this time she didn't plan to do it. She picked up the cup and sipped the chamomile tea.

"Maybe I have been a little distant, especially about the spa. I know business is good right now, but in this economy, things can change without warning and I guess it's got me a little spooked."

"I don't understand why. We're very careful not to overextend ourselves and we make sure we get the best prices for our materials. I stay well within the budget we set, and we've been in the black for over three years. Even if there's a change in the economy, the company has built up enough of a reputation that we should be fine."

"Can you compromise and give me a little more time?"

Why did she always have to be the one to compromise? She had done that at the beginning when they were deciding which of the businesses to start first. Now he wanted her to do it again. "I have been compromising . . . for a decade. When is it going to be my turn?"

Robert covered her hand with his. "Please, baby. Just another couple of months. I don't want to lose what we have. I want you to come back home."

Joy eased her hand from his. "I'll think about it."

"Joy."

"It's the best I can do." She really wanted to agree to give them another chance. However, the hurt in her heart wouldn't allow her to just erase everything that had happened over the past year. Besides, he hadn't said anything about love. The memory of that day in the kitchen when she'd asked and he didn't answer flashed in her mind. No, for now she would remain cautious. And keep her appointments to look at condos in the morning.

Chapter 11

Rochelle

ROCHELLE PLACED THE PLATE OF FRUIT AND CHIPS and dip on the dining room table between Haley and her classmates, then went back for the lemonade.

"My mom said she'd be here to pick me up at six," Tiffany said, bobbing her head to the music playing softly in the background.

Erin smiled. "Thanks, Ms. Winters. You're going home at six, Tif?"

"I don't know what you're talking about. You're going home at six too," Haley said to Erin.

Rochelle placed the small pitcher and three cups on the table and shot her daughter a glare. *This girl!*

Haley shrugged and mouthed, *What?*

She shook her head and, giving her one last look of warning, left the girls to their task. Pouring herself a small glass of lemonade, she headed to her bedroom to get started on her own task— finding something appropriate to wear for her date. The butterflies in her stomach took flight again, and, staring into the cup, she wished it was something a little stronger. *I definitely need to go shopping again and soon.* It took a good forty minutes of trying on one thing after another to settle on a navy skirt and gray wrap blouse.

"Girl, you'd better believe that if I had your curves, I'd be flaunt-

ing them every day. Embrace your beautiful curves, sis. And work it like you own it." Yvette's words came to her mind unbidden. Smiling and promising herself she'd keep working on loving herself, she laid the chosen outfit on her bed and went back out front to make sure Haley hadn't tossed the girls out.

"How's it going?"

Tiffany glanced up. "We're almost done."

She retrieved the empty plates and took them to the kitchen. Thankfully, Val had volunteered to bring dinner for her and Haley, so Rochelle would have one less thing to worry about. She rinsed and placed the plates in the dishwasher along with the few other things in the sink. The doorbell rang. Rochelle dried her hands and went to answer. She had expected to see one of the parents but saw her sister standing there instead with a bag.

"Hey, Val."

"What's up, sis? Ready for your big date?" Val stepped inside and hugged Rochelle, then headed straight toward the kitchen.

"I guess."

She stopped and turned. "Did something happen?"

"No. Why?"

"Just trying to figure out why you wouldn't be ready for a date with someone as fine as Warren. For a man in his forties, the brother has it going on—handsome face, sexy walk, nice body. I'd for damn sure be ready," she whispered, then laughed and continued walking. "Hey, Haley and Haley's friends," she called out.

"Hi," the girls chorused. She placed the bag on the counter. "What are you wearing tonight?"

The doorbell rang again, saving Rochelle from having to answer. Fortunately, both mothers had arrived at the same time to pick up their daughters, and Rochelle wouldn't have to worry about Haley badgering Erin about leaving. After a quick round of goodbyes, she and Haley joined Val in the kitchen.

"How did the studying go?" Val asked.

Haley peered into the bag. "Fine. We finally finished the project. What did you bring for dinner?"

"Wings, potatoes, breadsticks, veggies and dip. All the proper fixings for a Friday night. Of course, we have to make root beer floats too."

"Ooh, yay! Can I eat now?"

"As soon as you put your books away and wash your hands," Rochelle said.

"Okay," she grumbled and shuffled out.

Val chuckled. "You are such a mean mother, making your child clean up after herself and not bring germs to the table."

"I know, right? I'm going to get dressed," Rochelle said with a smile as she left the room. She had just taken off her earrings and placed them on the nightstand when Haley appeared in the doorway.

"Can I ask you something?"

She hoped it wasn't another one of those questions about changing the house rules because she didn't have time for a lengthy discussion. "Sure."

"Who is the guy you're going out with?"

"Mr. McIntyre."

Her eyes widened. "Are you talking about Uncle Joe's friend?"

"Yes."

She giggled. "Ooh, he's cute for an older guy."

Rochelle shook her head, then angled it thoughtfully. "How do you feel about me going out with him, or any guy for that matter?"

Haley shrugged. "Okay, I guess." After a long pause she asked quietly, "Why doesn't my father ever come over?"

She knew they would eventually have this conversation but wished it were at a different time. She patted the bed beside her.

"Come here, baby." She waited until Haley was comfortable before answering. "Sometimes people just aren't ready to be husbands and fathers."

"I heard you, Aunt Joy, Aunt Yvette and Aunt Diane talking one time, and they said he wasn't really nice, and that's why you left."

Rochelle sighed heavily. "That's true. He wasn't, and if someone is being hurt in a relationship, emotionally or physically, that person has to make the best decision for themselves. And that's what I did. It was better for you and me to be together without him." Haley had been less than two years old when Rochelle left, and the teen had no memories of the man who'd fathered her.

"Did he hit us?"

She had never lied to her daughter and wouldn't start now. "He never hit you, but he hit me once, and that's when I knew for sure I had to leave . . . to protect us."

Haley seemed to think for a moment, then she hugged Rochelle tightly. "I'm so glad you didn't let him hurt us, Mom. My friend at school is scared all the time because her dad hits her and her mom and brother. She said her mom is going to take them away soon. I promised not to tell anyone, but I wanted to tell you."

She wrapped her arm around her daughter's shoulder and gave it a gentle squeeze. "I'm glad you told me, and I hope they're able to get away." Rochelle wanted to press for a name with the intention of calling the authorities but sensed Haley's struggle with breaking a friend's confidence and didn't want to add to the burden. But then again . . .

"Would you like to tell me her name? Maybe I can figure out a way to get her mom some information about safe places."

Haley shook her head. "I can't, Mom."

"Haley—"

"I promised I wouldn't."

Sighing, Rochelle said, "Alright. But if she comes to you again, or if you think she and her family need something, please let me know." She just prayed things worked out for the family. She kissed Haley's temple.

"Okay. Thanks, Mom." They sat silently for a moment, then she said, "*Um*, shouldn't you be getting ready for your date?"

"Probably, since Mr. McIntyre will be here in about forty minutes."

"I really hope you have a good time."

"So do I."

Rochelle watched her daughter's departure with a smile. The rest of her marriage might have been crap, but having Haley was the most precious blessing in her life. She stood and went into the bathroom. After dressing, she viewed herself critically in the mirror. Everything fit okay, and the style of the blouse camouflaged her midsection reasonably well.

A knock sounded. "Can I come in?" she heard her sister ask.

"Yep."

Valerie entered and eyed the outfit. "That's what you're wearing?"

"What?" Rochelle sighed. "I knew this wasn't going to work." She glanced over at the clock. Warren would be arriving in less than five minutes, which didn't give her time to change into something else.

"Don't get me wrong, sis, you look good, but you're dressed more like you're going to a business meeting than on a date, is all I'm saying. It's a good thing that TV show *What Not to Wear* isn't still on. I'd nominate your butt in a heartbeat."

Rochelle skewered her with a look, and Val ignored it. "Joy, Diane and I went shopping last weekend, but didn't find anything. I had planned to go shopping this week but didn't get a chance. When we make our next trip to the mall for our Jamaica trip, I'll also be looking for some *date clothes*. Happy now?"

"There's hope for you yet, sister of mine."

The two shared a smile. "Whatever." Although, she was looking forward to finding some cute outfits, both for her dates and for their trip.

Valerie came over to where Rochelle still stood staring in front of the mirror. "Chelle, you are so beautiful. I know Kenny did a number on you—he was an ass—but Warren is a totally different man. This really is a good thing, sis."

She stared at her sister's reflection behind her. Valerie had always been her champion, even when Rochelle couldn't do it herself. "Thanks, and I know he is. I don't know what I'd do without you."

Valerie grinned. "Yeah, me either." They both laughed. "I think that's the doorbell. I'll get it." She rushed out of the room.

Rochelle drew in a deep, steadying breath, picked up her purse and started for the door. She paused to turn off the light, then made her way to the living room.

"Hi."

Warren whirled around. A grin made its way over his face as his gaze traveled slowly down her body and back up again. "You're more beautiful each time I see you." He closed the distance between them and brushed a kiss over her lips. "Hi, baby." He handed her a vase filled with the prettiest red roses she had ever seen.

"These are gorgeous. Thank you." She placed them in the center of her coffee table. Both Valerie and Haley were staring with huge smiles.

"Haley, I want to thank you for allowing me to spend some time with your mother. These are for you." He gave her a small bouquet of pink carnations.

Haley's eyes lit up like fireworks. "Wow! Thank you, Mr. Mc-Intyre." She gave Rochelle a thumbs-up.

Rochelle couldn't believe his thoughtfulness. "That was very nice of you."

"It's the least I could do. If I'd known your sister was going to be here, I would've gotten her some too."

Valerie waved him off. "Don't worry about me. Besides, my husband might lose his mind if somebody else bought me flowers."

Warren laughed and raised his hands in mock surrender. "Well, I certainly don't want to cause any problems." He turned to Rochelle. "Are you ready?"

"Yes."

"You kids have a good time, and *don't* hurry back," Valerie said with an exaggerated wink.

He chuckled, and Rochelle rolled her eyes. At the door, she turned back and saw her sister pretend to swoon, complete with a fall to the sofa, while Haley broke out in a fit of muffled giggles. Rochelle quickly closed the door just as Warren faced her. She smiled.

He helped her into the car, rounded the fender and got in on the other side.

"Sorry about Val. She doesn't have a filter."

Warren got them on the road. "I like her. I probably should've asked about giving flowers to your daughter. I apologize if I overstepped."

"You're fine. As I said, I think it was a nice gesture." She'd never introduced any of the guys she'd dated to her daughter and didn't know why she felt comfortable doing so this time. Haley already knew him, she reasoned, so Rochelle didn't see any harm in it. Although if things went south between them, it would be pretty awkward seeing him whenever they ran into each other at Joe and Yvette's house. "So where are we going?"

"I made reservations at Morton's downtown, if that's okay."

"Sounds good." As he drove she found herself studying the strong lines of his face, the way his large hands gripped the steering wheel and the bulge of his biceps in the navy polo shirt.

"Something on your mind?"

Rochelle jerked her gaze up to his face. "*Um*, no. I've never heard this song before. Who is it?"

Warren slanted her a knowing glance. "A local guy named Joe Leavy. On one of those rare times I was listening to the radio, they were advertising a concert of his and had him on live. They played a few of his tracks and they sounded pretty good. So a couple of my buddies and I went to check him out. He put on a great show and I downloaded some of his music."

"I like it." It was that good old R&B she rarely heard these days, except from a few of her favorites. She made a mental note to look him up.

"Since we're on the subject of music again, if you had the chance to attend a concert, who would you see?"

She leaned back and thought for a moment. She couldn't remember the last concert she'd attended, unless she counted the holiday music show at Haley's school. A sad statement she knew, one that said she needed to do more than just work and go home.

"I'd like to see Jill Scott, Lalah Hathaway, Maysa, Eric Benét, or Kenny Lattimore. Maybe Leela James. If I'm paying money for a concert, I need to see people who can actually sing like the album, instead of lip-synching while doing some complex choreographed dance routine."

He laughed. "You've got a point. I'd be pissed off if I paid good money to see somebody and found out they could barely hold the note and had their voices auto-tuned in the studio."

"Exactly! That's why I stick with the ones who are a sure bet."

"Then how about you and I make a date to go see one of those singers on your list the next time they come to town?"

Rochelle opened her mouth to say yes but closed it. Who knew the next time any of her favorite singers or groups would make it to the area? By then they might not even be seeing each other, but he seemed to assume otherwise.

"You don't want to go?"

She stared out the window. "That's not it. I was just thinking it could be a while before any of them have a show near here. We may not even be . . ."

"Oh, we'll still be dating."

She whipped her head around and met his gaze.

"Count on it." Warren refocused his attention on the road with a broad grin.

Rochelle didn't say another word until they reached the restaurant. The man was confident. Not in an arrogant sort of way, but more like someone who knew what he wanted. That made one of them. She had no idea what she wanted. True, she sometimes imagined how nice it would be to have a good relationship, but she was a realist. Not everyone had the same kind of love story as her parents, sister, and Joe and Yvette. Rochelle saw them as the exception, not the norm. She glanced up at Warren, and he gave her a smile that made her heart skip a beat. Rochelle returned it. Maybe this time would be different.

He led her inside the upscale steak house, and they were shown to a booth in minutes. A white linen cloth covered the table, and a candle with a soft glowing light sat in the center. Music played softly in the background. Once they received their drinks and had their orders taken, Rochelle summoned the courage to ask the question that had been nagging at her for days. "Have you ever been married?"

He let out a small chuckle. "Once, a long time ago. I'd just turned twenty-one, was at the end of my third year of college and thought I was madly in love. We both did. Our parents tried to tell us to wait until we graduated and found jobs, but we knew every damn thing, and no one could tell us anything. We were all the way grown." He shook his head and chuckled. "I argued that I'd been living on my own in the dorm and so had she, and we'd be just fine living in our own apartment."

Rochelle took a sip of her wine. "I take it you found out differently."

"Boy, did I. Reality hit us like a ton of bricks. Going from staying in a dorm where we had no household bills and a dining hall where we could go and eat virtually anytime to having to do all of those things on our own turned out to be far harder than we ever imagined." Warren told her about all their struggles but paused when the server returned with their meals.

"How long did you stay together?"

"We tried to make it work for almost three years, but it was just too hard. She knew it, and I knew it. Rather than ending up hating each other, we decided to end it."

They ate for a few minutes in silence.

"Do you still talk to her?"

She had no idea why she had asked the question. Did he still have feelings for the woman? She tried to tell herself it didn't matter one way or another, but inside she knew it was a lie. The more time she spent with Warren, the more she liked him, and it scared the hell out of her.

"We talk every now and again. She's remarried and has two children."

Rochelle stared. He didn't sound angry, bitter, or anything. As a matter of fact, he had a smile on his face and in his voice. She wouldn't be able to do the same when it came to her ex. Just the thought of Kenneth brought out an anger she never knew she possessed. She did have another question, however. "So, in all that time, you've never found . . . *um* . . . never married again?"

Warren shrugged. "Never found the right one, I guess."

Something had to be wrong with the women around here. From what he'd shown her, the man was damn near perfect—good job, great personality, a gentleman, sexy from top to bottom. Or was it all an act?

Okay, girl. Get a grip.

She snatched herself back from her trip down the rabbit hole, picked up her glass and took a huge gulp.

He leaned forward and pinned her with a searing gaze. "But I think my luck is changing."

Rochelle choked. Coughing, she set the glass down with a *thud*.

Warren was up and around to her side in a flash. "Are you okay?" He handed her a glass of water.

Embarrassed beyond belief, she accepted the glass and took a few cautious sips. "I'm fine. Really," she added when he didn't move. He scrutinized her a moment longer, then returned to his seat. Rochelle always made a practice of not drawing attention to herself, and with half the patrons in the restaurant staring at her, she wanted to crawl under the table or run out the door. Both of those choices would only make things worse, so she stifled the urge and concentrated on her food. She managed to get through the rest of the dinner without further embarrassment, but she remained curious about what he'd meant by the statement. When they finished eating, both declined dessert. Warren paid the bill and escorted her out to his car.

"I had a really good time tonight, Warren," she said as he started the engine.

"So did I." He leaned over, pressed a soft kiss to her lips and drove out of the lot.

They passed the time talking quietly, interspersed with moments of companionable silence, and Rochelle found herself becoming more and more comfortable with him.

Once they arrived at her house and he'd walked her to the door, Warren said, "I really enjoy spending time with you, Rochelle."

"Same here." She hesitated briefly. "Would you like to come in for a few minutes?"

"That would be nice."

She could hear the TV in the family room and, not wanting to be under her sister's and daughter's scrutiny, she led him to the living room. "Have a seat. Can I get you anything?"

"No, thanks." Ever the gentleman, he waited until she'd taken a seat on the sofa before claiming the spot next to her and easing his arm around her shoulder.

Her heart pounded and butterflies danced in her belly.

"You know I've had one thing on my mind since seeing you at the office on Wednesday."

"What's that?"

"Kissing you."

It was a good thing she was already seated because her whole body went weak.

"You have no idea how hard it was for me to sit in that chair with you so close to me and not be able to touch and kiss you." He stroked a finger down her cheek and pressed his lips lightly against hers. "Do you know what I mean?"

The contact sent a jolt of pleasure through Rochelle. She wanted to say something—anything—but words failed her, and all she could manage was a quick nod. Yeah, she knew exactly what he meant, and it was the reason she'd missed his mouth and sprayed his face.

"I have the perfect fix."

Before she could ask what, he slanted his mouth over hers in a slow-as-molasses kiss. His tongue swirled around hers with a finesse that further melted her against the sofa. Despite all her reservations about getting involved with a man, she found her guard dropping little by little.

Chapter 12

Diane

DIANE SAT IN HER OFFICE GOING THROUGH HER EMAILS. She went still upon seeing one from social services, and with a nervous hand, she quickly clicked on it. Her heart raced with excitement as she read.

"*Yes!*"

They'd been approved for the foster-adopt program. Doing a shimmy in her seat, she let out a little squeal. Diane leaned back and brought a hand to her chest.

"It's really going to happen. I have to let Jeffrey know."

Maybe now that the process was complete, he'd have a different mindset. She pulled out her cell and sent him a text: **Foster-adopt has been approved. Hallelujah!**

She sat there a moment longer, basking in her joy, then got up to finish opening the boxes that arrived. She had ordered several titles from the Bluford book series for Ebony's gift. The teen loved reading and had been hooked ever since Diane introduced the series to her. She had purchased duplicate copies for Haley, who would celebrate her birthday in the summer. It would give the girls plenty to discuss and keep their minds engaged during the school break.

Thinking of summer break reminded her that this year she would have her own. *Ten weeks to go.* She'd looked up some activities for her and her friends to do on their trip and taking a sunset cruise topped her list.

Her phone buzzed with a text from Jeffrey: **Glad it's finally over.**

Diane really wanted to ask him more but decided to wait until she got home. She set the phone aside and opened the rest of the boxes. Every year, she purchased a number of books for the students who attended the center full-time in the summer. Diane had instituted a reading challenge, and the students earned prizes for reaching different levels. A few of the school-aged students had already inquired about it and expressed their excitement. She spent the next hour sorting through the stacks and updating the checkout system.

Once she finished, Diane started preparing for the other activities that would also take place during that time. For the older students, that meant the annual weeklong camping trip, academic enrichment sessions twice a week to ensure they'd be ready for the upcoming school year, and a few other day trips, both educational and for fun. She had also arranged for one of the parents who was an artist to come in one afternoon a week for six weeks to do art lessons. The woman had mentioned tile art, canvas painting, sand art and a few other things. Diane thought she might like to sit in as well. She glanced at the time. The center would close in fifteen minutes. The last of the students were usually gone by five thirty. This gave the teachers half an hour to clean and prep for the following day. For once she would be ready to leave at six on the dot right behind the rest of the staff.

"Diane?"

She shifted her gaze from the screen to the door and smiled at the young teacher. "Hey, Jade. Everybody ready to pack up and leave?"

"Yes, but we have a problem. Tomiko's parents haven't picked her up yet. Everyone else is gone."

Diane frowned. "That's odd. They're usually here no later than five fifteen." The Franklins were one of a handful of parents who consistently showed up on time. "Have you tried calling?"

Jade nodded. "I called both cells and the home phone and left messages."

"Okay. Where's Tomiko?"

"She's curled up in one of the beanbags reading, but I can tell she's a little worried."

So was she, but Diane refrained from saying so at the moment. "If they're not here by six, I'll stay and wait with her. I know you have to pick up your little ones from your mother's house."

"I can call my mom and let her know I'll be a few minutes late. My kids would be ecstatic because it means extra time for them to be spoiled by Grandma," she said with a little laugh.

Diane smiled. "I can imagine." Once again, the empty feeling rose inside her. Her own mother had often said she couldn't wait to spoil her grandchildren. If things continued the way they were, her mother's only grandchildren would be Diane's older sister Shelby's thirteen- and fifteen-year-old sons. "Let me know when they get here."

"I will. I checked and saw the traffic on Highway 99 is a nightmare right now, so I'm guessing they're caught up in the mess."

"Most likely." Twenty years ago, Sacramento's rush-hour traffic had lasted about thirty minutes, but now she could count on the backup lingering up to three hours, especially on a Friday evening. When Jade left, Diane finished her task and powered off her computer. She straightened her desk and placed the box containing Ebony's and Haley's books on top with her purse so she wouldn't forget them. She made a mental note to stop at the store on the way home to pick up a card and gift bag.

Half an hour later, the Franklins still hadn't arrived, and Diane's concern mounted. If the expression on Tomiko's face was any indication, the little girl shared that worry. Diane sent Jade home and made a quick call to Jeffrey. "Hey, Jeff. Are you home yet?"

"I just walked in the door."

"I'm going to be a little late. One of my parents hasn't made it to pick up their daughter yet."

"It's already six thirty. Did they say what time they'd get there?"

"No. We haven't been able to contact them, which is unusual." She glanced over to where Tomiko sat and saw her start to cry. "I have to go. I'll let you know when I'm leaving. I took some chicken breasts out to thaw if you want to go ahead and start dinner."

"I'll wait."

She sighed inwardly. It used to be no problem for him to cook dinner on the rare occasions when she came home late. Now this was his standard response. "I'll talk to you later." Diane disconnected and stuck the phone in her pants pocket, then made her way over to the little girl.

Tomiko stood and wrapped her small arms around Diane's waist. "I want to go home. Where's my mom and dad?"

Hugging her and gently wiping the little girl's tears, Diane said, "They're probably in traffic and just running a little late. Are you hungry?"

She nodded.

Smiling, Diane took Tomiko's hand and led her over to one of the tables. "Let's see what snacks we can get into." She washed her hands and placed string cheese, four slices of salami, crackers and a handful of grapes on a plate. "How's this?"

Tomiko gave her a small smile. "Good."

She sat next to Tomiko while she ate and tried to engage the seven-year-old in a conversation, which was usually easy. But tonight the little chatterbox just leaned against Diane and was mostly silent. By seven o'clock, Tomiko's parents still hadn't shown, and

Diane's earlier apprehension returned. "Tomiko, I'm going to try to call your parents. You finish up, and I'll be right back."

"Okay."

She walked the short distance to her office, pulled Tomiko's file and made the call. Once again, it went straight to voice mail for both parents. She tapped her finger on the desk while observing the little girl through the window. Something was wrong. She could feel it. Diane picked up the phone again and called the person listed as the emergency contact—Antoinette Collins.

"Hello," came a soft, muffled voice.

"Hello. Ms. Collins?"

"Yes."

"This is Diane Evans from Journey Preschool and Childcare Center. Your name is listed as the emergency contact for Tomiko Franklin. I've been trying to get in touch with her parents because she hasn't been picked up, and it's far past closing."

The woman burst out crying, and the hairs on the back of Diane's neck stood up.

"Ms. Collins?"

"The police just notified me that Marjorie and Terrell were killed in a car accident on the freeway this evening," she whispered.

Diane gasped sharply. "*Oh no.*" Her knees went weak, and she collapsed onto the chair. How was she supposed to tell this baby that her parents were gone? "What's going to happen to Tomiko?"

"I told the police she attended the day care, and they're on their way with a social worker to take her to the receiving home and find an emergency foster care placement. I would do it, but I'm not family and I haven't done any of the things required to be a foster parent, so I'm not eligible."

She heard what sounded like regret in the woman's voice. *But I am.* There was no way Diane would let this baby be placed with some stranger. She'd lost enough. She heard a knock on the front door, and her head snapped around. They kept the doors locked after-hours. "I think they're here. My husband and I are licensed to be foster parents, and I'm going to see if they'll let me take her."

"I hope so. Please let me know if they do. Marjorie was not only my best friend, but I was also their family attorney." Antoinette sniffed.

Attorney? Why isn't a family member listed as next of kin? "I'll do that. I'm so sorry for your loss."

"Thank you."

Diane hung up, and with her heart heavy, went to open the door. The grim set of the officers' faces told all. She introduced herself and waved them in. With the two men was a young woman who looked to be no more than twenty-five.

The woman stuck out her hand. "I'm Casey Davis from the Department of Social Services."

She shook the proffered hand. "Diane Evans, the director here at Journey. I was just getting off the phone with Ms. Collins."

"Then you already know."

She nodded around the lump in her throat. She wanted to cry for the parents who would never see their daughter grow up and for the young girl who would be forced to live without her parents' love. And they had loved Tomiko.

"Where's Tomiko?"

Diane paused.

"Ms. Evans, I know this is hard, but she's going to need to come with us, and we'll find an emergency placement for her."

"My husband and I are on the list for approved fosters. Let me take her." The words burst out of Diane. She sent up a silent prayer of thanks that their home study had just been approved.

"I don't—"

"You just said she needs an emergency placement. I can do that.

This baby's world is about to be turned upside down. Wouldn't it be better for her to be with someone she already knows rather than a stranger?" When the woman seemed to hesitate, Diane said, "*Please.*"

Casey studied Diane. "I'll make some calls."

"Thank you."

"Don't thank me just yet."

She was prepared to fight the woman all night if necessary to make sure she'd be able to take Tomiko home. She went still. *Jeffrey.* "I need to call my husband. I'll be right back." Diane went to her office, leaving Casey and the officers in the lobby. Picking up the phone, she called Jeffrey, but he didn't answer, so she sent a text telling him what happened and asking him to call her as soon as possible. With that done, all she could do was wait and pray.

It seemed like forever before Casey appeared in the office, her features unreadable.

Diane waited, her nerves a jumbled mess. "Ms. Davis?"

"You can take her home," the woman said. "The emergency placement can last anywhere from three days to thirty while we locate a family member, which is preferable."

Diane nodded, following Casey back to the lobby. Now the hard part. Diane led them around a corner. Tomiko was still sitting at the table where Diane had left her a few minutes ago and turned at their entrance. She divided a wary gaze between the newcomers and Diane.

"Hi, Tomiko," Casey said. She took the chair next to Tomiko. "I need to talk to you about something, okay?"

"What?"

"It's about your parents."

"They're late. Maybe they got stuck in traffic again."

Casey shot Diane a sympathetic look. "Well, it's a little more than that." She slowly and painstakingly explained what happened.

Before Casey could finish, Tomiko's loud wail pierced the silence. "*Noooo!* I want my mommy and daddy."

"I know, but we're going to take care of you, and—" The woman reached out to touch Tomiko, and the little girl started kicking and screaming.

Diane quickly scooped her up. "It's okay, baby." She rocked and tried to comfort Tomiko as best she could while the little girl's whole world fell apart.

She took a moment to wipe Tomiko's face. The little girl buried her face in Diane's chest and continued to cry softly.

"I'm so sorry about your mom and dad."

"They're not coming back anymore."

"No, honey. I'm afraid not."

"Then who am I going to live with?" Tomiko started crying again. She threw her arms around Diane's neck and held on tight. "I want to go home with you. I don't want to go with the police and the lady. Please let me go home with you. *Please*," she wailed.

Diane's heart shattered in a thousand pieces. She tried to offer reassuring and comforting words, but she didn't feel any of those things herself.

She let out the breath she'd been holding.

"Tomiko," Casey rubbed the girl's back softly, "for right now you'll need to come with me, but afterward, Miss Diane will come and take you to her house." Casey shot Diane a look. "We can take her until you're able to get an approved car seat."

"We have some here." She hopped up and started from the office. "I'll show you." In the room next to hers, she gestured to the half a dozen car seats—from infant- and toddler-sized to booster seats for the older children. "They're for field trips when a parent forgets to leave theirs. I'll use one to take her home, then shop for another one this weekend."

While Casey looked through the inventory and filled out paperwork, Diane pulled out her phone, still holding Tomiko close to her side, and tried to call home again. She let out a frustrated sigh when the voice mail came on. *Jeffrey, I need you to call me back. It's important.* Pushing down her irritation, she looked down at Tomiko.

She sent a quick text to Joy and Rochelle with the same details, including that Diane might be taking Tomiko home and letting them know she wouldn't be able to go house hunting with them in the morning.

Joy responded almost immediately: **Oh, no! I'm so sorry. Keep me posted, and let me know if you need anything.**

It took another hour to finalize everything, including a stop at a local hospital for a checkup. Tomiko hopped into the back seat and strapped herself in.

"I guess you do this all the time, huh?" Diane asked with a smile.

Tomiko nodded solemnly.

She sent another text to Rochelle and Joy to update them, then tried Jeffrey again before getting into the car.

"Are you still waiting for the parents?" Jeffrey asked as soon as he picked up. "It's kind of rude of them to be this late without calling."

Diane mentally counted to ten. "Jeffrey, Tomiko's parents were killed in a car accident on their way to the center tonight," she said quietly.

"Oh. Wow. Sorry to hear that. What's going to happen to the kid?"

"That's why I've been trying to reach you for the past two hours. I'm bringing her home until they can locate a family member."

There was a long pause on the line. "Just like that? We need to talk about this."

"Again, I tried, but you didn't answer." It bothered her because she knew he was already home from the first time she called. "I'm going to stop and pick up a few things for her and some dinner. Do you want anything?"

"No. I already ate."

"Then I'll see you in a little while." The line went dead. She blew out a long breath and slid behind the wheel. "Tomiko, I'm going to stop at the store and get you a few changes of clothes, a toothbrush and stuff like that. Is there anything you want?"

"No. What about my stuff at home?"

Diane studied her through the rearview mirror. "We'll have to wait and see what Ms. Davis can do, but I'm going to work hard to make sure you can get your favorite things."

Though she knew Tomiko having her things might go a long way in making the little girl more comfortable, Diane also worried about how going to the house would affect her. The sadness in Tomiko's face tugged at Diane's heart.

After shopping, Diane headed home. She didn't look forward to the confrontation with Jeffrey that was sure to come. She just hoped he would table it until she could get Tomiko settled. As soon as she pulled into the garage, her heart started pounding.

"Okay. We're here."

She got out and helped Tomiko, then grabbed the bags. Tomiko clung to the stuffed animal Diane had purchased. The little girl had mentioned having a similar one at home, and Diane was doing her best to provide everything needed to make Tomiko more comfortable.

She opened the door leading to the kitchen and stopped short upon seeing Jeffrey standing there. "Hey."

Jeffrey glanced down at Tomiko, then back to Diane. "Hey. I'll take these." He relieved her of the bags and carried them over to the bar.

"Thanks." She took Tomiko's hand. "Tomiko, this is my husband, Mr. Evans."

Tomiko leaned closer to Diane and said in a barely audible tone, "Hi."

"Nice to meet you, Tomiko. I'm very sorry about your parents." Jeffrey ran a comforting hand over the little girl's head. To Diane he said, "I'll let you get her settled. We'll talk later." He pivoted on his heel and stalked out.

Diane sighed inwardly. For a split second he'd softened, and she thought things might not be so bad after all. *So much for that.* She took out the soft tacos and tortilla chips she'd gotten from Tomiko's favorite fast-food restaurant and placed them on the table. "We can eat first, then I'll show you your room."

They had purchased the four-bedroom house hoping to have at least two children. It hadn't happened the way Diane envisioned, but she'd take it. While they ate, Tomiko didn't talk and Diane didn't push her. The child's entire world had been tilted on its axis, and it would take time for things to become somewhat bearable. Once again, she wondered why no family member had been listed as the emergency contact. Did the family live too far away? Or were they estranged? The questions made her remember that she needed to call the attorney. A quick glance at the time showed it to be already after nine, so she'd call tomorrow.

"Miss Di, I'm done." Tomiko had eaten only about half of her food.

"Okay, honey. Is there anything else you want?"

Tomiko shook her head.

Diane cleaned up the remnants of the meal and tossed everything into the trash. She held out her hand. "Let's go get ready for bed."

She scooted off the chair and grasped Diane's hand.

On the way out of the kitchen, Diane grabbed the bag of clothes and toiletries she had purchased. Upstairs, she stopped at the first bedroom, which held a twin-sized bed. There was a bedroom downstairs, but she didn't want Tomiko to be that far away. The one next to hers and Jeffrey's was still unfurnished, as they had planned for it to be the nursery. "How's this?"

"Okay."

She smiled softly, stepped back into the hallway and pointed. "My room is right down the hall. If you need anything, you come get me. I'm going to leave the hall light on so you can see."

The light would also keep the guest room illuminated. Diane helped Tomiko take a bath, then settled her into the bed. Jeffrey never came out of the room.

Tomiko crawled into Diane's lap. "Why did my mom and dad have to die?"

Diane blew out a long breath. She had no ready answer because she still didn't understand why Yvette, who ate healthy, exercised, never smoked, and did all the things she was supposed to do, had gotten cancer and died. "I don't know, sweetheart. Sometimes terrible things happen to good people, but I know they're in heaven watching over you."

Tomiko stared up at Diane. "Really?"

"Yes, really."

"But I didn't want them to die," she said, her tears starting again.

Her own emotions rose again. Diane gathered the little girl closer in her arms and held her, murmuring every comforting word she could think of until Tomiko cried herself to sleep. She pressed a soft kiss on Tomiko's brow and slid off the bed carefully, so as not to wake her. She stood there a moment longer, then trudged to her room.

"I hope she can sleep through the night," she said, dropping down heavily on the bed.

"How long are you planning to keep her?"

She eyed Jeffrey. "The social worker said it could be anywhere from three days to a month while they try to locate a family member."

"I hope it's soon," Jeffery mumbled. "I don't know why you had to be the one to take her in, and without consulting me."

"Are we back to that again? *You* didn't answer the damn phone when I called multiple times," she gritted out. "That little girl has lost her *entire* world! This is not about you, Jeffrey. You, of all people, should understand what she's going through since you lost your mother two years ago. If you couldn't handle it at almost forty years old, how do you think a seven-year-old is going to deal with it?"

He jumped off the bed and paced. "How can you say this isn't about me, about *us*? This is going to impact my life just as much." He ran an agitated hand down his face. "Look, I get it, and I'm not saying she has to leave this moment, okay? But this is a huge responsibility and frankly—" The doorbell interrupted whatever he had planned to say. He glanced down at his watch and muttered a curse. "It's after ten." He stalked out of the room.

Diane sighed wearily. She was too tired to deal with this mess tonight. Was it too much to hope that they could have a civilized adult conversation about this? Yes, it would be a big responsibility and impact their lives in every way, but she could *not*, in good conscience, let them take that baby and just drop her off with anybody.

"Rochelle and Joy are downstairs. Did you ask them to come over?"

She turned, ignoring the accusatory tone in his voice. "No." She brushed past Jeffrey and rushed downstairs. "Hey. What are you

two doing here?" Without a word, Rochelle hugged her, then Joy
did the same. Tears misted Diane's eyes. Somehow they always
knew when she needed them.

"How are you doing, Di?" Joy asked.

"It's been a long day, to say the least."

Rochelle gave Diane's shoulders a comforting squeeze. "And
the little girl?"

"Finally cried herself to sleep. We can talk in the kitchen. I'm
going to make some tea. Do you want some?"

Both declined, and Rochelle said, "We stopped by only for a
few minutes to check on you. I don't want Haley to be alone too
long."

They all started in the direction of the kitchen. While Chelle
and Joy took seats at the kitchen table, Diane went about making
the tea and shared everything that had happened. When it was
done, she joined them at the table.

Joy shook her head. "That poor baby."

"I know." Diane took a tentative sip. "The crazy thing is that
the family's attorney was listed on the center's emergency contact
form and, apparently, as next of kin. It makes me wonder whether
they have any family."

"Or have any family they trusted," Rochelle said.

"My thoughts exactly. I'll be calling the attorney tomorrow."

"I know you won't be able to go house hunting with us tomorrow, but I think you should bring Tomiko to get her nails done."

"I don't know, Joy."

Rochelle leaned forward and clasped her hands on the table.
"Joy's right. It might help to keep her busy. I'll talk to Haley and
Ebony beforehand. Ebony will definitely be able to understand
what Tomiko's going through."

Diane hadn't thought of it that way. "You're right. I'll see if Joe
minds me bringing her to the party for a little while as well."

Joy patted Diane's arm. "Good." She lowered her voice to a whisper. "How's Jeffrey handling things? He didn't seem too happy to see us."

She shook her head. "Not well. In his mind I should've just let them take Tomiko to some foster home." She lowered her head as the tears welled in her eyes again. "But I couldn't do it, not when that little girl had just lost everything. I have no idea what I'm supposed to say and do, but I felt it would be better for her to be here with someone she knows."

"It is. Give Jeffrey some time. Yes, he's acting like a complete butthead right now, but he'll come around."

Diane smiled at Joy. Leave it to her to cut right to the chase. And Jeffrey *had* sort of said Tomiko didn't need to leave right away. "I hope so." She couldn't take the alternative.

Chapter 13

Joy

JOY HALF TUNED OUT THE REAL ESTATE AGENT SHOW-
ing her around the two-bedroom, two-bath condo. Although it
was nice, it didn't give her that sense of home she wanted.

"What do you think?" Rochelle asked. "It's nicer than the first
one we saw."

"It is, but I'm not feeling it." The other thing playing on the
edges of her mind was the conversation with Robert. Did he
really want a reconciliation, or was this just another way to keep
things going in his favor? Taking another glance around the
place, she let out a deep sigh. "I don't think this is the one I'm
looking for."

While it had been located on the second floor as she'd re-
quested, the place was dead smack in the middle of the row of
condos. She would much prefer something on the end or closer to
it. After being in a house for all these years, Joy enjoyed the peace
of not being connected to another residence. Maybe she needed to
turn her attention toward renting a small house instead.

The woman gave Joy an indulgent smile. "I understand totally.
We have one more, and I think you'll like this one. It's only ten
minutes away."

They all filed out, and as soon as Joy and Rochelle got into
Joy's car, Rochelle turned to her. "Okay, sis, what gives? You were

fired up about house hunting all week. Now, today, it's a different story."

Joy pulled off behind the Realtor. "I don't know. On one hand, I still am fired up, but on the other, it's hard to end a marriage I thought would last forever." She hesitated briefly before sharing what Robert had said. "What if he does want us to get back together?"

"Do you think he's sincere?"

"Honestly, I don't know. I have no idea whether we can get back everything that's been lost, or if I even want to at this point." Yet she continued to hesitate making the move.

"Well, if it's any consolation, I went through the same thing. You just need to ask yourself if you'll be better with or without him."

"Is it possible to fall out of love with someone?"

Rochelle snorted. "You're asking the wrong person. But my situation was different. My feelings for Kenny had been steadily going downhill after Haley was born, but I fell out of love with him the moment he raised his hand to me, and no amount of pleading would make me change my mind."

"That's one thing Robert hasn't done, though. Honestly, I've wanted to punch him a few times over the past few weeks," Joy mumbled. They both laughed. "I'm just so conflicted right now. When we were at the coffee shop, Robert seemed so . . . so . . . oh, I don't know. It reminded me of how things used to be." He'd held her hand and called her baby in the way that always grabbed her heart.

"Then maybe you should take a little more time to think about it. You can stay with me as long as you need."

"I'll see."

A few minutes later, they pulled up to a gated community in Rancho Cordova. Joy had decided to search for homes on this side of town because they were closer to the El Dorado Hills property she had her eye on for the spa. Inside, she found that she did like the spacious unit much better than the previous two. She added bonus points because it was on the end and had a private garage. In the end, Joy thanked the woman, then told her she wanted to think about it a little more before making a decision. She also planned to check out a few houses on Monday morning.

On the way back to Rochelle's house, Joy said, "I'm ready for some fun, and I hope Diane brings Tomiko."

"So do I. I already talked to Haley, and she said she and Ebony would make sure Tomiko has a good time."

"Those girls are such sweethearts."

"*Humph.* That's because you don't live with them. Haley has her moments, but the teenage life is about to give me fits."

Joy laughed. "And *that's* why I'm the godmother."

Rochelle smiled. "Yeah, yeah. Hush."

They had just enough time to change and collect the girls—Ebony had spent the night with Haley—and get to their appointment on time. To Joy's delight, Diane was already waiting. Joy took in the little girl clinging to Diane like Diane was her lifeline. In a way Joy supposed her friend did fit that bill for the time being. After a round of greetings, the three younger girls were ushered to the other side of the day spa. Joy, Rochelle, Diane and Yvette had been coming to Sweet Renewal Day Spa for years and loved the place. The owners had added an area for younger girls five years ago, and the first time they'd brought Haley and Ebony to get a mani-pedi, the girls had been hooked.

"Hi, Tomiko. I'm Haley. This is my godsister, Ebony. I'm sorry your mom and dad died."

Ebony slung an arm around the younger girl's shoulders. "I kind of know how you feel. My mom died a few weeks ago."

Tomiko's eyes widened. "She did?"

Ebony nodded. "We know you don't have any sisters, but you can be our godsister. So come on, let's pick out some colors for your nails." They led her away while telling Tomiko about all the fun they were going to have.

Joy dabbed at the tears in her eyes. "Those girls are going to have me doing the ugly cry in the middle of this place."

"You're not the only one," Diane said, wiping at her own tears.

Rochelle handed them a tissue and kept one for herself. "Same."

As soon as the girls were settled, the three women started their own services, which included glasses of iced tea. "I have so missed us hanging out together," Joy said, feeling Yvette's absence.

"We're going to have to get better at having our girl time," Diane said.

Rochelle chuckled softly.

Joy leaned forward. "What are you laughing at, Chelle?"

"Just remembering the last time we came." They all smiled. "I have never seen anyone move as fast as Yvette."

Diane nearly choked on her tea as she burst out laughing. "Oh my goodness. I forgot all about that."

"That girl was out the door so fast, you'd have thought she was back on the track team." Joy wiped tears of mirth from her eyes.

On their last visit, another woman had been there with her young son, and he had a rubber lizard toy. Somehow, while tossing it in the air, he misjudged how hard he'd thrown it, and the thing landed on Yvette's lap. She had screamed, jumped out of the foot spa, sending the poor woman who'd been doing Yvette's pedicure sprawling, and ran out the door yelling, *"Get it off me!"*

Rochelle hollered. "She left a trail of water from here to the car."

It had taken a good fifteen minutes to coax Yvette back into the place. The boy's mother had been apologetic and made sure that the lizard and all his other animals were kept out of sight.

"I haven't laughed like this in so long," Diane said wistfully. "I needed this."

Joy agreed wholeheartedly. "We all did."

"So are you ready for our girls trip?" Rochelle asked Diane.

"I have no idea," Diane said. "I need to find out what's going to happen with Tomiko first. If no family members step up, she may be staying with us, and I don't know if I want to leave her so soon with everything she's going through."

"We can just play it by ear," Rochelle said. "If we need to delay the trip by a few weeks, it'll be fine. You just do what you need to do for Tomiko."

Joy smiled. "Agreed."

Diane nodded. "Thanks. But maybe we can still do a little shopping next weekend. Just a couple of hours." She waved her glass of iced tea in their direction before taking a sip.

Rochelle groaned. "I wish. I have the family reunion next weekend. If I didn't think my mother would have a coronary, I'd skip it in a heartbeat."

"I totally forgot about that. How about doing it the weekend after?"

"Sounds good. We can do lunch at my house around noon on that Saturday," Rochelle said.

Diane toasted her with her glass. "Works for me."

Joy took out her phone. "I'm putting it on my calendar."

The conversation tapered off, and they relaxed while finishing up the pedicures and manicures. She thanked her technician and stood. "Oh, wait. This is *my* song!" "Candy Rain" by Soul For Real came through the speakers and Joy starting belting out the lyrics.

Rochelle bobbed her head. "Girl, yes. I used to think those guys were so fine," she said, giving Diane a high five.

Joy's friends joined in with her singing, complete with the

dance steps from the group's video. The three of them broke out in a fit of laughter.

Diane fanned herself. "I haven't danced in a long time. We need to make up a dance routine like we used to."

"Shoot, we were good." Joy recalled the four of them being at high school dances doing their choreographed moves and all the fun they'd had. "I think the last one we did was for that graduation party for Christina Jefferson."

"I forgot all about that," Rochelle said with a chuckle.

They were still laughing about it when they went to the other side of the salon to collect the girls. Haley, Ebony and Tomiko couldn't stop raving about the fancy designs on their nails and toes.

They all left and went over to Joe's for Ebony's birthday party. Joy had taken the liberty of bringing decorations and shooed the girls out until they were done. Ebony's favorite color was purple, and Joy had chosen a theme with varying shades of the color and added splashes of cream.

"I can't believe you did all this," Joe said, staring at the fully decorated sunroom.

"My goddaughter deserves some sunshine after these tough weeks." Joy gave him a quick hug. "And so do you."

Rochelle smiled. "You know we had to go all out. Yvette wouldn't have had it any other way."

He shook his head. "No. No, she wouldn't," he said emotionally. "Have I told you three how much I appreciate all you've done for us?"

"Not lately," Diane said with a grin. She waved a hand. "So go ahead. Tell us how fabulous we are."

Joe threw his head back and laughed. "Yeah, okay. Fabulous, amazing and all those other adjectives."

Joy was glad to hear him laugh. It seemed as though they all needed these few minutes of laughter and fun. With all the turmoil going on in her life, she especially craved this time with her friends.

"*OMGeeeeeeee!* I love it!"

They all turned at the sound of Ebony's excited screams. Joy opened her arms. "I take it you approve."

Ebony flew into Joy's arms. "Aunt Joy, this is so pretty. Thank you. I gotta go get my phone and take pictures." She ran from the room yelling Haley's name.

Joe gave her a grateful smile.

"I guess working with all those interior designers paid off," Rochelle said.

Joy glanced around at her handiwork and smiled. "Yes, it has." And she couldn't wait to employ the same techniques in her own business.

Chapter 14

Rochelle

"CHELLE, CAN YOU FINISH MAKING THE MAC AND cheese while I get these greens started?"

Rochelle went over to the counter where her mother stood cutting cheese and relieved her of the knife. "Sure."

She had gotten to her parents' house at eight Saturday morning for the reunion activities, and three hours later, she was already ready to go home. Her three cousins had arrived half an hour ago with Rochelle's aunt and her grandmother, the family's matriarch, and neither cousin had yet to enter the kitchen or offer to help set up one thing. She could see them sitting in the family room, legs crossed and sipping on whatever they'd brought from the coffee shop, acting as if they were royalty.

Val passed by muttering under her breath. "Lazy ass heifers. You best believe that I'll be dragging their sorry butts in here for the cleanup."

"And I'll help." It was the same every family reunion. Colette, Keisha and Lisa typically showed up late, ate enough for three people each, then left early with to-go plates piled high. They had come early today only because their grandmother demanded it.

"Rochelle, how've you been?"

She shifted to face her grandmother. "Good. Work and raising a teenager keeps me busy." *Three, two, one.*

"So when are you getting married again? You're still young and just because you fell off the bike once doesn't mean you don't get back on again."

Rochelle had known it wouldn't be long before the question was asked. Her mother and aunt paused in their tasks, waiting for Rochelle's response. Since her divorce, every family gathering centered around her finding another husband. Initially, her grandmother said she couldn't believe that Rochelle had walked away from such a "fine young man" and thought she should have stuck it out and tried to make her marriage work. However, the words *fine young man* stopped applying to Ken long before Rochelle ended their relationship. It wasn't until she'd told her grandmother about the verbal abuse that the woman backed off. No one in her family knew about the one time he'd raised his hand to her, and she planned to take that information to her grave.

"I know. If I find that special guy, I'll let you know."

Her grandmother smiled and nodded as if satisfied and went back to what she was doing.

Rochelle let out the breath she'd been holding. She and Val shared a look. Her sister was the only one who knew about Warren, and Rochelle planned to keep it that way for now in case things fell apart. In her mind, she didn't see her relationship with Warren lasting too long. He'd lose interest soon, just like the few other men she'd dated since her divorce. Val tossed her a wink and pantomimed zipping her lips.

Rochelle mouthed, *Thank you.*

She finished the mac and cheese, slid the pan into the oven, then cleaned up and started on the next dish. Over the next two hours more family arrived, giving Rochelle and Valerie a chance to leave the cooking to their many aunts and have some fun. They drifted out to the backyard where Frankie Beverly and Maze's "Before I Let Go" blared through hidden speakers. Young children chased each other with delightful squeals, Haley and the other teens were huddled together buried behind their cell phones, and adults sat around playing everything from spades to dominoes. With the sun shining and temperatures hitting eighty degrees, this first weekend in May turned out to be the perfect day for a gathering.

"Hey, baby girls," one of their uncles called out.

Rochelle leaned down and kissed his cheek. "Hi, Uncle Bernie."

"Who's winning?" Val asked, leaning down to hug him.

"Not us," he said with a chuckle. He threw his cards on the table. "I'm out. Val, you and Chelle can take our spot."

Val rubbed her hands together and took the seat Uncle Bernie vacated. "You let Darryl and Alan beat you?" Smiling, she divided her gaze between their two male cousins. "You know Chelle and I are the reigning family spades champions. Y'all sure you want some of this?"

Rochelle sat in the opposite chair. "Nah, they ain't ready."

Alan dealt the cards. "Oh, we're ready for you."

"*Mm-hmm*. We'll see." She looked at her cards and gave Val a coded look that let her know their reign wouldn't be over anytime soon. They laughed and talked trash throughout the game, and Rochelle thoroughly enjoyed herself.

"You only have two books, Darryl. Still think you're kicking us off the throne?" Val slammed another card on the table, scooped up the book and did a little dance in her chair.

Rochelle knew the game was over. She had both jokers and the ace of spades left in her hand. She stood. "Game *o-va!*" she said, slapping down each card for emphasis.

Darryl groaned. "That was pure luck."

She placed a hand on her hip. "Luck, my ass. We've been whipping your butts from day one. You'd think you would've learned some skills by now."

"Yes, girl." Valerie hopped up and they did a high five across the table.

Alan chuckled and raised his hands in surrender. "Alright, alright. You get this one." He rose to his feet and kissed each of them on the cheek. "I need a drink and a full plate to ease my pain."

They burst out laughing, and Rochelle said, "You're going to need more than that."

"Okay, everybody. Gather around and let's bless this food," Rochelle's mother called out. A table sat on the far end of the backyard ladened with all manner of bowls and platters.

Darryl slung an arm around Rochelle's shoulders as they joined the family in a large circle. He whispered, "I hope they don't let Uncle Gary bless the food this time. Hell, everything was damn near frozen by the time he finished."

She giggled and elbowed him in the side. "Hush." But he had a point. They'd had to reheat nearly all the dishes by the time he finished the prayer. Her grandmother had fussed for ten minutes. Apparently the woman remembered because when her uncle stepped up, she sent him a scathing look that had him ducking his head and backing up. Rochelle's father did the honors and, as a result, all the food was still hot when all was said and done.

"Thank you, Uncle Kirk!" Darryl called out, which brought on another round of laughter and a sharp look from their Uncle Gary.

Rochelle stared up at him. "I can't with you. You know you're wrong for that."

A grin curved his lips and he shrugged. "Just telling the truth. And don't act all innocent now, girl. The two of us got into lots of good stuff back in the day." He tossed her a wink.

"Whatever." Of all her cousins, she was closest to Darryl. Maybe because they were the same age. Growing up they had been two peas in a pod, from hiding out to avoid chores and sneaking off to the movies, to her running interference with girls he'd tried to dodge. Even after he moved to the other side of the state after college, she could count on a phone call or text at least twice a month. Whenever he made the trip to Sacramento to visit his parents, Darryl always made a point of visiting Rochelle as well.

After filling their plates, Rochelle and Darryl carried them over to a table where Val, her husband, and another distant cousin sat. To her dismay, her three lazy cousins made their way over. She didn't understand why since they had never been close.

"Well, if it isn't the three wicked witches of Winters," Darryl drawled. He used to say that every family had its share of evil, and Lisa, Colette and Keisha were their burden.

Colette, the oldest, shot him a look but didn't respond. Rochelle guessed it stemmed from the beat down he'd given her when he was ten and Colette was fourteen. Back then they'd teased him about being short, wearing glasses and loving science, and often pushed him around.

Apparently, "accidentally" stepping on his glasses had pushed the sweet, fun-loving little boy over the edge. When the dust settled, Colette had a black eye, split lip and bloody nose. Rochelle smiled inwardly at the memory and started in on her food. Rochelle had been waiting all day for the fall-off-the-bone ribs her father always cooked, her sister's potato salad and her grandmother's prized 7Up pound cake. Laughter flowed around the table as they caught up on each other's lives.

"Rochelle, I heard you're seeing someone," Keisha said halfway through the meal.

She went still. "What makes you think I'm seeing someone? Not that it's any of your business."

"Trina said you and some guy were quite cozy at Fixins." Keisha leaned forward and smirked. "I see you've gained a few pounds, so you might want to push that plate back and get some salad instead. Maybe this time it'll help you keep your man."

Before Rochelle could open her mouth and deliver the set down she'd been itching to do for two decades, Val said, "Keisha, you're a size two. That didn't help you keep your two husbands or that baby daddy you've got now, so you're the last person who needs to be giving out advice. Better yet, you need to mind your own damn business."

Gary choked on his drink, Val's husband shook his head, and Darryl outright laughed.

Keisha glared at Val but thought better about a comeback. "Go to hell!"

"Nah, girl. Ain't nobody coming to visit you," Darryl said, eliciting laughter.

She jumped up, snatched up her plate and stormed off. Her sisters followed.

"Not that I don't appreciate you having my back, sis," Rochelle started, "but I could've handled it."

Val reached over and squeezed Rochelle's hand. "Oh, girl, I know, but I couldn't help myself. The little bitch," she muttered.

"Anybody else smell the lingering scent of sulfur?" Alan asked, breaking the tension. Everyone chuckled and went back to their food.

Throughout the remainder of the meal, Rochelle picked at her food. She contributed to the conversation and pretended she was okay, but in reality, Keisha's comments had conjured up all the insecurities and questions she'd asked herself about Warren. She ended up throwing away her nearly full plate, and as the day went on, she found herself sinking further into the depression that had claimed much of her life after her divorce.

Rochelle couldn't have been happier when people started packing up to leave. All she wanted to do was go home and bury herself beneath the covers. She grabbed three large empty bowls off the table and carried them into the kitchen. She chuckled inwardly upon seeing Keisha, Lisa and Colette elbow deep in dishwater. "Don't forget these." She placed the bowls on the table and walked out. Two hours later, the last of the stragglers had gone.

Her mother dropped down heavily in her favorite recliner. "Hallelujah! My everything hurts."

Kirk Winters bent and kissed his wife. "Marie, you did good, baby. I've got dinner for the next week."

"Shoot, I wish my husband would cook for me an entire week," Valerie said, eyeing her husband, Bryan.

Bryan shook his head. "Whatever, woman. You know I cook for you."

Rochelle envied the soft smiles and adoration in the faces of her father and brother-in-law. "Mom, I'll take care of putting away the last few things and then I'm going home." She stood and started for the kitchen.

"I'll help," Valerie said, trailing Rochelle. As soon as they were out of earshot, she said, "Okay, missy, what's going on? And don't tell me it's nothing because I've been watching you all day."

She sighed heavily. "Just thinking about what Keisha said."

"I knew it. And that's why you basically starved yourself all day."

Rochelle spun around from where she stood at the sink. Obviously Val had been watching her more closely than she'd thought.

Valerie folded her arms. "Please don't let what she said make you fall back into those habits again."

She slumped against the counter. "It's kind of hard not to, and I have gained weight. I need to lose a good thirty pounds, *at least*."

"That's fine, but not eating isn't the way to do it. In fact, it'll make it harder."

"Maybe not, but none of my clothes fit right, and Warren . . ."

"Wait. Did Warren say you needed to lose weight?" Valerie slowly lowered her arms and took a step. Her expression gave the impression that she would hunt the man down tonight, if necessary.

"No, but—"

She relaxed. "I didn't think so. He looks at you like you are the answer to every one of his prayers," she said with a chuckle.

Rochelle ignored the comment. Yes, the way he stared at her sometimes made her entire body catch fire, but she was a realist and figured it would be only a matter of time before he took his affections elsewhere. "Aren't you supposed to be helping me put the rest of the food away?"

"Yeah, I am." Valerie came over, picked up an empty container and filled it with small portions of food. She placed a lid on it and thrust it toward Rochelle. "Take this home and eat. And don't even think about not doing it, because I'm going to enlist my beautiful niece's assistance in making sure you follow through. Oh, and I saved you this." She held up a Ziploc bag.

Her eyes lit up. "I thought all of Grandma's pound cake was gone."

"It was, but you know I wasn't putting that cake out without getting some for us first. Now, it's a small slice, so I don't want to hear that you can't eat it."

Rochelle swiped at the tears stinging her eyes.

Valerie hugged her. "I get that you want to lose weight. We all could stand to lose a few pounds, myself included." Valerie and Rochelle were both five eight, but Valerie's size tended to hover around a fourteen. "But you have to do it the right way, for the right reasons, and for *you*. Nobody else. Okay?"

She nodded. "Thanks."

"You know I love you and I'll help in any way. The thing I found that works for me is meal planning on the weekends."

That would probably help her as well. "I may take you up on it."

"Good."

Sharing a smile, they finished the task and Rochelle and Haley drove home.

As soon as they got inside the house, Haley said, "Aunt Val told me you were running around at Grandma's and didn't have a chance to eat. I'm supposed to make sure you eat your dinner. Do you want me to heat it up for you?"

Big sisters. "No, I've got it. I'm going to eat as soon as I take a shower and change." Between cooking and sitting around outside, she desperately needed to wash away all the perspiration of the day. She started toward her bedroom.

"Can I call Ebony?"

Rochelle paused in the doorway and checked her watch. "It's already after nine, so don't talk too long."

"Okay."

She closed the door, stripped and headed for the shower. Fifteen minutes later and feeling refreshed, she made her way back to the kitchen. She shook her head at the laughter coming from Haley's bedroom. No doubt her daughter was dishing all the dirt from earlier. Rochelle's stomach growled as she heated up her plate. She was starving and had to force herself to eat slowly. She eyed the slice of pound cake but decided to save it for tomorrow. The unhealthy pattern of starving herself, then bingeing had been one that took three years to get under control. It had gotten so bad once that she'd ended up in the hospital, and she couldn't allow the bitterness of her crazy cousin to send her back to that dark place again. Her cell phone buzzed just as she finished eating, and she saw Warren's name on the display. She wiped her hands on a napkin and answered.

"Hey, Warren."

"Good evening, beautiful. How did the family picnic go?"

"It went."

Warren laughed. "Sounds about right. It's never a dull moment when it comes to family."

"Amen to that."

"I know it's a little late, but would it be okay if I came by for a moment? There's something important I need to talk to you about."

Rochelle's heart rate kicked up. "What is it?"

"This is something that has to be said in person."

Keisha's words echoed in her head. She started to tell him no but decided that if he planned to break things off, she might as well get it over with tonight. No need to ruin her entire weekend. "Sure."

"Thanks. I'll see you in a bit."

She disconnected, tossed the phone on the table and blew out a long breath. That was the story of her adult dating life for as long as she could remember. Things never lasted beyond three or four dates, and it always ended the same—no one wanted to be with a big girl or one who couldn't serve as a piece of eye candy on a man's arm. But she had to give Warren props—at least he planned to do it face-to-face. The last man she'd gone out with sent her a don't-call-me-I'll-call-you text and said he wanted to be with someone who he could show off to his boys. Sure, when she and Warren had gone to dinner, he said they would still be dating a few months from now, but she knew, better than most, that things changed, *people* changed, and it could happen at the drop of a dime.

By the time Rochelle opened the door to Warren half an hour later, she had worked herself into such a state that she wanted to shout, "Just hurry up and break it off so I can go to bed!" Calming herself, she said, "Hey. Come on in."

"Hey, beautiful." Warren brushed his lips across hers and stepped inside. "I won't keep you long. Where's Haley?"

"She's in the shower," she said over her shoulder as he followed her to the family room. "Can I get you anything to drink?"

"No, thanks. I'm fine." He waited for her to sit before lowering himself next to her on the sofa.

The serious set of his face all but confirmed her thoughts. She had her speech ready: *I understand. We just didn't click. It happens like that sometimes, and sure, we can still be friends.* Rochelle knew the script by heart. Only this time she'd felt like they *had* clicked. Or maybe it had been just wishful thinking on her part.

He took her hands. "Rochelle, these last few weeks with you have been nothing short of amazing, and I want more. I want us to spend time getting to know each other better. *Exclusively.* I've waited a long time to find someone special like you."

Three, two . . . wait! What? She had been so engrossed in getting her speech ready that it took a moment for his words to register. "What did you say?"

Warren smiled. "I said I've found the woman I want to build a relationship with, and it's you."

She sat stunned, and it took a moment for her to find her voice. "I . . . *um* . . . wow, okay. I wasn't expecting you to—" She cut her rambling off.

Rochelle was so not ready for this conversation. A more accurate assessment would be that his words frightened her more than a little bit, and it was all she could do to sit there and not bolt from the room.

He must have read her expression because he chuckled. "No? What were you expecting me to say?"

"I don't know." Rochelle couldn't very well tell him what she'd been assuming—that he planned to relegate her to the friend zone. A million questions ran through her mind, the most prominent being whether she could trust his words. "Warren, I—"

Warren cut off the rest of her words with a soft kiss. "Baby, I don't want your answer tonight. I'm far past the age of playing games, Rochelle, and I need you to really think about whether you want this relationship as much as I do. And I'm not talking about some casual fling."

Her heart was pounding so fast, it made her light-headed. Good thing he didn't want an answer tonight because Rochelle couldn't utter a word if her life depended on it.

He stood and gently pulled her to her feet. "I'm going to go."

Without releasing her hand, he led her to the front door. He turned and slid his arms around her, and the contact made her suck in a sharp breath. The deep, passionate kiss that followed made her knees weak. His tongue swirled around hers, tasting, teasing, claiming. At length, he eased back.

A smile curved his lips. "Sleep well, beautiful." And he was gone.

She rested her forehead against the closed door. *What am I going to do?*

Chapter 15

Diane

"MS. COLLINS, PLEASE COME IN." DIANE GESTURED the brown-skinned, tall, slender woman inside. She looked to be less than thirty years old. "I appreciate you taking time out of your Sunday to meet with me."

"Please call me Toni, and it was no problem at all."

She gestured Toni to the sofa in the family room. "Would you like something to drink?"

"No, thank you." Toni glanced around the room. "Your home is lovely, Mrs. Evans."

"It's Diane, and thank you. How are you doing?" Although Toni served as the Franklins' family attorney, she remembered the woman saying she was their friend as well.

She smiled weakly. "It's been a rough couple of days. I still can't believe they're gone. How's Tomiko?"

"I think she's doing well, considering. The nights seem to be hardest." Diane made a move to stand. "She's asleep, but I can wake her."

Toni shook her head and waved a hand. "Don't do that. Let her sleep. I really want to see her, but as emotional as I am right now, it might do more harm than good." She took a deep breath and pulled a folder from her bag. "Has social services determined whether you'll be able to keep Tomiko?"

"No. I'm just the emergency placement for now." Diane got up the courage to ask the question that had been burning since Friday. "If I'm out of line, please let me know, but why wasn't a family member listed as next of kin?"

"You're not out of line, and it's a natural question." She hesitated briefly before continuing. "Off the record, Terrell's family never liked Marjorie and never forgave her for 'ruining' his life," she said bitterly, emphasizing her sentence with air quotes. "They were banking on the money Terrell stood to make playing professional football. But when Marjorie got pregnant their junior year of college, he decided he wanted a safer career and went to law school instead, like he really wanted."

She couldn't believe her ears. "When you say they were counting on the money, do you mean his family expected him to take care of them?"

"That's exactly what I'm saying. We all went to school together, and Terrell's two brothers and one sister barely graduated. Neither of them can keep a job for more than a few months. They didn't even show up to the wedding." Toni paused briefly, as if remembering. "When Tomiko was born, Terrell's mother told him she didn't want to see him, that bitch he married or their bastard child."

Diane gasped softly and brought her hand to her mouth. "How on earth could a mother say that to her child?" She couldn't imagine the pain that must have caused. And not to want to be part of her own grandchild's life? Diane's mother would have moved heaven and earth to see her grandchild, no matter the circumstances. Obviously there was more to the story, but Diane didn't think it was her business to pry. "What about Marjorie's family?"

She dearly hoped the young couple had at least some support and someone who might be willing to take Tomiko into their home.

"I've been in touch with her mom, and she'll be flying in from Atlanta this week to help with the service. She was devastated, and even more so because she knows social services won't allow her to take Tomiko because of her health, even though she's listed on the will as the guardian—they never got around to changing it. Mama Doris had a stroke three years ago. She can get around okay with a cane but has some residual weakness. And she's almost sixty-five."

This was getting worse by the moment.

"I recall a distant aunt on that side, but no one has been able to get in touch with her yet. But Mama Doris is actively involved in Tomiko's life, so that's a good thing."

"I agree. Then—"

"You want to know why I didn't take her?"

"I just assumed since you were listed as the emergency contact . . ." Diane let the sentence hang. Toni mentioned her and Marjorie being best friends, so it would stand to reason that she'd be given custody.

Toni gave Diane a sad smile. "Believe me, I would've taken Miko in a heartbeat because I love her as much as I love my own three children, but I'm in the middle of a divorce and dealing with my own custody issues. I wouldn't feel right bringing her into my toxic environment."

Marriage problems seemed to be going around. "I'm sorry." She could see the pain reflected in Toni's eyes.

"Thanks." She cleared her throat and opened the folder she'd been holding. "Now, on the record, there are a number of items I need to discuss with you." She detailed the provisions left in the Franklins' wills with regard to the monthly stipend the caregiver would receive, allowances for clothing and other things. "If you've purchased some things for Tomiko, just give me the receipts and I'll see to it that you're reimbursed."

Diane waved her off. "I don't need to be reimbursed. Save that money for something else she might need in the future."

She studied Diane a lengthy moment. "I'm glad Miko ended up with you for the time being."

"So am I." She'd known Tomiko since age three, when she started coming to the day care center, first as a student in Diane's class, then as one of the students in the after-school program. Diane usually bonded with all her students but was closer to a few of them, including Tomiko.

Toni nodded. "Do you have any questions for me?"

"I do. Would it be possible to get some of Tomiko's favorite things from her house—a stuffed animal, blanket or some other things? I think it might help her."

"Sure. I can stop by their house and set up a time with you to drop them off." Toni stood.

Diane followed suit, and they walked toward the front door. "Thank you so much. Again, I'm very sorry for your loss. Please let me know if you're able to contact the aunt." While she'd love to keep the little girl, Diane recognized that Tomiko being with a good family member would be better.

She smiled. "I'll be in touch about the service. If you think of anything else, just give me a call."

"I will." Diane closed the door and blew out a long breath.

A few minutes later, while seasoning the chicken she planned to have for dinner, she stifled a yawn and savored the quiet. She was exhausted. Jeffrey had gone out to play golf with a few of his friends, and Tomiko was still, blessedly, asleep. The poor baby had been up half the night crying off and on and asking for her parents. Diane had done the best she could to console her.

"Miss Di, may I have some water?"

She spun around at the sound of Tomiko's voice and smiled.

"Hi, honey. Of course." She washed and dried her hands, then got water from the refrigerator. "Are you hungry?"

Tomiko rubbed her eyes. "Yes."

Diane handed her the small glass and made a mental note to purchase a few plastic cups. "Anything in particular you'd like to have?"

"*Um* . . . do you have peanut butter and jelly? I like strawberry on mine." She drained the water from the glass, handed it back and laid her head against Diane.

Her smile widened. "I have some peanut butter and the best strawberry jam around. Have a seat at the table, and I'll make it for you." In addition to the sandwich, she added a few baby carrots and pretzels. As soon as she set the plate down, Tomiko bowed her head, recited a blessing, then dug in. The fact that she'd blessed her food without prompting told Diane the family must have done it regularly.

The doorbell rang. "Let me go see who's at the door." She wasn't expecting anyone but figured it might be Joy and Rochelle. Diane smiled when she saw her mother and older sister standing there. "Mom! Shelby! What are you two doing here?" They hugged, and Diane stepped back to let them enter.

Shelby held up a bag. "We wanted to come and check on you and see how you're adjusting."

"How's she doing?" her mother asked.

"I love y'all. This placement is only temporary, so she may not be here for long. Although her maternal grandmother isn't able to take her in due to her health, they're still looking for an aunt." She led them to the kitchen where Tomiko sat finishing her sandwich. "Tomiko, I'd like you to meet my mom, Mrs. Bailey and my sister, Mrs. Hall."

Tomiko dropped her head and said shyly, "Hi."

Diane's mother sat in the chair next to Tomiko. "It's so nice to meet you, Tomiko, and I'm really sorry about your mom and dad. But I know they're watching over you in heaven."

Her head came up. "That's what Miss Di said."

"And she's right."

"But I didn't want them to die," Tomiko said, echoing the words she'd said to Diane that first night.

Diane's heart constricted, and she made a move to hug Tomiko, but her mother's subtle shake of the head stopped her.

Janetta patted Tomiko's hand gently. "Believe me, baby, they didn't want to leave you either. Sometimes bad things happen in this world that we don't understand, and this is one of them. When my parents died, I cried for weeks. And it's okay to cry and be sad."

With the same tender loving care that she'd always experienced from her mother, Diane watched as Janetta displayed the same to Tomiko, knowing exactly what to say. Her mother had lost her parents early in life, and the shared bond seemed to make it natural for Tomiko to gravitate to the older woman.

Shelby sidled up next to Diane. "I swear that woman is a miracle worker."

"Yes, she is. And I'm so glad she's our mom." They shared a smile.

"Amen, sister. Amen."

While Tomiko chatted away with their mom, Diane and Shelby stepped into the family room, and Diane filled her in on the conversation she'd had with the attorney.

"Do you think any of the dad's family members will step up?"

The thought terrified Diane after hearing their history. "I hope not."

Shelby raised an eyebrow. "Money makes people do all kinds of things, and I wouldn't put it past at least one of them to try. I hope their will has some added stipulations, just in case."

"I wanted to ask, but that would probably be breaching some confidentiality laws. The attorney mentioned having a funeral service, and I wonder if any of them will come."

"They probably will, just to be nosy. Shoot, you're Tomiko's guardian now, and you need to know what you'll be up against." She made a show of thinking. "I might take off from work and go with you. If those folks show up, you're going to need some backup."

Diane chuckled. "I'm not going there to fight anybody."

"Humph. You might have to," Shelby said with a roll of her eyes. "Like I said, the scent of money brings out all the fools, and from the little bit you shared, boxing gloves might be in order."

"Girl, you are too old to go around beating up people." Growing up, Shelby had never been one to back down from a fight and was known for not putting up with any bull. No one dared mess with Diane.

She smiled and shrugged. "I'm just saying. How's Jeff taking this?"

Diane blew out a long breath. "Not good. We've been having problems for a few months, and this just seemed to make it worse."

"I talked to you three weeks ago and you didn't say anything."

"I know. I was hoping it would blow over, but it hasn't. We barely talk, and when we do, all it takes is one little thing and we're at each other's throats." She dropped down on the sofa and buried her head in her hands, then tearfully shared everything from the early menopause diagnosis to the growing battle with Jeffrey over possibly adopting. "First he said the timing wasn't right, and now it's too late. We took all the classes for foster parenting and adoption, and he was all in favor, but somehow now he's against that as well."

Shelby sat next to Diane. "Maybe you two can talk about why he's so against it."

"I've tried, Shelby. Multiple times. But he shuts me down cold each time. I don't know what else—" Diane cut herself off when she heard the garage opening.

"Well, I guess we'll have to table this little conversation for another time. You go wipe your face, and I'll run interference with my brother-in-law until you get back."

She grasped Shelby's hand and gave it a gentle squeeze. "You're the best big sister a girl could have."

"Yep. That's me," she said with a laugh and strutted off to the kitchen.

Diane went to the small half bath and washed her face. She studied her reflection in the mirror, satisfied that she didn't look like she had been crying. *That's the last thing I need him to see.* Taking a deep breath, she followed the sound of laughter coming from the kitchen. The sight of her husband smiling and laughing momentarily froze her. If he was putting on a show, he was doing a heck of a job because she couldn't remember the last time he'd been so open and relaxed. "Hey. How did the game go?"

"It was good." Jeffrey closed the distance between them and placed a gentle kiss on her lips.

The sweetness poured through her, and she hoped it meant their relationship was getting back on track. She'd missed his laughter, missed his kisses, missed *them*.

Diane couldn't have been more wrong. As soon as her mother and sister left, he began to distance himself, and by bedtime, he had all but shut down. Something had to give, and soon. They couldn't keep going this way. *She* couldn't keep going this way.

"Want to talk about it?" she asked when he came out of the bathroom freshly showered, a few droplets of water still clinging to his wide chest. For a man in his early forties, he kept himself in good shape. Her gaze made a slow path down his rich brown toned body, and the memories of touching and tasting every inch of him came back with vivid clarity. Just like always, her own body reacted and reminded her how long it had been since they'd last made love.

"There's nothing to talk about." Jeffrey tossed the towel onto a chair and pulled on a pair of boxer briefs.

"I think there is. We've been walking on eggshells around each other for the past several weeks, avoiding the elephant in the room. I need to know what's going on with you, Jeff."

"I'm fine. Everything would be fine if you stopped talking about this having a baby thing so much."

There. He'd finally said it. *Having a baby thing.* The words cut deeper than she had anticipated. Diane didn't understand his reluctance. He'd wanted children too. "Help me understand something. You said you wanted children. For the first five years of our marriage, that's all you talked about—having at least two little ones to fill this house. Now, all of a sudden, you want me to stop talking about it."

Jeffrey flipped the covers back on his side of the bed and sat. "I'm at a different place in my life now and much older. I'm not sure I want the burden of kids."

She couldn't believe her ears. He'd been the one who insisted on buying their four-bedroom home to make sure they had enough room, and while shopping for furniture he had dragged her over to the baby section to look at cribs and other decorations.

"A burden? Then why did we take all those classes to become foster or adoptive parents last year?" On one hand, Diane was ecstatic about finally experiencing motherhood, but on the other, she never imagined having to do it without the support of her husband.

"Because *you* wanted to."

The words felt like a slap to her face. It had never occurred to her that he hadn't wanted to take the classes. "You never said anything before."

"What was I supposed to say, Diane?" he yelled. "That's all you wanted, all you talked about."

"Lower your voice," she whispered harshly. "Tomiko is asleep."

Jeffrey threw up his hands. "Now I have to be quiet in my own damn house? This is some bullshit!" Although he'd lowered his voice, the words crackled through the room.

Diane jumped off the bed and was around to his side in a flash. "What part is bullshit—the fact that I asked you to lower your voice so you don't wake that sweet little girl or the fact that you've changed your mind about something we agreed on and refuse to say why?"

He stood and brushed past her. "You just can't let it go, can you?"

"No, I cannot. We're supposed to be partners in this relationship, and we can't even have a decent conversation these days. All I'm asking is for you to be honest with me." Once again, Diane tried to keep her mind from traveling down the path of their past. "You're the one who wanted at least two children and was always showing me some new thing we should buy. How is it that now you don't even want to talk about it?"

"Diane, I don't want to talk about it," he said through clenched teeth.

"You haven't wanted to talk about it for months. Well, I do. Why can't you just tell me what's going on with you?"

Jeffrey came back to where she stood, chest heaving, eyes darkened with anger. "You want to know what's going on with me? Fine! What's going on is every time you mention having a baby, it points to my failure." He pointed toward the hall. "And every time I see that little girl and the look of love you have for her, I know you would make a great mother, and it's a reminder that I couldn't give you the one thing you wanted most."

Diane's heart started pounding. "What are you talking about?" she whispered anxiously.

He dropped down on the side of the bed and buried his head in his hands. "You can't have children because I can't give them to you," he said resignedly.

The breath whooshed out of Diane, and she became so light-headed she had to sit down. "I don't understand. Are you talking about the fact that you have a slightly lower sperm count?" She searched his face for some hint of . . . anything, but all she saw was misery.

"The doctor said it shouldn't affect my ability to father children, but obviously *that* wasn't the truth," he said with a bitter chuckle.

For a moment she sat stunned, having no idea what to say. She'd heard about men with lower sperm counts still fathering children, and Jeffrey had never mentioned being bothered by those test results before. Surely he didn't believe it was his fault. However, when he met her gaze, she saw exactly that. "If you blame yourself for that, do you blame me for my issues too?"

"No. I don't blame you, Diane," Jeffrey said wearily. He scrubbed a hand down his face. "I've been thinking about my mother and her early onset Alzheimer's. What if the same thing happens to me? I wouldn't be around, and . . ." His jaw tightened. "And now you're all into this adoption thing. I've been reading the statistics, and some of those kids never bond with their adoptive parents. What if the kid we get doesn't connect with us—with *me*? What if I don't measure up?" He stared at Diane. "I don't think I can take that chance."

She placed a tentative hand on his arm. "Jeffrey—"

Jeffrey shrugged her hand off, stood and went over to the dresser.

He snatched out a pair of sweatpants and a T-shirt, dressed without a word and stuck his feet in his slides, then started for the door.

Diane jumped up and blocked his path. "Wait. Where are you going?"

"I need to get out of here."

"What time are you coming back?" She searched his face, her fear rising. He stared at her a lengthy moment but didn't reply. "Jeffrey?"

"I don't know." He grabbed his wallet and strode out.

Body trembling and tears running down her face, she watched him go.

Chapter 16

Joy

"MORNING."

Joy shifted her gaze from the computer to where Robert stood lounging in her office doorway. This was not how she wanted to start her Monday. They'd been staying out of each other's way, only communicating when necessary, until last Friday. "Good morning."

"How was your weekend?"

"Fine."

"Have you thought about what I said?"

She'd thought about it nonstop but had no intentions of telling him that. "Some."

Robert pushed off the doorframe, came over to where she sat and propped a hip on her desk. "Well, it's the only thing that's been on my mind. I miss you, Joy. I miss *us*," he said softly.

She leaned back in her chair and exhaled deeply. "Where is all this coming from, Robert? I haven't been able to get you to discuss our relationship for months, and now you want me to believe you miss us?" For months she had tried to push toward some kind of reconciliation, and not once had he been receptive. Now, all of a sudden, he wanted one. She searched his face, looking for something—*anything*—that would give a hint as to why he was so interested in their relationship after all this time. Was it the reality of her filing for divorce? Or the realization that she would no longer be there to help him run the business? Whatever the case, she still had very real reservations.

"You were right, and I want to apologize. I shouldn't have been so selfish. I know how important your retreat spa is to you." He gently pulled her to stand in front of him. "I'm going to do better to take care of your needs."

Before Joy could respond, Robert covered her mouth in a deep kiss. His tongue dipped in and out of her mouth in the way that always drove her crazy. The way that always ended with them naked and indulging in the most passionate and intense sex. She could feel the solid ridge of his erection pressed against the base of her belly, and a soft pulsing began in her core.

I can't do this.

She broke off the kiss abruptly and backed out of his embrace. For months she'd wanted this kind of connection with him, and not once had he reciprocated. Now he changed his mind? She couldn't dismiss everything he'd said and *hadn't* said just because he kissed her, no matter how much she missed the physical parts of their relationship. Her feelings for him had changed, and the love she once felt had waned and was all but gone.

"Why now, Robert? For nearly a year you all but ignore me, and you want me to do what? Fall into your arms as if none of it has happened?" She shook her head. "I'm not buying it. Again, why now?"

"Joy." Robert reached for her but didn't answer her question.

She put a hand up and shook her head but didn't say anything. She couldn't. She didn't want him to know how much she still craved his kiss, his touch. And that he still hadn't answered her told Joy everything she wanted to know. Nothing had changed.

His cell rang. Digging it out of his pocket, he checked the display and muttered a curse. "I have to take this. Can we have dinner tonight?"

"I'll think about it. You should answer that," she said, gesturing toward his still ringing phone.

Sighing, he answered and strode out of the office.

Joy ran a hand across her forehead. She was more conflicted than ever about what to do. Her mind conjured up a hundred and one scenarios about what could go wrong. She was so lost in her thoughts, it took her a moment to realize her own phone was ringing. She picked it up from the desk, saw her Realtor's name and answered the call. "Hey, Gretchen."

"Good morning, Joy. I'm checking to make sure we're still meeting to view a few more rentals today."

"I'll be there."

"Okay. You mentioned wanting to look at houses as well, and a listing just came up for a three-bedroom, two-bath in Rancho Cordova."

"Is it in good shape?" She wanted something move-in ready so she didn't have to shell out thousands of dollars in renovations. She needed to save those funds for whatever property she found for her business. Joy heard papers rustling for a moment, then Gretchen came back on the line.

"It says it is—new flooring, updated kitchen and master bedroom—but we'll find out for sure when we get there. I hope it's not like the last place," Gretchen added with a hint of disgust in her voice.

One of the foreclosed town houses the Realtor had shown Joy had been completely trashed on the inside by the previous owners, the appliances stolen and every room littered with half-eaten food and empty packages. She had wasted no time calling her office to complain.

"I hope not too. See you soon." They spoke a moment longer, then Joy ended the call. Going back to sit at her desk, she made a list of the flooring and bathroom tile samples she needed to pick up from the home improvement store for her afternoon consultation. Afterward she rotated toward the computer and opened the listings of the homes she'd be viewing and documented the pros and cons of each. As she'd told Gretchen, Joy preferred a house to a condo or town house. She'd gotten used to not sharing walls with other tenants and having her own backyard. The latter had been the place she sat at the end of the day to unwind, think and dream and she couldn't see herself giving that up. She'd given up enough already. Her phone chimed with a text message.

She smiled at the text Rochelle sent, asking if they were still on for Saturday to go shopping for their trip. Before she finished reading the message, she typed YES!

Rochelle: Lol! Are you anxious?

Joy: Girl, you don't even know.

Diane: Need this right now. Things not good with Jeff.

Rochelle: What happened?

Diane: Long story. Will tell you everything Saturday.

Joy: Sounds like we'll need wine.

Diane: Stronger!

Joy frowned. Of the four friends, Diane tended to be the one who stuck to wine and fruity mixed drinks. For her to mention needing something stronger meant things must be really bad. She wondered if it had anything to do with Jeffrey still having issues with Diane taking in Tomiko. Joy truly believed Jeffrey and Diane loved each other and hoped they could work through whatever problem they had by the time Saturday came around.

She finished making notes on each property, closed the window and powered off the computer. Making sure she had her shopping list, she retrieved her purse and headed out. On her way, Joy stopped by Stacey's desk to let her know she was leaving.

"What time will you be back?"

"Probably around one." It would give her plenty of time to put together the presentation for her two thirty appointment. "Can you let Robert know?"

Usually she stuck her head in Robert's office to tell him herself, but she didn't want any residual *feelings* she might have for him to cloud her judgment or make her have any more second thoughts.

"Sure. See you when you get back."

It took Joy only ten minutes to arrive at the first property. Although the two-bedroom condo had all the amenities she wanted, including several restaurants and shopping plazas nearby, it was located only a few miles from their office. She didn't want to chance running into Robert all the time, so she nixed it and followed Gretchen to the next one on the list. On the way, she thought about what had happened earlier with Robert and was, admittedly, somewhat conflicted. No woman wanted to add a failed marriage to her list of accomplishments, and she was no exception. However, at the same time, all the lonely nights, lack of intimacy and just the mere fact that Robert had yet to say he loved her gave Joy pause and reinforced her decision to stick with her current plans.

"I wasn't sure if you wanted to be downtown, but there are a lot of charming places, and you can't beat the ambience," Gretchen said as they entered a newer loft development.

Joy surveyed the space as she walked from room to room. "I can't deny the place is gorgeous, but I don't want to have to worry about constant foot and car traffic. There's also the issue of parking." She didn't want Chelle and Diane to have to deal with trying to find a spot on the street whenever they visited. Taking one last glance, she said, "This is a no too."

Gretchen chuckled. "I figured as much. I saved the best two for last."

"Two? I thought we only had one more." Everything she'd seen so far had been condos and town houses. The next stop was a house in the Greenhaven area of Sacramento.

"Remember the one I mentioned this morning?"

"Oh yes. The house in Rancho." It was in the opposite direction of the other property. Joy took a quick peek at her watch. She still had plenty of time to see both, pick up her samples, and make it back to the office on time. "Okay. Let's go."

She had liked the first house and the neighborhood, but the moment she stepped out of her car in front of the Rancho Cordova house, she fell in love. The one-story home was tucked away on a quiet street with manicured lawns, lush greenery and mature trees. "I like this."

Gretchen smiled. "Well, let's see what the inside looks like." She unlocked the door and stepped back for Joy to enter first. Following, she said, "Nice, open layout."

"I agree." Joy entered the open concept living room with vaulted ceilings and a wood-burning fireplace. It opened to a spacious eat-in kitchen with an abundance of cabinetry, counter space and pull-out shelving. She walked over to the French doors and opened them. A smile lit her face when she saw the covered patio area on the side of the house with its stone walkway. "I like this." She took the path to the backyard. Her heart started pounding in excitement. This would be the perfect place to relax and entertain, especially when it was her turn to host her girlfriends. She hoped the rest of the house met her standards.

As they went back inside, Gretchen said, "Did I mention it has inside and outside surround sound?"

She spun around and met the woman's smiling face. "No, you did not."

"My bad." Her laughter rang out through the house.

Smiling and shaking her head, Joy followed the petite redhead. The rest of the house proved to be just as nice. There were a few things she had questions about, but she figured they could be negotiated and mentioned them to Gretchen. The extra bedrooms would work well whenever her nephews or Ebony and Haley spent the night. She stepped into the primary bedroom and froze. "Oh. My. Goodness. Look at this *closet*. It's big enough to convert into another bedroom." It had built-in shelves and hanging rods in different heights. Joy could fit three of her current walk-in closets in there and still have room to dance around.

"So does this mean you want me to let them know you're interested? Apparently the house belongs to an older couple who can no longer live alone. Their children don't want to sell and are looking to rent it out as quickly as possible."

She opened her mouth to say yes, then closed it. *"I miss you, Joy. I miss us."* Robert's words floated through her mind. Once again she asked herself if she really wanted to give her marriage a second try. Robert seemed sincere, and the kiss . . . "Can I think about it?"

Gretchen studied Joy for a long moment. "Yes, but I wouldn't wait too long. The rent is already cheaper than most places around here, so it'll go fast."

"I know. I'll make a decision no later than tomorrow morning." If she accepted Robert's dinner offer, it would give her a little more time to feel him out and find out if he was genuinely interested in a reconciliation.

"Okay. I'll open dialogue with your earlier questions so they'll know there's an interested party, and I'll call you later."

They exited the house and the agent locked the door.

"Thank you so much, Gretchen."

"You're welcome. I'll talk to you soon."

"Yes, you will," Joy said, and with a wave she got into her car and headed to her next stop. She decided to visit the home improvement store near the office so she didn't get caught in traffic, which was already picking up. While driving, her thoughts strayed back to her dilemma. The months of neglect and lack of interest on her husband's part had taken their toll on her. A few months ago she might have jumped at the chance to patch things up in her marriage, but now, if she were honest, she'd admit to being unsure it was really what *she* wanted. When Joy arrived at the store she had to rush. She'd spent far more time at the house than she had planned, and she hastened her steps to the checkout.

"Hey, Joy."

She turned. "Grant. How are you?" Grant Mills and his wife, Leticia, owned Mills Interior Design, and they'd hired the husband-wife team for several of their projects.

"Doing well. I'll be even better once the merger with you all goes through."

Stunned, Joy stared. *Merger? What merger?*

"I couldn't believe it when Robert approached us on the last job. I guess he heard me talking about wanting to sell and just become an employee again," Grant said with a laugh. "With four kids, the long hours are killing us."

"I can imagine." She couldn't believe how calmly she'd spoken, particularly with the red-hot rage surging through her veins at the moment.

Oblivious to her lack of response, Grant continued sharing his excitement. "And you know Leticia made sure he knew we'd only agree to the sale if she could continue to work with you."

Her body trembled with anger, and it was all Joy could do to stand there. Deciding that she needed to leave before all hell broke loose, she said, "I'm sure we'll iron out all the details, but I need to get going. Tell Leticia hello." She was already striding away before he finished his reply. Thankfully, she was able to go through the self-checkout quickly. *Wait 'til I get my hands on that jerk!* All that sweet-talking had been nothing more than him trying to keep her from quitting and walking away until that sale went through. A thought occurred to her. Widiane hadth a merger, there wouldn't be any liquid assets to split the business, and he knew it. *Well, he has another thing coming.*

Back in her car, she had to take a few deep breaths before starting up the car. In her present state she'd most likely get more than one speeding ticket. As it stood, she was going to have to work hard not to knock the hell out of Robert when she saw him. Joy snatched up her cell and dialed the Realtor. "Hey, Gretchen," she said when the woman answered.

"Joy. Hi. I didn't expect to hear from you so soon. Did you have some other questions?"

"No. I want you to make an offer."

"*Um* . . . sure. Are you okay?"

"Just fine." Or she would be as soon as her divorce was final.

"I'll get right on it and let you know as soon as I hear something."

"Thanks so much." Joy disconnected. She started the car and roared out of the parking lot. She hadn't gone one block before her phone rang. She groaned and engaged the Bluetooth. "Yes."

"Whoa. Who pissed you off?"

"Sorry, Brent," she muttered, "but to answer your question, Robert." She told him about Robert's newfound affection and ended with what happened in the store. "And when I get to the office—"

"You're going to do nothing, sis. Let your attorney handle it."

SHERYL LISTER

"Then she'd better get to the office before I do. I've had it with the lies."

"Joy, I know you're upset."

"*Upset?* No, Brent, I'm *pissed.*" She hit the End button. She swerved around a car driving slow enough for her to walk beside and pressed harder on the gas pedal. The closer she came to the office, the madder she got, and by the time she arrived, she'd reached a boiling point. She was going to kick Robert's ass and let her attorney pick up the pieces.

Joy strode purposefully to the entrance and snatched the door open. She heard her brother's voice behind her and whirled around. "What are you doing here? And how did you get here so fast?"

"I was in the area and had planned to see if you wanted to do a late lunch, but I never got around to that part before you hung up on me." Brent laid a hand on her arm. "Don't do something you'll regret."

She snorted. "You should be making that speech to Robert. And the only thing I regret right now is marrying him in the first place." She pulled her arm away and marched off toward Robert's office like a woman on a mission, Brent following closely on her heels.

"Sis, wait."

"No! I've had enough." She raised her hand to the partially open door, but the voices inside stopped her cold.

"Rob, why do we need her?" she heard Stacey say. "I can help you run the company as well as she can."

"Just a little while longer, okay? I need this merger with Mills to go through, and then I'll be all yours. You know I love you, baby."

Joy's heart nearly stopped hearing Robert tell the other woman he loved her.

"Damn," Brent whispered and gave Joy's shoulder a sympathetic squeeze.

She glanced up at her brother, and tears burned the back of her eyes, but she willed them not to fall. She would *not* let Robert see her cry. Myriad emotions rushed through her—hurt, betrayal and white-hot rage. The latter won out, and she shoved the door open with such force it slammed against the wall. Robert and Stacey, in the middle of what looked to be a passionate kiss, sprang apart, eyes wide. It wasn't enough that he'd tried to absorb another company without her knowledge, but cheating . . .

And he was kissing me this morning.

Without a word, she crossed the floor and punched Robert in his face.

Robert staggered back and grabbed his jaw. "*Ow.* Shit!"

"You lying bastard!"

"Hey, you can't—" Stacey said.

Joy was in the woman's face in the blink of an eye. "Say *one* more word." The woman's eyes grew even wider and she jumped back, but she had the good sense to heed the warning. Joy pointed her finger in Robert's face. "Sign. The. Damn. Divorce. Papers. You don't want to test me. And I hope you have a good lawyer."

She flashed around to Stacey. Everything in her wanted to knock the trifling bitch on her ass, and it took supreme effort on Joy's part not to do it. "You're *fired.* You have ten minutes to get your *shit* and get out. And you might not want to test me either."

Robert would probably hire her back, but it gave her pure satisfaction to say the words. Sending one last glare his way, she stormed out and didn't stop walking until she reached the exit.

"I'm so sorry, baby girl."

Joy let herself be enfolded in her big brother's arms as the tears ran freely from her eyes. She was done with all the lies. She cried for everything that could've been—everything that *should've* been—but would never be.

Chapter 17

Diane

THE FOLLOWING WEDNESDAY, DIANE'S NERVES WERE stretched so thin, she felt as if she would snap at any minute. For the first time in her marriage, she slept in their bed alone. After returning late Sunday night, Jeff had gone downstairs to the guest bedroom and had been sleeping there for the past three nights. She really needed to get away for a few minutes to relax, but she didn't see that happening anytime soon. And they still had weeks before the Jamaica trip. *Why can't it be* this *week?*

She responded to Joy's message: **Still walking on eggshells. Slept alone since Saturday. Not sure how much more I can take.**

Joy: **Ugh! What is it with these men? Do you need anything?**

Rochelle: **Maybe Jeff will come around. And y'all are telling me I should start a relationship.**

Diane: **I don't need anything, Joy. Chelle, you can't let our drama affect you. Warren is a good man. Don't forget what Yvette said.**

Rochelle: **Low blow, sis . . . LOL!**

Smiling, Diane typed back: **Hey, gotta use what I can. Need to get back to dinner. We're still on for shopping Saturday, right?**

When both responded in the affirmative, she set the phone aside and refocused on dinner. The mention of Yvette made her wonder what she'd say about all the mess in their lives. Diane still half expected to see Yvette chiming in on their group texts. The grief surfaced again, and she could feel the tears stinging her eyes.

Her one bright spot, however, was Tomiko. She had already gotten attached to the little girl over the years, but having her in their home had tightened the bond. Diane stirred the spaghetti sauce, then glanced over at Tomiko sitting at the kitchen table doing her homework. "Do you need any help?"

"No, thank you," came the soft reply.

So far today, there hadn't been any tears, but Diane knew that grief didn't play by any rules and could rise up at any moment. She was just glad Tomiko hadn't been placed with strangers. While the sauce cooked, she added spaghetti to the pot of boiling water.

"Miss Di, may I have some water?"

"Sure, sweetheart." Diane got a cup, filled it and placed it on the table. She leaned down to check the reading comprehension sheet and smiled. All the answers had been neatly written. She gave Tomiko's shoulder a gentle squeeze. "Good job. If you're done, you can read a book or watch one of your TV shows."

Tomiko nodded over the cup as she drank. After finishing, she placed it in Diane's outstretched hand and silently left the table.

Diane went back to the stove, sighing and wishing she could wave a magic wand to bring the little girl's parents back. She heard the garage door open the same time as the phone rang. Her heart pounded, and her hands started shaking, not knowing what to expect from Jeffrey. Diane rushed to the phone and didn't recognize the number. "Hello."

"Mrs. Evans, this is Toni Collins."

"Hi, Toni, and please call me Diane. How are you holding up?"

"Some days okay, others not so much. How's Miko?"

"A lot like you. She doesn't talk much and has some crying spells. I imagine it'll be like this for a while." If it had been her parents, Diane would have difficulty getting through the days too.

"That poor baby," Toni whispered. She cleared her throat. "I'm calling to let you know that the service for her parents will be next Friday at eleven."

"Let me get a pen." Diane startled when she turned and saw Jeffrey standing there. After retrieving the pen and notepad, she wrote down the information. "Thanks so much. We'll be there."

"Sounds good. I want to warn you that some of Terrell's family members may be there, and my guess is that their only interest is the estate, and they won't hesitate to harass Tomiko to get the information."

She felt her anger rising. *They're not getting within ten feet of this baby!* "Thanks for the warning. I'll do whatever's necessary to protect her. I would like for her to have some time with Marjorie's family, if that's okay."

"She'd love that, and I'll make sure to introduce you. I won't hold you, but if you have any questions, please let me know."

"I appreciate your call. You take care." Diane hung up the phone and steeled herself for whatever might happen with her husband. Taking a deep breath, she turned. Jeffrey stood at the bar leafing through the mail. "Hey."

He glanced up briefly, then ripped open an envelope. "Hey."

I don't know how much more I can take. She really wanted them to finish their conversation from the night he stormed out, but she didn't have the strength for another shouting match. Instead, she opted to focus on cooking and try to find a safe topic. However, the funeral and what Toni said about Terrell's relatives weighed heavily on her mind.

"That was Toni, letting me know that Tomiko's parents' service will be a week from Friday."

"Do you plan to go?"

"Yes. As hard as this will be, she needs to be able to say good-bye." How Tomiko would react had her concerned, as did the distant relatives.

"*Hmm*," was all he said.

She had never mentioned what Toni disclosed about Terrell's family on her first visit, so she took a moment to tell him. "Now she's telling me his family members may be there and bother this sweet baby to get at her inheritance, and it has me worried."

Jeffrey loosened his tie and leaned against the counter. "Some people have no shame. Hopefully they won't bring that kind of crap to the funeral. That's the last thing she needs."

"I agree." She wondered if he was recalling the drama with a couple of his family members who'd been angry about being left out of his mother's will. "Dinner will be ready in about ten minutes."

He nodded and strolled out of the kitchen.

Diane released the breath she'd been holding. This had been the longest conversation they'd had without being at each other's throats. Granted, the discussion stayed off their relationship, but she'd take it. For now.

However, it was short-lived, as dinner turned out to be a strained affair with him muttering one-word responses and nearly bolting from the table the moment he finished eating.

"Can I help put the dishes in the dishwasher?" Tomiko asked, placing her plate in the sink.

Diane smiled. "I'd love that." Working together, it took them less than twenty minutes to return the kitchen to its former clean state.

She looked up at Diane with sad eyes. "My mom used to let me help her too."

This was the first time Tomiko had mentioned her mother

outside of questioning her death. "I can see why. You're a great helper." Bringing her in for a hug, Diane kissed her temple. "I tell you what, after your bath, we'll have popcorn and watch *The Lion Guard* on Disney+."

"Okay." Tomiko gave her a small smile, another hug and headed upstairs.

She took a moment to check the freezer for vanilla ice cream and the refrigerator for root beer. Seeing she had both, she thought adding small root beer floats would be a special treat.

"What are you doing?"

Diane jumped and spun around with her hand to her chest. "You scared me." Jeffrey had entered so quietly, she hadn't heard him. She got two cups, the ice cream scooper and a long spoon. "Tomiko and I are going to watch one of her Disney shows, and we're having popcorn and floats. You're welcome to join us." She took a wary glance over her shoulder to gauge his expression.

Jeffrey stared at her for the longest time, and for a split second, his features softened. Then he finally said, "Nah. You two go ahead. I'll be upstairs." He went over to the fridge, grabbed a bottle of water and walked back out.

She sighed and continued making the dessert. By the time Tomiko returned, Diane had everything ready. She picked up the bowl of popcorn, handed one of the floats to Tomiko and took the other one for herself. "Ready?"

"Yes, ma'am."

Diane had already placed TV trays on either side of the oversize recliner for their drinks. Once the two of them were settled, she started the show. These were the moments she had looked forward to having with her own children, and being here with this little one filled her with a contentment she couldn't describe. They laughed at the antics of Kion and his friends and enjoyed their snacks. She opened her mouth to ask Tomiko a question but went still at the sight of Jeffrey observing them from the kitchen. He quickly turned away and disappeared around the corner. She tried to get a read on what he might be thinking, but these days he'd been so closed off, Diane had no idea about his mindset.

"It's over."

So lost in her thoughts, Diane had missed the ending. "Okay. Time for bed. I'll take these into the kitchen while you brush your teeth." She lowered the recliner and Tomiko scooted out. "I'll be up in a minute." Using the remote, she turned off the TV, then carried the empty dishes into the kitchen, where she rinsed and added them to the dishwasher. Afterward, she made sure she hadn't missed any stray pieces of popcorn. Satisfied, she turned off all the lights, climbed the stairs and met Tomiko coming out of the bathroom. Hand in hand, they walked to the guest bedroom.

Tomiko climbed into the bed. "Miss Di, am I going to stay with you?"

Diane adjusted the covers around Tomiko. "I sure hope so." So far, she hadn't heard anything about potential family members— not that she wanted any of them near Tomiko—and she prayed the placement would be permanent. But then, what would it do to her marriage? Would Jeffrey come around eventually or decide he wanted out? Leaning down, Diane placed a kiss on the little girl's brow and caressed her cheek. "Good night."

"Good night."

When she got to her bedroom, Jeffrey was stretched out on the bed watching television. *Oo-kay.* She wanted to ask if he planned on sleeping there but didn't. Instead, she grabbed a gown and underwear from the drawers and went into the bathroom. Usually he would've retreated to the downstairs bedroom by the time she came out, especially since she'd taken a long, relaxing bubble bath. But tonight he hadn't moved. Diane crossed the room to the sitting area and picked up the romance novel she'd been trying to read for the past couple of weeks.

At least some couple will get a happy ending.

She tried concentrating but gave up after five minutes and pulled out one of her word search books. Her eyes started to glaze over after completing several of them. Deciding she'd delayed going over to the bed long enough, she tossed the book aside and made her way to the bed. "So . . . *um*, are you sleeping in here tonight?"

Jeffrey slowly turned his head toward her. "I had planned to . . . unless you prefer I didn't."

"No, I . . . You don't have to sleep downstairs. I mean, if you don't want to, I'm fine with you in here."

He sat up, clicked off the TV and slid off the bed. "I'm going to shower."

She nodded.

He stood there for a minute as if he wanted to say something. In the end he just said, "Night."

Truthfully, she was more than fine with him being back in their bed. She *wanted* him here next to her, holding her, loving her. Diane didn't think for a minute she'd get the last two, but for tonight, she'd take the first one. And hope for the others.

Chapter 18

Joy

"WHAT TIME IS DIANE GETTING HERE, CHELLE?" JOY called out from her borrowed room Saturday morning. The three of them were going shopping, then having lunch afterward. She needed to run by the office first, because in her haste to leave a week ago, she'd left two of the flash drives with her spa notes. Joy had waited until the weekend to avoid seeing Robert and figured she'd be in and out in less than two minutes.

Rochelle poked her head in the bedroom. "Around ten. She'll be here after her mother picks up Tomiko for the day."

"*Awww*, that is so sweet. Ms. Janetta has been campaigning for a granddaughter for years," she added with a laugh.

"I know."

"Since we still have an hour, I'm going to make a short trip to the office."

Rochelle frowned. "Do you want me to go with you just in case Robert is there?"

She shook her head. "I should be fine. It'll only take me a couple of minutes to get my flash drives. Then over lunch, I can tell y'all all the details of what happened."

Joy had only shared that Robert said something about giving him a little more time. She decided to drop the cheating bombshell and the fact that he tried to buy the interior design company over lunch and a strong drink.

"Wait." Rochelle lifted a hand. "There's more than him still taking his sweet time to live up to his promise?"

"*Way* more," Joy said, slinging her purse on her shoulder and grabbing her keys off the dresser. She chuckled at Rochelle's stunned look. "Be back in a few."

When she parked in the small lot several minutes later, Joy didn't immediately get out. She surveyed the building that had housed West Home Renovations for the past eight years and a myriad of emotions flooded her—pride, sadness and anger. The latter had a stronger grip on her. Blowing out a long breath, she hopped out of the car, locked the doors by remote and strode up the walkway. That she didn't see Robert's car gave her a measure of relief.

The sound of her sandals echoed on the polished tile floors as she made her way to her office. Joy unlocked the door and paused in the doorway, scanning the space. Everything was just as she'd left it the day she stormed out. She'd have to clean it out soon, but not today. She rounded the desk and opened one drawer, then another, moving papers and folders aside until she found what she needed.

"I didn't expect to see you here."

Joy let out a surprised gasp and whipped her head around to the door. *Just great.* Her soon-to-be ex-husband stood in the doorway with his arms folded. Ignoring Robert, she closed the drawer, stuck the flash drives into the outer pocket of her purse and prepared to leave.

"So you aren't going to say anything?" Robert asked, frowning.

"There's nothing left to say." She lifted a brow when he didn't move away from the door. "Do you mind?"

He stared momentarily, then stepped back just enough for her to exit.

After relocking the door, she breezed past him, then paused. "Oh yeah, I do have one thing to say. Sign the divorce papers, Robert."

"Joy."

"No. Just sign them. I'm sure you want to be free to date Stacey. You did say you loved her, right?" she added sarcastically. Without waiting for a response, she strode off before she was tempted to punch him again. *Asshole.*

Joy was still simmering by the time she made it back to Rochelle's house. But seeing Diane's car parked in front lifted her spirits some. Pushing thoughts of Robert to the furthest corner of her mind, she went inside. She wasn't going to let him ruin the day with her girls.

"Hey, girl," Joy said to Diane, hugging her.

"Hey."

"Things still strained between you and Jeff?"

Diane nodded, tears shimmering in her eyes.

She gave her another sisterly hug. "Well, we'll do a little retail and happy hour therapy, and hopefully we'll both feel better."

She laughed. "I'm down for both."

Rochelle strolled in with her purse. "I'll drive. We can go to the Galleria at Roseville again or Arden Fair."

"I vote for the Galleria. Trying to get into those small parking spaces at Arden is a pain," Diane said.

"For real," Joy said. The aisles were so narrow, sometimes it took serious maneuvering to get out if you drove a large car or SUV. "There are several restaurants in the area, so that works." The three women piled into Rochelle's Honda Accord, and she cranked up the music. They passed the drive discussing everything except the upheaval in their lives.

Joy was the first out of the car when they arrived. "Alrighty. Let's go get our shopping on. We need some more cute stuff for the trip. Maybe even a bikini or two." Her body didn't look like it did in her twenties, but she was still in reasonably good shape. Besides, no one knew her in Jamaica, and after all the mess she'd been going through, she planned to enjoy herself to the fullest. The good thing was that with summer a few weeks away, they'd still be able to find a good selection of clothing.

Rochelle shook her head and chuckled as they crossed the parking lot to the entrance. "I see right now we're going to be here for hours messing around with you."

"Hey, y'all know shopping is my hobby. We only had a couple of hours last time, but today we're going to have big fun," Joy said, rubbing her hands together with glee.

Diane burst out laughing. "Yeah, girl. And don't forget we have to find Chelle a few outfits for all those dates she'll be having with Warren."

Rochelle shook her head. "As long as you two don't get too crazy."

Grinning, Joy hooked her arm in Rochelle's. "We won't. So, come on. Remember, we're supposed to be finding you something that'll make his eyes bug out. I promise it'll cover all the essentials, but leave a little to tease, sort of like those sundresses."

"Gee, thanks," she said, rolling her eyes. Then she laughed. "I can't stand y'all sometimes."

Diane waved Rochelle off. "*Awww*, girl, you know you love us."

"*Mm-hmm*, whatever. So, Joy, where's the first stop?"

"I'm thinking some summer wear, then swimsuits. Shoes last because we'll know what styles and colors we need based on the clothes."

"Should've known Joy would have it all planned out," Rochelle said. "Come on, Ms. Shopping Queen. And don't try to have us in here all day."

Joy pointed to herself and asked innocently, "Who me?" then burst out laughing. "Hey, I'm just trying to keep my promise to Yvette to make sure this trip happens." They shared a moment of silence, then nodded. This was what she needed—time with her girls. Having Yvette there would have made the day perfect, but there was no such thing when it came to life.

Joy had a great time trying on and discarding one outfit after another as she searched through the racks.

Diane held up a short, halter multicolored sundress. "Joy, try this." She passed it over. "I think I'm going to get this one," she said of a knee-length, bright orange sleeveless V-neck dress.

Joy all but snatched the beautiful dress. "I love it." She added it to the pile on her arm and continued searching. She found a black-and-white cold-shoulder high low dress that would look fabulous on Rochelle, who'd been having difficulty finding something she liked.

"Chelle, go try this on. You can wear it on a date and on vacation if we decide to dress up for dinner one night."

Rochelle held it up, turning it one way, then another. "I actually like this."

They all made their way to the fitting rooms to try on the various outfits they'd found. Joy came out in her dress the same time as Rochelle. The door behind her opened, and Diane stepped out.

Rochelle held her arms out. "Well?"

Joy and Diane did a little squeal and Joy said, "Oh my goodness, sis. You look amazing."

"Turn around," Diane said, gesturing with her finger. "Girl, I just want to be there when Warren sees you in this dress."

A smile blossomed on Rochelle's face. "I can't with you two, but I really like it."

"I guess that means you're adding it to the keep pile."

Still admiring the dress, Rochelle said, "I most definitely am."

Joy had already selected four sundresses, three pairs of shorts and a wrap skirt, a few pieces more than her friends. The dress she had on stopped a few inches above her knees, had a slim-fitting bodice and flared out at the waist. "I'm getting this one too. What about you, Di?"

"Yep." She smoothed a hand over the fitted dress. "This will work well for casual or dressy."

"For a long time I hated shopping," Rochelle said, "but these last couple of times I've actually enjoyed it and am excited."

Diane hugged her. "*Awww*, we're glad we could help a sistah out."

"Me too. Now I need to find shoes to match after I take this off." She headed back to her fitting room.

"You're speaking my language, my sister." Joy almost skipped back into the fitting room. Dressed again, they found a few more pieces—casual and dressy—before beginning the search for shoes.

When they got to the shoe department, Diane pointed at Joy. "Joy, we are *not* going to purchase a dozen pairs of shoes."

Joy placed a hand over her heart. "I don't know what you mean," she said innocently.

"Let me move, just in case lightning strikes from that lie." Rochelle took an exaggerated step to the left.

"Forget y'all." Joy lifted her chin haughtily and strutted off, with Diane's and Rochelle's laughter trailing. Her friends caught up, and the three women headed straight for the sandals. After finding a couple of pairs each, Joy picked up a black peep-toe pump with a four-inch heel. "Chelle, I just found the perfect shoe for that black-and-white dress." She scanned the boxes in the cubby, found Rochelle's size and handed her the box. "Try these on."

Rochelle lifted an eyebrow. "*Um*, these look a little high."

"Remember, work it like you own it," Diane said.

She sat and put the shoes on, then tried to stand. She took four steps and started to wobble. "No. Just no," she said, nearly staggering back to the chair. "I hope that met your definition of 'work it like you own it' because that's the *only* work you're gonna see with these shoes." She snatched them off and tossed them back into the box. "Out here about to make me break my neck," she muttered, glaring at Joy.

Joy doubled over laughing. "Y-you have to practice." She could barely get the word out. "Oh my goodness. You should've seen yourself with that Frankenstein's monster walk."

Diane bit her lip to stifle her laughter but lost the battle too.

Rochelle rolled her eyes but was smiling. "I think I'll find my *own* shoes, thank you very much." She walked over, found another pair—a strappy sandal that had a slightly lower heel—and held it up. "*This* is more like it."

Joy and Diane were still chuckling. Diane said, "Hopefully you'll be able to walk better in those."

Rochelle removed the tissue paper from inside the shoe and threw it at Diane, hitting her in the chest. "Ha! Now hush. I didn't see you trying to walk in them."

"Because I know better," she said, cracking up.

Joy found her size in the high heels, slipped them on and stood. "See. It's easy." She did a strut past them as if she was a model on a runway, pivoted, started back and stumbled. Rochelle and Diane fell out laughing. Joy dropped down in the chair and laughed with them. "I think we need to pay for these shoes and get out of here."

They paid for their purchases and, loaded down with bags, carried everything to the car and placed them in the trunk.

"After all that shopping, I'm starving," Rochelle said.

Joy patted her stomach. "Same, girl." The three discussed options and ended up across the street at Yard House in the Fountains shopping plaza.

A hostess led them to a table, and by the time a server followed shortly after to take their drink orders, they were ready for the food as well.

The drinks—pink dragon margaritas—had barely hit the table before Rochelle asked, "Diane, are you and Jeff still sleeping apart?"

Diane took a sip of her drink. "Oh, that's good. But to answer your question, no, we are not sleeping apart. But we're still not really talking. I so want us to finish our conversation, but I'm afraid of what might happen if I bring it up." She shrugged. "We're going to have to broach the subject sometime soon, though. We can't keep going like this."

"Do you think he's seeing someone else?" Joy asked.

"Strangely enough, no. He's been coming home after work every day, like he used to do. We're drifting apart, and I have no idea how to fix it."

"I know you mentioned him not really interacting with Tomiko—"

Diane didn't wait for Rochelle to finish. "He's still not saying much of anything outside of a quick hello when he gets home. She seems to be adjusting, but I spoke with the attorney, and the funeral is next Friday."

Joy mentally went over her schedule. "Let me know the time, and I'll be there. I can see her father's crazy folks showing up and showing out. Vaseline may be needed." She saluted Diane with her drink and took a long draw from the straw.

Laughing, Diane said, "You sound like Shelby. She said something similar."

"Hey, she has a point." Joy loved Diane's older sister, who'd acted as a big sister to her and Rochelle. Shelby did not play when it came to protecting them. However, she did hope the family would act like they had some level of home training and keep the drama to a minimum.

"I'll try to take off work too," Rochelle said.

"Well, I have some news," Joy said, shifting the conversation. "I went ahead and filed for divorce and put an offer in on a rental in Rancho Cordova."

Rochelle frowned. "Wait. You didn't mention that this week. Granted, it's been crazy, and we haven't really had a chance to get into any deep discussions, but I thought you were going to hold off to see if you two could work some things out."

Joy had spent a couple of nights with her brother and one with her father trying to rebuild their relationship. "That was before I ran into one of the owners of the interior design company we typically use and he told me how glad he was that Robert had reached out and offered to buy them out."

"*What?*" Diane and Rochelle chorused.

"Yep. Then I went back to the office to confront him and busted him and Stacey kissing." That image had played over and over in her head, and each time it broke her heart all over again.

"You have got to be freakin' kidding me," Diane said, her eyes wide. She grasped Joy's hand. "Oh, sis, I am so sorry."

Rochelle shook her head slowly. "I don't even know what to say."

"He didn't either when I punched him in his face. Stacey tried to get in my face, and I was *this close*"—she put her thumb and index finger close together—"to knocking her on her ass too. I did fire her, though. But the worst part was hearing him tell her he loved her," she said softly. The same words he refused to say to Joy.

The server returned and placed chicken nachos, wings and spinach dip on the table. "Can I get you ladies anything else?"

None of them wanted anything, and the young woman departed with a smile. They each filled plates, then resumed the conversation.

"Girl, I cannot believe Robert. I hope you get everything you ask for in your settlement." Rochelle made a face of disgust.

Joy bit into a wing covered in barbecue sauce, chewed and swallowed. "He does not want to mess with me. The good thing is that Brent happened to be with me and saw the whole thing, so Robert can't lie." Since the incident, her big brother had called every day, sometimes twice, to check on her. He'd also teasingly suggested that he wouldn't have a problem paying Robert a visit. She still hadn't said much to her mother. "Okay, that's enough about my mess. Chelle, how are things going with Warren? We need some good news to counter all our problems."

Rochelle scooped up some spinach dip on her chip. "He said he wants us to date exclusively," she said casually and stuffed the chip into her mouth.

"And I know you told him yes," Diane said, pointing a drummette her way.

"After listening to you two and recalling all the crap Kenny put me through, I'm not sure I want to put myself back out there again. I agree that Warren is very different from Kenny, and I like him, but it's hard. Warren didn't want me to answer right then. He asked me to think about it and be sure."

Joy laid a sisterly hand on Rochelle's arm. "I know it's hard after going through what you did and now hearing about our issues, but please don't close your heart to him. He's been around us for years and has always been a good man."

"Besides, if he does anything to hurt you, Joe will definitely handle him," Diane added with a smirk.

Rochelle nodded. "True."

"Just think about it. If I get a second chance at love, I'm taking it," Joy said. "Life is too short not to take advantage of our blessings." She said the words, but with her heart in tatters, would she really be open to another relationship? Their trip to Jamaica would start the healing process, and she was counting down the weeks and days. *Just eight more weeks.*

Chapter 19

Rochelle

SATURDAY AFTERNOON AFTER SHE RETURNED FROM shopping, Rochelle drove over to her sister's house to pick up Haley.

"Hey, sis. Come on in," Val said, hugging Rochelle, then stepping back for her to enter. "How was shopping?"

"Long," Rochelle said with a chuckle, following Val to the kitchen. "You know we had to pry Joy out of the stores." She didn't hear the usual chatter between Haley, Bryan Jr. and Amari. "Where are the kids? It's never this quiet."

"You got that right. We figured we had some time before you got back, so Bryan took them to the movies. They should be here in the next twenty or thirty minutes. I figured I'd do dinner early and you and Haley can join us. I'm keeping it simple with steak sandwiches and fries. I'll be having a salad with mine."

"Sure. That means one less thing for me to think about when I get home." While out earlier, she, Joy and Diane had googled *Jamaican food*, and her taste buds were ready, but tonight she'd have to set the desire aside and enjoy this meal. She hung her purse on the back of a chair, then went to the sink to wash her hands. "I'll help."

Val smiled and gestured to the mushrooms, bell peppers and onion. "You can slice those while I do the steak."

Rochelle got another cutting board and bowls for the vegetables. Val handed her a knife. "This feels like old times, when we were growing up." Once they reached their teens, they'd been responsible for preparing dinner once a week. They would put in one of their favorite CDs and dance and sing while cooking. She and Val shared a smile.

"It does." They worked in companionable silence for a few minutes, humming along to the music playing, then Val asked, "Any updates with you and Warren?"

"How did I know that would be the first thing you'd ask?"

"You know me—I have to make sure you haven't cut the brother off without giving him a chance first." She paused for a minute. "I know you too," she added pointedly.

"I haven't cut him off. Last week he called after I got home from the reunion and said he had something serious to discuss. I figured it would be the same 'things didn't work out, we should just be friends' speech like every other guy, but it wasn't."

"Girl, with the way that man looks at you, I wouldn't be surprised if he skipped the whole dating thing and went straight to a marriage proposal. The heat in his eyes makes *me* warm."

Rochelle skewered her sister with a look. "Seriously, Val?" But she totally agreed. Sometimes she thought her clothes would melt right off her body under his intense stare. "He wants us to be in a committed relationship." She shared the details of the conversation and that he wanted her to think about whether they were on the same page. "I was so shocked, I couldn't say one word."

Val paused in her slicing. "Well, what are you going to tell him?"

"I don't know." Blowing out a long breath, Rochelle set the knife down, faced her sister and braced a hip against the counter.

"And before you say anything, I agree that he's a great guy. I just don't want to get hurt again."

The abuse she suffered at the hands of her ex rose in her mind, as did the earlier conversation with Diane and Joy. She didn't want to go through the same thing again.

"I get it, but not all relationships are that way. Every woman deserves love. *You* deserve love. Not the kind that causes pain and heartache but one that's sweet, full of passion and with someone who loves you just as you are. I truly believe Warren can be that person."

She nodded. Warren had been the opposite of pretty much every guy she'd dated. Looking back, Rochelle had tolerated less than she deserved for so long. Maybe it was time for something different. This time she wouldn't settle for less than anything but what was best for her well-being.

"So?" Val asked, a smile playing around the corner of her mouth.

"I'll call him tonight."

"*Yes!*"

Rochelle playfully bumped Val's shoulder. "Hush. Shouldn't you be slicing that steak?" She went back to the task of slicing vegetables and singing under her breath.

"Aw, yeah. This is my *jam*." Val snapped her fingers and shook her hips to the mid-tempo groove "Don't Waste My Time" by Usher, featuring Ella Mai. She sang along with the chorus, then said, "Warren won't be wasting your time. He's gonna give you that good lovin', sis."

"Whatever."

But if his kisses were any indication, Val might be right. One part of Rochelle wanted to find out, but the other part reminded her that it had been a good two, three years since she'd had sex, and it had been so bad, she decided her battery-operated boy-friend would be a better option. She pushed the thoughts aside and placed the sliced vegetables in a bowl. "You want me to start peeling the potatoes?"

"Could you please? I know the frozen kind are easier, but for some reason, freshly cut potatoes taste better to me. Oh, I've been meaning to ask if you decided to do the meal prep we talked about."

"I thought about it, but there's so much information about eating plans that I don't even know where to begin." Rochelle had searched online and found everything from low carb and keto-genic to plant-based and intermittent fasting. After more than an hour, she'd been so overwhelmed, she'd shut it down. "I just want something simple to help me get back on track," she added, start-ing on the second potato.

"I hear you. With all these fads out there, it does make it diffi-cult to figure out what's best."

"What have you been doing because you look like you've lost a few pounds since I saw you."

"Not dieting, that's for sure," Val said with a chuckle. "Like I mentioned at Mom and Dad's, I do a lot of my cooking on the weekends and divide the food into containers so I don't have to think about it after getting home from work. I've cut back on the red meat and focus on fish and chicken mostly. I started walking at least three days a week too. One of these days, I'll get back in the gym." She came over and helped with the potatoes.

"It sounds so simple when you say it. And didn't you say you'd give me a few recipes?"

"Yeah. I'll make a copy of the ones I did last month. And if you want to go walking, let me know."

They heard lively chatter and laughter, and the teens barreled in discussing the movie they'd seen. Val's husband brought up the rear. After a round of greetings, the kids rushed off, and Bryan went to watch television.

Thirty minutes later, the family sat down to dinner, and Rochelle realized she'd missed hanging out with them. She made a mental note to talk to Val about doing it more often.

Val declined help with the dishes when dinner ended and whispered, "You need to go home and call Warren."

Rochelle told herself earlier that she would, but now she started to get cold feet.

"And you'd better not chicken out. I see that look on your face."

"Sometimes I can't stand you," she muttered. "Big sisters are overrated."

"Whatever. As long as you make that call. You know I love you."

"Yeah, yeah. I'm going home." She called out to Haley, said her goodbyes and got on the road.

The closer Rochelle got to home, the more nervous she became. And by the time she pulled into her garage, she was close to changing her mind. *Girl, you know you like the man. Just make the call.* She did like him—a lot—and he had always been a perfect gentleman.

"Did you have fun with your cousins?" Rochelle focused on Haley instead of obsessing over Warren.

"Yes. At the movies we saw this girl who likes Amari. He can't stand her, so he asked me to pretend to be his girlfriend." Haley laughed. "You should've seen her. She was too mad. I gotta call Ebony and tell her."

Rochelle wanted to chastise her, but she had run interference with Darryl and Alan when they were teens as well. "Don't be on the phone all night."

"I won't."

Shaking her head, she sauntered down the hall to her bedroom and kicked off her shoes. She flopped down on the side of the bed and gave herself a pep talk before opening her text thread with Warren. The last few days it had been silent, him giving her time.

It was a little past seven o'clock. Not too late to text, not too early. She could do this. She scrolled to his number: **Warren, I hope your week has been . . .** She paused, and then deleted. Too formal. *Just ask the man to coffee, don't use the phrase* we need to talk.

She started again: **Hey! I was hoping we could grab a coffee this week. I've been thinking about what you said the other day.**

There. Friendly, open, not weird. She pressed Send.

Immediately, her phone chimed with his reply. Rochelle quickly hit the button.

Warren: **Are you free tonight?**

Rochelle released a nervous breath.

Warren: **Just finishing a workout then I could stop by. I've been thinking about you too this week.**

She wondered what type of workouts he did and whether he'd be willing to give her some tips. She typed back: **I'm free.**

Warren: **Is eight o'clock too late?**

Rochelle: **Not at all. I'll see you when you get here.**

Warren: **Sounds like a plan, beautiful. See you in a few.**

Rochelle's heart beat double time as she set the phone on her nightstand. She decided to shower since she'd been out much of the day.

Afterward, she went to Haley's room and found her stretched out on the bed laughing on the phone.

"Hold on, Ebony," Haley said when she saw Rochelle in the doorway. "You need me, Mom?"

"No, baby. I just wanted to let you know Mr. McIntyre is going to stop by in a few minutes."

A wide grin spread across her lips. "Go, Mom. Don't worry, I'll stay in my room," she added with a giggle.

"Whatever, girl. Tell Ebony I said hello."

Still laughing, Haley went back to her call. "My mom said hi." A second later she said, "Mom, she said hi."

Back in her bedroom, Rochelle put on a pair of jeans and a short-sleeve tee. She took her ponytail down and combed through the long strands that extended past her bra line. Lately she'd been considering cutting her hair for easier maintenance but always changed her mind because it meant she wouldn't be able to throw it up in a ponytail when needed. At the last minute she added lip gloss, then stuck her feet in a pair of flat sandals.

Warren rang her doorbell at precisely eight, and when she opened the door, Rochelle felt like a teenager with her first crush. "Please come in." When he entered, the scent of whatever cologne he wore drifted into her nostrils. The warm, citrus and earthy fragrance smelled so good and was perfect for him.

He dipped his head and placed a soft kiss on her lips. "How are you?"

The brief contact seared her, and it took her a moment to find her voice. "I'm good." She led him to the family room. "Did you finish your workout?" she asked, sitting on the sofa.

Warren lowered himself next to her. "Pretty much. I was almost finished when you texted and only had one more upper body exercise to do. I'll just pick it up tomorrow or Monday." He shifted to face her and draped his arm across the back of the sofa. "So tell me what's on your mind."

You can do this. "I thought about our last conversation."

"About us being in a committed relationship?"

Rochelle nodded. "I want that, too, but it's been a long time for me, and I'm not even sure I know what that looks like now." She wrung her hands. Truthfully she couldn't recall much good in any of her relationships, which added to her apprehension.

A smile inched up on his full, sexy lips. He covered her hands with one of his large ones. "You don't know how happy you've made me." He scooted closer. "It's been a while for me, too, and I know you're still a bit nervous, but I'm going to do everything in my power to make sure you don't regret taking this chance with me." Warren stroked a finger down her cheek. "As far as what a relationship between us will look like, I'll be glad to tell you." Holding her gaze, he lifted her hand and placed a kiss on the back. "Our relationship will include long walks through the park and romantic candlelight dinners either in a restaurant or prepared by me in my home." Still staring intently at her, he turned her hand over and kissed the center of her palm. "We'll spend hours laughing and talking about everything and nothing and hold hands just because."

The lazy kisses moved up to Rochelle's wrist and made her pulse skip. His words were hot, his gaze hotter, and she could barely breathe.

"There will be trips with you, Haley and me, and getaways with just us two. We'll stroll along a moonlit beach, dance to music only we can hear, and enjoy passionate kisses that take our breath away."

Have mercy! He trailed kisses up her arm, then slanted his mouth over hers in a deep, slow-as-molasses kiss that made her senses spin. Somebody moaned, but she didn't know who. She'd never been kissed this way or had a man share his feelings so eloquently, and she wanted to stand up and shout, *this! All. Of. This!*

Warren lifted his head, but his lips remained a mere inch from hers. "What you need to know, Rochelle, is that I will always respect you, and this relationship will be my first priority. *You'll* be my first priority. So what do you say? Are we going to do this?"

The sincerity in his voice went straight to her heart, and she'd be crazy not to take the risk. "Yes."

He smiled. "Thank you. I promise you won't regret taking this chance on me. I think we need to seal this deal with a kiss."

Rochelle laughed softly. "I thought we just did that."

"When it comes to kissing you, one will never be enough."

He always knows the right things to say. She shrugged and leaned closer. "In that case . . ." She wanted this. Wanted him.

Chapter 20

Diane

DIANE WISHED SHE COULD SNAP HER FINGERS AND BE in Jamaica.

Today.

But it was only the third week in May.

Walking out of the church where Tomiko's parents' funeral had been held, it took all her self-control not to curse out Terrell's family members. When Toni told her about these people, Diane figured there might some moments of drama, but nothing like this. She had never seen such a blatant display of foolishness in all her life—falling out over the casket and screaming out randomly. She'd gotten more than a few hostile glares and heard a few rude questions from them, asking about insurance policies and the house. She wrapped a protective arm around Tomiko's shoulders and guided the still weeping child toward the bathroom.

Inside, she grabbed a couple of tissues and hunkered down in front of the little girl. "I know that was hard, baby, and I'm so proud of you."

Diane gently wiped her tears and gathered Tomiko in her arms. If anyone had a right to lay out over those caskets, it was Tomiko. Yet she'd shown more dignity than those grown-ups. Once she seemed to be calmer, Diane rejoined her sister and two friends.

"Those fools need their butts beat, coming in here showing out like that," Val said quietly.

Joy nodded. "I agree. They basically disowned him because he didn't do what they wanted, and now that he's gone, they have the nerve to act like they're so sad about his death."

Rochelle just shook her head. "I can't with them."

"Hey."

Diane whirled around. "*Jeffrey?* What are you doing? When did you get here?"

Jeffrey ran a comforting hand over Tomiko's head. "I got here halfway through the service but didn't see you, so I sat in the back. Are you okay?" He kissed her forehead.

She didn't know if his comments and the kiss were for the benefit of their audience, but she didn't care at the moment. She was just glad to see him. Joy, Val and Rochelle all stared with raised eyebrows. "I'm okay. Worried about some of the family members, though."

He greeted each of the three women with a hug. "They're a piece of work."

"Amen," Val said.

Diane spotted Toni coming toward her with an older woman with a cane. "Hi, Toni." She introduced her to everyone.

"This is Marjorie's mother, Mama Doris," Toni said.

Diane shook her hand. "It's so nice to meet you. I'm very sorry for your loss."

"Thank you," Mama Doris said.

"Hi, Grandma," Tomiko said in a small voice.

Mama Doris held her arms out to Tomiko. "Come here, sweetheart." She held and rocked her granddaughter, then placed a tender kiss on her cheek. "I'm going to be here for a few days. Would it be okay for me to visit?"

Diane glanced up at Jeffrey, who nodded. "Of course. Just let us know when. You're more than welcome to stay in our home, that way you can spend as much time as you'd like with her. We can pick you up from your hotel."

The older woman smiled. "That's a very generous offer. I accept." She and Tomiko shared a smile and another hug. I'll be right back so I can get your phone number and we can make the arrangements. There are a couple of people we need to talk to before they leave."

"I'll wait here." She and Toni headed toward a small group of people standing a short distance away.

"I need to get back to work," Rochelle said. "I'll call you later."

Both Val and Joy said the same thing, and Val added sotto voce, "I really need the 4–1–1 on what's up with Jeffrey."

Diane didn't reply to that comment but said, "Sounds good. Thank you so much for being here. I can't tell you how much I appreciate you." After a round of hugs, the women departed, leaving her with Jeffrey. "Do you have to go back to the office?" Before he could answer, two women who Diane recognized as Terrell's relatives approached.

"Hi, Tomiko. Do you know what's going to happen to your house?" one of the women asked.

"How much money are you getting to keep her? I think she should be staying with her family instead of a stranger," the other one spat.

Diane couldn't believe her ears. Tomiko wrapped her arms around Diane's waist and burrowed into her side. If what Toni said was true, these women didn't even know Tomiko. "I'm not a stranger. I've known Tomiko since she was three."

"She still doesn't belong with—"

"Enough!" Jeffrey said.

The women froze, and so did Diane.

"Don't come over here badgering my wife or this baby who's

lost her parents. Show some respect." He picked up Tomiko and patted her back. "It's going to be okay."

They looked like they wanted to say something else, but Diane didn't know if it was Jeffrey's six-three height or the dark glare he shot their way, but they stormed off, muttering. *This* was the man she'd married. Her champion. "Thank you."

"You're welcome. And I took the rest of the afternoon off."

She looked over and saw Terrell's mother barreling toward them with a frown on her face. She sighed. "Here we go again."

"What?"

That woman coming is Terrell's mother, she mouthed.

He rolled his eyes.

"Hello," Diane started, trying to be polite when she really wanted to snap her fingers and transport them somewhere far away from the craziness. "I'm Di—"

"I'm not interested in who you are. I came for my granddaughter." Dismissing Diane, the woman glared at Tomiko. "Where are your manners, little girl? Turn around and speak to your grandmother," she said harshly.

"You're the one who needs to get some manners," Mama Doris said, rejoining them.

Diane and Jeffrey shared a look, then he said, "I'm going to take Tomiko for a little walk. We'll be back in a few." Jeffrey gave the woman one last glare before striding off.

Mama Doris pointed her cane at the other woman. "Who do you think you are talking to Tomiko that way? Weren't you the one who called my daughter a two-bit whore and a bitch? And didn't you call *my* granddaughter a bastard child? You don't even know her, so don't you dare stand here and pretend to care about her."

"I have as much right to her as you do, and I will fight to get everything I'm due."

"All you see are dollar signs, but I'm warning you," Mama Doris said, "if you come near her, I will come down on you so hard, you won't know what hit you. And before you open your mouth, you don't want to try me because, as the kids these days say, I have receipts. Now take your greedy, hateful behind and go."

Diane seriously wanted to ask what those receipts were, but she didn't dare move for fear she'd be next. Apparently the other woman must have known because she stormed off without another word.

"The old evil bat," Mama Doris muttered. "Sorry about that, but she works my last nerve."

"*Um* . . . no apologies needed." She dug her phone out of her purse. "If you'll give me your number, I'll call you this evening after you're settled, and we can discuss a time to pick you up." She input the number the woman rattled off. "I'm going to find my husband so we can leave, but I'll be in touch."

"Thank you, Diane. Toni spoke highly of you, and it's my prayer that my baby will be able to stay with you permanently." She gave Diane's hand a little squeeze.

"It's mine as well." They spoke a moment longer, then she started across the courtyard in the direction Jeffrey had gone. She found him a short distance away and took some time to observe him talking to Tomiko. He was squatting down next to the little girl, holding her close, and whatever he was saying had her nodding. Her heart melted at the sight, and Diane wished he could see what she did—that he'd make a wonderful father. As if sensing her presence, he turned.

"You ready?"

She nodded. As he walked her to the car, they didn't speak, but she took comfort in him being with her.

Jeffrey helped Tomiko into the car, and she gripped the front of his suit coat.

"*Nooo.* Don't leave me."

His expression softened. "We're not leaving you, okay? You're coming back home with us," he assured her. He offered more soothing words, and she finally allowed him to leave her in the car.

Diane got Tomiko strapped into her booster seat, then closed the door. Jeffrey was still standing there staring into the back seat. She placed a tentative hand on his arm. "I'll see you at home."

"Okay."

He waited while she got in and started the engine. With one last glimpse into the car, he pivoted on his heel and strode off.

Diane was emotionally drained when she got home and would've loved to go upstairs and lay across her bed, but Tomiko needed her.

"How about we change out of these dresses and do something to make us feel a little better?"

"My mommy always made me cookies when I got sad."

"Then we'll do that."

They climbed the stairs and went to their separate bedrooms. She'd just stepped out of her dress when Jeffrey came through the door. She assessed him for a long moment, not sure what would happen now that they weren't in public.

"How did Tomiko do on the ride home?" Jeffrey asked, tugging his tie loose and tossing it along with his suit coat on the chair.

"She was pretty quiet." She retrieved a pair of leggings and an oversize T-shirt from the drawer and put them on. "We're going to make cookies. She said her mother did it when she was sad. I hope it will give her a little lift. I'm thinking about just picking something up for dinner."

"That's fine."

They stood staring at each other, and she waited to see if he would say anything else. When he didn't, she said, "I'd better get started," and walked out.

Downstairs in the kitchen, Diane quickly did an inventory of ingredients and was glad she had everything. Tomiko came in a few minutes later. "We can make chocolate chip or sugar cookies. Which is your favorite?"

"I like chocolate chip."

"Sounds like a plan." They gathered what they needed and went about the task.

"Maybe we should make some for Mr. Evans because he always looks sad too."

Obviously she'd noticed the tension between them, and Diane wished a simple batch of cookies could straighten things out. "*Hmm*, that's a good idea. We should ask him what kind he wants." She went still upon seeing her husband and had no idea how much of or if he'd heard the conversation.

Tomiko spotted him as well. "Mr. Evans, do you want us to make you some cookies so you won't be sad?"

He walked slowly over to the island where they were putting together the dough. "What kind are you making?"

"Chocolate chip. It's my favorite," she said, carefully pouring in the sugar Diane had measured.

"It's mine too. Sure, I'll take a couple." Jeffrey watched them a short while longer, then went into the family room and turned on the TV.

Diane wished she knew what he was thinking, but his expression gave nothing away. She refocused her attention on helping Tomiko place the cookie dough on the baking sheet. She had longed for moments like this and could see them doing more things together for years to come. "These look great, Tomiko." Tomiko smiled up at her and Diane lost another piece of her heart. "I'll put them in the oven, and while they bake, you can read or watch something on the television in the guest room. Let's wash your hands first."

"Okay." She hopped down from the stool and followed Diane to the sink. After drying her hands on a paper towel, she skipped out of the kitchen.

A smile curved Diane's lips. This was the most animated she'd seen the child, and she had to wonder if there was something to Marjorie's claim about baking cookies. She went into the family room and sat in the second recliner opposite Jeffrey. "Is there anything in particular you'd like to have for dinner?"

Not taking his eyes off the television screen, he said, "No. Just order it, and I'll go pick it up."

Oo-kay. "I'll check out some of the take-out menus and let you know." He'd surprised her for the second time today. She really wanted to bring up the issues in their relationship, but she didn't want to shatter the guarded peace they had going. Tomiko came in with a book, and Diane opened up her mouth to ask if she wanted to sit with her, but she walked straight to Jeffrey and climbed into the recliner with him.

Jeffrey wore the same shocked expression as Diane, but to his credit, he didn't question it. He just made room for her and draped his arm loosely around Tomiko's shoulders. She didn't say anything but opened her book and began reading. Jeffrey gave Diane a questioning look.

She shrugged, smiled inwardly and made herself comfortable until the oven timer went off. Lowering the chair, she removed the cookies and placed them on a rack to cool. While waiting, she leafed through the many restaurant menus and finally settled on BJ's Restaurant & Brewhouse since they had a lot of options.

They spent a low-key evening together and while she still felt tension between her and Jeffrey, it seemed to have lessened. When it came time for Tomiko to go to bed, Diane tucked her in, as always.

"Can Mr. Evans come tuck me in too?"

She wasn't too surprised by the request because since they'd returned home from the funeral service, Tomiko had been glued to Jeffrey's side. Diane chalked it up to his timely intervention with the wicked grandmother.

"Well, I'll go ask."

On her way to the master bedroom, she sent up a silent prayer that her husband wouldn't turn down the request. She found him standing near the bed, typing something on his phone. He'd changed into shorts, a tee and a pair of running shoes. She didn't recall him mentioning going anywhere.

Jeffrey looked up at her entrance. "Something wrong?"

She shook her head. "*Um* . . . Tomiko wanted me to ask if you'd tuck her in tonight. After that knight-in-shining-armor rescue earlier, I think she's gotten attached to you," she said with a small teasing smile, hoping he'd take it as such.

A slight smile tilted the corner of his mouth, but it vanished so fast, Diane might have imagined it. He tossed the phone on the bed. "I'll be there in a minute."

Diane made her way back to Tomiko's room. "He'll be here soon."

Jeffrey entered on the heel of her words. "Ready for bed?" he asked, sitting on the side of the bed.

Tomiko nodded and lifted her arms.

Tears misted Diane's eyes as she watched Jeffrey hug the little girl who was steadily worming her way into Diane's heart. And now, apparently, Jeffrey's.

He appeared to hesitate briefly before placing a fatherly kiss on Tomiko's brow. He tucked the covers around her. "Sleep well," he whispered, then rose to his feet. With one last glimpse over his shoulder, he brushed past Diane and silently went back to their bedroom.

Diane turned on the small night-light and followed. She found Jeffrey pacing.

He stopped and dragged a hand down his clean-shaven face. "I know we still need to talk, but not tonight, okay? I can't do it right now."

She was emotionally drained and sensed he might be as well, so she wouldn't argue. "Sure."

"Thanks." He closed the distance between them and brushed a kiss over her lips. "I'm going for a short run."

She stood stunned. It was the first time in, she couldn't remember how long, that he'd kissed her. The one at the church earlier that day didn't count. Though the contact was brief, it sparked a longing in her that only he could satisfy. Diane hoped it meant that just maybe they'd make it.

Chapter 21

Joy

JOY SHOULD'VE STUCK TO HER FIRST THOUGHT OF coming into the office in the evenings after business hours. Robert took every opportunity to plead his case. By midweek she was wound so tight, she thought she might snap. She'd give anything for a massage right now. She moved her head one way, then the other, trying to relieve the kinks in her neck. All the more reason to get her business off the ground. However, at the moment she had to finish transferring all her files from the renovation company to a drive. She would have loved to just walk out and let Robert figure everything out on his own, but she couldn't do that to the customers. It wasn't their fault she'd married a liar and cheater.

Since filing for divorce, Robert had made several attempts to reconcile, and she'd shot down every last one. Why he thought she'd take him back after busting him in a lip-lock with another woman right after him spouting nonsense about them staying together and kissing *her* baffled Joy. He could beg for the rest of his life, and she still wouldn't take him back.

"Have you thought about what I said? You could at least think about us trying marriage counseling."

It was as if she'd conjured Robert just by thinking about him. "Nope. Nothing to think about." *Marriage counseling? Seriously?* After all the times she'd tried to convince him to work on their marriage, now he wanted to do counseling? Joy stifled the urge to roll her eyes. "I should have the rest of the files downloaded and the folders divided by the end of the week."

"So that's it? You're going to end over thirteen years of marriage just like that?" Robert snapped his fingers.

Joy wasn't going to dignify that foolishness with a response. He knew damn well nothing had happened *just like that*. She used the mouse to drag the next few files over. Moving one stack of manila folders aside, she searched for the spreadsheet she'd created to track the accounts. Robert still lounged in the doorway, but she ignored him. Finally, he got the message that she had nothing more to say and left.

As soon as this batch downloaded, she was leaving to meet with the rental company's manager to sign the papers for her new home. As much as she appreciated Rochelle opening her home to her indefinitely, Joy wanted to be in her own space. She just hoped nothing happened to delay the move-in. Joy placed the folders in a bankers box behind their respective tabs. As soon as the last of the files transferred, she shut down her desktop, made sure she hadn't left anything behind, and locked up. On her way out she passed the empty desk where Stacey used to sit. She hadn't seen the woman since the day she'd fired her, but it wouldn't surprise her in the least if Robert had already rehired her. *I don't even care. Friday, I'm out.*

Half an hour later, as Joy sat signing the mound of paperwork, she felt a degree of sadness for what this meant—her marriage was really over—and excitement about moving forward into the next phase of her life. But she was realistic enough to know that she'd probably be on an emotional roller coaster for a while. Tonight Joy would celebrate with her sister friends over dinner, then tomorrow she'd take each moment as it came and let the future take care of itself.

Rochelle was already home when Joy arrived and met her with a strong hug.

"How did it go?" Rochelle asked.

"Okay. It's kind of a weird place to be in right now, though."

"Believe me, I know. One minute you're fine, and the next you're bawling your eyes out and can't figure out why."

"Exactly." Joy found herself crying at the oddest times, and the triggers ranged anywhere from lyrics in a favorite song to a random memory that popped up.

"You'll get through it, and you know we'll be here for whatever you need, just like you all were for me. Oh, Diane should be here shortly. She's bringing Tomiko. I told Haley, and she's already picked out a movie for them to watch while they eat." She shook her head. "Haley said, 'I know you and the godmothers want to have some girl-talk time, so I'll take care of Tomiko.'"

"I love that girl," Joy said with a chuckle. "Let me go put this stuff down, and I'll be back to help."

"There's nothing for you to do. I kept it easy with a fajita bar."

"That sounds heavenly, and I'm starving."

Her stomach cosigned with a loud growl. They both laughed. She headed to her borrowed bedroom while Rochelle went to the kitchen. Sitting on the side of the bed, she unbuckled her sandals and kicked them off. Joy checked her emails on her phone and deleted the multitude of spam messages. "How do these people get my email address?" she mumbled. She paused when she saw one from her real estate agent and opened it. Although she rarely did commercial properties, Gretchen had promised to check into the former gym in El Dorado Hills that Joy had found. The owners had given the okay for a walk-through and had included dates and times they would be available. Joy accessed her calendar, then replied with her preferred appointment times and hit Send.

She sat there a moment longer before going back out front. "Hey, Haley."

"Hi, Aunt Joy." Haley hugged her and continued toward her bedroom.

The doorbell rang, and Joy called out to Rochelle, "You want me to get that, Chelle?"

"Please."

She opened the door to Diane and Tomiko. "Hey, girl." The women embraced.

"Hey, Joy. It smells good in here."

"Thanks to Chelle. Hi, Tomiko."

"Hi," she said shyly.

They all went into the kitchen, and after hugs and greetings, Haley and Tomiko fixed their plates and took them into the family room. Joy and Diane followed with trays and lemonade.

"Okay, grab what you want, then we can get this celebration started," Rochelle said when they came back.

Joy made one each of the steak, chicken and shrimp fajitas, added her toppings and carried her plate to the table. She returned with the pitcher of lemonade and placed it in the center.

Once everyone had their food and was seated, Diane lifted her glass. "Joy, congratulations on your new home. Here's to the start of something new and better."

"Amen." Joy touched her glass to both women's and took a sip. "I'm excited but in a weird kind of space, if that makes sense."

Diane nodded around a bite of fajita. She swallowed. "It makes perfect sense. You're losing something that you thought would be forever."

"Yeah." Memories of her wedding day rose unbidden in her mind. She'd been so sure she had found a once-in-a-lifetime love. They didn't even make it to the twenty-year mark, let alone forever. She waved a hand. "Okay, this subject is off-limits for the night. It's supposed to be a celebration. I can't wait for you to see the house." She'd only shown them the few photos from the listing.

"You know we'll help you move," Rochelle said.

"Thanks, sis. I'm keeping my fingers crossed that everything goes smoothly." They ate in silence for a couple of minutes. "Oh, Diane, what was up with Jeff and that kiss at the funeral?"

"I was going to ask the same thing," Rochelle said. "And the fact that you didn't even tell us he was going to be there."

"I couldn't tell you something I didn't know, but I was so glad he came." She told them about the confrontation with Terrell's mother and what Marjorie's mother said.

Joy burst out laughing. "Honey, I really want to know about those receipts."

"Same. The one good thing was that Jeffrey took Tomiko away from the drama."

Rochelle stared. "Wait. I thought you said he barely says two words to her."

"Until then, that was the case. Whatever he said to her, she's been clinging to him ever since and even wanted Jeffrey to tuck her into bed."

"Awww, that's so sweet." Joy paused mid-bite. "He did it, right?"

Diane nodded. "And he actually kissed me that night. It was just a little peck on the lips, but it was the first one in a while that wasn't for show. He knows we still need to talk, so we'll see what happens after that."

"I really hope you two can put your marriage back together. One of us has to make this work," Joy said. Even though her own had crashed and burned, she was still pulling for her friend. "What about you, Chelle? Did you ever talk to Warren?"

Rochelle divided a glance between Joy and Diane. "Yes. He came over Saturday evening while you were gone."

Diane lifted a brow. "And? Don't keep us waiting, girl. What did you tell the man?"

"I told him yes."

"*Hallelujah!*" Joy clapped and did a little shimmy in her seat. "My girl has got a *real* man. So, how are his kisses? Since you're the only one getting the good stuff, we have to live vicariously through you."

They all burst out laughing.

She hesitated briefly, then said, "Oh my goodness, the man can *kiss*! He makes me forget my name." Rochelle leaned back in her chair and fanned herself.

They screamed with laughter. Joy and Diane exchanged a high five, and Diane said, "That's what I'm talking about."

A sly grin played around the corner of Joy's mouth. "Now aren't you glad you bought that cute cold-shoulder dress?"

"Oh, shut up," Rochelle said, trying not to laugh. "One more thing: I'm going to start back working out. A coworker mentioned that her cousin teaches a cardio class on Saturdays. I want to check it out, but I don't want to go alone."

"I'll go with you," Joy said.

Diane wiped her hands on a napkin and picked up her drink. "So will I. As long as it's not one of those fanatical on-steroid classes."

Rochelle saluted her with her glass. "Girl, you ain't said nothing but a word."

They spent the rest of dinner laughing, and for Joy, it was exactly what she needed. But Yvette was never far from her mind. She wondered what her friend would say about the divorce, then recalled her last words: "*Robert can either get on board or get his ass out of the way. You helped him live his dream, and now it's your turn. Promise me.*" Somehow Yvette most likely already knew the outcome. She always did.

"Do you want anything else?" Rochelle asked as they finished eating.

"No, thanks. I'm full, and it was so good." Joy stood, stacked their empty plates and took them to the sink. "Since you cooked, I'll clean." She came back to the table. "I forgot to tell y'all Gretchen sent me an email to set up an appointment to see that closed down gym in El Dorado Hills, the one I mentioned that could be a possible spa location."

"That's fabulous. When are you going?" Diane asked.

"I sent her back a couple of dates, so as soon as I hear back, I'll let you know. The great thing is that it was one of those smaller women's fitness centers, and I'm hoping it will work. Financially I'm still in pretty good shape, and Brent said he'd help out."

"You know we've got you too."

"Thanks, Chelle. You two have always had my back."

"And we always will," Diane pledged. "That's what friends and sisters do."

Smiling, she nodded, her heart full. "I just need Robert to sign the divorce papers and stop acting like there's a chance for us to get back together." When they both stared at her, she said, "Yeah, you heard right. He brought it up again today, and I ignored him. He even had the nerve to say we could go to counseling."

"We need something stronger than lemonade for this conversation." Diane shook her head. "I can't believe he's acting like he didn't get caught cheating."

"Definitely need something stronger. I can't wait until we get to Jamaica so I can be away from all this craziness." By then, she hoped to be in her new house, have a potential spot for her spa and have the divorce papers signed and her delusional husband on his way to being an ex.

With it being a school night, they cut their time short. Diane headed home, and Rochelle got a FaceTime from Warren and retreated to her bedroom. Joy cleaned up the kitchen and went to call her father.

"Hey, Joy," her father said when he picked up.

"Hi, Dad. Did I catch you at a bad time?"

"It's never a bad time to talk to my baby girl. What's on your mind?"

Every time he said something like that, her guilt surfaced all over again. He'd told her more than once he didn't blame her and that they had to leave the past behind and start fresh from here. She was working on it. "Do you think I'm doing the right thing by filing for divorce?" Joy had told him about Robert's cheating, lack of support and affection for the past year, but took a few moments to give him the latest updates.

"Wow, I'm really sorry, sweetheart, but what's important is do *you* think you're doing the right thing? Baby, you have to do what's going to be best for your heart, for your peace of mind. No one else's opinion matters."

"Thanks, Dad. Hearing you say it confirms what I'm feeling." She'd missed being able to talk to him and wished she could go back in time to recapture more of these precious moments. But as he'd said, the only way was forward.

"Anytime. How are you doing with all of this?"

"Okay, I guess. It hurts, but not as deeply as it did at first." Joy speculated whether her lack of mental anguish could be attributed to the fact that her love for Robert had waned steadily over the past year, leaving only numbness in its place.

"It'll take time, but you'll make it through. Are you still staying with Rochelle? You know you're welcome to stay here until you get on your feet."

"Yes, but I found a house and I'm hoping to move in within a week or two." She'd spent a couple of nights at his house, and they had been some of the best times she could remember with him. They'd watched old movies and cooked together. She'd even shared her dreams about opening a spa, and he'd pledged to assist in any way he could.

"That's wonderful, Joy. Be sure to let me and Brent know when you're moving so we can be there to help."

She smiled. "I'll do that."

"Now, have you talked to your mother yet?"

Her smile faded, and she blew out a long breath. "No," she mumbled. They hadn't spoken since the day her mother had dropped the bombshell, and every time Joy picked up the phone to call, her anger would bubble up, prompting her to put it off yet again. "I know what you're going to say, and I'm working on it."

"Honey, don't let this go on too long. You don't want that kind of bitterness to take root in your heart, because it'll kill you. Trust me, I know. It took me a long time to forgive Marsha, but I had to, not for her but for me. And my health was better for it. You won't truly be able to move on until you let go."

Joy digested her father's words and prayed she'd be able to forgive and let go soon. However, at the moment, as she'd just told him, she was working on it. It was the best she could do under the circumstances.

Chapter 22

Rochelle

SATURDAY, ROCHELLE PACED HER BEDROOM, THINK-ing about her date that evening with Warren. They were heading down to Oakland to see Eric Benét in concert. Since agreeing to an exclusive relationship, she'd been second guessing herself all week, and it had nothing to do with Warren. Just her. Plain and simple, she was afraid. Every *what-if* scenario had bombarded her mind. What if a month from now he changed his mind about them? What if the negative emotions from her past surfaced and ruined everything? What if Haley decided she was uncomfortable with Rochelle dating?

Rochelle was beginning to like Warren far more than she let on, and she really needed her inner voice to shut the hell up. Forcing the crazy thoughts out of her mind, she went to the closet and, after a minute, decided on the black-and-white dress she'd purchased during the shopping trip. She'd definitely take it to Jamaica but decided to take her friends' advice and wear it for her date.

"Mom, can I come in?" Haley called through the closed door.

"Yes."

She entered and flopped down on the bed. "Are you going out with Mr. McIntyre again?"

"I am. Well, Mr. McIntyre and I are going to be . . . We're . . ." She searched for the right words.

Haley giggled. "Is he going to be your boyfriend?"

That's one way to describe it. "Something like that. What do you think about that?"

"I think it's so romantic." She pretended to swoon. "He's always nice, even when we're at Uncle Joe's house, and I want you to have somebody nice, Mom."

"I think he's nice too." And fine, a gentleman, an amazing kisser, all of which Haley didn't need to know. "I just want to make sure you're okay with it, since he's going to be around more."

Haley playfully bumped Rochelle's shoulder. "It's cool, Mom. Are you guys going to get married?"

Rochelle sucked in a sharp breath so hard she almost choked. "*Married?*" she said, still trying to clear her throat. "Just dating, child. Go get your stuff packed so you'll be ready when Aunt Val gets here."

The original plan had been for her to hang out with Ebony for the evening, but she'd contracted a virus, so Val graciously agreed to step in. Or more specifically, demanded Rochelle pack Haley's bag to spend the night rather than stay a few hours, saying she didn't want Rochelle to have to rush this first serious date, especially since the drive would be almost two hours, longer if there was traffic.

Haley burst out laughing. "I'm just sayin'. You said he's nice, right? And Uncle Joe would tell you if he wasn't, so . . ." She shrugged.

"Out," she said, trying to hide her smile.

Still laughing, Haley jumped up and started for the door. "I'm going, but if you do get married, I want to be in the wedding. Me and Ebony."

Before she could form a response, Haley walked out, closing

the door behind her. Rochelle shook her head. She hadn't even gotten used to the fact that she was in a relationship. Marriage seemed light-years away. Pushing to her feet, she went to take her shower.

Rochelle had just finished curling her hair when she heard the doorbell. She tied the belt on her robe and went out front to answer the door. "Hey, sis."

"Hey, girl." Val followed Rochelle inside. She hugged Haley and kissed her cheek. "Are you all packed?"

"Yes. I just need to get my tablet."

"It's no rush. I'm going to talk to your mom for a minute."

Haley nodded and went back to watching her television show.

Once out of earshot, Val wiggled her eyebrows and asked, "Ready for your big date?"

Rolling her eyes, she said, "You act like I've never been on a date."

"According to you, they were, and I quote, 'a big waste of my time.' So I'll ask again because I *know* Warren ain't wasting one single second. In fact, I'm willing to bet he's making every one of them count."

"Why you always bringing up old stuff?" And Rochelle wasn't touching the comment about Warren.

Chuckling, Val hooked her arm in Rochelle's. "*Awww*, you know I love you, and I'm just excited you're finally going out with a *real* man. Any brother who brings flowers to my niece as a thank-you for allowing him to spend time with you is all good in my book." She fluffed Rochelle's hair. "I wish my hair would grow this long and thick. It hasn't been the same since those two pregnancies," she grumbled. She wore her hair in a chin-length bob.

They continued to talk while Rochelle applied light makeup and slicked her lips with a deep burgundy color.

"Ooh, I like this, and it's called Thicker than Water. Why

didn't I know MAC had a *Wakanda Forever* makeup line?" Val asked.

"I have no idea, especially since you're the one who wears makeup regularly." Rochelle could count on one hand how many times she'd worn makeup of any kind in the past six months.

Val set it on the counter and whipped her phone out of her back pocket. "Oh good. They still have some available for shipping." In less than two minutes, she'd made her purchase. "Okay, now what are you wearing? I should've taken you shopping."

"Aren't you leaving? And I already went shopping."

Her eyes lit up and she rushed out of the bathroom.

Rochelle followed, took the dress from the closet and held it up. "Does this meet with your approval?"

"Honey, I think I'm going to hang around until Warren gets here. His eyeballs are going to pop out when he sees you in this dress."

Laughing, she said, "How do you know what it's going to look like on me?"

Val pushed her toward the bathroom. "Hurry up and put it on."

"You are so bossy sometimes."

She waved her off. "Yeah, yeah, I know."

Inside the bathroom, Rochelle smiled. As much as she fussed, she wouldn't trade her big sister for all the money in the world. She took off the robe and slipped into the dress. Aside from the midweek celebration dinner with Joy and Diane, she'd started doing the meal planning and making small modifications in her diet. She'd even gone walking twice. With those simple changes, she'd already started to see a difference. While she'd lost only a pound, her stomach wasn't as bloated, and the dress fit even better across her midsection than when she'd tried it on in the store. She surveyed her look once more, then went back to the bedroom for her shoes—black strappy sandals with three-inch heels. Val had stepped out but came back just as Rochelle stood.

"Oh. My. Goodness. I was right. Girl, you're going to have to pick up his eyes *and* his jaw." Val brought her hands to her mouth. "You look amazing. Now this is the confident baby sister I know. Work it, my sister!"

She smiled. Tonight she did sense that young, confident girl emerging. "Thanks. And thanks for the meal prep tips. They're actually helping."

"I'm glad."

When the doorbell rang a minute later, Val nearly sprinted out of the room. Rochelle slung her purse over her shoulder and picked up her wrap. Even though June was a few days away, the temperatures in Sacramento had hit the nineties already, but she knew the Bay Area would be cooler, particularly since Yoshi's was near the water. Taking one last look in the mirror and feeling satisfied with her appearance, she turned off the lights.

"Let the date night begin," she mumbled.

She stopped in her tracks when she rounded the corner to the living room and saw Warren standing there in a tailored charcoal-gray suit that fit him to perfection, a pale-gray shirt, coordinated patterned tie and expensive black loafers. She hadn't seen him in a suit since Yvette's funeral, and she'd been too overcome with grief to notice how good he looked in one. But not tonight. She took in every inch of his six-foot-plus fit body. The man was downright sexy without trying.

Finally finding her voice, she managed a soft, "Hi." He continued to stare. *Good, I'm not the only one affected.*

Val chuckled and mouthed, *I told you,* to Rochelle.

The soft laugh seemed to bring him around. He closed the

distance between them and kissed her cheek. Handing her yet another bouquet of red roses in a crystal vase, he said, "I didn't think you could improve on perfection, but I was wrong. You are absolutely stunning, Rochelle, and I'm honored to be the man by your side tonight."

Have mercy! "Thank you." She chanced a glance at her sister. Val stood with her mouth hanging open, and Haley stared wide-eyed.

"We'd better get on the road. It's Saturday, and I know there will be some traffic."

"Here, I'll take this," Val said, relieving Rochelle of the flowers. "We'll lock up, so don't worry."

Rochelle hugged Haley. "Be good. I'll pick you up tomorrow around one."

"I will, and okay. Have fun," she added with a little giggle.

Minutes later, they were on the way. "Are you okay with eating at Yoshi's? I made reservations there for six thirty to give us plenty of time to get there and enjoy dinner before the show starts. But if you want to go somewhere else, we can."

"Of course it's fine. Don't they reserve your seats if you dine there?" She had been to the venue only a couple of times, and it was a few years ago, so she didn't remember exactly.

"Yes, they do, and I just figured it would be easier to already be in the building."

"Sounds good." Rochelle made herself comfortable for the drive and hummed along to the song playing. During the drive, they discussed his job and that he couldn't wait for school to be out.

"We only have two more weeks, and I can't wait for the summer break—no alarms, no students complaining about their grades. Just peace and quiet."

She laughed. "You sound like Haley. She's already decided that sleeping in will be her new summer hobby."

"I may have to join her, but I'm sure my definition of sleeping in is completely different than a teenager's."

"You've got that right. I do have to admit that I'm a little jealous. While you two are lounging around, I'll be working. What do you plan to do with all your free time?" She wouldn't know what to do with herself if she had the entire summer off.

Warren slanted her an amused glance. "Don't hate. But to answer your question, there are a few renovations I'd like to have done around the house. Maybe Joy and her husband can give me a few pointers."

Rochelle didn't want to spread her friend's business, but she also didn't want him to bring it up if he ran into Joy. "Unfortunately they won't be working together anymore. They're getting a divorce."

"Wow. I'm so sorry to hear that. Is Joy okay?"

"She's hanging in there." That he asked about Joy's well-being earned him some brownie points.

"Glad to hear it. The other thing I'll be doing is setting up my home gym. It's starting to be a hassle accessing machines when I go to the fitness center. Some people tend to hog the equipment just talking and scrolling on their phones."

"That would frustrate me too." He'd just given her the opening she'd been looking for when it came to working out. "Do you think you'd have some time to show me a few things? I need to get these pounds off."

He paused. "Sure, but I want you to know you're beautiful just as you are."

"I appreciate you saying that." And when he did, she felt beautiful. "I'm not trying to be skinny and whatnot; I only want to be healthy."

"Okay. We can work out together, and before you say anything, I won't have you running miles or doing anything crazy. You can let me know your comfort level with different activities."

"Humph. It's a good thing you won't be trying to get me to do any running because you'd definitely be out there alone. I hate running. Back in high school, my PE teacher was the track coach, and he acted like we were part of his team. When I got out of his class, I told myself I was never running again, and I meant that. I will walk, but running is out. For-eva."

Warren had started laughing halfway through her little speech and was still doing so. "That was . . . passionate. So no running. Got it. Anything else on the I'm-not-doing-that-ever list?"

Smiling, she said, "Not that I can think of at the moment, but I'll let you know." Rochelle thought it would be awkward and embarrassing to talk to him about exercising, but it wasn't because he didn't judge or criticize. He only offered his help, and she appreciated it. They spent the remainder of the drive discussing workout routines, healthy eating and a host of other topics. There were small pockets of traffic here and there, but not too much, and they still had thirty minutes before their reservation.

"How about a short walk near the water?" he asked as he helped her out of the car.

"I'd love to." He entwined their fingers as if it was the most natural thing to do, and they started a leisurely stroll up the block toward the waterfront in companionable silence. They didn't need to fill every moment with conversation, and it was something she'd never experienced. She couldn't remember a time when she'd felt such contentment with a man. Her ex certainly hadn't made her feel this way. Thinking back, Kenny had fallen short in a lot of areas, and she'd put up with far more than she should have. However, that young, naive girl was gone, never to be resurrected again. It had taken some time, but Rochelle knew she deserved better, and she wouldn't settle for anything less. The man walking beside her embodied better, and for now, she was going to go with the flow.

She hadn't been to Jack London Square in a long time, and several things had changed. The big Barnes & Noble bookstore had been replaced with a restaurant and entertainment spot that included bowling, and many of the small shops had closed. Once they reached the water, she stood at the rail enjoying the peaceful view. A slight breeze kicked up, and she tightened her wrap around her.

Warren moved behind her and pulled her into his arms. "I haven't been here in a while, and I'd forgotten how nice it is out here."

"I was thinking the same thing." They stayed that way a few minutes longer, then she felt the warmth of his lips against her neck. Her eyes slid closed, and she moaned softly.

Warren turned her to face him. "I've been wanting to kiss you since the moment I walked into your house. May I?"

Rochelle had never been into public displays of affection, but at this moment she wanted nothing more than his lips on hers. "Please." He touched his mouth to hers once, twice, then slid his tongue inside. The mingled taste of mint and his own unique flavor filled her with pleasure, and the sweetness poured over her like warm honey.

"There's just something about you that makes me want to keep right on kissing you," he murmured. "But since we're outside, I'd better stop." He checked his watch. "We should probably head back."

"Yeah, probably," she said, still trying to get her breathing under control.

They retraced their steps to Yoshi's and he gave his name to the hostess. They were shown to a table a minute later. Evidently, many people had the same idea, if the packed restaurant was any indication. She thoroughly enjoyed the dinner and the conversation, and when they were led to third-row-center seats, she had to agree that eating there was the perfect idea.

"I don't think I've ever been this close to the stage before."

However, in the intimate space, there wasn't a bad seat in the room. Efficient servers weaved in and out of the tight area, and soft music played through hidden speakers. She, along with everyone else in the room, cheered when Eric Benét hit the stage. Rochelle swayed and danced in her seat, sang along to every song, and had a fabulous time.

Warren whispered in her ear during the song "Real Love," "I don't think I planned this right."

"What do you mean?"

"I'd rather be holding you in my arms while this song is playing than sitting in these seats."

The seductive tone of his voice and the banked heat in his eyes sent a sharp jolt of desire through her. She didn't have a comeback that didn't involve them finding the nearest bed, so she merely smiled and turned her attention back to the stage and enjoyed the remainder of the concert.

"Did you enjoy yourself?" he asked as they filed out with the rest of the patrons and headed to the parking garage.

Rochelle laughed. "You couldn't tell with all the dancing I was doing in my seat?"

He smiled. "Yeah, that might've given you away."

"I can't wait to do it again," she said.

Giving her hand a gentle squeeze, he pressed a kiss to her temple. "Neither can I."

They spent the drive home sharing their favorite parts of the concert, which songs they wished had been included and laughing about some of the overzealous female fans who tried to plaster themselves all over the singer as he crooned his way through the audience. Because there was no traffic, the drive took only an hour and a half. "Would you like to come in?" she asked after Warren helped her out of the car.

"For a few minutes."

Rochelle was admittedly nervous, and it must have shown because he gathered her in his arms and just held her for the longest time. After a couple of minutes, she relaxed. He always seemed to have that effect on her.

"Thank you for spending the evening with me. It was the best time I've had in a long while."

"Same here, so thank you."

"There is one thing I'd like to do before I go." Warren released her and dug his phone out of his pocket. "Do you have a stereo system where I can sync my phone?"

"Yes. Why?"

"I'd like to dance with you, if that's okay."

She hadn't danced with a man in she didn't know how long, but she wanted to be in his arms. She powered on the system and waited for his phone to pair. Once it did, the soft strains of "Spend My Life With You," the duet Eric sang with Tamia, flowed through the speakers. He circled his arms around her and pulled her close. They started a slow sway in time with the beat. Rochelle wound her arms around his neck and rested her head against his shoulder. She was falling hard for this caring and sweet man, and it felt . . . wonderful.

Chapter 23

Diane

"OH MY GOODNESS, CHELLE, I'M SO HAPPY FOR YOU," Diane said, adjusting the phone on her ear. "Sounds like you and Warren had a fabulous time last weekend." Because the three of them had been so busy during the week, it had taken her, Joy and Rochelle until the following weekend to connect and hear about the concert date.

Rochelle's laughter came through the line. "Girl, Eric was all that and more. I'd forgotten how great Yoshi's is for concerts. Every seat has a nice view of the stage, and we were in the third row right at the center."

"That's what I'm talking about," Joy said. "I just want to know what happened *after* the concert."

The three women screamed with laughter, then Rochelle said, "We danced. Right in my family room, and it was . . . amazing. He's so very different from every guy I've dated, and in a good way. I'm really glad y'all talked me into giving him a chance."

Diane smiled. *"Awww,* you know we love you. You deserve a good man. We'll really have something to celebrate in Jamaica."

"Especially if Warren curls her toes before then," Joy cracked, which brought on another fit of laughter. "I'm just kidding, sort of. But really, sis, I'm glad it's working out. On my front, yesterday was my last day in the office, and I'm so happy to be done. Add my celebration to the list, Di."

"Noted."

"Any more news on Tomiko?" Rochelle asked, changing the subject again.

"Nothing other than the house and insurance policies will be held in her name. I spoke with Toni, and she said Marjorie's mother is leaning toward renting out the house so it doesn't sit empty for the next several years, so we'll see what happens. I still don't know whether we'll be able to keep her, but I'm keeping my fingers crossed."

Every time Diane thought about those crazy relatives, it made her shudder. She'd been sending up constant prayers that none of them would think about trying to claim Tomiko after all these years of acting like the child never existed.

"I really hope she stays. And you and Jeffrey?"

"I don't know how to describe it, Joy, but even though we still haven't talked a lot, it doesn't feel as tense. We're actually going to talk things out today. On one hand, I'm looking forward to clearing the air, but on the other, I'm afraid of what he might say. What if he wants out? I don't know what I'll do."

"Girl, you know I know, and I'm praying hard it doesn't turn out like mine. With the way Jeffrey acted at the funeral, I really don't think it will."

"The fact that he even showed up says something," Rochelle added.

"That's true, I guess." He had to care about her at least a little bit to be there, in Rochelle's opinion.

"Do you want me to pick up Tomiko so you don't have to worry about her possibly listening?"

"Thanks for the offer, Chelle, but her grandmother is here. We invited her to stay here so she could spend as much time with Tomiko as possible before flying out. Mama Doris is supposed to be leaving sometime next week but might be here a little longer to deal with the house and all the contents."

"I'm so glad she has at least one family member who loves her," Joy said.

"I agree." Diane couldn't imagine how devastated Marjorie's mother was losing her only daughter. Thankfully, she could still be there in some way for her granddaughter. If Diane was fortunate enough to remain in Tomiko's life, she would make sure the relationship between grandmother and granddaughter stayed strong. The conversation moved to whether Robert had finally signed the divorce papers.

"I think he's finally gotten the message that there's no chance for a reconciliation. My attorney hopes that after meeting with his attorney on Tuesday, Robert won't contest anything. One, because he was caught cheating, and two, he won't want a messy divorce to interfere with the business. And you know word will get around."

"Basically it'll be in his best interest to give you what you're asking for and move on quietly," Rochelle said.

"Exactly. And it may keep us from having to go to court."

Voices in the kitchen caught Diane's attention. Tomiko was asking Jeffrey something. She seemed to be getting closer to him. He'd been patient, but Diane had no clue how he really felt, considering their last conversation—or a more accurate description would be a blow-up. She tuned back into the conversation.

"I'll let you know what happens," Joy said.

"Hopefully he'll just sign and keep it moving." Diane caught her husband's gaze, and she smiled at him as he squatted down in front of the petite little girl, who had her arm wrapped around his shoulders so she could tell him something. To her surprise, he smiled back, and it made her heart flutter the way it did when they first met. "Hey, y'all. I need to get off and get ready to go. Keep me posted."

"You'd better do the same," Joy said.

"I will." They spoke a moment longer, then ended their three-way call.

Diane pushed up from the lounger on the back deck and went inside. She closed the screen and then the glass door and locked it, then went to find Jeffrey and Tomiko. She found them in their bedroom relaxing on the bed and watching some animated show on television.

"Joy and Rochelle doing okay?" Jeffrey asked.

"Joy's still waiting for Robert to sign the papers, and Chelle is dating Warren."

"Joe's buddy?"

"Yep. He's liked her for a long time, but they've only recently started going out." She sat on the side of the bed. "What are you watching?"

"It's *Moana*," Tomiko answered, not taking her eyes off the screen. "What time is Aunt Toni coming to pick me and Grandma up?"

"She said two o'clock, and it's almost that time, so she should be here pretty soon."

"Okay." She gave Diane a small smile, then went back to the movie.

Less than fifteen minutes later, Toni arrived.

Tomiko ran into Antoinette's arms. "Hi, Aunt Toni."

"Hi, precious. Are you and your grandma ready to go have some fun?"

Tomiko nodded vigorously. "Yes. Come on, Grandma."

Smiling, Mama Doris planted her cane and slowly pushed to her feet. "Okay, okay. I'm ready."

Antoinette said to Diane, "We'll be back around seven or eight."

Diane nodded. "Have a great time." She and Jeffrey walked them out and waited while Antoinette secured Tomiko in the booster, then waved as they drove off.

Back inside, Jeffrey said, "How about we go to the park so we can talk?"

"Okay. Let me put my sneakers on." She figured they'd have their talk here at the house, but maybe a change of scenery would be a good thing. He followed her up and changed his shoes as well. Diane stuck her driver's license and credit card into a small card case and stuck it into the back pocket of her shorts, and put her phone in the front pocket.

Jeffrey grabbed his keys off the nightstand. "Ready?"

She nodded. The park was a short five-minute drive. With the nice weather, the lot was almost full, and several groups of people had snagged the covered areas, while others sat on blankets placed on the grass.

"Do you want to walk and talk or sit?"

Diane shrugged. "We can do a little of both, if that's okay." At the moment, she had too much nervous energy to sit with not knowing how the conversation would go.

He gestured her forward, and they started down the walking path. For the first few minutes, neither spoke, then Jeffrey grasped her hand. "I owe you an apology, Di."

Okay, so maybe they should sit. That was so not what she expected him to say, at least not right off the bat. "I'm sorry too. I shouldn't have pushed so—"

He cut her off with a kiss. He stopped at a bench. "Let's sit." He waited until she sat, then lowered himself next to her. "Yes, you did push some, but I should've told you how I felt. We promised each other that we would talk things through, and I didn't live up to that promise. That's on me. And I'm sorry."

Diane couldn't stop the tears that flowed down her cheeks.

"I love you, Diane, and I don't want things to continue the way they have been between us." Jeffrey draped an arm around her shoulders and pulled her closer. "Why are you crying, baby?"

Hearing him say he loved her only made the tears come faster. "Because I was scared you were going to tell me you wanted out, that you didn't love me anymore."

Gently, moving her hand aside, he used the pad of his thumb to wipe her tears. "You're the only woman who has my heart, and though things haven't been great with us, that hasn't changed. It *won't* change."

"I love you too." She buried her face in his neck, relieved that they might be able to regain the closeness they once shared. Her tears slowed, then stopped, and she basked in having his strong arms around her.

"I talked to Aaron and my dad."

Her head came up sharply. "You did?" His older brother Aaron lived in Southern California, as did his father. "You told them about our . . . I mean . . ." She waved a hand, trying to find the right words.

"I did. It wasn't easy, but I needed someone to talk to about all this."

"What did they say?"

Jeffrey chuckled. "Aaron told me I was acting like a dumbass. Dad said the same thing, only nicer." He shifted to face her. "They were right, though. I should've let you know how angry it made me to find out that my chances to be a father had decreased significantly. I felt like a failure as a man and as a husband."

Diane caressed his face. "Jeff, honey, you're not a failure, and I never saw you that way." It broke her heart to hear the anguish in his voice.

"I knew that here." He pointed to his temple. "But in here," he pointed to his heart, "was a different story. You know, my boss let me know yesterday that I had gotten the promotion, but I couldn't even be happy about it because you were the one person I wanted to celebrate with. But because I'd caused this rift between us, the promotion didn't matter."

"You didn't even mention it. Despite us going through our problems, you know I would still be happy for you, and I am. You worked hard and deserve it."

"Thanks, but having all this . . . this anger and stuff inside me made it worthless. Honestly, I'm still angry, but I'm trying to work through it."

"You're not the only one who's been angry."

"I know, and I dropped the ball on that one too." Jeffrey leaned his forehead against hers. "I shouldn't have let you cry alone when you got that letter from your doctor. I should've validated your pain and held you while you cried so that you'd know we were in this together. Then when you brought that sweet little girl home, I didn't support you in that either. I have so much to make up for. Forgive me," he whispered, his voice cracking.

The tears started again. "I do. I do. We'll get through this. We're a team. Whatever you lack, I've got you, and vice versa."

"And I've got you, sweetheart. I've got *us* . . . forever. Can we get back to what we had? I know it won't happen overnight, but I want to try."

Diane nodded, feeling like a boulder had finally been lifted off her chest. "Yes. A thousand times *yes!*" The kiss that followed was one of pain, forgiveness, healing and love.

"Come on. Let's go home."

She smiled the entire drive, and the kisses started again as soon as they were inside the house. It had been so long since he'd touched and kissed her this way, and her body was on fire. Her hands slid under his shirt and moved across his flat abs and strong chest.

Jeffrey groaned. "Di, baby."

"Stop talking and make love to me."

He stared down at her. "Are you sure? I mean, I know we're—"

She placed a finger against his lips. "Yes, we still have a lot of work to do, but I've missed being with you this way."

"I've missed you too, more than you know, and I'm going to show you just how much."

In the blink of an eye, he whipped her shirt over her head and tossed it aside, then did the same with his own. The farthest they got was to the family room. He drew her down onto the blanket he'd spread out on the floor. He slowly removed her clothes, then kissed and caressed every inch of her body, lingering in some places longer than others.

"Can you feel how much I've missed you?"

Diane felt everything, *everywhere*. "I feel it," she said with a sigh. Her hands were as busy as his. Touching, caressing, loving . . . remembering and relearning.

Their eyes met, and for the first time in a long time, Diane felt her heart ease. This was the man she'd first fallen in love with.

"I missed being with you like this. I could stay here forever."

She palmed his face and locked her gaze on his. "Then stay. Forever." A gentle kiss, soft, passed between them. Each new touch felt like a dream, a memory, bringing them closer and closer together. Afterward, Jeffrey braced himself on trembling arms. "I love you, baby. You are my everything."

"And you are mine." *We're going to make it.*

Chapter 24

Joy

THURSDAY AFTERNOON, JOY PARKED IN FRONT OF HER mother's house and cut the engine. She'd been trying to get up the courage to stop by for the past week, ever since the conversation with her father. Part of her wanted to restart the car, drive off and stew a little longer; the other, more mature part of her said it was time to deal with the anger and hurt that had been festering right below the surface and making her feel off-balance and irritable.

After debating with herself for a good five minutes, Joy drew in a couple of calming breaths, got out and headed up the walkway. Instead of using her key, she rang the doorbell. While waiting, her stomach knotted up, and she absently ran a hand across her midsection.

"Joy. Hey. Come on in," her mother said when she opened the door. Staring at Joy with uncertainty in her features, she stepped aside for Joy to enter. "*Um* . . . I didn't expect you."

Marsha wrung her hands as she shuffled down the entryway and through the kitchen to the family room. Her mom took a seat in her favorite recliner, and they sat in awkward silence for what seemed like hours. She trained her eyes on whatever television show she'd been watching.

A few tense seconds longer, Joy sat on the sofa opposite the chair and said, "I'm really angry with you, Mom, and I don't know what to do with all that's inside me right now. How could you lie to us? You watched me ignore and pretty much treat Dad like crap, and you said nothing. The worst part is that he didn't deserve any of it."

All the bitterness rose up so swiftly, it nearly overwhelmed her. Tears ran unchecked down her face, and her breathing accelerated. Joy grabbed her chest and struggled to get control.

"You don't understand."

"You're right. I *don't* understand how you could leave a man who worked hard, provided for this family and loved you. Yet you want me to stay with a man who doesn't love me and *cheated*."

"Joy, I didn't say I wanted you to stay with him. I only wanted you to be sure, because sometimes things aren't what they seem. That maybe you were just assuming he's been cheating because of how bad things are between you two."

Joy stared at her mom as if she'd lost her mind. *Assuming? So catching him with his tongue damn near down Stacey's throat is an assumption?* Then she remembered she hadn't talked to her mother since that incident. "Would you consider hearing him tell another woman he loved her, then catching them kissing, cheating?"

Her mom whipped her head around and her mouth fell open.

"So yeah, Mom, things are *exactly* as they seem. And he tried to buy out another company behind my back. As far as I'm concerned, he doesn't respect me either." She hoped Sondra would have some good news when she called later. The meeting with Robert's attorney had been changed from Tuesday to earlier today, and she wondered if it was just one more stall tactic.

"Oh, honey, I'm really sorry. I had no idea. So you're filing for divorce?"

"I've already filed, and he's finding every reason to delay signing the papers."

Her mother nodded. "I'm also sorry about your father," she said softly. "At the time, it was easier to blame him than to look in the mirror and realize that I'd been a fool."

"I don't understand, Mom."

"Join the club," she muttered. Sighing, she said, "Back then, all my girlfriends and their husbands seemed to be traveling, going to music concerts and parties, and generally having fun. Because your dad was focused on working, we didn't do many of those things. He tried to tell me that we'd get to do them and more once we were both stable in our careers. At that time, he only had an entry-level position that didn't pay much. Then I started listening to my girlfriends, who convinced me that I was missing out on the best years of my life." Marsha shook her head. "Worst thing I've ever done in my life." She swiped at the tears flowing down her cheeks.

While Joy's heart went out to her mother for her bad choices, the resentment she felt didn't lessen.

"You have every right to hate me, but I hope one day you can forgive me. All of you."

"It's going to take some time, Mom," she said softly.

"I know."

Silence stretched between them. "I have to get going." Joy stood. "Thanks for telling me the truth. It helps." She hesitated briefly, then placed a kiss on her mother's cheek. "I'll see you later."

In the car she leaned her head back, closed her eyes and blew out a long breath. While she still faulted her mother for what happened to their family, a part of her could see how it happened. She had a few acquaintances who'd subscribed to the proverbial grass-is-greener-on-the-other-side move and had it backfire as well. Hopefully she could get past her anger soon.

Sitting up, she checked her messages and saw she'd missed a call from Gretchen. She dialed her voice mail and listened: *"Hi,*

Joy. Just got off the phone with the owners of the gym, and if you're available today before five, we can do a walk-through. Give me a call and let me know if you can make it, or if I need to schedule for another time. I also found something else you may like better."

Joy immediately returned Gretchen's call. It was only three thirty, and she should be able to make it to El Dorado Hills from her mother's Orangevale home in plenty of time.

"Hey, Gretchen."

"Oh, Joy, good. I was hoping you'd call. I know you mentioned wanting to check out the old gym, but there's a day spa not too far from there that I think you might like. The owner wants to retire, so he's a little anxious to sell."

"Oh wow. That might be nice." Then she wouldn't have too much in the way of renovations, depending on the size and layout. "Is it possible to see both today?"

"I'm just leaving another client and can meet you at the gym in about thirty minutes. We can look at the spa afterward. I'll call the owner and see if today's a good time."

"I'd appreciate that. I'll meet you at the gym in thirty." Joy ended the call and did a little squeal. She started the car, plugged the address into her GPS and drove off.

Gretchen was already waiting when she arrived. Getting out of the car, Joy took in the parking lot and building, wanting to get a feel for the area. The one-story building was located in the middle of a strip mall that housed two small eateries, a liquor store, furniture store and nail salon. Although it was located in a nice area, all the buildings were connected, which she really didn't like.

"Hey, Joy," Gretchen called out as she approached. "First thoughts?"

"Not too fond of it being in the middle because it takes away from the whole serene ambiance I envisioned, but let's see the inside."

They found the owner sitting in the empty front area working on a laptop. He glanced up at their entrance and stood. "Hello. I'm William Atkins. Welcome."

They introduced themselves and followed him around. "Do you mind if I take a few photos?" Joy asked.

"Not at all."

"Thanks." She whipped out her phone and took several pictures and a couple of videos. On the positive side, it had a sauna, Jacuzzi, and plenty of locker room space. It also had three smaller spaces that could be used for treatment rooms and an office space in the back. However, she would have to do extensive renovations and wasn't sure her budget could handle them at the moment now that she had to factor in rent.

Once the tour ended, they thanked him and Gretchen told the man she'd be in touch. Outside, she asked, "Well, what did you think?"

Joy listed all the positives, then pointed out the negatives. "The biggest thing is the amount of work needed. I'm not sure my budget can withstand it."

She nodded. "Okay. We'll check out the other space and you can think about what you'd like to do." After giving Joy the address, she strode off to her car.

The second building was far more to Joy's liking, and she gave it bonus points for being a freestanding building. The lot had ample parking, and mature trees gave it a more secluded feeling. "So far, so good." She opened the door and could immediately envision the space being hers. Excitement flowed through her veins.

"I like this myself," Gretchen said with a little laugh.

This time the receptionist showed them around because the owner had already moved out of the state. When she led them to the private grounds out back, Joy was sold. She took more pictures and couldn't wait to show them to Diane and Rochelle.

Her phone buzzed with a call from Sondra, and as much as she wanted to answer, she let it go to voice mail. She'd return the call in the car.

As Joy and her agent headed back out to their respective cars several minutes later, she said, "I really like this place."

"I could tell. And all of the equipment is in the asking price. When I spoke to the owner today, she mentioned that the eight employees were willing to stay on as well."

"Okay, that's something else to think about and might make things a little easier. Can I have a couple of days?"

"Of course, dear. How about we talk on Monday or Tuesday at the latest?"

"Sounds good. Thank you." The two women talked a few minutes longer, then went their separate ways.

In the car Joy connected the Bluetooth and called Sondra.

"Hey, Joy," Sondra said.

"Hey, Sondra. Please tell me you have some good news." Her heart rate sped up in anticipation.

"I take it you didn't listen to the message," she said with a chuckle. "Robert isn't going to contest the divorce and has signed all the paperwork. His attorney tried to play hardball until I mentioned that his client would have to go before a judge who might not take too kindly to him cheating with an employee and trying to purchase another company without the co-owner's knowledge, particularly since you're listed on the business as equal partners. Not to mention the negative publicity that could jeopardize his business."

"Thank you, thank you!" Joy yelled in the car. "This is the best news you could have given me, girlfriend. I appreciate you more than I can say."

"I have a few more things for you to sign, so stop by tomorrow when you get a chance. I should be in the office after one thirty."

"I'll be there."

"Go home and celebrate, and I'll see you tomorrow."

"Alright. Have a good evening." This time when the tears came, they were tears of joy. Though California had a six-month waiting period, she could finally close this chapter in her life and move forward. She still had some lingering sadness, but she knew it would take time for the sting of betrayal to fade. For now she would take Sondra's advice and celebrate.

Joy would see Chelle when she got to her home, but was so excited, she couldn't wait and sent a text to her and Diane: **BEST. DAY. EVER! Robert signed papers . . . Six months and I'm FREE! And I may have found the perfect place for the spa.** She attached a few of the pictures, then with Mary J. Blige's "Just Fine" cranked up to the highest volume, drove home.

Rochelle grabbed Joy up in a big hug as soon as she walked through the door. "Oh my goodness, sis, I'm so excited for you. And that place does look perfect. Did you already put a bid in for it?"

"Not yet. I wanted to take a couple of days to see if something else pops up and to work out the financing."

"Let me know if you need some help."

"I will." Her phone chimed in her purse. She dug it out and laughed at the GIF Diane sent of a Black woman dancing: **Yassss! Way to go, sis. Doing a happy dance for you.** She turned the phone so Rochelle could see, eliciting more laughter.

"Can you tell we're excited?" Rochelle asked.

"I love y'all so much. I need to go call Brent and my dad." Joy nearly skipped down the hallway to the bedroom. The first call went to her big brother.

"Hey, baby girl. What's shaking?"

"Robert finally signed the divorce papers and he's not going to contest anything," she blurted with excitement.

"That's good news, sis. I still want to break him in half for hurting you, though."

"I know, and if we were teens, I'd say go for it."

Brent chuckled. "Yeah, don't think my wife would go for me punching out folks now. But I'm glad you can move on."

"Guess what else?"

"What?"

"I think I found the spot for my spa, and it won't require as much as the gym I told you about because it's already a day spa." She told him about the renovations she wanted to make and about the employees being willing to stay on. Gretchen had also relayed that the financials on the company were solid, which was even better. "I'm going to send you a few of the photos I took."

"Sounds good. I have to say that Rob is a fool. You could've done so much together and have not one but two amazing businesses. If you need some money, let me know. I don't want you overextending yourself."

"Yeah, but sometimes things don't work out the way we want. And I will." Yes, that had originally been her dream, but now she'd had to shift to a new one, and as Mary J. said, Joy was just fine with it. "I know it's probably close to dinner for you all, so I'll let you go. I just wanted to share my good news."

"I'm glad you did. Have you told Mom and Dad yet?"

"Not yet. I'll call Dad after I hang up with you. I stopped by to see Mom today and we talked. She did apologize, but it's still going to take some time for me to work through all of my anger."

"I'm glad to hear it, and it's a start."

"It is. I need to go, so tell Kim and the boys I said hello. I'll get by there soon."

"Will do. Talk to you later, Joy, and thanks for the good news."

Joy ended the call, scrolled to her father's name, and hit the Call button.

"Hey, sweetheart," her father greeted when he answered.

"Hi, Dad. Did I catch you at a bad time?" She heard voices in the background.

"No. I'm just over at a friend's house. We'll be sitting down to dinner in a few minutes, but I have some time to talk to my favorite girl."

She giggled. *"Awww,* Daddy. I love you too. And this friend wouldn't happen to be a woman, would it?" He had never mentioned seeing anyone. Then again, Joy hadn't asked.

His booming laughter came through the line. "As a matter of fact, it is. Her name is Vera, and I hope to introduce you soon."

"Well, alright now. It must be serious."

"It's getting there." He sounded happy.

"Good for you, Dad. I can't wait to meet her. I was calling to let you know that Robert finally signed the divorce papers, and he didn't contest anything, which means my Christmas present will be freedom."

"I'm glad it worked out, but I am still disappointed in him. He promised me he'd take care of your heart, and he didn't."

Even though things had been strained between them when she and Robert got married, her father had still walked her down the aisle. She recalled them standing at the entrance to the church and her father saying to her, *"Robert's a good man, and he promised me he'd always take care of your heart."*

Thirteen years later it was over, and her heart had been broken in every way imaginable. Not wanting to dwell on the memories, she changed the subject. "The other reason I called is to let you know I'm going to get that spa off the ground, sooner rather than later." She repeated the information she'd shared with Brent.

"That's wonderful, honey. Just so you know, I'm going to put up half the cost."

Joy blinked. Had she heard him correctly? "Dad, I can't ask

you to do that." Now she wouldn't turn him down if he wanted to contribute, but she wouldn't feel right having him drop a quarter of a million dollars in her lap. There were some things that needed to be repaired, and she hoped they could knock a little off the asking price, but it still was a lot of money.

But far less than if you'd gone with the gym, a sage inner voice reminded her.

"You didn't ask me to do anything. I'm offering, and I won't take no for an answer. I'll also help with the renovation costs. Have you found a contractor yet?"

Still stuck on his declaration, it took her a moment to find her voice. "Thank you so much, Dad. I love you," she said around the lump in her throat. "And no to the contractor. I haven't even put a bid in yet."

"Well, don't wait to get it in. I can hear how excited you are about this place. You don't want someone else to grab it up while you're thinking about it."

She smiled around the moisture in her eyes. He'd always been no-nonsense and straightforward. "I'll call my real estate agent in the morning."

Things are finally looking up.

Chapter 25

Rochelle

"I DON'T KNOW WHAT I WAS THINKING," ROCHELLE muttered as she put on a pair of sweats and a tee. She'd forgotten about the Saturday cardio class she, Joy and Diane were going to this morning and had told Warren she'd be available later to work out with him. *Probably because when I agreed, it was after one of those mind-stealing kisses.*

"You ready, Chelle?" Joy called through the closed door.

She walked over and opened it. "I guess."

"Did you ever find out the level of the class?"

"I asked Summer, and she said it was for all levels, which is a good thing because it's been a minute since I've done anything aside from walking." She was proud that she'd kept up with getting walks in a few times a week. Warren had joined her once that week. With it being mid-June, school had finally ended, and he'd told her he was looking forward to the best summer of his life. If she were being honest with herself, she was looking forward to it as well.

"Oh good, because I haven't either. These bones are closer to forty than not, and I know I'm probably going to need a long soak in the tub afterward."

"At least you didn't sign yourself up for a second workout in one day." At Joy's confused look, she said, "Warren agreed to show me some weight lifting techniques . . . today."

A sly grin spread across Joy's face. "I bet that'll be one workout you'll never forget. Sexy man spotting you, standing behind you to show you the proper technique . . . Yes, honey, sign me up!"

A vision of Warren standing behind her with his hands all over her body filled her mind and sent a jolt straight to Rochelle's core.

"See, you know *exactly* what I'm talking about," Joy said, laughing.

Rochelle waved her off and strutted past her. "I'm not talking to you." But she was smiling. "Haley, we're leaving. I should be back in about an hour and a half. You know the drill."

"I know. Don't open the door, don't answer the phone unless it's family, and don't leave the house. I won't."

She bent and kissed her daughter's forehead. "See you later."

Today, Joy drove, and they slowly made their way down the street searching for the address. Rochelle pointed out the building in the middle of the block. The studio was located in a mixed business and residential area.

"I don't see Diane's car yet," Joy said. "She'd better not chicken out."

She chuckled. "Right. Misery loves company, as the saying goes." Scanning the parking lot once more, she saw her friend turn into the parking lot. "There she is." Rochelle and Joy got out of the car and waited for Diane to park.

"Hey, y'all." Diane hugged them. "Are we ready to be tortured?"

Rochelle noticed how much more relaxed Diane looked now that things between her and Jeffrey had improved. "Like I told Joy, my coworker said it's for all levels, so hopefully it won't be so bad."

They entered the building and followed the music to a room near the rear. All three women froze in the doorway. "I'm going to strangle Summer."

"I take it she didn't mention this part," Diane said with a hand on her hip.

"No, she did not. There is no way I'm staying in a twerking class."

"Hell, if I drop it, it might not come back up," Joy cracked.

As people continued to trickle in, all over the room women were in various positions practicing shaking their butts, and Rochelle stood mesmerized as the woman she figured was the instructor did a move where each isolated cheek bounced up and down, taking on a life of its own. Rochelle was further stunned when the woman went from standing to bent over to squatting, and ended in a plank position, all without missing a beat.

"Damn," Diane whispered. "Maybe I should stay and learn a couple of these to spring on Jeff."

"After he recovers from the heart attack he's sure to have, I'm sure he'd have you naked in a flash," Rochelle said. They laughed.

"Probably, but it'll be worth every second. You'd probably get the same results if you use this as your 'workout'"—Diane made quotation marks in the air—"instead of lifting those weights."

The image popped into Rochelle's mind and sent heat flowing through her. "*Um . . .*"

Joy did a little move, trying to imitate the instructor. "*Ow*! I think I pulled something." She rubbed her hip.

"Welcome, ladies. Is this your first time?" The instructor smiled and crossed the room to where they still stood near the door.

"Yes," Rochelle answered. "But—"

"Great. Come on in, and don't worry if you can do all the moves. Just have fun while getting some cardio work in." She waved them into the room.

Rochelle shared a look with Diane and Joy, who both shrugged. They found spots in the back of the room.

"When I get to work on Monday, I will be talking to Summer. She should've warned me. I can't believe that girl."

"Well, since we're here now, let's try to make the best of it," Joy said.

"And try not to break something in the process," Diane cracked.

"Ain't that the truth." Rochelle scanned the room and saw women of all shapes and sizes. A couple of them looked to be a few years older than her.

"Okay, ladies. Let's get started," the instructor finally said. She waited until she had everyone's attention, then turned on the music. She started with a side-to-side movement to warm up.

"Okay, I can do this," Rochelle said.

After a couple of minutes, the instructor said, "Now we start the TikTok jump squat." She demonstrated bouncing her hips, alternating each side for a count of four, then doing a squat and jumping forward. "Let's go!"

After the second one, Diane said, "My thighs are on fire already."

"Same." Rochelle was really contemplating canceling that workout with Warren.

They continued with several more exercises, then the instructor called out, "Ready to learn the booty clap?"

Joy stilled. "Booty what?" The instructor demonstrated, then she asked, "Is my booty clapping?"

Rochelle muffled her laughter. "I don't know about it clapping, but it's doing something. I don't know how these women get their butts to move separately from their bodies. My everything is clapping."

Diane and Joy giggled, and Diane said, "Mine ain't even close to a clap. More like a gong."

A woman in front of them turned and said, "Hallelujah! Finally I'm not the only one in here who has no clue how to get this booty moving."

Rochelle, Diane and Joy couldn't hold back their laughter.

Halfway through the hour-long class, Rochelle was winded and wanted nothing more than to lay out on the floor, especially when the instructor had them doing a crab walk on their hands and feet while executing the same clap movement. More than a few women ended up stretched out on the floor laughing, which made her feel better.

The next move had them laughing at Diane as she tried to imitate booty clapping with her hands on her knees while walking. "Sexy, right? Jeffrey's not going to know what hit him when I pop into the room like this." She added a little extra dip on the next one.

"Get it, girl," Rochelle said with a chuckle. "The only thing popping on me is my knees right now. I think I'll stick to that hip sway with a dip move from the warm-up."

At the end of the class, they all sat on the floor. Joy moaned. "I don't think I can move."

"My everything hurts. I hope I can drive home," Diane said with a laugh, sounding winded.

Because another class was coming in, the three women trudged out to the lobby area and collapsed in the chairs. "Oh, a soft surface. This feels so good. Joy, you need to hurry up with this spa because I seriously need a massage right now," Rochelle said.

The last time Rochelle had done any pampering of any sort had been when they'd taken the girls out for Ebony's birthday. And that was only a mani-pedi. However, her last massage had to be at least two years ago.

I'm way overdue.

In her quest to be the best version of herself, she planned to be more intentional about her self-care.

"I called Gretchen yesterday and asked her to make an offer," Joy said. "There are some repairs needed, and she's going to see if the owner will drop the asking price by twenty or thirty grand."

"I really hope she can get it down," Diane said. "I can't wait to see it."

"We all need massages," Joy said. "As much as I'm into all this, taking care of me has been on the back burner for a long time."

"Girl, I was just saying that to myself," Rochelle said. "My body would probably go in shock if I tried to get any sort of massage."

Diane laughed. "Chelle, you are so right. Mine too. We need to do better. We spend so much time taking care of everyone else, it's time to prioritize us for a change."

"Yvette was always the one who kept us on track. Man, I miss her," Joy said quietly.

They lapsed into reflective silence for a minute, then Rochelle said, "I think she'd be happy to see that we've all stepped out of our comfort zones." A wry smile curved her lips. "Actually, she'd probably say it's about damn time. Although I don't know what she'd say about this whole twerking class."

"Knowing her crazy behind, she probably would've hopped to the front row and yelled, 'work it, sisters.'"

Diane shook her head and chuckled. "She would, too, Joy. But I have to say, I'm pretty happy myself. Jeff and I have been spending more time together. There's laughter at the dinner table, and he's been such a great father figure to Tomiko. That little girl loves him, and he can get her to smile far easier than I can."

"I am so happy for you two. I knew he'd get himself together."

"So am I. I'm just glad he opened up about how he blamed

himself for us not being able to conceive. We've both come to realize that God had a different plan for us, and we're coming to grips with it."

"You both have good men," Joy said.

"I know you're not ready now, but if another man comes along, don't block your blessings, my sister."

"You know you sound like Yvette, Chelle."

"She said it to me so many times, I hear it in my sleep." But Rochelle's friend was right. Giving Warren a chance had been the best decision she'd made in a while. If she were being honest with herself, she'd admit that she was falling in love with him. The fact that he always took Haley's feelings into consideration only made her fall harder. Twice he'd invited her daughter along with them for dinner as if they were a real family. Haley had told her more than once how much she enjoyed those times, making Rochelle realize how much she needed a father in her life. Sure Rochelle's dad, Val's husband and even Joe had filled a little of that role, but it wasn't enough. The past two months with Warren had been like something out of a dream and proved that there were still good Black men out there.

And one of them is mine.

"Yeah, Yvette was right," Joy said. "And Rochelle's going to be working out with Warren later."

Diane swung her head in Rochelle's direction. "You're going to be working out with Warren? I'd love to be a fly on the wall to see that. All those muscles on display, his hands all over you to show you how to use the machines." She fanned herself.

Joy pointed toward Rochelle. "Ha! See, I said the same thing."

"Y'all get on my nerves. Just come on and be quiet."

Rochelle stood and tried hard not to think about Warren's big, strong hands on her body. By the time they made it to the car, once again she seriously considered canceling. However, the desire to see him outweighed her current discomfort. With any luck, after a hot shower her muscles would be relaxed. "What are you doing for the rest of the day?"

"Jeff and I are taking Tomiko to the Jelly Belly Factory in Fairfield. They don't have the live tours on the weekend, but we'll be able to watch the videos of how the jelly beans are made."

"I love it," Rochelle said. "I remember taking Haley there several years ago. I must've bought every flavor of jelly bean they had in the store." The company had the regular flavors but also offered unique ones like glazed blueberry cake and jalapeño. They even had an assortment of cocktail flavors, including margarita, piña colada and mojito.

"I love that, Diane. While Chelle's out getting her 'workout' on"—Joy made quote marks in the air—"I'm going to have dinner with my dad. He wants to introduce me to his new lady friend."

"Whaaat?" Rochelle and Diane chorused.

"I know. I said the same thing. But he deserves some happiness after what my mom put him through. Anyway, you'd better get going, Di. It takes a good hour to get to Fairfield without traffic, and you know there'll be some at noon on a Saturday with folks heading to the Bay Area."

"I know. I'll see you guys later." After hugging Rochelle and Joy, she got into her car and drove off.

Rochelle and Joy followed suit. When they got back home, both headed straight for the shower. Rochelle felt infinitely better when she finished. Going down the hallway, she stuck her head in Haley's room. "Did you eat already?"

"Yes. I had a boiled egg and one of the cinnamon apple muffins. Are you still going to hang out with Mr. McIntyre today?"

"I am." Haley would be finally spending the night with Ebony. "You good with it?"

She sighed audibly. "Mom, I already told you I like him. You don't have to keep asking me."

"Okay. Anyway, he should be here in about an hour, so have your stuff ready."

Haley's smile widened. "I packed last night."

"Figures. Make sure that bathroom is cleaned before you leave."

"Awww, Mom. You always know how to ruin my day."

"*Mm-hmm*, I know." Chuckling, Rochelle went to the kitchen and took out the last container holding one of her prepped meals—a shrimp Caesar salad—added a little dressing and sat at the table to eat. She flipped through the mail, discarding the junk and setting the bills aside. Not seeing anything that needed her immediate attention, she picked up the romance novel she'd borrowed from Val and picked up where she'd left off.

Rochelle got so lost in the story, she startled when she heard the doorbell. *Oh, shoot! I'm not even ready.*

She took a hasty glance at the clock—it read two o'clock on the dot, and Warren was never late. She hopped up from the table and rushed to the door, glancing down at herself to make sure she hadn't spilled anything on her top and smoothing a hand over her ponytail. Drawing a calming breath, she opened the door.

"Hi." It came out breathier than she intended. In the basketball shorts and fitted tee that showed off his muscled chest and biceps, the man looked good. Realizing she was staring like a starstruck teen, she backed up and waved him in. "Come on in."

"Hey, baby." Warren slid his arm around her waist, dipped his head and kissed her.

She heard giggling behind her and moved out of his arms. She shot her daughter an amused look.

Haley clapped a hand over her mouth, but her eyes sparkled with mirth. "Hi, Mr. McIntyre."

"Hey, Haley. Are you glad school is out?"

"Yes. *Finally.* No homework for two months."

He chuckled. "I know the feeling."

"Oh, that's right, you work at a high school. Summer is awesome, huh?"

"It is, indeed," Warren agreed.

"Are you ready to go, Haley?" Rochelle interrupted their conversation.

"I just have to go get my bag." Haley bounced out of the room.

"She's a great kid, Rochelle," Warren said, smiling.

"Unless you have to live with her every day. The child can tap-dance on my last good nerve sometimes."

"Which is true for all teenagers, from what I understand. But I still would've liked to have one or two," he said.

Instinctively, Rochelle knew he would've made a phenomenal father and wished her daughter could have had a man like him instead of a lying, cheating, deadbeat jerk. "Well, if you want to borrow some, I'm sure Joe and I will be happy to let you have our three."

Warren threw back his head and roared with laughter. "The funny thing is, he and Yvette did say that a few times."

"*Uh-huh*, but I don't ever recall you taking them up on their offer," she teased. "Have a seat while I go grab my stuff."

She figured she'd bring a change of clothes because she had no intention of sitting around in sweat after working out. When she came out, Warren and Haley were sitting together on the sofa looking at something on her iPad. Whatever it was had them both laughing.

When Warren noticed Rochelle, he rose to his feet. "Ready, babe?"

She nodded. "What are you two laughing at?"

"Haley was showing me one of those videos that someone made

265

of a dog and cat fighting, but the person has done a voiceover. These people have a lot of time on their hands to create this stuff." He eased the bag from her hand, then picked up Haley's. "Shall we, ladies?" He did an elaborate bow.

Haley strutted past him with her head held high, as if she were a queen. "We shall."

"Lord, this child of mine," Rochelle said and followed them out. She had to admit that she enjoyed their interactions, and if the smile on Warren's face was any indication, so did he.

They kept up a running stream of conversation during the drive, and he patiently answered the many questions Haley asked. By the time they arrived at Joe's, Warren had promised to help Haley with her basketball skills because she planned to try out for the team next year. Rochelle didn't comment, but that was several months away. Would they still be seeing each other then? The thought that they might not didn't sit well with her. She really wanted this relationship to work.

"Hey. Come on in," Joe said, dividing a smile between her and Warren. The two men shared a one-arm hug. "Looking good, bro." He pulled Rochelle into a brotherly hug. "I'm happy for you, Chelle. It's been a long time since I've seen my boy smile so much, so thank you. Oh, and my wife was right about you two being perfect for each other."

Rochelle elbowed Joe playfully. "I don't know what I'm going to do with you."

"You can send me the first invitation to the wedding."

Her mouth fell open. But before she could form a reply, Ebony and Ian rounded the corner. She hugged them both, as did Warren. Then they were gone, leaving just the adults.

"Warren, you're taking good care of my girl, right?"

Warren lifted a brow. "You mean am I taking good care of *my* girl? The answer is I will always take care of Rochelle."

He said the words to Joe, but his eyes never left Rochelle's. Her pulse skipped.

Forever the instigator, Joe said, "Always is a long time, my brother."

"When it comes to Rochelle, always isn't long enough."

If she knew how to swoon, she would have right there. Rochelle didn't dare look at Joe. "*Um*, we should probably get going."

"You're right," Warren said. "We'll see you later." He and Joe did a fist bump.

"You kids have fun. Chelle, I'll bring Haley home around two or three tomorrow so they can sleep in, because I know they'll be up all night giggling."

"That's for sure," Rochelle said with a little laugh. They reminded her of the way she, Yvette, Diane and Joy used to be when they had sleepovers. "See you later."

As Warren helped her into the car, she could still see Joe standing in the doorway smiling. She threw up a wave.

Warren rounded the fender and climbed in on the driver's side. "Ready to get this party started?"

She gave him the side-eye. "Party? Since when did working out become a party? More like torture."

"*Awww*, sweetheart, it won't be that bad, I promise. Are there any specific areas you want to focus on?"

Every one of them. "I want to tone up, lose some inches. Just generally get healthier."

"We can do that."

"How often do you work out?"

"Depends on the week. The goal is at least four days a week, but sometimes it ends up being only once or twice. Seems like since I hit forty, I have to work harder to get the same results. But that's how it goes, and I've been doing it since I was fifteen, so it's pretty much ingrained. If I had to start now, I probably wouldn't be as consistent."

"Sounds like my problem. I've started and stopped so many times over the years." The last time she'd been consistent was a few months after Haley's birth, but then she had gone to the extreme, exercising three or four hours a day, and barely ate. All in the name of what was supposed to be love. It wasn't. And now she could see it for what it really was—abuse. Rochelle never again would allow anyone else to have that kind of control over her. "I've neglected my own self-care for so long, and it's time to get back to taking care of me."

Warren's eyes left the road briefly to glance her way. "You spend the most time with yourself, so it should be a priority. I've watched you over the years grow into a confident and even more amazing woman, and I applaud you taking charge of your life. I gotta tell you, though," he said with a wry smile, "after seeing what your ex put you through, there were several times when I wanted to snatch him up and teach him some manners."

The fury in his tone took her by surprise. Outside of her father and Joe, she'd never had a man champion her the way Warren did. Rochelle laid a hand on his arm. "Thank you for saying that. I can't tell you how much it means. It took me a while, but I learned my lesson well." She'd broken her own heart over and over again trying to make her marriage work, when clearly it wasn't meant to be. She couldn't force Kenny to care, to be loyal and to just be the man she needed him to be, and she'd stopped trying. After two years she realized she'd lost herself in an effort to fix what needed to stay broken. But she knew her worth now, and she was done with anything that didn't bring her peace. She still believed in love and would hold out for the kind she witnessed between her parents and her sister and brother-in-law.

"The thing is, you shouldn't have had to learn that kind of lesson, Rochelle. You deserve to be with a man who respects and loves you. One who honors you for the rare and precious jewel you are, and who will protect and give his life for you."

Those last words were spoken directly into her eyes after Warren had pulled into the driveway of a beautiful one-story home in the West Roseville area. His intense stare and passionate words pierced her heart so deeply, she could barely breathe. Rochelle had never, ever met a man like him.

He leaned over and kissed her sweetly. "I'll come around to help you out."

She got out on shaky legs, still reveling in his words. "This is nice. How long have you lived here?" she asked as he guided her up the walkway.

"Almost ten years." He unlocked the door and gestured her forward.

"Wow. This looks like a house you'd see in one of those magazines." The entryway led to a formal dining room on the left and another hallway on the right that she guessed housed the bedrooms. They kept straight and ended up in the kitchen, which opened up into an elegantly decorated family room. The black, gray and white color scheme definitely had a masculine feel. "It's gorgeous. How many bedrooms?"

"Four, but one of them is now my home gym." Warren took her hand. "I'll give you the ten-cent tour, then we'll circle back to the gym."

The guest bedrooms were all tastefully furnished, and the home gym had everything a person would need to get a full-body workout. However, the huge main bedroom stopped her in her tracks with its fireplace, sitting area and outdoor patio.

"I can't believe you live here all alone."

SHERYL LISTER

"I figured if I ever got the family I wanted, it would be large enough that we wouldn't have to move." He set her bag on the bed. "Let's go get our workout on."

Rochelle wished she could be as enthusiastic.

He turned the lights and music on. "We'll start with a few stretches, then do some light weights."

She followed his lead, stretching her upper and lower body, then he handed her a set of five-pound dumbbells. Standing behind her, he demonstrated the movement for a bicep curl. The heat of his body surrounded her, and she had a difficult time focusing on his words. All she wanted to do was lean into him, feel his hands . . .

"Rochelle, are you okay?"

"Huh? Oh yeah. Fine. Just listening to your instructions." *Focus, girl.*

She managed to get through the three sets of arm and leg exercises pretty well. Her abs were a different story. Rochelle struggled after four crunches, and by the time they got to the mountain climbers, she was close to saying "never mind," but she finished and was proud of herself.

"You did a great job." He powered off the stereo and lights as they left the room. "If you want to shower, you can take the one in my bedroom. I'll use one of the guest bathrooms." She opened her mouth to protest, and he cut her off with a kiss. "This isn't up for debate, sweetheart." He showed her where he kept the towels and made sure she didn't need anything before grabbing a change of clothes for himself and exiting the room. "I'll meet you in the kitchen when you're done."

His shower stretched the length of the wall, had a bench at one end, three showerheads and could easily fit three people. Rochelle quickly showered and went to the kitchen, where she found him pouring two glasses of what looked like iced tea. He handed her one.

"We can go sit out on the patio for a while, if you want."

"Sounds good." They settled on the swing that sat on one side. "I like this."

Warren smiled. "I have a confession to make."

"What's that?"

"I bought this swing a week ago specifically to sit here like this with you."

She stared up at him and lost another chunk of her heart. It also brought to mind his comments about always taking care of her. "Did you mean what you said to Joe earlier?"

"If you're talking about me always being here for you, I meant every word." He placed his glass on the table next to him, then shifted to face her. "Rochelle, you have to know that I'm in love with you, and I'm in this relationship for the long haul."

Oh. My. Goodness. Did this man just say he's in love with me? Her heart started pounding in her chest. "We've only been dating a couple of months."

Warren smiled. "That may be true, but I've loved you from afar for a good two years before getting up the nerve to ask you out those twenty-five or thirty times. It was worth every no for the pleasure of getting to that one yes." He tilted her chin and held her gaze. "And, baby, me saying that is no pressure on you in any way to say it back. I'm a patient man, and I can wait for you to fall in love with me the way I have with you."

Rochelle wanted to say it back because she loved him too. He made it hard for her not to fall. "I'm there, Warren."

"You don't know how long I've waited to hear those words," he said emotionally. "Come away with me for the weekend. Again, no pressure. I just want a few days of uninterrupted time with you."

If you don't say yes, I'm going to seriously hurt you. She could hear Yvette's voice in her head as surely as if her sister friend was sitting right next to her.

But was Rochelle ready for this next step? The answer came back a resounding yes!

"Okay."

As soon as the word was out, he slanted his mouth over hers in a kiss so achingly tender, it brought tears to her eyes. In it, she felt his desire, his passion and, most of all . . . his love. He had been one of the best surprises in her life, and she wanted everything he had to offer.

Chapter 26

Diane

FRIDAY, DURING HER LUNCH, DIANE SAT IN HER OF-fice texting with her girls: **Are you ready for the big move tomorrow, Joy?**

Joy: **YES!! I need to get out of Chelle's space now that she has a new man. Oh, and have an intro meeting with a contractor in the afternoon.**

Rochelle: **Oh, hush. And you don't have to rush out on my account. Besides, Warren's house is bigger than mine, so . . .**

Diane: **Wait! Exactly what does that mean? Did you and Warren get your freak on and you ain't tell nobody?**

Diane couldn't have been happier for her friend, and she hoped the relationship ended in marriage. Warren loved Rochelle like he loved breathing. Everyone around them could see it.

Joy: **Girl, I was about to ask the same thing. And I've been living here!**

Rochelle: **Both of you need to hush. And my lips are sealed.**

Diane laughed when she and Joy both sent back GIFs of excitement.

Rochelle: **And what about you and Jeff, Di?**

Diane: **It's been good. Better than good.**

A smile played around the corner of her mouth. She and Jeffrey had been spending time together laughing and talking about where they went wrong, so as not to repeat the same mistakes. It had been a healing time for both.

Rochelle: **Glad to hear it. Gotta get back to work.**

Diane: **So do I. See you both tomorrow.**

Chuckling, she set the phone down and finished the last of her chicken salad sandwich. Diane leaned back in her chair and reflected on the past couple of weeks. She and Jeffrey had come a long way in a short time. They still had a little ways to go, but both were putting in the effort. A thought popped into her mind. She wiped her hands on a napkin and picked up her phone again. After making sure the short, layered strands of her hair were in place, she slicked on another coat of lipstick and hit the Record button. Diane sent Jeffrey a video describing all the ways she was going to love him tonight. She giggled like a teenaged schoolgirl, then settled down to work.

Five minutes later, her phone chimed, and she saw a message from her husband: **Di, don't tempt me. I can be at your office in 20. And I won't be coming to talk. I'm going to show YOU all the ways I'll love you . . . on the desk, against the wall. Just say the word.**

Desire hit Diane hard and fast, and it took everything inside her not to reply: **Bring it on!** She grabbed a flyer off her desk and fanned herself. *Mercy!* The man could still turn her on with his words. *I am not touching that comment.* Instead she replied: **What do you want for dinner tonight?**

Jeffrey: **How about I take care of dinner, and then you later?**

Thinking it best to not respond and to keep herself from doing something foolish that might get her busted having sex in her office, a *daycare center office*, she wisely dropped the phone into her purse and locked it in the desk drawer because, at the moment, he wasn't the only one tempted. She spent a few more minutes going over some paperwork, then went out to help prepare the afternoon snack.

With one of their teachers out sick, she'd taught one toddler class earlier and now stood in the kitchen cutting up strawberries and apples while two of the teacher assistants filled cups with pretzels and Cheez-Its. String cheese and apple juice would complete the snack.

They'd almost finished when Jade stuck her head in the door.

"Diane, there's someone here to see you."

"Okay. I'll be out in a second." The other two young women assured Diane they could finish the preparations, and after washing and drying her hands, Diane rushed out.

She froze upon seeing Jeffrey standing there wearing a navy tailored suit, looking as if he'd just left a cover shoot, and holding a vase with a dozen red roses. "Jeff. What are you doing here?"

"I came to see you, baby." He closed the distance between them and brushed his lips across hers. "And to tell you I love you." He handed her the vase.

Diane was so overcome, she couldn't speak.

"This is so romantic," she heard Jade say.

She agreed, accepting the flowers. "I love them, and I love you. Let's go to my office." Once there, she placed them on the small round table in the corner. She sauntered back over to where her husband stood leaning against the closed door and draped her arms around his neck. "This was the best surprise. The flowers are gorgeous, but seeing your handsome face . . . Nothing is better than that."

The hazel eyes that had ensnared her all those years ago bore into hers ablaze with passion. It wouldn't take much for them to explode.

"I feel the same. I had already planned to surprise you, but those texts had me damn near sprinting out of my office to get to you," Jeffrey said, nuzzling her neck.

Diane laughed. "If it makes you feel better, I was seriously considering telling you I'm down."

His head popped up. "Be careful, sweet baby." He playfully growled and nipped her bottom lip before releasing her and stepping back.

Diane giggled. "Are you going back to the office after you leave?"

"Actually I took the rest of the afternoon off. I'd like to take Tomiko home with me so we can hang out."

She stared in shock. "*Um*, sure. She'll probably enjoy it. Let me call and have her teacher send her over." Diane made the call, then put the receiver back on the cradle. "What are you two going to do?"

Jeffrey shrugged. "Don't exactly know. I'll see if there's some favorite place she likes and go from there. That little girl has stolen my heart in a way I never expected," he confessed.

She smiled. "Mine too." A soft knock sounded, and she opened the door.

"Hi, Miss Di. Ms. Miller said you—" Tomiko let out an excited scream and launched herself at Jeffrey. "Mr. Evans!"

He swung her up into his arms and kissed her cheek. "Hey, baby girl."

Tears stung Diane's eyes seeing their twin wide smiles.

"How's your day going?" he asked.

"Okay." She wrapped her little arms around his neck and hugged him tight.

Jeffrey placed her on her feet. "What do you think about you and me taking off and going to have some fun before Miss Di gets home?"

Tomiko's eyes got even wider and she bounced up and down. "Yes, yes. I wanna go."

"Then tell Miss Di you'll see her later, and we can leave."

"See you later, Miss Di."

"Bye, baby. You two have fun, and I'll see you when I get home. Jeff, do you want me to take care of dinner since you're going to have your hands full?"

"Nope. We can handle dinner, can't we, Tomiko?"

She nodded. "We can handle it."

"There you have it," Jeffrey said.

"I'm going to leave a little early and should be home around four."

"Sounds good." He kissed Diane. "See you when you get home, baby."

Tomiko giggled. "My mommy and daddy used to kiss all the time too."

Diane tickled her. "That's because they loved each other and loved you too. And that means you're a special little girl." It had been almost two months since her parents' deaths in late April and her extended emergency placement, and every now and again, Tomiko had bouts of tears. But since the funeral, overall the child seemed to be adjusting, and Diane was grateful. She waved and watched them leave.

The time seemed to fly, and leaving the assistant director in charge, Diane was striding out the door at three thirty. When she got home the delicious smells of whatever Jeffrey was cooking hit her nose and made her stomach growl. She heard their laughter before she saw them. They were at the bar, and he was helping Tomiko take cookies off a tray and place them on a rack to cool.

They noticed Diane at the same time, and Tomiko said, "We made your favorite cookies, Miss Di."

She came closer, placed her roses on the opposite end of the bar, and saw the oatmeal raisin cookies. "Ooh, can I have one now?"

"You can't have cookies right before dinner, Miss Di," Tomiko said sagely.

Jeffrey chuckled. "I guess it's a good thing dinner is almost ready. By the time you put your bags down, everything should be on the table."

"Thank you for this." She kissed both of them and floated up to her bedroom. Diane took a moment to change into a pair of shorts and a V-neck tee before going back downstairs. "Wow."

He'd set the table with their wedding china, crystal glasses and cloth napkins.

He came around and pulled a chair out for her, then did the same for Tomiko, who smiled up at him. Going back to the counter, he picked up a large platter and carried it to the table.

"Everything looks and smells so good," Diane said. He'd done steaks on the grill, fried potatoes with onions and peppers and roasted asparagus. They served themselves, and she took a moment to cut up Tomiko's meat. The first bite of the tender, juicy steak made Diane moan. "Oh, this is amazing, baby."

He smiled. "Thanks. It's been a while since I fired up the grill. The weather wasn't as hot today, so I figured it would be a good time."

The three of them laughed and talked while eating, and when dinner was over, Tomiko brought the plate of cookies to the table.

"Now you can have a cookie. And I helped make them."

Laughing, Diane snagged one and bit into it. "This is delicious. You did a great job. Try one."

She took a big bite out of one and chewed. "*Mmm*, it's good," she said around a mouthful.

The doorbell rang. Diane started to get up, but Jeffrey waved her back down. "Sit. I'll get it."

He came back a minute later, and the look on his face set off warning bells in her head.

"What is it?" she asked, her heart starting to pound.

His jaw tightened, and he motioned for her to go to the living room. Pasting a smile on her face, she patted Tomiko on the hand. "We'll be right back. Don't eat all the cookies while we're gone."

"I won't," she said, munching away.

As soon as Diane rounded the corner, she saw the same social worker who had come to the center that first night. *No, no, no!*

"Hello, Mrs. Evans."

"Ms. Davis."

"I'm sure you know why I'm here. We've located a family member who's willing to take Tomiko in, so she'll need to come with me."

The *family member* could only be one those nasty aunts or cousins she'd met at the funeral. "Why now when she's finally getting adjusted? You always say you want to do what's best for the child, and going to live with strangers doesn't seem to fit the bill," Diane said angrily. "They don't even know her and have never spent one minute with her, but you're just going to uproot her like this? It's not as if she's a baby and won't know the difference."

She knew they only wanted her because they figured they'd be able to get their hands on her money. Diane had no idea whether Toni already knew, but whichever family member wanted Tomiko would have a rude awakening because they'd have to go through the attorney for every penny.

"Children are better served being with families, and her aunt will make sure she's well cared for."

"*Nooooo!*"

Diane and Jeffrey whirled around at the same time. Tomiko screamed no over and over again. Jeffrey held and rocked her, trying to console her, but none of them could be consoled.

It took a good thirty minutes for the social worker to get To-miko out of the house, and Diane felt as if her heart had been ripped from her chest, especially when the woman told them it would be best that they have no further contact to help with the bonding process. She could still hear Tomiko's screams as the car backed down the driveway. As soon as it was out of sight, she broke down and sobbed.

"She was finally getting settled," she cried. "I wish she could've at least gone to her grandmother."

Jeffrey carried her inside and sat on the sofa with her in his lap. "I'm so sorry, and I know," he whispered, his own eyes filled with tears. "It won't take away the pain, but when you come back from Jamaica, maybe we can talk about adoption."

She searched his face, saw the same misery, and nodded. Though she appreciated it, he was correct that it wouldn't take the pain away. Diane didn't know if her heart would ever be whole again.

Chapter 27

Joy

JOY RUSHED AROUND SATURDAY MORNING MAKING sure she had all of her belongings from her borrowed room and bathroom and loaded them into her car. Her excitement was tempered by Diane losing Tomiko. After what she'd witnessed at the funeral, she was appalled that the social worker would even consider any of the distant family members, particularly since they'd never spent time with Tomiko, according to what Diane had learned.

Jeffrey had called her and Rochelle and asked them to come over last night, and the sound of their friend's cries had broken all their hearts. Even now, she felt her emotions rising again. The one bright spot was Jeffrey and the way he'd been there for Diane. He'd confided in them that Diane was thinking about backing out of their trip, and he wanted them to convince her to go. Joy was with Jeffrey on this one, and she wished they could be boarding the plane today, instead of three weeks from now.

"Is that everything?" Rochelle asked, cutting into Joy's thoughts.

"I think so." She gave her a strong hug. "Thank you so much for opening your home to me for these past couple of months. I don't know what I'd do without you."

"Girl, you know it was no trouble. I was glad to do it. You were right by my side during that mess with Kenny, and I could do no less for you."

They shared a smile. "I'm leaving to meet my dad and Brent over at the house to pick up the rest of my things and the pieces of furniture I purchased for my sitting room. They said they'd be there by eight thirty." Joy wasn't looking forward to seeing Robert and hoped with the buffer of her family there would be no drama.

"I'm glad they're going. The last thing you need is worrying about Robert acting up. Text me when you're on the way to your new place and I'll meet you there. I called to check on Diane, and she said she's still coming." Rochelle shook her head. "I still can't believe it. Tomiko was doing so well with them."

"Girl, don't get me started on this system." She took a quick peek at her watch. "Okay, let me get going. I'll text you both."

Joy made the twenty-minute drive to the house and saw her father and brother already there and waiting in the trucks. She directed them to back their pickup trucks into the driveway, and she parked out front.

This is the last time I'll be using this key, she thought as she unlocked the door and stepped inside.

A riot of emotions bubbled up in her—the love and laughter they'd shared, the peace of her outside oasis and the pain of rejection and betrayal.

"Joy?"

She spun around and brought her hand to her chest. "Robert, you scared me. *Um . . .* I'm just here to get the rest of my stuff. It shouldn't take long."

"You found a place." It came out as more of a statement than a question.

Joy nodded. "Moving in today. Dad and Brent are outside."

"Fine. I'll get out of your way," Robert said tersely.

He stood there a moment, and she thought he might say something else, but he just walked away toward the back of the house. Sighing, she got to work. It took about an hour for them to load up everything. She did one more walk-through to ensure she hadn't left anything behind. Joy didn't want to have any reason to return.

"Is that it, baby girl?" her father asked.

"I think so. Where's Brent?"

"He's outside tying the larger items down in the bed of the truck. I'll go help. Did Rob come out?"

"Okay. And no."

She hadn't seen him since she first arrived. No, they weren't parting on the best terms, but she was a little disappointed that he hadn't even offered to help.

He nodded and gave her shoulder a sympathetic squeeze. "Come on out when you're ready."

"I'll be right there."

After he left, she glanced around the room once more, then went into the kitchen. She removed the key from her ring and laid it on the counter next to Robert's coffee cup, a place where she knew he would see it. Joy ran her hand over the granite countertop that she'd picked out, then with a bittersweet smile, walked out for the last time.

"Are you guys ready?" she asked, approaching the trucks.

"Ready when you are," Brent said. "We'll follow you."

"Sounds good." She climbed into her car, took a moment to text Chelle and Diane, then drove away. Joy didn't look back.

The closer she got to her new home, the more excited she became. Starting over was scary, yet exhilarating at the same time, but she couldn't wait to see what her new life had in store.

Diane and Rochelle arrived a few minutes after Joy, and she welcomed them into her place. She gave Diane a strong hug. "How're you holding up?"

"I'd like to say I'm okay, but it would be a lie," Diane said with a sad smile. "I didn't sleep all night. I tossed and turned worrying about Tomiko." She waved a hand. "Hopefully this will give me a distraction so I don't have to think about it."

Nodding, she hugged her one more time. "Let me show you two around." She proudly led them through the three-bedroom, two-bath home, then outside to the backyard.

"Oh, I love this stone patio," Diane said.

Rochelle leaned to see farther in the yard. "It's gorgeous, and the yard reminds me of your other one."

Joy smiled. "That was a selling point for me. After we get back from Jamaica, I'm hosting the first get-together. Alright, we'd better get started. I know you probably have some other things to do today."

Diane stepped around a planter. "You're still meeting with the contractor too, right?"

"Yes. At two." Which gave her three hours to get everything inside and get the rest of her furniture delivered. She'd put it all away at her own leisure.

"We'll start with the little stuff that goes into the kitchen and bathroom," Rochelle said.

"That works." And it allowed Joy to guide her dad and brother.

Over the next couple of hours, they worked in a sort of organized chaos. To Joy's delight, her furniture was delivered earlier than the estimated time.

Rochelle stuck her head in the main bedroom where Joy stood observing the guys from the furniture store putting together her bed frame.

"I'm going to grab us some sandwiches. What kind do you want?"

"Turkey on whole wheat with lettuce, tomatoes and honey mustard."

She typed it in her phone. "Okay. Be back in a few."

After Rochelle left, Joy went into the kitchen and found Diane washing dishes. "What are you doing? And where did these come from?" She'd never seen the elegant but simple black-and-white-patterned china before.

"Chelle and I figured since you didn't plan to bring anything from the old house, you'd need some new stuff, so we splurged and got you a whole set. We bought water glasses and wineglasses, as well as silverware and dish towels." She placed another glass in the dish rack.

"I so appreciate you, Di."

No matter what life threw at them, they'd always showed up like the cavalry for each other in every situation. And she'd be right there for Diane as she went through this latest heartbreak. Smiling, she picked up a towel and started drying. Joy had planned to shop for her kitchenware after meeting with the contractor, but thanks to her friends, she had one less thing on her list to do today.

After washing up all the dishes, Joy and Diane wiped down the insides of every cabinet and drawer, then filled them with her new wares.

"Lunch is here." Rochelle strolled into the kitchen carrying two large bags.

Joy hurried over to help. "Thanks."

"I already gave your dad and Brent theirs. They said they'd eat outside on the patio."

"Okay." She removed the remaining sandwiches, chips and drinks and placed them on the kitchen table. "Diane, which one is yours?" she asked.

"I have the hot pastrami." Diane read the labels, picked up hers and took a seat.

After they'd all settled down with their food, Rochelle asked between bites, "I know you mentioned the spa needing repairs. Are you planning to make any other changes?"

"I am. Right now the manicure and pedicure stations, receptionist desk and waiting area are all in one room. I want to wall it off so that only the waiting area and receptionist are out front and all the treatment areas have that private feel. There are also a couple of huge rooms they've been using to store old equipment, but I'm going to turn one of them into a small kitchenette. Not sure about the other one yet, but it definitely won't be a graveyard for broken chairs, tables and whatnot."

"I don't understand why they didn't just throw that stuff away," Diane said, picking at her sandwich but not really eating.

"Girl, same. Some of that stuff looked like it had been there for years based on how much dust was covering it." She had so many ideas and was glad she'd taken time to write down her vision. It would make it easier in the long run.

"Have you ever worked with this contractor before?" Rochelle popped a chip into her mouth.

"No, but I've seen their work, and they've done some fantastic projects, both residential and commercial. And it's minority-owned, so that's a plus in my book."

Joy had gotten a business card from Hidden Gems Renovations during the business luncheon that she'd stormed out of a couple of months ago. So much had happened since then, and it dawned on her from Robert's comments that day about them expanding the business that he'd already been plotting the interior design acquisition. He'd broken her trust in so many ways.

Pushing the infuriating memory aside, she asked Rochelle, "How did the workout with Warren go?"

"It wasn't as bad as I thought. I'm starting slow, and he's been really patient." She paused. "He asked me to go away with him for the weekend."

"I hope you told him yes, Chelle," Diane said. "And if you need me to keep Haley, just let me know."

Rochelle smiled. "Thanks. I did say yes, and she's going to stay with my mom. We're driving down to Monterey Bay. I'm a little nervous, to tell you the truth. It's been so long since I've spent time alone with a man. I feel like a fish out of water."

"Chelle, I don't think you have anything to worry about," Joy said. "I guarantee Warren is going to go out of his way to make sure you're comfortable."

She sighed. "I know. He always does. I've never met anyone like him, and he's been so amazing."

Diane laid a hand on Rochelle's arm. "Then go with that, sis. Let him love you the way you deserve to be loved."

Rochelle nodded. "I'd better get going. No telling what Haley's gotten into by now."

They all laughed, and Diane said, "I need to go home too."

Joy's heart went out to Diane. "Thank you both for helping me out today. Two more weeks, and we'll finally be heading to Jamaica."

And Yvette could rest.

Joy gave them both grateful hugs and saw them out.

A few minutes later her father and Brent also departed, leaving Joy in her new space alone. She breathed a sigh of contentment, then went to shower before her appointment.

Nervous flutters gripped her an hour later as she parked in front of the spa that would soon bear the name *Amani*. And thanks to her father and brother putting up the capital and suggesting she have their names on the deed for the time being, she wouldn't have to worry about it being caught up in her divorce proceedings as an asset. Joy got out and went inside. She greeted everyone as she headed to the office, happy to see the place still bustling with activity.

"Joy, there's a guy out front to see you," the receptionist said in the open doorway. "Should I send him back?"

"Please." The smiling young woman departed, and Joy took out the folder with her wish list.

"Ms. West?"

Joy blinked. In her doorway stood a tall, good-looking brother. He had to be every bit of six five or more, had coffee-with-cream skin, well-groomed goatee and dark-brown eyes. The black tee showed off his muscular chest, abs and arms, and the well-worn jeans showcased long legs and thick thighs.

Construction really does a body good. Realizing she was staring, she shook herself mentally and rushed around the desk. "Hello. Please call me Joy." She stuck out her hand.

"Micah Bennett. It's a pleasure to meet you, Joy."

He grasped her hand, and a shock of awareness shot through her. *What in the world?* She quickly but gently eased her hand from his and chalked the sensation up to going more than a year without a man's touch. Yet his frank appraisal and lifted eyebrow gave her the impression that he'd felt it as well.

"Have a seat."

"Thanks."

Joy reclaimed her chair.

"I took the liberty of checking out the place before coming back and saw a few things that definitely need attention. Why don't you tell me what your vision is for the place."

My vision. She immediately liked him. Opening a folder, she handed one copy to him and kept the other, then launched into a detailed explanation of what she wanted. "Is this something you believe your company can handle?"

Micah nodded. "Absolutely. I also have a background in architecture, so if you don't mind, I have a few additional ideas I'd like to share with you."

They shared a smile. "I don't mind at all." She was all for anything that would make this a five-star place.

"Could we do it at the coffee shop down the street? I've been running since six this morning and need a jolt."

"Of course not. I'll follow you over." She stood and gathered her belongings, and he followed suit. Micah gestured for her to go first, towering over her by almost a foot.

"Actually," Micah said, placing a staying hand on her arm, "why don't you give me a tour first so I can see things through your eyes."

"*Um* . . . okay."

Why did she feel a warmth that had nothing to do with the hundred-degree July temperatures? Joy led him through each space in the building, pointing out what she wanted to change. Then they toured the outdoor grounds.

"What do you think?"

"I think you're going to make this place a showpiece. Would you like to go out to dinner sometime?"

She blinked.

Micah's eyes widened. "My apologies. I . . . I meant no disrespect. It's just that you're an intelligent and beautiful woman." He dragged a hand down his face, clearly embarrassed. "I don't even know if you're married. Again, I'm sorry."

Joy would be lying if she said the man didn't intrigue her, but until the ink dried on her divorce papers, she didn't feel right about starting up with another man, no matter how fine he looked. "No disrespect taken and apology accepted. I'm actually a little flattered. However, I'm going through a divorce right now, so . . ."

He smiled. "Then how about we work on being friends for now, and you can let me know if and when you're free for that dinner?"

"Sounds like a plan." *Well, now.*

Chapter 28

Rochelle

FRIDAY, ROCHELLE SAT LISTENING TO HER MOTHER go on and on about how Warren was such a nice man.

"I know he's nice, Mom," she said with a chuckle. "Do you need me to get anything else for Haley before I go?"

She and Warren would be leaving for their weekend in Monterey in an hour, and she needed to make sure she hadn't forgotten anything. Rochelle had always been a last-minute packer, but this time she'd packed her bag two days ago and double-checked it at least half a dozen times since then.

"No, I think we have everything. If not, I know where the store is and how to get there. You just go on and have a good time."

Rochelle stood. "I will." When her mother started to rise, she said, "Don't get up." She leaned down and kissed her cheek. "See you on Sunday. We should be back late afternoon."

"Bye, Mom," Haley said, coming over to hug Rochelle. "I hope you and Mr. McIntyre have fun."

"Thanks, and listen to you grandparents."

"I will."

She gave her daughter a few more instructions, then drove home.

Once there, she checked her bag one last time and, satisfied that she had everything, took it into the living room. Warren had asked her to bring a dressy outfit for dinner one night, and she was glad she'd relented on that second shopping trip and purchased three more dresses. Even Val had approved, saying, *"It's about time you dropped those business dinner outfits and got you something worthy of a date night. Now I won't have to put you on that television show."*

Admittedly, Rochelle was nervous. She'd never taken a weekend trip with a man, not even her ex, who'd deemed it a waste of money. As far as the men she'd dated afterward, none of them had been worth the time it took to change clothes. But now she had a man who loved her and whom she loved.

"Yvette, I let him in, sis. And you were right," she whispered as tears filled her eyes.

The doorbell rang, and she hastily wiped her eyes. It was time to go get her man.

Any worries about feeling awkward spending concentrated time with Warren disappeared within thirty minutes of their road trip. After an easy and fun ride down to Monterey and a quiet night, Warren took Rochelle to the Monterey Bay Aquarium, and she felt like a kid all over again.

"I can't believe we spent four hours in there," she said. "Haley would love this place."

"Then we'll bring her and Ebony next time."

"It'll have to be later in the summer because we're headed to Jamaica next week."

"Oh yeah. I forgot about that. Joe mentioned that Yvette left tickets for you three to take that girls trip."

"Yeah. I wish we hadn't put it off for so long. We always figured that whenever we got around to it, it would be the four of us. Never could we have imagined her not being here. Life does not play by our rules."

"I hear you. That's why I'm a firm believer in living life to its fullest and taking those risks because you never know what's going to happen in the future."

Rochelle nodded. If Yvette's death had taught her anything, it was exactly what he said, and it was one of the reasons she'd said yes to that first date after making excuses for so long.

When they got back to the room that evening after a wonderful dinner, she went out to the balcony. Thinking of Yvette had stirred up the sadness and grief all over again. However, she also remembered the fun times, the laughter they'd shared and all the shenanigans with the four of them. A while later, she heard the sliding glass door open.

"You okay, sweetheart?" Warren braced his forearms on the railing next to her.

"Yeah. Just thinking about Yvette and missing her."

"I sensed that, so I wanted to give you some time to yourself."

She leaned against him. "That's one of the things I love about you. You always seem to know what I need, sometimes before I do."

"Girl, I've been trying to tell you that for years," he teased.

She chuckled. "Yeah, yeah, I know." She cupped his jaw. "Thank you for not giving up on me, for hanging in there."

He kissed the palm of her hand. "I plan to be here for you forever."

Her brow lifted. "And that means?"

Warren straightened to his full height. "This isn't exactly how I planned to do this, but . . ." He dropped to one knee.

Rochelle's heart stopped and started again. *Oh. My.*

He grasped her left hand. "I wish I could explain how the sound of your voice gives me butterflies. How your smile makes my heart skip a beat, and how every time I'm with you, I feel complete. When I first saw you, I felt like I knew you, and I couldn't imagine my life without you. All of me loves *all* of you. I want forever, and I want to spend it loving you. I will also love and cherish Haley as if she's my own daughter. Will you marry me?"

She was crying so hard she could barely get the word out. That he thought enough to include her daughter in his proposal only made her love him more. She wanted forever too.

"Yes, yes, I'll marry you." He withdrew a small, blue velvet box from his pocket, opened it, and there in the fading sunlight he placed the heart-shaped solitaire on her finger. "It's *amazing.*" She threw her arms around him and kissed him with everything within her.

On the drive home the next day, Rochelle couldn't stop looking at her ring, and her cheeks hurt from smiling so hard. "I still can't believe this."

"Believe it, baby. It's you and me forever. If it's okay with you, I'd like to talk to Haley and get her permission, because she's part of this too. I don't want her to ever doubt that she's loved and wanted."

"No, I don't mind, and I appreciate you including her."

A couple of the men she'd dated had made it abundantly clear that they weren't going to be playing daddy to a kid that wasn't theirs, not that she'd asked or wanted them to fill that role.

When they arrived at her parents' house to pick up Haley, Rochelle slipped the ring off her finger. Sensing Warren's scrutiny, she said, "I want to keep it to myself for a few days. If my mother sees it, everyone within a four-hundred-mile radius will know."

Warren nodded. "Are you going to tell Joy and Diane?"

"Yep, but not until we get to Jamaica."

He chuckled.

"I've been so excited that I forgot to ask whether you want a long engagement."

Slanting her an amused glance, he said, "My definition of a

long engagement is anything past next week. So to answer your question, absolutely not. I can't wait to make you my wife."

"Great minds think alike."

"Really?" His eyes lit up. "You wouldn't tease a brother, would you?"

Rochelle burst out laughing. "You asked the same thing when I agreed to our first date. I wasn't kidding then, and I'm definitely not kidding now."

Warren pumped his fist and shouted, "*Hallelujah!*"

Usually they stayed around to visit for a while, but this time she was anxious to get home so they collected Haley and were out the door in five minutes.

"Did you guys have fun?" Haley asked as they carried everything into the house.

"We did," Warren confirmed.

He and Rochelle shared a look.

Haley divided a wary gaze between them. "What's wrong?"

Rochelle kissed her temple. "Nothing's wrong, baby."

"I'd like to talk to you about something, Haley." Warren gestured to the sofa.

Still staring at them, she perched on the edge.

"Haley, I want you to know that I love your mother, and I want to marry her, but you're a part of this, too, and I'd like to know if it's okay with you."

She brought her hands to her mouth. "*OMGeee*! I'm so excited. Yes." She hopped off the sofa and grabbed Rochelle in a big hug, almost knocking her over. Then she hugged Warren. Haley reclaimed her seat and rubbed her hands up and down her thighs. "*Um* . . . can I ask you something?"

"Sure," he said.

"Would it be okay if I called you Dad?"

Warren lowered his head, seemingly trying to control his emotions. When he looked up, Rochelle saw the tears standing in his eyes, mirroring the ones in her own.

"I'd be honored, Haley." He hugged her again, then reached for Rochelle's hand.

"I told you, Mom," Haley said, grinning.

"Told her what?"

"That you were going to marry her and that me and Ebony want to be in the wedding."

Warren laughed. "I'll see what we can do."

Rochelle just smiled. She'd taken the risk and won.

Chapter 29

Joy

"WOULD YOU LOOK AT THIS?" JOY SPREAD HER ARM around, marveling at her surroundings—soft waves crashing against the shore, fragrant smells from the food being prepared and music from a band set up on the beach.

"It's amazing," Rochelle said. "Ooh, we need to get in line and get us a rum punch."

Diane started in that direction. "Say no more. Joy, why don't you grab us seats before they're all gone, and I'll bring your drink."

"Gotcha."

They'd arrived in Jamaica earlier that day and found out that the resort was having a huge cookout on the beach, complete with a band and dancing. Joy quickly snagged a table with seats closer to the water and offered greetings to the three other people already seated there. She inhaled deeply and let it out slowly, releasing all the tension she'd built up over the past three months. She turned at the sound of Rochelle's voice and relieved her of one of the stacked plates, as well as the filled glass Diane had braced in an arm.

"Since we were passing the food table, we decided to just get a plate too." Rochelle sat across from Joy.

Diane took the chair next to Joy. "*Mmm*, this looks and smells so good."

"Agreed." They immediately dug in, and while eating, Joy moved in her seat to the infectious rhythm playing. She lifted her glass. "Here's to a time of fun and sisterhood."

Diane and Rochelle touched her glass, and they all sipped before continuing to enjoy the meal.

"I booked us spa appointments for tomorrow," Joy said.

"I can't wait," Rochelle said, finishing off the last of her jerk chicken. "I hope it gives you some inspiration for your own."

"I'm counting on it. When I went down earlier, the woman I spoke to was so nice. She gave me some great pointers on how to enhance the clients' enjoyment of their services."

The woman had told Joy to always remember the clients' well-being came first and had even given her a few essential oil blend samples for her to try.

"I'm looking forward to implementing her ideas, but in the meantime this music has me ready to get my groove on."

Several other people had the same idea and were up dancing.

"As long as it's not on a table, fine," Rochelle said, laughing.

Joy rose to her feet. "*Ha ha.* The best way to keep me off the table is to join me."

"You're on."

"I'm coming too." Diane hopped up from her chair.

The three women danced their way over to the small crowd of people swaying and singing along to a popular reggae song. Joy threw her arms in the air, tilted her head back and swayed her hips in time with the beat.

The song ended a couple of minutes later, and the band launched into Montell Jordan's "This Is How We Do It."

Rochelle said, "*Whaaat?* They play this here?" She did a hip swerve and dip and started singing.

Joy and Diane joined in, belting out the lyrics as if they were part of the band.

Then Joy said, "Wait, is this how you do it?" and tried to do one of the moves from the twerk class.

Diane let out a bark of laughter. "Work it like you own it, girl."

"That's about all I got," she said, smiling and going back to her original moves. She hadn't felt this free in a long time and let herself go. The music group played a mixture of old and new reggae, along with R&B and rock classics from the States, and the three women danced and danced as the sun dipped below the horizon.

"Oh my goodness. This is so much fun," Diane said, fanning herself when the evening ended. "I haven't danced this much in a long time. I need another one of those rum punches before they close down."

They all went back to the bar.

Rochelle studied the menu. "I think I'm going to have a pineapple daiquiri this time."

"Make that two," Joy said. After getting their drinks, they found some vacant loungers and relaxed in the moonlight. "Now *this* is how you start a vacation." And she couldn't wait for tomorrow. *Thank you, Yvette, for seeing what I needed—what we all needed.*

She'd promised Yvette that she would ensure they took the trip, and she had, but Joy also knew her friend didn't mean it just for this one time, but to continue it. To keep the bond of sisterhood strong.

Joy reflected on all that had happened since Yvette had died and how she'd never imagined having to start over again as a single woman, but she was doing it. She was close to realizing her dream and excited to see her vision come to life. Then there was Micah. Since his faux pas, they started over and worked well together. She chuckled recalling the look on his face.

"What are you laughing at?" Diane asked.

"Just thinking about the contractor I hired. He asked me out."

"What?" Diane and Rochelle chorused.

"It was kind of cute actually, because he sort of just blurted it out. He was so embarrassed."

"What does he look like?"

Joy grinned. "I knew you were going to ask that, Chelle. The man is fine, with a capital *F*. After he apologized and I told him I wasn't free to date at the moment, he told me to let him know if and when I was free."

Diane let out a little squeal. "Alright now, girl. You go. I may have to pop on over to the spa to check him out."

Joy sipped her drink. "You want to know the crazy part? I'm attracted to him. There was like this weird thing I felt when he touched me." She shifted her gaze and found them staring at her. "What?"

"It's not weird, Joy. It just means you're a woman with needs—ones that haven't been met," Rochelle said. "Believe me, I know."

"I know," Joy responded. Micah looked at her the way she'd wanted her husband to, as if she was special. "Micah—that's his name—is a gentleman and respects the boundaries we've set. Other than talking over coffee and working on business, he hasn't tried anything."

"Even if it turns out he's not the man for you, don't do like I did for so many years and close yourself off from love. You don't want to look back and see all the time you wasted."

Joy squeezed Rochelle's hand, knowing she was referring to all the years she'd ignored Warren. "I'll try not to." But she didn't plan to rush into anything either.

Chapter 30

Diane

DIANE SAT ON THE BEACH THE NEXT MORNING, DUG HER toes farther in the sand and lifted her head to the sky. Although it was only nine in the morning, the day promised to be a warm one. Drawing her knees to her chest and clasping her arms around them, she contemplated the hand life had dealt her. Foremost in her mind was Tomiko. The aunt had taken her out of the after-school program, so she had no idea how the little girl might be doing.

The other thing weighing heavily on her was the early menopause. She'd honestly thought she had accepted it but realized after the "why me" questions had come back with a vengeance that she still harbored so much anger inside her—at life, at God. Diane swiped at the lone tear that escaped.

Releasing a deep breath, she closed her eyes and prayed for forgiveness, for help in coming to terms with her infertility, for her to be a better person for whatever child she and Jeffrey would be blessed with having and to accept if it didn't happen. She prayed that Tomiko would be safe and the aunt would come to see what an amazing child she was and love her. She also thanked God for putting her marriage back together, for Joy and Rochelle, and especially for Yvette. Though their time had been cut short, not a day went by that Diane didn't feel her presence or hear her friend's sage words of advice in her mind.

It was time for Diane to accept her lot in life. She wasn't the first woman to experience this and certainly wouldn't be the last. It was up to her to make the best of the situation and believe that things would work out as they should. More tears escaped, and soon she was crying, letting go of the disappointments, the pain, everything. And for the first time she felt the light penetrate the darkness that had gripped her soul. No, it wouldn't instantly erase all she'd endured, but it was a step in the right direction.

After a while, the tears slowed, then stopped. Diane sat there a few minutes longer, then stood, dusted the sand off her shorts and headed back to the room for their scheduled massage.

As soon as she opened the door, Joy and Rochelle were there, both with concerned expressions on their faces.

Rochelle asked, "You good, sis?"

She smiled and hugged them both. "I will be. Just working on letting go and accepting some things."

"Okay. As long as you're alright."

"What time do we need to be at the spa, Joy?"

A grin played around the corners of Joy's mouth. "We're not having our massages at the spa. We're doing them here. On the balcony. With the ocean breeze."

Both her and Rochelle's mouths dropped open.

"Oh, I didn't tell y'all that part? My bad."

"Yeah, *yo'* bad," Rochelle said with a wide smile.

Joy shrugged. "I figured we needed some extra pampering, and since we had the choice of having the massages at the spa, in the room or outside in the gazebo, I chose here."

"Thank goodness," Diane said. "I don't think I want to be outside where everybody could see us. It would be just my luck for somebody to walk by just as a breeze kicked up and the sheet flew up, exposing my naked butt." Diane much preferred the clear view of the water from their second-story balcony.

"Mercy. The vision I just got if that happened to me." Rochelle shuddered, then laughed.

They burst out in a fit of laughter, and Joy said, "Yeah. No. I think we'll just do it here."

A knock sounded, and Diane walked over and opened the door. She smiled at the three women carrying massage tables and stepped back for them to enter. "Please come in."

"Good morning," the first one said in accented English. "We'll need a few minutes to set up. You can remove everything except your underwear and put on one of the robes."

"Great. Thanks."

They retreated to their bedrooms to change, and when they returned were surprised by the transformation. The women had positioned the tables next to each other, leaving room to walk between them, but with the wide balcony, she, Rochelle and Joy would still have a great view.

Minutes later, they climbed onto the tables, and with the therapists obstructing the view by holding up sheets, they disrobed and lay face down.

Diane moaned softly as soon as the woman started kneading the tight muscles of her back and shoulders. The gentle strokes, coupled with the uplifting, yet calming scent of lemongrass relaxed her so much that she felt herself drifting off.

Halfway through, they were asked to turn over, and Rochelle said, "Joy, you're going to have to figure out how to make house calls or find us a spot like this monthly."

They all laughed softly, including the therapists.

"I'll see what I can do."

By the time the massage ended, all three women were slow to rise. The therapists left with a promise to return in a while for the tables, so they decided to take advantage and lay there a few minutes longer.

"Every muscle in my body is so relaxed, I could lay here for hours," Joy said. "This is what I want to provide for the women—and men—who come through the doors of my spa. I want them to leave rejuvenated, relaxed and their balance restored."

"Girl, that sounds like something you should have on your brochure," Rochelle said.

Diane agreed. "*Mm-hmm.* Rejuvenate, relax and restore. Perfect." After another few minutes she said, "We should probably get up if we plan to make that tour."

They were doing the Appleton Estate Rum Experience, which included a guided tour, rum tasting and lunch.

"I guess," Rochelle said.

Finally, they got up and dressed, then made their way to the lobby to check in for the tour. It turned out that they were the only three booked at that time, so they piled into the appointed taxi. Diane expected to take in the beautiful scenery. What she hadn't expected was a harrowing ride up the curvy mountainside with lanes so narrow it felt like they were either going to pitch over the side of a cliff or be forced to run into the wall of rocks on the other side. She clutched the door every time a car approached.

"Wow, these are some narrow roads," Joy said, speaking Diane's words out loud. "What do you do if a big truck comes by?"

The driver responded, "Small up yuhself."

What the hell does that mean? And how do you small up a car? Diane heard Rochelle's chuckle next to her. "What?"

"Your face when he answered."

She opened her mouth to say something else but tensed and nearly jumped into Rochelle's lap when a car whizzed by so close she could see the color of its interior. Again, her friend laughed, and Diane skewered her with a look. "I'm going to need an entire bottle of that rum by the time this is over." And she'd probably need another massage as well.

Chapter 31

Rochelle

ROCHELLE HAD REALLY ENJOYED THE LAST THREE days in Jamaica. She chuckled, recalling Diane's reaction on the ride to the estate. Her friend had indeed tossed back the rum like a sailor and purchased a few bottles to take home.

They had only one more day before returning home. Today they had decided to have their celebration for Yvette, so she'd gone downstairs to pick up the orchids she'd ordered—blue because they symbolized the rare and natural beauty of their friendship, and yellow to represent new beginnings and joy. The flower had been Yvette's favorite.

"I'm back," she said, entering the suite.

"Those are so gorgeous." Diane gently fingered a petal. "As soon as we cut the stems, we can go."

"I also have something Joe gave me." Joy held up a box.

"What is it?" Diane asked.

"I have no idea. I mentioned that we were going to have a little celebration for Yvette, and he told me to open this when we do."

It didn't take long to take care of the stems. Rochelle placed the blooms in a basket she'd also purchased, and they made their way down and out to the beach. The sun was just beginning to set, and they chose a spot farther down and away from the crowd.

"Why don't we open the box first?"

"Sounds good to me." Joy lowered herself to the sand and waited for Rochelle and Diane to do the same.

They sat in a circle facing each other. Joy removed the box from her tote. For a moment she just sat and ran her hand reverently over the top. Steadying her emotions, she carefully opened it. On top was an envelope with the words *Read First* written across the top in Yvette's handwriting. She withdrew the sheet of paper and read it aloud:

"*To the sisters of my heart, you finally made it! Whew! I thought I was going to have to come back and drag your cute little butts to Jamaica. Thank you for honoring this small request. Did you ever imagine that when we pinky swore in third grade to always be best friends, to have each other's backs no matter what, that we'd end up here? We may not have had a clue about what true friendship meant in that moment, but we learned along the way, and it became a lifeline for all of us. This is why I wanted you to take the trip: to remind you of what this bond means. Not many people can boast of a friendship like ours. Hell, there are real sisters out there who aren't as close as we are.*"

Joy paused as they all laughed a little, then she continued:

"*Always remember that day over thirty years ago. I know life has thrown us more curveballs than we can catch, but as long as you have each other, you can win this game called life.*"

"*Joy, I wish I was there to see your vision come to life, and I'm sorry that you're having to do it without the support of the one person who you thought you could count on. Honey, I know Robert didn't get his stuff together (don't ask how I know, I just do), but you've got this.*"

"She called that one," Joy said with a shake of her head.

"*Diane, keep holding on, sis. You're going to get your chance at motherhood. Whether it's a child of your womb or one of the heart, he or she is going to be blessed to have a mother like you. Don't worry,*"

Jeffrey's going to get his act together, if he hasn't already. He loves you, and I know he's going to be a great father because I watched him with Ebony, Ian and Haley. Oh, and I'm still calling dibs on being a godmother.'"

Diane broke down and cried. "She's right. Jeff is an amazing father, and I am going to hold on."

Rochelle hugged her. "It's going to be okay."

"'Chelle, by now, you and Warren should be rowing in the same direction. I only wish I was there to see you fall in love with him the same way that he's loved you for the past two years. That's a long time to make a brother suffer. Put him out of his misery and be happy, sis.'"

Rochelle laughed around her tears. "She told me to let him in, and it was one of the best decisions I've ever made. And yeah, we're rowing in the same direction now."

The three women shared a smile.

"'Okay, there are two small numbered boxes for each of you with your names on them. After you open them in order, read the second letter. I'll wait . . .'"

Joy handed out the boxes. "What is this woman up to?" They opened the first box to find a travel package of tissue.

Diane opened it and wiped her lingering tears. "I'm afraid to open the next box."

"You're not the only one," Rochelle said. "Okay, let's do this."

Inside the second box was a beaded bracelet with a heart-shaped charm that read *Sisters of the Heart*. On the back, it had all four of their names inscribed, which brought on a fresh set of tears.

"It's beautiful," Joy said, fingering the purple polished beads interspaced with rhinestones. She slipped it onto her arm. Diane and Rochelle did the same. She opened the second envelope.

"'I hope you like the bracelet as much as I do. This is a reminder that no matter what happens, you have each other. And you have me in your heart. I'm wearing mine too. Now dry those tears, grab a

cocktail and turn up! Live your lives, sisters. I love y'all forever and a day. Until we meet again.

Yvette'"

Joy set the letter aside and grasped Rochelle's and Diane's hands. "We have our marching orders. We can do this because we have each other. I'm not going to sit on the sidelines and let life pass me by, and I'm definitely not going to close my heart to the possibility of finding love again."

Diane smiled and gave Joy's hand an encouraging squeeze. "As soon as I get back home, I'm going to sit down with my husband and discuss how we can make our dream of having a child a reality. I won't ever get over losing Tomiko, and no child can replace her in my heart, but there's room enough for another one who needs our love."

"I don't know what I would've done without you all," Rochelle said. "Thank you for pushing me, for encouraging me to grasp the happiness that Warren brought in my life. Because you did, I was able to do this." She dug into her pocket, slipped on the ring, and then held out her left hand. "I said yes."

Joy and Diane screamed, and Joy, sitting nearest to her left hand, grabbed it to get a closer look at the exquisite ring. "I am so happy for you, Chelle."

"So am I," Diane said. "I guess that weekend getaway turned out pretty well."

"It was amazing, and the words he said about my smile making his heart skip a beat and that he couldn't imagine his life without me . . ." She brought her hand to her heart. "But the best part is that he asked Haley if she was okay with it."

"I know she is," Joy cut in.

"Yeah, she is. Then she asked Warren if she could call him Dad."

Diane's hand flew to her mouth. "Oh my goodness. I know he was surprised."

"He was, and he told her he'd be honored."

Joy pulled out another tissue. "I thought I was done crying. First thing tomorrow, we start planning this wedding. We have to find a venue, a dress, get the invitations going—"

Rochelle held up a hand. "I will need your help pulling this together, but we can talk about it when we get home." She stood with the basket, and Joy and Diane followed suit. They walked closer to the water. "Over fifteen years ago, we pledged our sisterhood and promised we would always be there for each other. Today we renew that commitment."

Diane continued. "To accept each other with all our flaws, give encouragement and hope, support each other through the laughter and tears."

"To listen with an attentive ear and kick each other's butts into gear when needed, and to celebrate the beauty and joy of this bond . . . forever," Joy finished.

"We love you, Yvette, and were blessed to have you as a sister and friend. This is not goodbye, just see you later. Until we meet again . . . To friendship, sisterhood and living life with no reservations."

They released the blooms into the water, then with their arms around each other's waists, focused their gazes toward the ocean. The sun was setting on this chapter of their lives, but tomorrow the sun would rise again and bring new life.

Diane's phone rang and Rochelle said teasingly, "Tell Jeffrey it's only been a few days."

Smiling, Diane answered. "Hey, baby." She listened for a moment, then said, "*What?* You have got to be kidding me." Diane held up a finger, asking Joy and Rochelle to wait a moment. "Absolutely, yes. I'll be there as soon as I can."

Joy lifted a curious brow. "What's going on? Is Jeff okay?"

"The social worker called. The aunt that took Tomiko changed her mind, and she wanted to know if we wanted to take her back." She grabbed up the empty boxes. "I know it's a day early, but I need to go home."

"There's nothing to be sorry about," Joy said. "But there's one thing you've got wrong. *We* have to go home. Let's get upstairs and change some flights."

"I love y'all," she said around her happy tears.

Rochelle gave Diane's shoulders an affectionate squeeze. "That's what this is all about. Friendship and sisterhood." And she'd always be grateful to have them in her life.

*". . . I love y'all forever and a day. Until
we meet again."*

Yvette

Six months later

WITH THE SUN SETTING OVER THE OCEAN AND A GEN-
tle breeze blowing, Rochelle stood beside Warren at the Monterey
hotel reciting her vows. The last time she'd done this, she'd been
nervous and stumbled over her words. But not today. Today her
words came out loud and strong, and she'd almost beat the minister trying to get them out.

She laughed inwardly, thinking about the conversation with
her grandmother earlier. When she'd told the older woman she
wasn't nervous, her grandmother had replied with: *"That's good.
The only reason you should be nervous is if you don't know what
you're getting at the end of the aisle."*

Staring up into Warren's eyes as he spoke his vows, she knew
exactly what and *who* she was getting. Nervous? Not a bit. Excited, anxious, ecstatic? Absolutely!

Finally the minister pronounced them husband and wife, and
her first kiss as Mrs. Rochelle McIntyre was everything she expected and more.

"Thank you for marrying me, sweetheart. You made me the
happiest man alive today."

"Thank *you*. Thank you for loving me when I didn't love myself. For being my heart, my safe place. Thank you for letting me
dream, letting me fly. You are and have been proof that my heal-

ing wasn't in vain, and falling in love with you has been the best thing I've ever done. You are my everything."

"Rochelle, you are all that to me and more, and we're going to have an amazing life together."

"Then let's get this party started."

Laughing, they strolled up the aisle amid raucous applause and whistles. The reception turned out to be just as beautiful, and Rochelle smiled so hard her cheeks hurt.

"Hey, Warren. Can we steal our girl for a few minutes?" Diane asked as she and Joy approached.

"Sure thing." He kissed Rochelle and melted into the crowd.

Rochelle followed Diane and Joy outside where it was quieter.

"You did it, Chelle," Joy said. "And, girl, the way you two were looking at each other, I thought you were going to burn the place down."

Diane fanned herself. "For *real*. Be happy, sis."

"I am. More than I ever thought. Thank you for always being there for me. You saw me through the worst times in my life, and . . . *whoo*." She forced back the tears threatening to fall. "I don't know how I would've made it without you."

"We wouldn't be anywhere else." Joy held up her arm, showing the bracelet.

She embraced them, holding on long enough to communicate what her words couldn't convey.

"Okay. No more tears," Diane said with a laugh. "It took that woman half an hour to put this face together, and I can't be ruining my makeup before the party's over." They laughed. "And in my Yvette voice, 'Okay, sisters, dry those tears, grab a cocktail and *turn up!*'"

Howling with laughter, they reentered the ballroom. Rochelle spotted Warren talking and laughing with Joe and Jeffrey. She hugged her girls one last time and headed in his direction.

Warren caught her gaze, excused himself and met her halfway. "Missed you, Mrs. McIntyre."

Chuckling, she said, "I was only gone five minutes."

"That's five minutes too long without you."

"*Awww*, you say the sweetest things."

He wiggled his eyebrows. "You ain't seen nothing yet, sweet thing."

Many of the guests had started to leave. She and Warren would be spending the night at the hotel, then leaving tomorrow evening for a week in Hawaii. Haley would be staying with Val.

"Are you ready to head upstairs?"

Rochelle smiled. "Ready." They said their goodbyes and slipped away. As they passed the reception desk, she remembered Val's note. "Oh, I need to stop at the desk to get something Val left for us."

"Okay." He waited off to the side until she returned. "What is it?"

"I have no idea, but since it's from my sister, nothing would surprise me." Her big sister was confident, outrageous and outspoken, and Rochelle was getting back to being the same. In their suite, the first thing she did was kick off her shoes. "Those things were killing me."

"Maybe, but they sure looked good on your feet."

Shaking her head, she dropped down in one of the chairs facing the balcony and removed the ribbon from the box. She opened the lid and burst out laughing.

Warren peered over, lifted the slinky piece of material that left more bared than it covered and smiled. "I love her style."

"There's a note for you." She passed it to him.

He opened it, and this time he laughed. "She said I could thank her later." He gently pulled Rochelle to her feet and trailed kisses along her neck. "How about you slip into this little number, and we'll see how long it takes to get you out of it?"

Feeling bolder than she had in her entire life, she slid her arm up over his well-defined chest and around to his neck. "How about we do that next time and just skip to the good part?"

"You ain't said nothing but a word." Warren swept her into his arms, carried her into the bedroom and placed her on her feet. He turned her around and slowly, erotically removed each piece of her clothing. Her body was so on fire that by the time he entered her, she came with a soul-shaking intensity that left her gasping for breath.

"This is how it's always going to be with us, sweetheart. Forever," he said, kissing her and starting with slow, deep thrusts.

Forever. And I'm here for every second of it.

Diane

Diane sat in the corridor of the courthouse anxiously bouncing her knees.

Jeffrey placed a gentle hand on her thigh. "Relax, baby. In a few minutes we're going to walk out of here with our daughter."

Our daughter. The words made her heart swell. She glanced over to Tomiko, who was talking to Ebony and Haley, and smiled. The three had become close, reminding her of the bond she shared with her friends. She only hoped the bond would remain strong.

"The judge is ready for you, Mr. and Mrs. Evans," the clerk said.

It took everything in Diane not to sprint down the hallway. The woman ushered their family and friends into the judge's chamber, and Diane was excited to see that the judge was a woman and not too much older than she.

The judge smiled warmly. "I'm Judge McKenna. It's nice to meet you." She shook Jeffrey's and Diane's hands, then turned to Tomiko. "And it's very nice to meet you, Tomiko."

Giving the judge a shy smile and shaking the proffered hand, Tomiko said, "Nice to meet you too."

"I see you have quite the crowd here, and that tells me you all have a great support system."

Judge McKenna retook her seat, then asked Diane and Jeffrey to confirm their intention to provide Tomiko with a loving home. She asked if they had something they wanted to say.

Jeffrey said, "Your Honor, we have this remarkable little girl, and I want to make sure she grows up with all the love I know her parents would want her to have. I know we can give her that."

The judge smiled. "Thank you, Mr. Evans."

Because Tomiko was old enough, the judge asked her if she wanted the adoption to take place, and she responded with a resounding "*Yes!*"

"Then by the power invested in me by the State of California, from this day forth, you shall be known as Tomiko Evans."

A cheer went up in the room, and Tomiko started crying. She threw her arms around Diane and Jeffrey. "I love you, and I'm so glad you're going to be my mom and dad."

Diane couldn't stop the tears flowing down her face. *Mom.* She'd waited a long time to hear those words. After many rounds of hugs from hers and Jeffrey's families, and her sisters of the heart, they took a mound of pictures to document the day.

Jeffrey kissed Diane's hand and placed it on his heart. "She's ours."

She placed her hand over his, feeling the strong, steady beat. "Yes, she's ours."

"I love you, Diane."

"I love you too." *An incredible husband, a wonderful little girl— everything is right in my world.*

Joy

Joy ran around her new spa Saturday morning making sure everything was in place. She'd been bouncing off the walls all week. It had taken almost six months to transform Amani Day Spa into a space that would nurture the spirit and well-being of everyone who stepped through its doors. From the majestic shades of purple and gold that highlighted the lobby to the peaceful and relaxing blues that made up the treatment rooms, everything had turned out better than she'd expected.

And Micah, bless his heart, had worked his butt off without complaint when she changed her mind a million times. But she couldn't have pulled it off without his expertise. His architectural eye had been a godsend when he suggested changing the metal lockers to a light-colored wood. It had enhanced the beauty of the locker room so much that she'd added oversize wooden chairs with purple cushions to the lobby area as well. A frosted sliding door painted with greenery to close off the manicure and pedicure stations had been his idea, too, and was more cost effective than building a wall.

Smiling, she went to her office where Diane and Rochelle were waiting. "I can't believe it's finally happening," she said, collapsing into her new office chair.

"Believe it, girlfriend," Diane said.

"And we brought a little something to celebrate your double

blessing." Rochelle withdrew bottles of champagne and pineapple-mango juice from her tote.

"Yes, girl. Pour me one. I'm so glad to finally close the door on that chapter of my life. I'm ready for everything coming my way." She'd received her divorce decree earlier that week and had done a happy dance in her house for a good hour.

Diane set the flutes on the desk while Rochelle poured. Once glasses were filled, Diane held hers up. "To new beginnings." They touched glasses and sipped.

"This place is fabulous," Rochelle said. "I've already booked massages for the next three months. I've decided that my self-care is going to remain a priority from here on out."

"I feel the same way. And Jeffrey is in total agreement. I only booked one month, but I think I'm going to add a few more." Diane took another sip of her mimosa. "Oh, and I love how you transformed that storage room into a private room for small parties."

A smile tilted the corner of Joy's mouth. "I can't take the credit for that one. It was Micah's idea. I mentioned having special packages for bridal parties or girls' nights out, and he suggested it."

He'd also recommended adding the covered gazebo out back for the same thing. They'd become good friends over the past several months, and not once had he tried to hit on her or make any romantic overtures, and she appreciated that about him.

"Micah, huh?" Rochelle said with a sly grin.

Joy was spared from answering when her assistant stuck her head in the door.

"Sorry to interrupt, but I think folks are starting to gather. We have about fifteen minutes before showtime."

"Thanks. We'll be right out." Downing the rest of her cocktail, she stood. "Time to turn up." The phrase had become a running joke between them.

Laughing, the trio danced their way to the front, where there was, indeed, a growing crowd. Joy spotted her family off to one side and waved. She and her mother had been slowly working through their issues, and she was hopeful that they'd reclaim some of the closeness they once shared. She smiled seeing her father with his new wife. Ms. Vera was a sweet lady and perfect for him.

At precisely noon, she and her staff gathered in front of the double doors, and Joy tapped the portable microphone to get everyone's attention. She waited until the crowd quieted. "First, I'd like to thank everyone for coming out to celebrate the grand opening of Amani Day Spa. I chose this name because the word Amani is Swahili for peace, and that's what I hope to provide to everyone who comes through these doors.

"There are so many people I have to thank for this. I'm going to start with my amazing staff, who without their graciousness, there would be no spa. I appreciate you from the bottom of my heart. My family, who has been in my corner from day one."

Joy paused to get her emotions under control. Her father and brother had surprised her by paying off the remainder of her mortgage. She'd been humbled and grateful.

"To my sisters of the heart, Rochelle McIntyre and Diane West, y'all already know." She searched and found Joe. "And to my sister, my friend, Yvette Stephens, who isn't here to see this dream fulfilled but who spoke the words of encouragement I needed. Love and miss you, sis." Joe acknowledged her with a nod. "Okay, let's cut the ribbon and get this party started."

She handed off the mic to one of her staff members, who passed her a pair of scissors in exchange. Joy stepped up and made a snip. The purple ribbon floated away, and a loud cheer went up.

The crowd streamed inside, many of them stopping to congratulate her.

She spent a few minutes talking to a few more people before her mother came up.

"Joy, this is wonderful, honey. I'm very proud of you."

"Thanks, Mom."

"I've got to go and enter that drawing and make me an appointment. I'll see you later." And she was off.

Her father and Ms. Vera came up next.

"It's beautiful, Joy, and I've already booked your dad and me a couple's massage," Ms. Vera said.

"Go, Dad," Joy said with a laugh.

"Hey, I might as well see what I paid for."

"You can have any service you want for free, forever. I love you, Dad."

"Love you, too, babycakes." He gestured for his bride to go through the doors.

Joe approached and wrapped her in a brotherly hug. "I'm proud of you, girl. And I know my baby is smiling down from heaven." He scanned the building. "You did good."

"Thank you so much," she whispered, hugging him again.

He went inside and she continued to greet those gathered. Joy laughed and hugged so many people, she lost count.

"It's a good turnout."

Joy whirled around at the sound of the deep, masculine voice. "Micah, hey."

"What do you think?"

"I think it's fabulous, and I have you to thank for helping me get this done."

Micah glanced around. "We make a good team."

"Yeah, we do," she said softly, feeling somewhat shy.

She glanced up and saw Rochelle and Diane behind Micah gesturing wildly and pretending to swoon. She bit her lip to stifle a laugh.

"Did I miss something?" Micah asked, glancing over his shoulder.

"No." Her friends halted their antics when he looked their way but started up again when he turned back toward Joy.

"Are you sure?"

"*Mm-hmm.*"

He didn't look convinced but said nothing else. "Well, I just wanted to come by to congratulate you. I'll let you get back to your guests." He stood there a moment longer, then said, "Take care of yourself, Joy."

He started to walk away, and both Diane and Rochelle pointed to their bracelets, then gestured with their heads toward Micah. She nodded and drew in a deep, calming breath. She placed a staying hand on his arm. "Micah."

"Yeah?"

"I'm free for that dinner date now."

A wide grin spread across his face. "Does that mean what I think it does?"

"Yes." Joy spread her hands. "I'm a free woman now."

Micah gathered her closer and slid his arms around her waist. "Are you free for me to do this?" he asked, his head descending.

"What?" Her heart pounded as his lips moved within an inch of hers.

"This," he murmured.

Before she could form her next thought, his mouth came down on hers . . . *hard*. His tongue swirled around hers, tasting, teasing. She hadn't been kissed like this in . . . well, never, and she felt her legs shaking.

"*Yes!*"

They both snapped their heads around. Diane and Rochelle stood there clapping and giving her the thumbs-up.

Micah chuckled. "Friends of yours?"

"No. They're much more. They're the sisters of my heart."

"Then maybe you should introduce me because I want to be part of your life—if that's okay with you," he added.

Hell yeah, it's okay. "Yeah, I'm good with it." Smiling, they headed toward her friends, and she heard Yvette in her head: *Yasss, sis! Claim your man.* Joy planned to do just that.

Author's Note

Dear Reader,

No Reservations is a story about friendship, sisterhood, and not being afraid to take risks. But at its core, it is also about love and taking stock of what's really important, like spending time with the special people in your life. Just like the three women in this story, I've been guilty of putting off get-togethers, trips, and the like because I believe I'll have time to do them later. Yet, that's not always the case. Time doesn't wait until everything is perfect . . . There will never be a *perfect* moment for that coveted girls trip or quick getaway. Joy, Rochelle, and Diane certainly learned this and so have I. I hope, after reading, that you will be inspired to grab your besties and do *that* thing you've always wanted to do. You won't regret it . . . *Trust me.*

Love and blessings,
Sheryl

Acknowledgments

My Heavenly Father, thank you for my life and for loving me better than I can love myself.

To my husband, Lance, you will always be my #1 hero! Thank you for your unwavering support and love.

To my children, family, and friends, thank you for your continued support. I appreciate and love you!

Thank you to Cindy Cain for answering my many questions pertaining to social work, and to Leslie Wright and Tracy Hale for being my sounding boards . . . and talking me off the ledge many times. I love y'all!

A special thank you to my incredible agent, Sarah E. Younger, who believed in this story when it was just a thought, and to the wonderful team at Harper Muse for your editorial guidance and support.

Thank you to all the readers who have supported and encouraged me throughout this journey. I couldn't do this without you.

Discussion Questions

1. Do you have a core group of friends like those in *No Reservations*? What roles do your friends play in your life? What do you contribute to their lives?
2. Which character is most like you? Which character reminded you of one of your friends?
3. Each woman goes through trials as her story progresses. Which character's situation did you most sympathize with?
4. Although Yvette was only on the page briefly, in what ways did her presence impact the story?
5. Did any part of this book strike a particular emotion in you? Which part, and what emotions did the book make you feel?
6. How would you adapt this book into a movie? Who would you cast in the leading roles?
7. How have the characters changed by the end of the book?
8. Female friendship is a key theme of this story. Discuss the importance of the bond between Joy, Diane, and Rochelle.
9. Do you feel satisfied with how each woman's relationship and life is resolved at the end of the story? Why or why not?
10. What are some rituals you have with your closest friends? Do you believe those rituals play a role in sustaining your relationship with them?

About the Author

Photo by Ashley Taylor of Taylor'd Shots Photography

SHERYL LISTER IS A MULTI-AWARD WINNING AUTHOR and has enjoyed reading and writing for as long as she can remember. She is a former pediatric occupational therapist with over twenty years of experience and often says she "played" for a living. A California native, Sheryl is a wife, mother of three daughters and a son-in-love, and grandmother to two special boys. When she's not writing, Sheryl can be found on a date with her husband or in the kitchen whipping up delicious meals and desserts to satisfy her inner foodie.

sheryllister.com
Instagram: @sheryllister
Twitter: @SherylLister
Facebook: @sheryllisterauthor